Cotton in
AUGUSTA

Cotton in
AUGUSTA

To Val,
I hope you
enjoy Myra's story
of long ago,
God Bless,
Shirley Twiss
11-17-11

SHIRLEY PROCTOR TWISS

To order additional copies of this book, contact:
Xlibris Corporation
1-888-795-4274
www.Xlibris.com
Orders@Xlibris.com
40421

DEDICATION

*In loving memory and in thanksgiving for the lives of
Albert Hammock Twiss, Vida Sheppard McIntyre,
and Ruth McIntyre Reynolds.*

Acknowledgments

Many thanks to my family and friends, who supported and encouraged me in realizing the dream of publishing my story.

Very special thanks to

My daughter, Erin Ryan, for proofreading my work, for the computer assistance, and for the patience in helping me through the discouraging times.

Judy Lemmons for proofreading my work, for encouraging me to continue, and for the many book discussions over cafeteria dinners.

My cousin, Cliff Reynolds, for the photos.

Melvie Stephens for taking me to a cotton patch and sharing stories of long ago.

~ 1 ~

Hard-packed red clay pounded Myra's bare feet, and dry red dust scattered in her wake as she raced away from the schoolhouse toward home. Her shoes hung by the strings around her neck. Shoes made her feet feel like they were in a stranger's house, so she pulled them off as soon as she left the schoolhouse door. The feel of her toes digging into the red clay gave her a contented feeling. Shoes were hard to come by in her family. She hoped this pair would last, since her feet must've stopped growing. Her papa would be relieved to have one less pair to buy when he got his crop money in the fall.

Myra liked to go to school when she had the chance, but she raced out of the little one-room school ahead of all the other young'uns as soon as the teacher rang the bell at the end of the day. Running at top speed down the road was the only game she knew.

Her race was with the sun. She had to get home to help Papa in the field while there were still a few hours of daylight. She could not remember when she first started working in the fields. Her first memory was trailing behind Papa to pick the white cotton boll from the thorny petals, holding it captive. Papa had made a little burlap tote sack to sling over her shoulder, and she was as proud of this as she would have been of anything. She had never owned a toy, and the only game she'd ever played was running with her brothers.

Papa believed in schooling, but putting in the crop came first. She had never been to school long enough to learn much. She had to stay out to work in the fields or to help Ma so often that it seemed as though she stayed out more than she went. She couldn't read and could barely write her name. Papa had taught her numbers and to add and subtract on her fingers. Working with her hands always came easier than book learning. She knew she was a good worker, and she was proud to do her share.

Her papa was a sharecropper. The cotton crop was the only way he had to make cash money for such necessities as shoes and vittles to last through the winter. In a good crop year there might be a little extra for hard candy and new warm socks for Christmas. Everything in their life depended on the cotton crop. Times were always hard for the family, but Papa kept them going by working from sunup to the last light after sundown. Ma was little help in providing for the seven young'uns. She usually was in one of her spells where she just sat and did not talk or lift a hand to help with anything.

Sharecroppers owned no land but provided the labor to make a crop. The harvest was divided between the landowner and the tenant according to their set deal.

Plowing was the first step in making a crop. It took a big, strong man to hold onto the plow handles and manage the mule at the same time. A sad feeling would come over Myra when she saw her papa struggle behind the plow.

After the land was plowed and ready, the seeds were planted. Sharecroppers valued every seed and tried hard not to lose a single plant.

In early spring, the little cotton plants started breaking through the hard-packed mounds of dirt, and the grass and weeds were right there to choke them out. Chopping weeds out by their roots was the only way to protect the little plants. The chopper had to bend over, hold the hoe at the bottom, and be very careful to chop out the weed and not the cotton plant. This hard, backbreaking work was done for many weeks until the cotton was tall and strong enough to stand above the weeds.

The cotton was open and ready in early fall, and the cropper put every hand in his family into the field to get it picked. After a day in the cotton field, the pickers were so tired they could hardly make it back home. That was the only way to make a crop, and a sharecropper had to make a crop.

When Myra reached the path that led up to their place, she put two fingers in her mouth and let out a shrill whistle to let Papa know she was on her way. In a minute he sent the whistle back to her. She and Papa had special signals that no one else knew.

She passed through the house just long enough to take off her school dress and put on overalls and her straw hat. She always wore a long-sleeved shirt and a big straw hat to keep the sun off. She hated the way the sun made her skin dark. Her skin always turned brown as a berry every summer no matter how much she kept it covered. Her skin came from Ma's side of the family where there was some Indian blood. All the young'uns, except Myra and Joe Wiley, had light hair and fair skin like Papa. Papa's eyes were as blue as the sky, but all the young'uns had brown eyes. Myra, Joe Wiley, and Ma had the same coal black hair, skin the color of honey, and eyes that were as dark as pitch. Joe Wiley never paid this any mind, but Myra couldn't figure out why she was the one who had to look like an Indian. Sometimes she tried to picture herself with feathers in her hair, and this made her laugh.

When she reached the field, Papa and Will Rob were chopping far down the row. She just picked up her hoe and started making the dust fly as she chopped. Most folks would think this work was too hard for a girl just into her thirteenth year, but Myra was strong and could chop out a weed with one swing. The plowed dirt was soft and felt comforting to her feet. The three of them worked silently up and down the rows. When the sun was low in the sky, Papa called out.

"Little Girl, finish up that row and then get on to the house to help yore ma get supper on the table."

At the end of the row, she looked at the work she had done and felt her mouth curling up in a smile. Her rows were clean and clear of weeds, and she knew she had done a good turn of work. On the way to the house, she stopped at the well, drew up a bucket of water, turned it up, and drank until her thirst was gone. She knew that one of the best things on God's earth was cool water from a good well. The remaining water was poured into an old bucket, so she could wash up. Finally, she just put her whole face down in the water, and that made all the miseries of chopping leave her.

Now it was time to think about supper. This was the time of year when all the cured meat and dried peas had been eaten up, and they were getting close to the bottom of the flour barrel. Soon the spring garden would be coming in, and they would have fresh greens, but tonight's supper would be biscuits and flour-water gravy. She could feel her empty stomach pinching her backbone.

None of the family had much to eat during the day. She carried a syrup bucket of leftover biscuits for her and her little brothers. She always took the boys to the end of the schoolyard before she opened the syrup bucket and divided their biscuits. It made you even hungrier to watch the other young'uns opening their buckets and taking out their lunches. She tried hard to keep from smelling when she walked past, but she always got a whiff of fried meat, and her mouth would water.

"Hey, Myra, what ya got in yore bucket? Y'all so pore I bet you proud to have a hickory nut and a rock to crack it," one of the ol' boys would yell at her.

Myra had to squeeze her eyes shut to keep from squalling and balled up her fists tight so he wouldn't know that what he said bothered her. Her oldest brother, Joe Wiley, had taught her that before he ran off.

When she got closer to the house, there was a good, sweet smell in the air. She knew it was coming from the oven of the wood stove, but it couldn't be what she thought it smelled like. She went in the kitchen, and Ma was grinning as she opened the oven door to show Myra ten fat sweet taters, baked just right and already oozing out that sweet, sticky stuff that made them taste so good.

"Ma, I know we ain't got no sweet taters left. We et'um all right after Christmas."

"We shore put one over on ya, Myra. I told yore pa not to tell ya. The boss man came and got Will Rob this morning to help him clear out some brush. Then he gives him these sweet taters for his work."

To Myra, ten sweet taters were good pay for a morning's work. She hurried to get the little young'uns washed and to the table before Papa and Will Rob came up the path. Her older sister, Annie Lou, came in holding Dolly, the baby, and sat down at the table as if she was invited company. She got to go to school every day and never worked in the field. Myra didn't know why this was so, but she just accepted it and went on doing her work.

The table looked like Sunday dinner. The tops of the biscuits were browned just right. A jug of fresh milk from the cow had been cooling in the well, and even the flour-water gravy looked thick and filling. Ma broke up the taters so everyone would have a piece. Then they bowed their heads for Papa's grace.

"Oh Lord, we are thankful for these and all other blessings.

"Keep us ever mindful of the needs of others."

"I'd just like to know who these others are with more needs than us," her older brother, Will Rob, always whispered to Myra.

One time Papa heard him say it, and he just looked at Will Rob for a long time. Then he told them a story about how hard it was for the colored folks after the big war. One time Papa saw a man gathering up acorns to take home to feed his young'uns. After that tale, Will Rob just dropped his head and didn't eat nearly as much as he usually did.

Myra filled the little young'uns' plates twice. Papa's plate was full, but he hadn't eaten a bite. He was just feasting his eyes on watching his young'uns fill their bellies. Ma was holding the baby, Dolly, and was feeding her mashed tater. Myra hoped this meant that Ma was over the bad times she always had after a new young'un came. She saw Papa watching Ma. His eyes were bright blue and not cloudy and sad like when Ma was not herself. A peaceful feeling came over her, and then she knew just what Papa meant when he said his grace.

Every evening after supper, Papa and Will Rob sat on the front porch and smoked their corncob pipes. A wild tobacco grew in the woods. Everyone called it rabbit tobackey. Papa pulled some every fall and hung it from the barn rafters to dry. He did enjoy smoking his pipe on the porch in the evening. Will Rob had taken up the habit. Myra thought he liked being able to be like Papa more than he liked the smoking. She always tried to hear them talking while she was cleaning up the kitchen and putting the little young'uns to bed. When everything was tidy and the little boys had settled down, she went outside to sit with them.

Most nights they just sat without talking and enjoyed the soft, quiet feeling of the night. In the distance, all kinds of critters were making their night noises, and the sweet rabbit tobackey smoke perfumed the air. On this night, there wasn't a moon or a star in the sky that they could see. The only light came from the lamp inside the house where Annie Lou was getting her lessons at the table. Kerosene for the lamp was almost gone, and the only time there was light was when Anne Lou was doing her lessons. A breeze was blowing, which meant there probably would be a shower before morning. That would be good for the little plants. Papa knew a lot about telling what the weather was going to be. He just knew a lot about everything.

On Sunday, Papa always read to them from the Good Book. He would tell them about heaven and what a fine place it was to be. On evenings like this, Myra got a good feeling all inside of her, and she thought that might be the same kind of feeling that you would have up there.

This was one of the nights when Papa got to talking. "Young'uns, we got a chance of gettin' a little ahead this year. The land here is good, and the boss man is a fair and honest man. Looks like every seed I put down will make a plant, and we gonna get the rains and sun just when we need it."

"You reckon that's right, Papa? We ain't never had that kind of luck."

"Will Rob, I know that's right. I've seen signs in my dreams. Boy, you got to dream, and you got to follow yore dreams. One of these days we just might have cotton in Augusta."

They had heard Papa talk about cotton in Augusta before, and they had no idea what this meant. In fact, they did not even know where Augusta was.

This time, Will Rob got more interested in thinking that they just might make better this year.

"Why would we want cotton in Augusta?"

"Well, Son, that's what folks can do when they have more money left over from settling up than it takes to run them for the next year. Then they can have some of their cotton put in the warehouses up in Augusta and have it held until the price goes up later in the year. That's how rich folks get richer."

Tenant farmers in Georgia did not often get a chance to think about dreams. Myra didn't understand the system of sharecropping that kept her papa and other Georgia tenants in bondage to working land they would never own. Papa didn't outright own anything except a houseful of young'uns, a wagon, an old mule, a cow, a few tools, and their housekeeping stuff. Land meant a better life, and, as Papa often said, he didn't even own a cupful of soil. He had to sign on with a landowner to work for a part of the crop in exchange for a shack to live in, seed, fertilizer, and the use of plows and tools. Most boss men would stake you when you ran short of necessities before the year was out. Of course, all this was taken out of your share on settlement day.

Every year the tenant's worst fear was being "counted out." This meant you owed the boss man more than your share of the money. Anytime this happened, the tenant's family faced a hungry winter. This had never happened to Papa. He could deal with the landowners better than most tenants. Maybe it was because he could read, write, and talk as good as the boss man. He always wrote down how much the boss man had staked him.

When Papa went to town with the boss man to settle up, he prayed that he wouldn't be "counted out," and he could come home with a little money in his pocket. On a year with a good crop, he would think his prayers were answered until the boss man started taking out. Even though Papa wrote everything down, the boss man always found things to take out that he hadn't expected. Papa was a proud man, and he was thankful when he could stretch the little bit of money enough to get shoes for all the young'uns, rations to last through the winter, and a little something for Christmas.

Sometimes Papa would decide to try another year with the same landowner, and other years he would look for a better place. The only thing that ever changed year to year was the tenant shack. Actually, these weren't really different, just in different parts of the county.

This year had seemed different. Papa came home and told the family that he had signed on to make a crop for a man who lived on a good-sized farm about ten miles from where they were living. He had heard this landowner was always decent to his tenants, and Papa sounded really hopeful. They moved just before the cold weather started.

Papa loaded up the wagon with everything they owned. They had eaten all the chickens, even the fighting rooster. When he went in the dumpling pot, everybody cheered. They had learned that it just didn't pay to move chickens, since they made such a mess when they were penned. Queen Easter, the cow, was tied and walked behind the wagon. Papa, Ma, Annie Lou, and the baby, Dolly, rode in the wagon. The rest of the young'uns—Will Rob, Myra, Jesse, and Arno—walked along behind. They didn't have to walk fast because the heavily loaded wagon barely crept along. Will Rob carried a stick to prod the cow when she didn't move fast enough. When the little boys got tired and started to whine, Will Rob would take turns letting them ride on his back. Will Rob wasn't a big strapping boy like the oldest brother, Joe Wiley. He was not much taller than Myra and was skinny as a rail. All the same, since he was the oldest boy at home, he tried to act big.

Joe Wiley had not lived with them since cotton pickin' time a year ago. He hired out and did work for other farmers. He and Papa never did get along. He had a hard way of talking. It tended to be sort of the way Ma talked at times. Papa did not like for him to say hurtful things to the others. One day Papa got on to him something terrible for talking mean to Will Rob.

"I think it's time for me to go on down the road," he muttered under his breath, but loud enough for Papa to hear.

He packed up everything he owned in a croker sack and left. Papa stood and watched him from the gate until he couldn't see him any more. They heard that he was living with some folks around Riddleville and that he was sweet on their daughter. Myra missed him a lot, and she knew Papa did too.

It took all day to travel the ten miles across Washington County. They reached the new place just after sundown. The house stood right by the road, and even in the November wind, it looked tight and sturdy. The front steps hadn't been broken up for stove wood like they had been in most of the other tenant houses. There was a wide porch across the front to sit on at night after supper. A big chinaberry tree in the yard was just right for a swing.

They walked through the house and looked everything over. The front fireplace room was big enough for Ma and Papa's bed and the little bed for Annie Lou and the baby. They could put the eatin' table in there too. Papa had made the table from boards that he could take apart every time they moved. They took great pride in owning a chair apiece. Papa did love for all of them to sit down together and eat their meals. In the cold weather, they set the lamp on the table, and Papa wrote stuff down in his tablet while the young'uns did their lessons. That was one good thing about the cold weather.

Right off the front room was the kitchen with the stovepipe sticking out the sidewall. A shelf was built across one side to set things on. Behind the kitchen was a little porch where they could put out water buckets. The well was right beside the porch, so they could stand there and draw water. Papa dropped the bucket in and drew it up full of water. He gave everyone a drink of the sweet, cool water. He said the well was deep so they would always have plenty of good water.

Best of all was a shed room on the back that the boss man had built for them. It didn't have a ceiling, and the tin roof sloped down in the back so you couldn't stand up. It was just right for Myra, Will Rob, Jesse, and Arno. Ma had plenty of soft, warm quilts, and there was enough floor space for Myra and the boys to make pallets.

In the back was a woodshed, smokehouse, and a little pen for chickens. The new boss man had promised to give them a start of chickens. He sounded different from any other boss man. The only thing Ma didn't like was the outhouse being way back in the field from the house. Papa thought this was better than having it close to the house, and they would all get used to it. It was a fine house.

"Ann, we are going to have a real home here. I know our luck has changed," Papa said as he put his arm around her.

As soon as they moved into the house, the boss man, Mr. Clyde, came by and brought the chickens just as he said he would. After that, he came by the house real often and talked to Papa on the porch. He looked Papa right in the eye and called him Martin.

All the other boss men had looked at the dirt when they talked to him and called him Stuart. One boss man had even called him "Boy." Every time Mr. Clyde was there, Papa pulled out his tablet, and they figured out things about the crop.

Myra expected a slim Christmas that year. Papa was trying to hold onto what little cash he had. She figured there would be some hard candy, at least for the little boys. On the day before Christmas, Mr. Clyde came by and brought a big bag of oranges, a sack of sugar, a little stuffed doll for Dolly, and a pair of wool socks for each of the young'uns. He said his wife wasn't able to do much, but she did like to knit and made the socks for them. When he started to leave, Papa tried to thank him, but he just kept on walking.

"Martin, you're a good man with a fine family. I am proud to have you on my place." Then he climbed up on his wagon seat and drove away. Papa seemed to stand up straighter after that, even when he was worn-out from the fields.

Christmas Day was warm and sunny like a spring day. Ma made a big pot of greens with fatback in it and used the sugar to make custard filled with eggs from the new chickens and milk from Queen Easter. After dinner, Papa took the family out in the woods to walk around and look for roots and herbs that could help you get over bellyaches and things. Papa knew a lot about things like that. He even found some leaves to bring home and boil to make tea. Everyone had a cup, and it tasted like the cookies they gave out at school before Christmas. It was the best Christmas they ever had.

When school reopened after Christmas, all the young'uns, except Will Rob, started to the little one-room school at the crossroads about two miles from their place. One teacher taught all twenty-one students. School had always been a hard place for Myra. Learning didn't come easy to her like it did to Annie Lou and Arno. She never got into jumping rope, playing jacks, or joining the singsong games that the girls played at recess. There was always some ol' boy to aggravate her. Most of the teachers did not have any patience with helping her catch up after she had been absent for a long time. She often asked Papa if she could stay home and work every day like Will Rob, but he wouldn't even talk about it.

This year was different. Her teacher was a pretty young lady named Miss Caroline Wommack. She always smiled and talked to Myra, but she didn't know what to do with her. Myra was too big to study with the young group, and she didn't know enough to be with the older students. Miss Caroline had to teach everyone, and it was hard for her to spend much time with any one student. Since Myra couldn't read the textbooks, she wasn't given many assignments. Annie Lou spent most of the day reading and writing. Arno had almost finished the Blue Back Speller and could recite everything in it. Little Jesse hadn't learned much yet, so he sat and played with some wooden blocks with the alphabet on them. Myra sat quietly and made little squares from pieces of yarn she had found. She didn't have much yarn, so she just braided it and then unwound it and started over. She really liked to do this and didn't care if it made the others laugh at her. It passed the day, and Miss Caroline seemed to like to see her do this. Annie Lou would tell Ma that Myra was shaming herself at school with that crazy string twisting. Sometimes Ma whipped her for it, but Myra never told Papa.

Lightning flashed in the dark sky, and in a minute rain pattered on the tin roof of the porch. Myra jerked her head up and realized that she had been lost in her own thoughts.

Will Rob had already gone into the house when Papa said, "Come on, Little Girl, we need to get in before the lightning gets sharp. This here rain is just what our crop needs, and besides that, it makes for good sleeping under the tin roof."

The next day Myra sat in the classroom trying to make sense out of what the teacher was saying about how people had come from across the water to settle the country. It didn't make much sense to Myra. She couldn't figure out why they would cross water to come over to these woods. No mention was made of the Indians, so she wondered if they were already there or if they came with the people.

She was about to fall asleep when she felt a spitball hit her head. The glob of chewed paper fell and spattered on her skirt. It didn't hurt, but thinking about the wad of spit sure turned her stomach. It came from a boy named Willie Sconyer, who always picked on her. He had done this before, so this time she was ready for him. On the way to school, she picked up a handful of big acorns and hid them in her pocket. She slipped one out, waited for Miss Caroline to look the other way, and then she popped him on the back of the head. He jumped up and hollered as though he had been shot.

"Myra done hit."

"I seen her do hit. She had them acorns in her pocket. She meant to do it."

"Willie hadn't done nothin'. She just chunked at acorn at 'em."

Most of the class started yelling to tell what had happened. Myra trembled. She didn't want Miss Caroline to be mad at her, and she knew she had done wrong.

The teacher told the class to be quiet and then said, "Willie, I think you will live. Myra, I want to see you after school lets out."

Most of the class, including Annie Lou, looked at Myra, and their eyes were saying, "You are going to get what you deserve now. We wouldn't want to be in your shoes."

Myra felt bad and didn't know what she would say to Miss Caroline. She knew Annie Lou would hurry home to tell Ma all about it, and that would surely mean a switching. The day seemed to never end. Finally, Miss Caroline rang the bell, and everyone left but Myra. She just kept sitting in her desk while Miss Caroline went outside to watch the others leave. When the teacher came back inside, she sat down on the bench facing Myra.

"Hold up your head, Myra, and look at me."

"Yes'um." She was squeezing her eyes hard to keep from crying.

"Myra, you work so well with your hands that I have a new assignment I think will be more important for you to learn."

Myra looked right at Miss Caroline's eyes, but she didn't say a word. She just knew the assignment would be lining up the alphabet blocks with Jesse. The teacher went to her desk and brought back a sack. When she reached inside, Myra expected her to bring out the blocks. What she pulled out was a long shiny needle and a ball of heavy white thread. She also brought out some pretty scarves and pieces made from different colors of the thread.

"Do you like these pieces, Myra?"

"Yes'um"

"This is crocheting, and I think you would be very good at this. Would you like for me to teach you?"

"Oh, yes'um. I want to learn to do that more than I have ever wanted anything in my life." She couldn't wait to get the needle in her hand.

The teacher took out her own needle and ball of thread and told her to watch and try to follow. At first, her hands would not work with the needle any better than they did with a pencil. Soon she got the hang of how to make a stitch, and in no time she had a row of stitches. Miss Caroline clapped her hands and laughed. Both needles clicked and clicked as more and more stitches were added. Myra's stitches were beginning to make a square. Every stitch seemed to get easier and better. She didn't even think about the time and needing to get home to help Papa.

Miss Caroline stopped her needle and said, "Oh, Myra, it is getting late. I hope your folks won't be worried about you, but I know Annie Lou told them that you were staying after school. You better get on home. Take the thread and needle with you to practice on tonight. Every day during dinnertime we can work together. I am happy you are doing so well with this."

Myra ran out of the room and headed down the road as fast as she could run. Annie Lou had surely told Ma, but she didn't know just what kind of light her sister might have put on it. It was almost dusk dark when she ran panting into the yard. Ma was waiting at the door with a switch in her hand. Ma always took whatever Annie Lou said for the gospel truth, and Annie Lou was spiteful and tried to keep Myra in trouble. Ma didn't wait to hear Myra's story. All she knew was that Myra had to stay after school, and that was bad. She started switching, and her sister sat across the porch grinning. The peach switch stung like fire on her bare legs. Myra danced around trying to avoid the switch, but she did not shed a tear. She was holding the bag with the crochet stuff all through the switching. Ma was too busy switching to notice. Myra knew she had to find a place to hide the needle and thread. This was not the time to show Ma and hear her say there was no need for such foolishness and to give the stuff back to the teacher.

There was no way Myra would ever give up her chance to learn to crochet. She just had to find a way to keep it from Ma. She hurried out to the barn, put the needle and thread in one of the hen boxes, and covered it with straw. She hoped none of the hens would decide to nest in that box.

Papa and Will Rob would be coming in for supper soon. Myra walked into the house and was relieved to see a fire had been started in the stove. There wasn't time for the oven to get hot enough for biscuits. Neither Ma nor Annie Lou made a move to start any supper, so Myra knew it was up to her. The little young'uns were hungry and had already started whining and fussing. The sweet taters were gone, and she couldn't find anything but a little flour in the bottom of the barrel and a dab of hog grease. She could put together a supper of hoecake and flour-water gravy, but Lord, what would they eat the next night? She went out to the well and was thankful to find a jug of cool milk from Queen Easter. After she pulled up the milk, she looked across to Will Rob's garden and could see some little green sprouts. She hurried out there and found a few of the onion plants had sprouted and had little roots on then. She knew it was way too soon to pull them, but her stomach told her how good that gravy would taste flavored with onion. She pulled up a few and prayed that Will Rob wouldn't be mad.

There was just enough flour to make two hoecakes with a little leftover to thicken the gravy. She chopped the onions and browned them with the flour in a little of the grease. Then she filled the pan with milk and let it cook down. The gravy was ready just as she took off the last hoecake. The top and bottom of the bread was browned just right, and the middle was soft and warm. She put the food and the jug of milk on the table just as Papa and Will Rob walked in the door.

"Myra, when we came up to the porch and smelled them onions, I knew you had cooked us a good supper," said Will Rob.

"Yes, sir, this looks mighty fine, Little Girl. Now let's bow our heads for grace."

The supper wasn't much, but it filled their bellies. Myra joined Papa in giving thanks, but she also asked the Lord to help her find something for tomorrow night's supper.

-2-

When Papa left for the field the next morning, Myra felt relieved. She was so afraid that he would say he needed her to stay home and help in the field. She knew it was coming, but she hoped be able to go to school long enough to learn the crocheting

All morning as she sat in the classroom, crocheting was all she could think about. The hours until dinnertime seemed to take forever. When Miss Caroline rang the bell, Myra took out her piece of hoecake and gave the bucket to Arno to take outside and share with Jesse. She got a dipper of water and finished her piece of bread before Miss Caroline came back into the room. The teacher sat down and brought a little basket from under her desk. She had a biscuit with a slab of something yellow inside it. It smelled kinda strong and didn't look like anything Myra had ever seen before. She was glad it didn't have a good smell like fried meat, so her mouth wouldn't start watering. There was also a red apple and a tin cup on a little piece of cloth. It seemed funny to Myra to see her teacher eating. She never had thought about teachers eating and doing things like other folks.

"Myra, dear, you just sit here and eat your dinner with me. First, I need a cup of water."

"Ma'am, I done et my dinner, but I will fetch you some fresh water from the well." Myra was pleased to have the chance to get water for the teacher.

"Goodness, you did eat fast. Now let's get started. I can eat and crochet at the same time. I do it all the time."

They worked all through the dinnertime and stopped only for Miss Caroline to help Myra when her stitches got tangled. Most of the other students, including Annie Lou, kept peeking in the window. They thought

Myra was getting some kind of punishment for hitting Willie with the acorn. She didn't care what they thought and was more excited than she had ever been in her life.

"Myra, dear, you are taking to this faster than anyone I have ever taught before. Now I have to ring the bell for the others to come in for the afternoon, so stick the needle into the thread and go to your seat."

Myra tried to think of something to say to show how much she enjoyed the crocheting, but all she could say was, "Yes'um."

When the teacher rang the bell for the end of the day, she motioned for Myra to come up to her desk. Myra still feared a punishment was coming.

"Myra, my mother and I make a big garden every year, and she puts up everything we grow. There is just the two of us, and we can't eat it up before we need the jars again. Could your mother use these stewed tomatoes?"

"Oh, yes'um, we'se shore could use 'em."

"I'd appreciate you helping me empty these jars, but you be sure to bring them back to me." Miss Caroline sat two big jars of tomatoes on her desk. Myra eyed the jars and knew there would be something for supper that night.

"Oh yes'um. We love stewed maters. We ain't had none in a long time. I'm much obliged to ya."

Myra took a jar under each arm and headed for home. Now she had something for supper, but she had no flour for biscuits to put the stewed tomatoes over. When she got home, she was surprised to see Papa sitting on the porch.

"That is mighty kind of yore teacher, and we will be glad to help her empty out her jars. You just be shore you don't break 'em and get 'em back to her. Now you get on in the kitchen. The fire is already started for you to make some of yore good biscuits."

"Papa, I can't make no biscuits without flour and grease. We used the last up last night."

"Well, you just look in the kitchen and tell me what you see."

Myra opened the flour barrel and found it nearly filled. Sitting on the table was a can of hog grease, a ham bone with plenty of scraps for seasoning, and a croker sack of dried peas to be shelled. Myra knew she had prayed last night for help with supper, but she didn't really believe the Lord would just come down and put this in their kitchen. Papa sat with his blue eyes twinkling and watched her puzzlement.

"I sat out there on the porch last night and figgered and figgered how I could get enough vittles to keep us going 'til the garden started makin'. I never had to ask a boss man to carry me before, and I shore didn't want to ask Mr. Clyde. We'll need all the cash we get for the crop next fall. If we start eatin' up the money now, we'll run even shorter. It worried me something fierce, but I knew I couldn't let y'all go hungry.

"So I knocked off early this evenin' and went to talk to Mr. Clyde. I told him I wuz just at the end of my rope. It didn't seem to bother him one bit. He told me that he and his wife still are in the habit of stocking up on vittles just like they did when they had a houseful of young'uns. Now it's just the two of them, and there is always more than they need. He said every year he ends up throwing out flour that has weevils in it, and the grease gets rancid. Well, what happen is, he just plain gave me all these vittles. I figure it is enough to tide us over. Don't you think so, Little Girl?"

"Oh yea, Papa. We can get by on this fer a long time." Myra's mind was racing as she thought of all the good suppers she would be cooking.

"He is shore a good man, and he didn't make me feel like I owed him a thing. 'Course, I thanked him plenty and offered to work it off around his place. He said I would more than pay him back by my work with the crop."

Maybe the Good Lord hadn't brought that stuff right into their kitchen, but He sure had provided a way for them to get it. She got busy and made a big pan of biscuits and stewed the tomatoes with some of the hog grease and a few of Will Rob's onions.

Ma and Annie Lou had been in the back taking in the wash, and then they just stayed outside playing with Dolly. Myra figured they stayed out because they didn't want to face cooking supper with no flour. Everybody was surprised to be having such a good supper.

In a few days, Myra knew as much about crocheting as Miss Caroline, and the teacher said she couldn't tell Myra's work from her own. Most days she had Myra wait when the others left, and she always had more jars to be emptied. The next day it was soup mix with tomatoes, okra, corn, and beans in it. Then it was green snap beans and little white taters. One day it was peaches that were sweet enough to eat right out of the jar. The Stuarts had never eaten so much good stuff.

Myra started thinking about how she could get some of those jars. There was always plenty to eat in the summer with the vegetables and all the wild fruits and berries growing around, but there was no way to keep it through the winter. Now she knew how, if she could just get some jars.

During the next few weeks, Myra tried to learn all that she could about the crocheting. Almost every day, Myra took home more jars to be emptied. The family had a good filling supper every night. Myra usually cooked, and she loved seasoning things up with the meat scraps. These were the best days that she had ever known, but she knew a change was coming. She hurried home every day after school and tried to work even harder. No matter how hard they worked, she could see the weeds getting ahead of them.

Finally, one night after supper Papa told her, "Little Girl, I shore hate to have to do this to you. I know you're likin' school better this year than you ever have, and I'd give anything if you could go on and finish up the term. It can't be helped. We got a fine crop coming on if we can keep the weeds down. All this rain we've had is good for the plants, but it makes the weeds grow just as fast. Starting tomorrow, I need you to stay home and help us all day. I could keep Jesse and Arno out, but they just ain't the help that you are. I'm shore sorry, Little Girl."

"It's all right, Papa. I know you got to have the help. Besides, I done learned about all I will learn this year."

That was what she said, but she was glad Papa couldn't see the tears in her eyes. Myra went over and sat on the floor by his feet. She wanted to be close to him. She wanted to tell him that it didn't matter to her, and she knew he wouldn't keep her out unless there was no other way. She didn't know how to say that, so she just leaned her head against his leg. That was all right, because Papa was the kind who knew how you felt without you saying the words.

They sat in silence for a few minutes, and then Will Rob said, "Heck, Myra, Papa might even let you smoke."

All three had a good laugh, and then Papa got to talking.

"More than anything, I want to get us a little place of our own. The best chance I have is to stay on with Mr. Clyde for a few years and try to put back some money. I've heard of a lot of small farmers that are giving up on farming and moving into town to find work. I just might be able to pick up a few acres in a year or so.

"But I won't be planting cotton. Cotton breaks yore heart and yore back. I don't know what it'll be, but I will put in another cash crop.

"Now, young'uns, when layin' by comes, we're going down to the river and fish all day. That evenin' we will go to Side Robert's little store at the crossroads and get us a block of ice, some tea, and sugar. He knows I have a good crop coming in, so I don't mind asking him to carry that little bit 'til the crop is settled. Then we are going to have us a fish fry and ask Mr. Clyde and his wife to take supper with us."

"We better get some cornmeal and grease too, Papa."

"Shore, we'll get what we need. When the cotton is ginned and me and Mr. Clyde settle up, I'm takin' yore ma and all of ya to Tennille for the whol' day. We're gonna make out a list of what we need, so we won't run short next year. Then we are going to that café and eat us some ice cream."

Since Papa was acting as if he knew they would have enough extra money to buy these things, Myra had something to ask.

"Papa, could we buy some canning jars so I can put up some stuff from summer to eat through the winter."

"Shore, Little Girl, I will if you promise to can some blackberries so we can have cobbler on Christmas Day."

That all sounded fine to Myra. She could have talked like this all night, but they were all getting sleepy. Papa said they had best turn in because tomorrow would be a long, hard day. Just as they stood up to go inside, they heard the *who-o-o* of an owl off in the distance. They didn't say anything, but they all knew that some folks said owls hooted when there was going to be a death nearby. Myra had never known of this happening, but all the same, the mournful *who-o-o* gave her a cold chill.

Next morning they started out at daybreak for the field. Myra was not even sleepy, for she wanted to get started on the chopping. Papa lagged behind, and Myra noticed that he didn't look right. She figured he was tired since they stayed up so late. They started to work, and before Myra was halfway down the row, she noticed Papa was way behind her. He stopped and leaned on his hoe. Myra had never seen him do this before. She went to the water bucket and brought him a dipper of water. He bathed off his face and drank the rest. She asked if he was all right, and he said he just needed a drink of water.

Will Rob was chopping far up the row and had not looked back. Myra wanted him to come back to see about Papa, but she didn't want to call out to him. When Papa left and went to the bushes, she ran up and told Will Rob.

They waited a little, and then Will Rob went to check on him. He went behind the bushes and hollered, "Myra, come quick."

She ran over to them and found Papa in an awful fix. He was crumpled up on the ground and had vomited all over himself. His skin was white as milk, and his lips looked plum blue. Sweat was breaking out all over his forehead. He couldn't hold his head up, and he didn't make a sound when they talked to him. All they knew to do was get him to the house to lie down. Somehow they got him up and put his arms around both of their necks and dragged him to the house.

When Ma saw them bringing him in, she went to hollering. They laid him on the bed and bathed his face with cool water. Ma told them to get on back to the field and let him rest. They didn't want to leave him, but they knew he would want them to keep on chopping.

They had just picked up their hoes when Ma came running, carrying Dolly and yelling. "He's had another spell. He shook so hard he nearly came off the bed, and now he's just sleeping. I can't wake him up. Will Rob, you gottta go fer the doctor."

Will Rob ran to hitch up the mule. Ma gave him a few coins tied in a handkerchief and told him to get Doc Mercer and tell him she would pay him the rest somehow. Will Rob took off, and Myra just followed Ma back to the house. Papa looked whiter than milk now, and you could hear his breathing out in the yard. They didn't know anything to do for him, so they just sat by him and bathed his face with cool water. Dolly had just started walking, and she kept walking around the bed and pulling Papa's hair. She wanted him to play with her like he usually did. Myra took her outside and tried to keep her quiet.

The time passed, and Annie Lou and the boys came in from school. When she saw Papa, Annie Lou started hollering and begging God to help Papa. Myra found something for the little young'uns to eat, and then they all sat on the steps and watched for Will Rob and the doctor. Myra knew they better get there soon. Papa couldn't keep up that hard breathing and live much longer.

She thought about praying, but she didn't know what to say to God, since they had never met. She hadn't ever been to a real church house that had a steeple and a graveyard by it. Those church houses were for the folks who owned land and didn't move around like tenants. Papa always tried to take them when a tent revival came close enough. They did love to go to those revivals, and most of all, they loved the singing and seeing someone get the spirit. Anne Lou got it last time they went, but it didn't last very long on her.

Ma and Annie Lou started screaming louder, and Myra ran inside.

"He's gone, young'uns. There ain't nothin' we can do to help him now. Yore pa is dead."

Everybody was crying. Myra sat down on the floor and could hear nothing but her own sobs. Arlo and Jesse didn't know what being dead really meant, but they knew if Myra was crying, it was a bad thing. Just at sundown, Will Rob returned with Doc Mercer. The doctor listened to Papa's chest and held his wrist for a long time.

He shook his head and said, "Ann, there wasn't a thing I could have done even if I had got here. He had the heart dropsy. I have treated a lot of his kin for it, and it runs in families. I've known Martin all his life, and I sure hate for him to go like this."

It was a real surprise to hear the doctor talking about Papa like he knew him well. They had only seen him one other time, and that was when the mule kicked Jesse.

"Ann, I'll go by and tell Clyde. I know he will see to it that you get some help in getting him buried. When I get back to Tennille, I will make sure some of his kin knows."

"My oldest boy, Joe Wiley, stays somewhere around Riddleville. I'd be shore thankful if ya could get word to him."

"I'll try my best to get word to him."

The young'uns were surprised to hear that Papa had kin. They had never heard anything about Ma or Papa having any kin. Myra did think about it one time when they were in Tennille, and Papa gave them all a penny to buy candy. Instead of going to Mr. Roundtree's big store, they walked all the way to the end of the boardwalk to a little store that didn't sell much, but it had a lot of jars of candy in the window.

A real pretty lady stood behind the counter in the store, and there was something that just kept Myra looking at her. Somehow, the lady knew all their names. After they picked out their candy, she filled the bags up to the top. Besides that, she gave them each a piece of every kind of candy. Myra couldn't stop looking at her. She kept smiling at them, and Myra felt a funny feeling toward her. It was kind of like she felt when she gave Dolly a bath and she was all clean and smelling good. Myra figured if she ever got another penny, she would go back to that store because her candy was much cheaper than Mr. Roundtree's. There was enough candy to eat on all the way home.

When they got to the wagon and showed it to Papa, he had a funny look, and then he said, "Don't any of you ever go in that store again. I give all of my business to Mr. Roundtree, and he wouldn't like it if he knew you bought somewhere else."

Every time they went to town, Myra walked past that store. She always hoped the lady would come out, and she could speak to her.

Doc Mercer closed Papa's eyes. Myra hadn't even noticed that they were open. He covered him up with a sheet, and then he left. He didn't say anything to Ma about giving him more money, and Myra noticed the coins Will Rob had taken with him were on the table and still tied up in the handkerchief. Everyone just kept sitting there, and in a little bit, Mr. Clyde and his wife came in.

"Miz Stuart, I can't tell you how much I hate that this happened to Martin. He was a fine man."

Miz Clyde went into the kitchen and started setting out some stuff that she had brought from her house for them to eat. She said it wasn't much, but she just brought what she had already fixed. There was a big pan of biscuits, a bowl of sweet clabber, preserves, slices of crisp fried fatback, and baked sweet taters. Myra figured if this was what they ate on a regular week night, they must really eat good stuff on Sunday. Everybody ate except Myra. She didn't feel hungry and didn't think she could ever eat again. She could feel a big knot in her throat that wouldn't come up and wouldn't go down. She was glad to see the boys eat and Annie Lou feed Dolly.

Mr. Clyde was sitting at the table talking with Ma in a low voice. Myra knew better than to listen in, but she couldn't help overhearing.

"I am going straight to my preacher and ask him and some of the church folks to come tomorrow and help lay him out and see about the burying."

None of them knew what laying out meant, but they guessed they would find out tomorrow.

The next morning the folks did come. There was a mess of them—men folks, women, and the preacher. They brought a bunch more vittles and bouquets of cut flowers. The preacher prayed a long prayer, and then he told Ma that he would preach Papa a funeral, and they could bury him in the church graveyard.

Then he said something surprising. "I have always known the Stuarts, and some of them have been in my church in other parts of the county. I know they wouldn't want it any other way."

Ma seemed glad about having a place to put Papa, but she didn't say thank you or nothing else to the preacher.

They got through that day, and a lot of people came to see them. Myra didn't know that so many folks knew Papa. Some of them were colored folks who came to the back porch and said for her to tell Miz Stuart how sorry they were and that Mr. Stuart was always good to them.

She remembered one time when a colored family was passing by with all they owned strapped to their backs as though they were moving. There was a bunch of little young'uns, and they asked Papa for some water. He told them to come and sit in the shade on the porch. It was summertime, and the garden was bearing more than they could eat. Papa went in the house and brought back a big pot of peas that Ma had just cooked and a pan of corn bread. He gave it to them, and they ate it right out of the pot like they hadn't eaten in a long time.

Most of the time, Ma would have given Papa a tongue-lashing for giving her cooking away. All she said was, "Well, Martin, we will just have to make do with what's left."

There was still plenty of okra, tomatoes, cucumbers, and cold biscuits left from breakfast. That was when they lived in another part of the county, but she figured these colored folks must have heard about Papa being good to some of their folks.

Two of the men folks bathed Papa and put his good pair of overalls and best shirt on him and laid him out on the bed. That morning Mr. Clyde took Will Rob to his house and let him use his hammers and saws to make Papa a coffin out of some pine wood that he already had cut. When they brought it into the house, Myra didn't know what it was until Will Rob told her. She was glad to know that Papa wouldn't have to lie right on the ground. Mr. Clyde and Will Rob lifted the body up and put it in the coffin. Folks who came by said that he looked real good. Myra looked at him, but she didn't like to see him like that. He looked like he was asleep, but he never had slept in his best clothes. She tried to go in and sit by him, but she just couldn't do it. It seemed like she was with him more when she was on the porch. Ma or Annie Lou sat by him all day. Will Rob sat up beside him all night.

Papa's burial was the next morning. When it was time to go, all the young'uns, except Dolly, lifted up the coffin and put it on the wagon. Even King Solomon looked sad. Thinking about how Papa always said Solomon had pretty teeth usually made her laugh. The knot in her throat was still there, and it wouldn't let laughing come out. Heavy dark clouds were threatening, but it never rained. A crowd of folks were already at the graveyard when they got there.

Myra was surprised to see the pretty woman from the store standing beside a man who looked just like Papa, except that he had a mustache.

They were dressed in nice clothes and stood off to themselves. The preacher talked some about how he had heard that Papa was a fine Christian man and a loving husband and father. He prayed a long prayer and asked the Lord to take Papa in and to watch over all his loved ones. Then they put Papa's coffin in the ground and covered it up with a big mound of dirt.

Mr. Clyde had helped Will Rob carve Papa's name, birth date, and death date on a board, and they stuck that in the mound of dirt. Will Rob said he wanted to put "Loving husband and father" on it, but there wasn't enough room. Since Mr. Clyde had been so nice, Will Rob didn't want to ask him for more board.

Myra thought about going over and saying something to the candy store lady. The preacher walked over and talked to them after the burial, and then they got in their buggy and drove off down the road.

Back at home, Myra didn't know what to do or how you were supposed to act when your papa died. She just walked around the house and touched things and thought about how just two days before Papa had been touching those things. She picked up his hat from the hook and smelled it. It smelled just like Papa. She took it out to the woodshed and hid it so she would know it was there to smell any time she had that sick, lonely feeling. Papa's pipe was on the porch rail where he left it every night. The rabbit tobackey smell was still in it. She got to thinking that Papa should have taken his pipe with him 'cause she knew he would still want to smoke every evening. Since those times they sat together while he and Will Rob smoked seemed like what heaven must be like, she figured folks got to smoke in heaven. She decided she would go back to the church graveyard and dig into that mound of dirt over Papa and put his pipe with him. She didn't think he would need no tobackey 'cause rabbit tobackey grows everywhere. There was probably plenty in heaven.

She walked out to the field and looked at the cotton. In the three days they had missed chopping, the weeds had started choking it out again. Tomorrow morning they had to get back to work. She didn't know how they would do it without Papa, but they would sure try. Then she thought about a day awhile back when they were all chopping and she was fussing 'cause she had a worse row than anyone.

"You shore do have a tough row to hoe, Little Girl. That's the way it is in this ol' life, but you just have to keep on chopping."

When they were working close by each other in the field, Papa always talked to her about things like that. He told her to always look for something good that might come out of things that happened to her. He had a way of making her feel as though she could be a help to people. That was real important to Papa.

He said things like, "Little Girl, you got a good spirit and a brightness about you. Don't keep that hid."

Now that he was gone, she could see no brightness ahead for her, but she knew that Papa wouldn't want her to think that way.

She thought about what that preacher had said when he was praying over Papa's grave. He said Papa was safe in the arms of Jesus now. She had seen a picture of Jesus on a fan at a tent meeting one time, and she thought he looked like the kind of fellow whom Papa would like to spend time with. Papa never liked no cussin' or rough talk, and he tried to say something nice about everybody. When she fussed about Annie Lou, Papa always told her that it always made you feel better if you said something nice instead of something mean. That was when he told her about the mule teeth.

He said when he looked at their poor ol' mule, King Solomon (Papa always named the animals from the Bible, and he specially liked the king and queen names), he always thought that the ol' mule might be swaybacked and worn-out looking, but he sure had pretty teeth. Myra had never thought about mule teeth being pretty so that made her laugh and forget about being mad with Annie Lou. She figured that Jesus would talk that way too, so he and Papa would do just fine walking around heaven together.

She walked back on the porch, and the first thing she heard was Mr. Clyde and Ma talking. Annie Lou and Will Rob were sitting at the table with them. Her eyes rested on what was in the middle of the table. There was a middling of smoked meat that looked as if it hadn't even been cut, a big bag of grits, a bucket of cornmeal, and a croker sack full of peas in the shell, dried and ready to be beaten out. She didn't take a seat but just stood over to the side.

Mr. Clyde was saying, "I shore am sorry, Miz Stuart. Martin was the best tenant I ever had, and I had hoped to have many good years with him. You all work hard, but these are just young'uns, and I can't turn this big crop over to them. I've got too much at stake here. I have to find someone to take it over."

"Please, Mr. Clyde, this is my papa's crop, and we'll bring it in if it takes all of us working night and day. I promise." Tears ran down Will Rob's cheeks as he pleaded.

"I know you will do everything you can, but it just can't be done. We'll all end up losing everything. I will make it right by you for your pa's time, and you can stay on here for the rest of the year. I will have to hire someone to come in. You can help with the picking, and I will pay you for that."

"Mr. Clyde, it wouldn't be right. My papa wanted this crop to be his best, and we ought to be the ones to do it." Will Rob continue to plead.

"Well, son," said Mr. Clyde, "you would be the one to run everything, and you are just a boy. How old are you?"

Will Rob stammered for a minute, but he knew he had to tell the truth. Papa had always told them that telling a lie got you into a worse fix.

"I'm old enough. I turned fourteen last November."

Mr. Clyde smiled, shook his head, and said, "You know, if you were a few years older or if there was an older boy, I just might take the chance. The way it is, I just can't do it."

If there was anything left of Myra's heart to break, this did it. They just couldn't let go of Papa's crop. She couldn't believe her ears at what she heard next.

"There is an older boy, and he is back to take care of his family." Everyone looked to the door, and there stood Joe Wiley as big as life. He must have grown a foot up and across since he left home. He sure looked big enough to handle that crop. He came straight to Ma and did something they have never seen him do before or since. He put his head down in Ma's lap, and he cried out loud like little lambs cry when they are taken away from their ma.

"Ma, I come as soon as I got the word. I shouldn't have ever left, but I'm back now, and I will take care of all of ya."

Myra wondered how this would set with Mr. Clyde. When Joe Wiley stood up, he looked as if he could pull a plow all by himself.

Mr. Clyde walked over to him and stuck out his hand. "Well, son, a handshake was good enough for your pa when he took over the place, is it good enough for you?"

"Yes, sir, I always do things the same way as my papa."

Mr. Clyde shook his hand and then he shook hands with Ma and Will Rob and patted the rest of them on the head before walking out the door.

Myra still had the lonely feeling but somehow not as bad. She remembered Papa saying that Joe Wiley would come home when the time was right, and she figured this was surely the right time. Her papa did know about things.

~3~

After Mr. Clyde left, Joe Wiley ate some of the vittles from the church folks. There was a gracious plenty of food for several days. Myra didn't feel hungry, but she knew she'd get weak if she went too long a time without eating. To keep up her strength, she put a piece of fried ham between a biscuit and poured a cup of milk. She took a bite, but when she tried to swallow, it came right back up. She made a run for the toilet to throw up, but there wasn't anything in her to come out. The knot caught in her throat wouldn't come up no matter how hard she heaved. It did seem to be moving down into her chest, but it still wouldn't let anything past it. She had hardly said a word to anyone since Papa died. When folks talked to her, she just nodded her head. She didn't think anyone had even noticed, since nobody ever listened to her except Papa and Will Rob. Now Papa was gone, and Will Rob had been real busy.

She stopped at the well and picked up the gourd to get a drink of water. Her thoughts went back to last spring when she had planted the gourd seeds to run on the split rail fence at the last house. They always planted a gourd vine, because gourds were the best way in the world to drink well water. She had a drink from a tin dipper a few times, but she didn't like the way it changed the taste of the water.

Papa always gave her the job of growing the gourds, and she loved to watch the vine grow and cover the fence. By the end of summer, the vine was always covered with gourds which they left on the vine to dry out. Just before they moved, Papa told her to bring the gourds in so he could carve them into dippers. Only six were good enough to use. The rest had rotted, or birds had pecked them. It wouldn't do to have a leaky gourd. She remembered sitting on the porch and watching Papa cut a big drinking hole and shake out the seeds. She picked up the seeds and wrapped them in paper to save for planting the next year. Papa scraped the inside real smooth and rubbed the outside until it shined.

"These long, crooked handles are just right for dippers. You growed a mighty fine crop of gourds this year, Little Girl."

Myra had felt so happy that day. She stood there rubbing the gourd and thinking about how much she needed to see Papa. She felt like stomping on the gourd until it was in little pieces, but then she knew that wouldn't help. The gourd hadn't done a thing to cause Papa to die. She drank a big gourdful of the sweet well water and went back into the house.

When she came in, the boys had gone to bed in the shed room. Since Joe Wiley was sleeping in her place, she had to find a new place to sleep. Ma was sitting up in the rocker fast asleep. Myra tried to wake her and tell her to go to bed, but she mumbled that she would stay where she was. Myra didn't want to sleep in the bed either, so she just crawled in the single bed with Annie Lou and Dolly. Annie Lou fussed for a little about being squashed and then she got up and went to sleep in the big bed. That is how they slept every night, for as long as they lived in that house. Ma slept sitting up in the rocker. Dolly and Myra slept on the single bed, and Annie Lou had the big bed all to herself. That was all right with Myra, except for the nights that Dolly wet the bed. This was nothing new to her since she used to sleep with Jesse, and he was bad to do it.

There was just too much going through her mind for her to sleep. Things like what was the heart dropsy? Would they all have it too? Why was the store lady at Papa's burial? She figured if she ever got to go to Tennille again, she would walk right into that store and ask the lady. Papa had told her not to ever trade there, but she wasn't going to trade—just talk. The question in her mind, most of all, was how the preacher could say that God loved her when he took her papa away.

Just when she finally fell asleep, she heard the bantam rooster crowing. The bantams belonged to Will Rob, and he purely loved them. They weren't good for anything. The eggs were too little, and, of course, he wouldn't let the chickens be eaten. There wouldn't have been but a few bites on them anyway. A colored man came by one day with a rooster and two hens in a croker sack. Will Rob begged and begged until Papa bought them for a dime apiece. When she heard the crowing, Myra jumped up and was thankful that she wasn't wet. She hurried to start her first real day without Papa. The boys were already stirring around in their room.

Ma was still sitting in the rocker, but her eyes were open. She answered whatever she was asked, but she didn't have anything else to say. Everyone ate a bite from the cold vittles left on the table and drank a cup of milk. Myra wrapped up some biscuits and fried meat for them to take to the field. Will Rob poured water in a jug just like Papa always did. It was a surprise to see Annie Lou up and dressed for the field. This made Myra worry about Dolly, since Ma seemed to be slipping back into one of her spells.

"Myra, bring me the baby to feed. I'm gonna take her for a walk outside after that 'cause the pore little thing hasn't had much done for her lately."

That was good to hear, so Myra felt like Ma would take care of her. Jesse and Arno went to the field too. They couldn't do much, but anything they did would be some help. They were bad to fight if they were left alone. While they were walking to the field, the little boys started running and throwing dirt clods at the others. Joe Wiley got a switch and told them that he would switch them just like Papa if they didn't behave. They looked at him with surprise and were no trouble to anyone after that. Myra never went to school again. From that day on she knew she had moved over to the grown-up side of the family.

Papa would have been proud to see how everyone pulled together and got the cotton laid by. Six days a week they went to work right after daybreak. No matter how much the work was needed, Papa never allowed them to work on the Lord's Day. The whole family, except the baby and Ma, were in the field from sunup to sundown. The work was hard, but it seemed to help them feel better. They joshed and sang and really had a good time. When they stopped to eat a bite at noon, it sounded like a church social. There was still plenty of the middling, and Myra cooked enough every night to have some to put between biscuits to take to the field. She finally was able to eat and keep it down, but the only time she ate was in the field. When they sat down to eat their dinner, they talked a lot. It seemed as though they were all needing to be together like this. Every night after supper, Joe Wiley and Will Rob went out on the porch to smoke their rabbit tobackey. That was the one thing Myra just could not ever do again, so she stayed inside and worked on her crocheting as long as the daylight held.

Will Rob ran everything in the field, and Joe Wiley didn't seem to mind taking orders from him. They were just different sorts. Will Rob liked to think about how to do things and then tell the others what to do. Joe Wiley just liked to work and not have to make any plans. He was strong and could do a lot of things that Will Rob wasn't heavy enough to do. Mr. Clyde knew this after a few days, but the crop was looking so good that he didn't care how old Will Rob was.

Everything went just right with that crop. Papa must have had a talk with Jesus and explained to him how important it was that they make a good crop that year. The rains came just right. As soon as a little sprig of weed came up around a cotton stalk, one of them was there with the hoe to chop it up by the roots. The warm days made the stalks grow full and strong. Every time the stalks started to look dry, a good rain would come. The rain even seemed to know they needed help. It always came late in the evening and lasted long enough to soak the ground just right. They never had to miss a day in the field because of rain. In the middle of summer, while the cotton grew tall and full, the boys could handle the fieldwork. This is the time that farmers call laying by, and it is a break from their long, hard days in the field.

Myra was grateful to have the free time. The first garden was coming in, and this kept her busy. Every morning she picked the garden vegetables and put them on to cook for dinner. The middling was down to just scraps, but it flavored up the beans and peas. The young hens were starting to lay enough eggs for their needs. Myra wanted to make custard for them, but she didn't have sugar. The blackberries were getting ripe too, and she knew how much everyone wanted a cobbler, but you had to have sugar for that. She came up with a plan.

She picked a big bucket of berries and took them up to Miz Clyde's back door. She knocked and Miz Clyde came to the door.

"Mornin', Miz Clyde, I picked ya this bucket of berries to thank ya for all that y'all done fer us when Papa went."

"Oh, I love blackberries, and these are fine ones. I can't get out to pick 'em anymore and besides that, I'm scared of snakes. Me and Clyde gonna enjoy these berries with milk and sugar on them."

"They's plenty of 'em just goin' to waste. I'll pick you a bucket every day fer as long as they last."

"Why, Myra, that would be so sweet of you, but I can't let you do that without giving you something in return."

"No, ma'am, that ain't right 'cause you already done plenty for us."

"Surely there must be something I have in my kitchen that you are running low on. I know I always ran short sometime when I had all my family at home. It must take a lot for all those boys."

"Yes'um, all them boys can eat a pile of vittles. We a might low on sugar to make a cobbler, but we got plenty flour."

Miz Clyde got a jar and started filling it up with sugar. She must have put a whole pound in the jar. Myra could just see the boy's faces when they smelled that cobbler.

"I shore am thankful for this, ma'am, 'cause we ain't had cobbler this year. I'll take care of yore jar and bring hit right back."

"Oh, that won't be necessary. I've got more jars than I know what to do with. I used to put up a lot every year when my children all were living at home. Now with just me and Clyde, it's not worth the trouble."

Myra raced home and used the biggest pan she had to make the cobbler. It was so big that she didn't cook anything else for supper. Everyone just stuffed on the cobbler and sweet cream from Queen Easter.

That night Myra thought of another plan. She remembered how she had asked Papa about buying canning jars. After he went like he did, she just let that thought go out of her head. She thought if Miz Clyde didn't need the jars, maybe she could do some work to pay for them.

In the summertime there was always more of everything than they could eat, but when the frost came, it was all gone. They could keep sweet taters, onions, and dried peas—but even that ran out in the middle of the cold weather. If Myra had jars, she could put up enough to help them eat through the winter. They could have pole beans and blackberries on Christmas Day. Since she didn't need to spend so much time in the field now, she decided to go up and ask Miz Clyde if there was something she could do to help her. Myra knew Miz Clyde could use help around the house, since she was getting up in years and had the head swimming.

The next morning, she put on a big pot of soup made from all the vegetables and the rind of the middling. She made a low fire and left it on the back of the stove to cook. Annie Lou was there to watch it. Otherwise, she wouldn't have left it 'cause Ma was still not acting right. She spent all her time with Dolly and did not pay attention to anything else. Myra would have been afraid that she would let the house catch fire. She played with the baby as though she was a young'un herself. Sometimes it was right funny to listen to them playing. They tried not to laugh 'cause it didn't seem right to laugh at your ma.

Myra had saved a good helping of the cobbler, and she hurried up to Miz Clyde's and knocked on the door.

"I'm glad to see you, Myra. I'm feeling right poorly today. You just brightened me up."

"I don't want to bother ya if'en you ain't feeling like it. I wanted you to taste my cobbler." She handed the bowl of cobbler to her.

"Mmm, this is shore tasty. I hadn't ever had a better cobbler. I could eat it all right now, but I'm gonna put the rest up for Clyde to eat with his dinner."

There was no smell of dinner cooking, so Myra wondered what they were going to eat. She knew Mr. Clyde would be coming in from the field soon and would be hungry.

"You couldn't have brought this on a better day, Myra. This is one of the days that I just am not able to do much. You see, I have the head swimming from high blood, and it makes me feel real bad. Clyde will just have to make do with leftovers from last night."

"Miz Clyde, if it suits you, I can cook ya some okra and maters and hot biscuits fer yore dinner."

Myra's voice sounded shaky when she talked. Miz Clyde smiled, reached right out, and gave her a hug as though she was happy.

"Why, Myra, that would taste good, and we have plenty of both on the back porch. I've got some fried meat grease from breakfast to flavor it. I hate for Clyde to have to eat cold dinner. I wouldn't let you do it if it wasn't for him."

"Ma'am, you just go sit on the side porch where there's a breeze. I'll fix y'all a real good dinner in no time."

She started a quick fire in the big stove with the short pieces of stove wood stacked right on the back porch. There were plenty of tomatoes, okra, cucumbers, and onions. She stewed the tomatoes and okra and made biscuits. She cut the cucumbers and onions, and found vinegar to put over them. While the biscuits were baking, she ran home to see about the dinner she had left cooking and quickly made a hoecake of corn bread and put it in the oven.

"Annie Lou, I'm cooking dinner for Miz Clyde 'cause she's feeling poorly. I got to run right back down there. I left their biscuits in the oven. You can finish up dinner here.

"When the bread is ready, put dinner on the table for the boys. Feed Dolly. Tell Ma to eat. Save me some."

As she ran down the steps, she almost ran into the boys coming in from the field. She hurried back to check on the biscuits, and they were browned just right. Mr. Clyde was already there and sitting on the porch with Miz Clyde.

She poured some cool water from the well, filled their glasses, and put the bowl of okra and maters, the pan of biscuits, and the cucumbers on the table. She put out their plates and eating ware and went to the porch to tell them dinner was on the table.

"I'll be back to clean up the kitchen." She ran home to eat her soup and corn bread.

"Myra, you been running like a wild thing this morning. I know you done gone plumb crazy now that you're cooking Miz Clyde's dinner."

Annie Lou always enjoyed saying Myra was crazy.

"Yea, Myra's crazy just like a fox is crazy, but he still gets our hens," Joe Wiley said, and that gave him and Will Rob a big laugh.

Mr. Clyde was walking down the lane when she got back to their house.

"We both enjoyed our dinner. It was mighty tasty. Sara ate more than she has in a long time. I told her to lie down and take a nap. Yes, sir, that was a filling meal."

Since he called her Sara, Myra figured that is what she was named. Now she would know to call her Miz Sara instead of Miz Clyde.

"I'm proud you and Miz Sara liked the dinner. I'll be glad to help you out when you need me."

"Well, now that the boys don't need you so much in the field, how about working for me every morning and helping Sara out some. She's not doing well at all and just can't keep up with things. It worries her real bad, and you would be a big help. She'll enjoy having the company too. I'll pay you."

Myra knew Papa was still telling things to Jesus 'cause that is just what she had been hoping he would say.

"Yes, sir, I shore will."

"Before you say yes, I want you to ask yore ma and be shore it is fine with her for you to be up here every morning."

Myra wasn't worried a bit about Ma caring what she did. Most of the time, it seemed as if Ma didn't even know her. She could already picture all those canning jars filled up with blackberries and whatever else she could gather.

She drew a big bucket of water from the well and put it in the dishpan with the soap. Then she washed all the dishes, wiped down every thing else in the kitchen, and used the dishwater to scrub the kitchen floor. She wanted to make that house shine, so she went out and swept the front yard. There was enough left from dinner for a little supper, so she was finished for the day.

She hurried home to tell everybody what Mr. Clyde had asked her to do. She wouldn't have to cook supper that night either 'cause there would be plenty of soup left.

When she got to the house, everybody was sitting around the table talking. The first one she heard was Ma.

"I want you to go on and do it, Will Rob. Ya got the time now, and it is only fittin' as good as them church folks were to us."

When she sat down, they told her the rest of the story. An old woman in Mr. Clyde's church died that day. Since they remembered how good Will Rob had made Papa's coffin, they had sent someone to ask if he would make a coffin for the old lady.

"If y'all think I ought to do it, I'll get on over to Mr. Clyde's and try to get it made before dark."

After Will Rob hurried out the door, Myra thought it was a good time to ask about working for Mr. Clyde.

"Ma, while I wuz up there at Mr. Clyde's, he asked me if I could come up there every morning and help out Miz Sara. She's ailing and not able to do what needs to be done. He said fer me to ask and make shore hit wuz all right with you. I ain't needed in the field right now, and I can do that and what I need to do here at the house."

"You do that, Myra. There ain't no reason fer you not to help them out."

It was a nice surprise to find Ma so agreeable.

"What's he going to pay ya, Myra?" Annie Lou asked.

"I hope he will pay me in jars."

"Jars! Now I know you gone plumb crazy."

"It don't matter what he pays me. It'll be more than I have now."

Will Rob didn't get in until way after dark. When he hit the steps they knew he was excited. He came in and told them all about the coffin.

"When I got to Mr. Clyde's, the old lady's son was there and had all of the wood and other things that I'd need. The wood went together just right, and I sanded off all the edges and made them look like curves. Then I rubbed the wood all over with some oily rags until it just shined. The man told me that I had a born knack for making things, and he was shore proud to have such a fine coffin for his ma to have her final rest.

"Ma, I tried not to take this, but they said I had to, and Mr. Clyde told me to take it."

He reached in his pocket and pulled out two dollar bills. That was the most money that had been in their house in a long time. Ma didn't tell him that he had done good or anything like that, but everyone knew she felt it. She put the money in a sock to keep for when they needed something real bad.

The next day Myra started working for Miz Sara. Some days she washed, some days she ironed, some days she swept and dusted the house, but every day she cooked a big dinner with enough left for their supper. Her days were real busy. She had to put the family's dinner on to cook before she left in the morning, run home to check on it, and tell Annie Lou how to finish everything up and cook bread.

Annie Lou didn't seem to mind helping out like she used to before Papa went to Jesus. That is what Miz Sara said he did, and Myra liked to think about him like that. She tried to be real helpful to Miz Sara. When she had a head-swimming spell, Myra gave her a cool drink of water and fanned her 'til she felt better. Miz Sara let it be known that she sure liked to have Myra there—and Myra liked being there. They just talked all the time. Well, she talked most, and Myra listened most. One day she asked Myra how much Mr. Clyde said he would pay her.

Myra thought her words out real well before saying, "Well, we ain't talked about hit, but I was hopin' to make enough to buy some of them jars that ya don't need."

Miz Sara just looked at her, laughed, and said, "Why, honey, you can have all of those jars that you want. I don't have any use for them, but you will need to get some new lids and rings. Those old ones are too rusty. When Clyde pays you, we will get him to take us to Tennille and buy what you need. I haven't been there in a long time, and we can see my sister. She lives right outside of Tennille."

Myra couldn't believe what she had heard. Now she could get her jars and have a chance to ask the store lady why she came to Papa's burial.

In the next few weeks, word seemed to have spread about Will Rob and his coffin making. Three more people came to get him to build a coffin for somebody who died. They would come in a wagon to get him and then bring him back home. Every time, he had two dollar bills to put in Ma's sock. Myra and the big boys were starting to feel better about their chances.

The cotton was almost ready to pick, and they knew Mr. Clyde would do right by them. Ma's old sock was getting filled with money from the coffins. It was accepted that they would have to move on after the crop was finished. Mr. Clyde would need the house for a tenant that had a lot of hands to work. They knew he would hate to do this, but that is just how things were.

They also knew that Joe Wiley wouldn't stay with them much longer. He didn't like working a crop because he never had any spending money like he did when he hired out. Also, he was missing his gal over in Riddleville. They were thankful to have him, but they always knew that he was just there to keep them going until they figured out how to get along without Papa.

Myra knew Will Rob was trying to think of a plan for them and a place that they could go after the crop was gathered. Finally, he told her.

"Myra, I'm thinkin' of moving us to town. I think I can make us a good livin' makin' coffins. I don't want to farm no more."

"I figger you can too. If there's one thing this county is never short of, hit's dead people. I know you'll like that better. I just hope ya can make somethin' else 'sides coffins. That's just sad, even if you don't know the folks."

Myra was beginning to worry about going to Tennille. Cotton picking would start soon, and she would be in the field every day. Finally, on a Friday at dinner Mr. Clyde told her to come back early the next morning and be ready to go to Tennille for the day. Then he laid two dollar bills on the table and said she had been a lifesaver for them.

The next morning, Myra was there right after daybreak and was ready to go. She had washed and ironed her school dress, shined her shoes, and washed her hair and put it up on rags to make it curl. After being twisted on the rags all night, her hair was still as straight as a board. When she got to their house, she had to sit on the steps until she heard them stirring. They hadn't meant to leave that early.

She heard them walking and went into the kitchen where Mr. Clyde was frying eggs and making coffee. The kitchen was filled with the good smell of coffee and eggs frying in hog lard. Papa loved coffee, but that was always one of the first things to get used up.

Mr. Clyde and Miz Sara were all dressed up, and they were laughing and smiling as though they were planning to have a big time. Mr. Clyde put the fried eggs between leftover biscuits and poured each of them a cup of coffee. This was Myra's first taste of coffee. She put milk and sugar in it just like they did, and it did taste good. She rinsed out the dishes while they finished getting ready, and then they set out.

Mr. Clyde had a fine buggy, and there was a place for Myra to sit right behind the front seat. Myra was enjoying the ride and was listening to Miz Sara talk.

"Myra, dear, how much do you know about canning?"

"I know you can put stuff in jars and keep it to eat in the winter."

As soon as the words left her mouth, she knew canning must have more to it than that. She hoped Miz Sara wouldn't think she was just plain dumb. She had not even heard of canning until Miss Caroline started asking her to empty jars.

"Not many people know the things that you have to do to put up food the right way to keep it from spoiling. A lady who worked for the government came to Tennille once and gave a class on it. That is how I learned, and now I get the honor of teaching you."

"I'm mighty proud to have the chance to learn to can the right way. I figgered there was more to it than just puttin' stuff in jars." Myra felt better about what she had said earlier.

When they got to Tennille, Mr. Clyde tied the horse to a rail in front of the post office.

"I have some business to take care of before we do any shopping. Do you want to go with us or would you rather just walk around town? I know you will be all right on your own."

"I'd like to just walk around and see the town. I ain't been here in more than a year. I'll meet you at Mr. Roundtree's store, Mr. Clyde."

"After we finish our shopping, we are going to my sister's house for dinner. I wrote her a letter, so she is expecting us. Myra, she said she would be real proud to have you eat with her."

Myra knew just what she wanted to do, and she was glad to be able to go to the lady's store without having to explain.

Tennille wasn't much of a town, but it was the biggest one Myra had ever seen. There was just one street, so she wasn't afraid of getting lost 'cause she could look down the street and see the buggy.

"Myra, I know you have plans on how to spend the money you made and you will give what's left to your Ma, but I want you to buy yourself something with this."

He reached in his pocket and handed her a quarter. Myra knew that since Papa was with Jesus now, Mr. Clyde must just be the best man left on earth.

As soon as they walked into the post office, Myra headed straight to the little store at the end of the street. When she went in, a little bell rang. In just a minute the lady came in from the back room.

"Myra, how did you get here?"

Myra looked at the lady and saw the same blue eyes that she used to see when Papa looked at her.

"I come with Mr. Clyde in his buggy."

"Well, come back here and sit down with me. I can hear the bell if someone comes in."

They went in the back to a nice little room with a table, chairs, and icebox. The first thing Myra spied was a big roll of crochet thread and a piece of handwork on the table. The lady invited Myra to sit down and without asking brought out a pitcher from the icebox and poured some lemonade. Then she put out a plate of teacakes and told Myra to help herself. Myra wasn't ready to eat or drink until she said what she had to say. After sitting and looking at each other for a minute, Myra got the nerve to speak right out.

"I saw you at my papa's burying."

"Yes, I saw you too, but I didn't want to interfere with you and your family."

They just kept looking at each other as though there was more to say, but neither knew how to begin.

"Myra, I want you to promise not to say anything about this to your ma 'cause she has enough to worry with now. I have thought about it a lot, and I believe it is something that you and the other children should know." Myra nodded her head and waited for the lady to go on with the story.

"I am your papa's real blood sister. We were raised up together just like you and your brothers and sisters. I loved Martin better than anything when we were young'uns. The man you saw at the funeral with me is your uncle. His name is Joe Early, and he is the youngest in the family. There were just three of us. He lives on the old home place on the other side of Tennille and has four young'uns.

"When we were growin' up, your papa was smart and a hard worker. Everybody loved him. When he met your ma, our papa didn't like it a bit.

He had something against the folks your ma came from. Your grandpa told Martin that if he married her, he was out of the family forever, and none of the rest of the family could have anything to do with him either. Your papa loved your ma enough to give up everything, and he went on and married your mother. It broke all our hearts to do it, but we had to do what Papa said and not see Martin anymore. Your grandma cried and begged Martin to give up the girl, but he was determined. I kept up with Martin all through the years and missed out on knowing his family, but I am sure glad to know you now."

Myra sat and listened, but she just couldn't take in that she had all this family. She had always known that Papa turned sad at times like something was troubling him.

"My name is Mary, and I would love for you to call me Aunt Mary. My husband is a preacher named Daniel Coleman. He serves several churches in the county. We have never been blessed with children. I run this little store to keep myself busy while he is off holding services in other parts of the county. When your grandpa died, he left all the land to Joe Early, and he has done real well with it. He worried about having so much while Martin did not have anything of his own. I know your papa must have been very happy, because he married someone he loved enough to give up everything for."

Myra didn't know what she meant by that, but she knew it must have been right. They talked on, and Myra found herself talking instead of listening. It seemed just like talking to Papa. She told Aunt Mary about all of the family—about how smart Dolly was, how Will Rob was making coffins, and all about her crocheting and wanting to can.

"Myra, you are pure Stuart all the way through. We all worked hard, and we like to make things better any way that we can."

That made Myra real proud, and all of a sudden the knot in her chest moved down to her stomach and didn't seem quite as hard to live with.

"I got to go now and meet Mr. Clyde and Miz Sara. They're waitin' fer me at Roundtree's store."

"I'm so glad you came. Please come back anytime you can."

"I'm comin' to town when we settle up on our cotton, and I'll come back then."

"I will look forward to that. Bring the other children with you. I want to meet them all. Now remember, you can tell your brothers and sisters about our talk, but don't tell your ma."

"I know what you mean, Aunt Mary. Sometimes hit's better fer Ma not to know everything."

As she was leaving, Aunt Mary went in the store and counted out seven little sacks, just the same number as there were young'uns. Then she filled each sack to the top with candy and tied a string around each sack so the candy wouldn't spill out. She put the little sacks in a big sack for Myra to carry. In another sack she put three big balls of crochet thread, a new needle, and a little pair of scissors. Myra had been biting the thread off. Myra didn't know how she would get this in without Ma knowing, but she would figure it out on the way home.

When she started out the door, Myra looked back, and she could almost feel that she saw Papa looking at her with his blue eyes. She ran back to her aunt as fast as she could. Aunt Mary wrapped her arms all around Myra and pulled her down to sit in her lap in the rocking chair. Myra cried and cried, and Aunt Mary cried right along with her. Myra cried until there wasn't a tear left in her. Aunt Mary just stroked her hair and told her to go ahead and let it all out. When she had got down to just snubbing like Jesse and Arno did after they had a switching, Aunt Mary pulled out her lace handkerchief and told Myra to blow her nose. It was a shame to blow on that pretty thing, but she was so full that she had to blow hard. Myra looked on the front of Aunt Mary's dress, and it was all wet from her tears. Myra told her that she had to go to meet Miz Sara, and then she ran out fast. Right then and there, Myra knew she would love her aunt Mary Coleman for the rest of her days.

~4~

Mr. Clyde and Miz Sara were waiting in the store when Myra walked inside, but they didn't say anything about her taking too long.

"Well, here's our girl, and I think she has some shopping to do, Horace."

"Sir, do you have any jar lids and rings that I could buy?" The only thing she had ever bought was penny candy so her voice was shaking.

"Why yes, ma'am, I keep a good supply in the summer. How many do you need?"

Myra looked at Miz Sara, because she had no thought on how many jars there would be for her. Miz Sara went over behind the counter and brought out two large boxes of each.

"This should be enough for everything you have to can. How much will this be, Horace?"

"Well, I usually sell them for ten cents a box which would come to forty cents. Since Myra is a new customer and bought four boxes, I will let her have them all for twenty-five cents." Before she put the quarter on the counter to pay, she thought about how she had candy to take home to the young'uns, but she didn't have a thing for Ma.

"Sir, I would like to add on a nickel can of snuff." She didn't want to break one of her dollars, but she moved one of the bills into her hand with the quarter.

"Since you are buying so much, I can let you have the whole bit for twenty-five cents."

Two whole dollars could go in Ma's sock. She hoped Mr. Clyde would think she spent his quarter on the thread and needles that Aunt Mary gave her. That wasn't lying. It was just not saying.

They climbed into the buggy and rode about a half mile out of town to Miz Sara's sister's place. Miz Grace—that's Miz Sara's sister's name—her daughter, and three young'uns were waiting on the porch for them. Everybody hugged and kissed like Myra had never seen grown folks do. They even kissed her on the cheek and told her how glad they were to see her. Good smells of cooking came from the kitchen, and for the first time since Papa went, Myra felt really hungry. She waited for the knot in her stomach to knock out her being hungry like it always did. This time it didn't happen. It just wasn't there anymore. Maybe, it had been washed out with all her crying.

"What smells so good, Grace?" Mr. Clyde went in the kitchen, and everyone followed him to the good smell.

"Dinner is gonna be a real treat today. I know y'all love mullet, and as luck would have it, a truck from Florida come through yesterday with some really nice ones.

"I cleaned them, and they were fat and full of roe. Mavis is frying them up now, and we'll eat as soon as H. V. comes in from the pasture."

"Can I help, Miz Mavis? I'll do anything you need fer me to do."

"No, honey, I have everything taken care of. You go on out in the back and play with the young'uns. Susie, show Myra the cat and kittens under the steps."

Myra followed the young'uns outside, but she didn't know what to do She couldn't even remember what it was like to play. The little young'uns were from about Jesse's age on down. After showing her the cat and the kittens under the steps, they went off to make a playhouse under the chinaberry tree. Myra looked at the old cat for a while, but she'd never had time to think about petting animals and didn't care much about them. She just waited under the porch to be called for dinner. There was a lot for her to think about.

All the grown folks were sitting in the kitchen while Mavis fried the fish. From where Myra was sitting, she could hear them talking. She never had been one to try to listen in on grown folks. Ma would switch her good for that. When she heard someone say "Myra" she started to listen.

"That Myra is a sweet little thing. You can tell she is like the Stuarts. It's such a pity that she couldn't have ever known any of them." The voice belonged to Miz Sara's sister, Grace.

"All those young'uns are fine, and they know how to work. Grace, do you know anything about why the family turned Martin out?"

"Sara, I don't know much. Living so far out, I don't hear much of the goings on in town. I do know that the old man Stuart had something against the girl's folks. Their name was Block, and they came through and worked around Tennille for a while. Folks here didn't think much of them, and I did hear the brother caused trouble. Most folks were a little scared of them because they didn't look like our kind of people. They just went from place to place, and folks never wanted them around for long.

"The girl was real pretty with long black hair and skin that looked like honey. When Martin saw her, he just fell plumb in love and vowed to marry her. His papa put up a big fuss and threatened to kick him out of the family forever if he married her. Well, Martin went right on and married her and went against what his papa said. They left and stayed gone somewhere for a year or so, and then they came back with two little young'uns and started sharecropping. Mr. Stuart would never even say his name again, or let anyone else in the family say it either. Both his ma and pa went to their graves without ever seeing him again."

When Miz Sara spoke again she sounded like she was crying.

"That is just heartbreaking. Martin has a fine family. I just wish the Stuarts could have got to love these sweet young'uns. Mary Alice and Joe Early were at the funeral. Maybe it's not too late. These sweet young'uns could really use their help."

"No, sir," Myra said to herself, "it shore ain't too late."

She went out to the chinaberry tree so they wouldn't see her under the steps when they came out to call dinner. She didn't want them to think she had been listening. It gave her a good feeling to know more about her folks.

Soon dinner was called, and Myra went in and sat down to a meal like she had never seen. A platter was filled with crisp pieces of fish, and bowls were filled with all kinds of other good stuff. There was even a dish of sweet pickles, and by every plate was a big glass filled with ice and sweet tea. Mr. H. V. prayed a long blessing and said he was thankful to Jesus for bringing their loved ones and Myra to their table. While he was praying, Myra thought about Papa's plan to buy ice and tea and have a fish fry with the fish he and Will Rob would have caught from the creek. Now here she was, having all that good stuff. She had never seen or heard of mullet fish before. They didn't look a bit like the little fish that Will Rob brought home from the creek, but they did taste good.

After dinner, Mavis wouldn't let anyone help clean up. She shooed them all out to sit on the porch. In a few minutes, Mavis came out to join them. They talked and laughed and enjoyed being together. Myra hoped that someday, she and her brothers and sisters could enjoy good times together like this. She sat in the swing and was so full that she almost fell asleep. She was enjoying feeling better now that the knot in her stomach had washed out.

Soon Mr. Clyde said, "We best head home, if we want to get there in time to feed up."

As they started to leave, everybody did all that hugging and kissing again. Myra thought it was all right the first time, but she didn't think it needed to be done twice.

When she got home, everybody was at the supper table, but she was still full from dinner. The supper didn't look like much since Annie Lou had cooked. The boys were fussing at her about the peas not being salted and the bread being burned. They were ready for the candy when she brought it out. Ma seemed prouder of her snuff than anything she had gotten in a long time. After Myra gave everything out, she put the two dollars on the table. Ma picked it up quickly without saying a word and put it in the sock with the rest of their money. After Ma went to bed, they dumped out the sock and counted the dollar bills. They now had twelve dollars.

Myra was too tired to talk that night. Tomorrow, when they were sitting together after dinner, she planned to tell them all that she had learned today. She felt like they had the same right to know. The next day was Sunday, so nobody went to the field. She was waiting for a good time to tell what she had learned. After dinner, Ma took Dolly and put her down on a pallet under the trees down away from the house. Myra noticed that she took the snuff with her. Jesse and Arno were playing with some little colored boys.

When they were sitting on the porch, she started from the beginning of the day and told the whole story. As she started the part about her visit with Aunt Mary, you could have heard a pin drop.

"I knowed it, I knowed it, I knowed there was somethin' about that lady in the store that bothered Papa. Now we know what kind of folks we come from. I always knowed Papa was not like most folks who share crop. He was used to being much better off. I am proud to be a Stuart."

Will Rob was so excited that he was pacing around the porch while he talked.

"I betcha he named me fer his brother. When we go to town to settle up, I'm goin' to see him and shake his hand and say, Joe Early Stuart, I'm Joe Wiley Stuart."

They were glad to know more about who they were, and all looked forward to seeing Aunt Mary when they went to town.

Annie Lou had just listened until she said, "There's more to tell. I know about something that I haven't ever told. It all makes more sense now, so let me tell you. Joe Wiley, you were there too, but I don't think you noticed.

"A long time ago when we lived on a place right outside of Tennille, Papa decided it was time for me and Joe Wiley to start to school. I was seven and you were eight, Joe Wiley. Jesse and Arno hadn't even been born." She looked at Myra and Will Rob and said, "And you all were too little."

"The closest school was the one right in town. The day we wuz to start, Papa wrote down our names, birthdays, and his name on a piece of paper to give to the teacher. When we went in and gave the paper to the teacher, she told us to sit down and wait for a few minutes. Then she came over and said that we couldn't go to that school. So we just left and went home. I cried all the way home, but you were glad, Joe Wiley, 'cause you knew you wouldn't like sitting in the schoolhouse all day.

"That evening, when Papa came in from the field, he wanted to know about the new school. We told him what the teacher told us. Papa was real puzzled and said he would take us the next morning and see what the problem was. Even though I was only seven years old, I remembered it like it was yesterday.

"Papa went early before the school was to start, and he told us to sit on the steps. Joe Wiley did, but I went by the window so I could hear."

This didn't surprise Myra. Annie Lou was always one to try to listen in when grown folks were talking, and she has got more than one switching about doing it.

"I heard Papa saying, 'I know you are still angry with me, but I didn't think that you would take it out on these little children. You are a teacher, and they need to go to your school.'"

"The teacher said, 'Now, Martin, you knew better than to bring these children here. I can't let them go to school. It is against the law.'"

"What do you mean? What kind of law?"

"Oh yes, the state has a law against letting Indian children go to school with white children."

"Papa yelled out, 'What do you mean Indian children! They ain't more than one-eighth at most, if that much. There ain't a soul in this part of the country without that much Indian blood, and that includes you and me. Many of the early settlers took Creek wives 'cause there wasn't many white women. This used to be the Creek's land. It was an all right thing to do. You're still trying to get back at me.'"

"The law is the law. If other people have Indian blood, we don't know about it, but we do know that these children are part Indian. You should have thought about things like this before you broke our engagement and took up with her kind."

"I couldn't marry you, Virginia, when I loved someone else. I didn't take up with her. I married her, and I am proud to be her husband. I will take my children to another school 'cause I don't want to have to even think about how mean and bitter you have turned out to be. You should have married someone who loved you and had a family of your own, and then you would know how I feel."

They had always known about Indian blood on Ma's side of the family, but until now, they never knew that was bad.

"It don't matter what kind of blood we have. I'm proud of my papa and how much he loved Ma and us. Annie Lou, I can't believe you knew about this all these years and never said a word." Tears ran down Myra's cheeks as she thought about how much her papa had been hurt.

"When I came home that day, I had sense enough not to ask Papa about it, and I shore wasn't about to ask Ma. Joe Wiley didn't care, and you and Will Rob were too little. I just forgot about it. Now it all makes sense."

Knowing about their kin explained why some of the things in their life had happened. Myra didn't know what difference it would ever make to them, but she felt as though this was something worth knowing about.

"The next day, Papa took us to another little school farther down the road. We went there for the rest of the year. The next year we moved again, and nobody ever said anything about us being Injuns or not being able to go to school again."

"I know one thing about them schools. I never went to one where the teacher didn't nearly beat me to death. I wuz shore glad when Papa let me quit." Everyone laughed at Joe Wiley.

The next morning Myra picked the last of the blackberries. She meant to make that cobbler on Christmas Day like she had promised Papa. The little boys picked a tubful of butter beans. There was no work to do in the field that day, so everyone got busy and helped shell the beans.

Myra took the berries to Miz Sara and received her first lesson in canning. They scalded the jars before putting in the berries. Then they put the jars in Miz Sara's big canning pot for processing. Miz Sara said processing meant boiling long enough to kill all the things that would make canned goods turn sour. The last thing to do was tighten the rings. As each ring was tightened, the lid made a popping sound that showed the seal was good. Myra loved hearing that sound. They had worked all morning on the berries, and now twenty-quart jars of berries were sitting on the table. Myra was so happy and proud. They would have some good suppers of stewed berries over biscuits next winter.

The boys came in right after dinner and brought the shelled butter beans. They walked round and round the table, admiring the jars of berries. Myra wanted to start right in on the beans, but she was afraid Miz Sara felt too tired.

"Don't you worry about me being tired. I'm through with the canning for today. You, girls are going to put up these beans. I'm just going to sit back and tell you how."

That evening sixteen quarts of butter beans were sealed in the jars. Just as they finished, Mr. Clyde came in with a tub filled up with late peaches. They decided to wait and do the peaches the next morning.

Miz Sara cooked dinner that day and really seemed to be feeling much better. The trip to Tennille did her a lot of good.

That evening before dark, Myra and Arno went back to the garden to see if they could find anything else. There was a lot of okra, but the tomatoes were about gone. Okra and tomatoes on biscuits made a good dinner and made good soup. They cut the okra, and Myra tried to think of a way to get some tomatoes.

The next morning, the girls sat on the porch peeling the peaches. Arno and Jesse sat by the bucket where they were throwing the peels and pits, and ate the little bits of peach that was left on every pit. Myra was still thinking about the okra.

"Miz Sara, we got that big pan of okra already cut. It tastes good, but it ain't much fillin' by hisself."

"Let me think. The other day I saw tomatoes still in the patch of the colored family down the road.

"Run on over there, Arno, and ask if they are willing to give us some, and we will split the canned okra and tomatoes with them."

Myra thought that sounded like a better deal for the colored folks than it did for her. She didn't have any choice, but she was afraid of losing her jars.

Arno took off, and in about an hour he came back with two little colored boys about his size. All three were carrying a big bucket of tomatoes.

'These are fine tomatoes, boys, and we thank you. This is going to take longer than the beans or berries. You have to scald the tomatoes to get the skins off."

Myra didn't care how long it took to put up the okra and tomatoes. She kept remembering the night she first cooked the tomatoes that Miss Caroline gave her. She had to remember to tell the colored boys to be sure and bring back the empty jars.

Arno, Jesse, and the little colored boys sat on the back steps the whole time they were working on the okra and tomatoes.

"You boys can run on home and come back tomorrow to get your share. The jars have to cool before you can take them."

The boys just looked at Miz Sara and didn't say a word. They kept on sitting on the steps until the canning was finished. They didn't have anything else to do.

That was the last of the canning. The garden and the jar tops had run out at the same time. Myra took everything home and sat it in the woodshed for now. She would have to bring the jars in the house when the weather turned cold. Miz Sara told her that freezing would make the jars crack open. She didn't know where they would be then, but she did know they would have some good things to eat.

That summer they had plenty on their table at every meal. The garden just outdid itself with all the rain. Joe Wiley and Will Rob both liked to fish and brought home a good mess two or three times a week. One time they brought home a bunch of eels and wanted Myra to cook them. She told them they weren't that hungry yet. There were still things that made them sad. Everyone would always miss Papa. Dolly wouldn't remember anything about him, but the others would tell her what a good papa he had been. They had some good times together and talked a lot, mostly about the things they had learned about the Stuarts. They were looking forward to settling and going to Tennille.

Cotton picking started right at the middle of September. Other young'uns were going to school, but that didn't bother them. They were so proud of their crop and wanted to finish it up.

Picking cotton is about the hardest work you could ever do. You have to carry a big cotton sack over your shoulder, and the more you pick, the heavier it gets. You have to bend yourself down and stay like that all day.

Some folks would stay on their knees to pick to save their back. Real fast pickers went between the rows and picked two rows at a time. The cotton plant is thorny, and you get all scratched up. Sometimes a thorn will get stuck real deep in you, and someone has to dig it out with a knife. A plant, beggar's-lice, grew around the cotton, and it caught on your clothes.

Papa always told a story about Myra that made them all laugh. One time, when she was too little to be of any use in the field, Papa came in from the cotton patch for dinner. He had beggar's-lice all over his clothes. She had just started talking.

"Stand still, Papa, and let me pick these damn devils off of you." They didn't know where she learned that bad word. Papa never said it.

Every morning before they left for the field, Myra put their dinner in a big bowl and covered it with a dishcloth to keep the flies off. The meat was all gone, so she had to find something else that would fill them up and wouldn't turn sour in the heat. Fall comes late in Georgia, so the sun was still plenty hot all through cotton picking. The best thing she found was boiled taters and corn bread. They all liked that, and there were still plenty of Irish taters from the ones they had scratched in the spring. Jesse and Arno picked every day just like the others. It was a surprise to see how much they could pick. Maybe it was because they were so much lower to the ground. Papa always said he could put his young'uns in a cotton patch, and they would outpick anybody.

One day they had started their day of picking, and Myra put the bowl of taters and corn bread under a shade tree. They noticed a goat eating grass and wondered how she got there. Will Rob said he would watch, and if she didn't seem to belong to anyone, he would take her to the house. He would feed her and milk her until someone claimed her. Joe Wiley always let Jesse and Arno rest often because they weren't used to working yet. They didn't really rest but went off to play. They had gone out of the patch to play under the shade trees, and in just a minute, they came running back. Jesse was yelling and carrying on.

"Look, Myra, I found Ma the prettiest bowl. It was just sitting there under that big mulberry tree, and it ain't even dirty."

Will Rob looked at Myra, and Myra looked at Will Rob, and they started to laugh.

"Jesse, that's our bowl. That old goat must have et up our dinner." Myra had to laugh.

It was funny then, but it wasn't too funny late that evening when they were starting to get really hungry. They never saw that goat again. She must have just stopped by to have dinner.

They worked hard and fast and had a good time in the field. Mr. Clyde came by almost every day. Some days he would bring sweet tea with ice in it that Miz Sara had made for them. When you are hot and tired from picking, cold sweet tea is probably the best tasting stuff in the world. One day at dinnertime Miz Sara came with him, and they brought a bunch of fried chicken and some peach tarts. Every night Myra asked God to help her find a way to pay back all their goodness to her family.

When they had picked enough to take some cotton to the gin, Mr. Clyde let Joe Wiley go with him to learn how it was done. Everyone knew Will Rob wished he could have been the one to go, but the oldest gets first chance at things like that. They were down to just picking the scraggly places by the middle of October. They had really made some cotton. Myra thought Papa was right that every one of the seeds made a bale. They knew their share was going to be good, and they knew Mr. Clyde would do right by them.

About this time, Annie Lou caught a feller. A lot of girls her age were already married, but she hadn't ever had a feller. She was picky, and there wasn't many around to pick from. This fellow's name was Horace Morris, and he was a cotton buyer. A cotton buyer was a fellow that went around to farmers who were having a hard time waiting until settling up. They were running out of everything and really needed some cash money. He offered to buy their crop and gave them money right then. They had to finish getting the crop in, and then he would get their share when it was time to settle up. That sounded pretty good, but the bad thing was, he didn't give them even half of what they would get if they waited. Mr. Clyde had told them about these buyers. He said the cotton buyer would cheat them and warned them not to even talk to any that came by. Mr. Clyde promised that he would see they didn't suffer and asked them to let him know if they got in a bind.

When Horace Morris stopped at their house, Joe Wiley told him exactly that. Joe Wiley had a way of talking that let you know he meant business. The buyer left, but the next week he came right back. Joe Wiley went to meet him before he tied up his horse.

"There ain't no need in you even getting down. I done told you I don't want to deal with ya."

"I believed you, and I'm not here to try to make a deal for your cotton. I just thought since I was passing, I would just stop and say howdy."

He came up and sat on the porch with Myra and Annie Lou. He was all dressed up in church-going pants, a white shirt, and tie. Myra could tell Annie Lou thought he was something special. He had a fancy buggy too. He talked about the hot weather for a few minutes, but you could tell there was something more he wanted to say.

"Before I leave, I wonder if I could talk to yore ma for a minute."

"There ain't no need in talking to Ma about making a deal on the cotton. I'm the one with the say-so, and I done told you no."

"Oh no, I won't bother you all anymore about that. I want to ask if I can call on Miss Annie Lou and take her for a buggy ride next Sunday."

"Well, ain't you a mite old fer her."

"Oh no, I am much younger than I look. Some folks think I'm older 'cause I lost my hair early. I'm just twenty-one years old."

"Well, you don't need to bother Ma. Annie Lou is the one to say."

Annie Lou said right away, "Oh yes, Mr. Morris, I would love to go to ride in your pretty buggy."

"Well, that makes me proud, ma'am. I will see you next Sunday right after dinner."

Annie Lou didn't think about anything else until the next Sunday. She washed and ironed the only dress she owned and worked on her hair. Myra thought he might just be fooling, but sure enough, right after dinner on Sunday Mr. Morris drove up in his buggy. This time he was really dressed up and had on a derby hat. He helped Annie Lou get up in the buggy, and off they went. Will Rob and Joe Wiley made all kinds of jokes about him, but Myra was glad. She thought he seemed just right for Annie Lou.

After that, he came every Sunday, and they went for their ride. They were never gone but about an hour, and then he left. He lived a long way off in a place called Glencoe, but he traveled all through the country trying to buy cotton. Annie Lou said he told her that he always made sure he ended up every week close to their place. Every week, he brought Annie Lou something that cost money, so they could tell he must make a lot of money buying cotton. One time he brought a big box of candy, and another time he bought her a parasol.

Annie Lou was wide-eyed when she told them how he described his home in Glencoe. He said it was the best place to live in all of Georgia, a really up-to-date town. They had railroads, lumber mills, stores carrying all kind of things that you couldn't find anywhere else, gas lights on the streets, and plenty of ways for folks to make a good living besides farming.

His grandpa was a judge, and he owned many acres of land. There was a lot of building going on in Glencoe, so his family made money cutting timber for lumber.

"Gal, since ya been courtin' that ol' fancy man, ya been prancin' round here actin' like ya got cotton in Augusta."

"Joe Wiley, I don't know what you mean by that, but it shore don't sound right. Papa wuz the only one I ever heard say that."

"Hit means someone acts uppity 'cause they think they got better than other folks."

"Y'all can laugh if you want to, but I might have something even better than cotton in Augusta."

~5~

One day near the end of picking time, they came to the house to eat dinner and were surprised to see a horse tied up to a bush in front of the house. They were even more surprised to see a fat, grizzly looking man sitting at the table with Ma and Annie Lou. The man and Ma were already eating, and he seemed to be putting it away pretty fast.

"This here's my brother, Bunk. Y'all say howdy to yore uncle."

None of them had ever heard Ma mention a brother. This fellow didn't look like he was any kin of theirs. His hair was all matted, and his clothes must never have seen a washpot. Myra immediately remembered what she had heard Miz Grace say about Ma's brother causing trouble in Tennille.

"I jess heared 'bout yore pa dyin'. I come to see how y'alls doin' and hep out."

"Well, we thank ya, but we're doin' just fine," Joe Wiley said as he looked straight at him with the hardest look he could give.

"Bunk wants us all to go and stay with him where he lives over in Johnson County. He's got a place big enough fer all of us, and he says we can work with him on his crop. We're gonna have to leave here anyway. So I figger that's what we need to do."

No one said a word. The shock of discovering a new uncle and Ma saying what they were going to do overwhelmed them. She hadn't said much of anything since Papa went, and they had pretty much been doing as they pleased.

"I best be getting on. I'll be back to get y'all after ya settle up. Now you young'uns behave yoreselves and mind yore ma."

"Well, Ma, don't you think we ought to have somethin' to say about this. We don't know nothin' about this uncle. It's funny to me that he didn't come lookin' fer us until he musta got wind of us havin' a good crop and makin' a good share," Joe Wiley confronted Ma as soon as Bunk walked out the door.

"Now you just hush up, boy, I need to be close by our man kin to help me take care of y'all."

Suddenly, Will Rob pitched a fit like they had never seen him do and started hollering at Ma.

"The only men folks you have now are sittin' right in this room This so-called Uncle Bunk is just tryin' to cheat us out of the money we gonna make on the crop. We ain't goin' nowhere, 'cause Mr. Clyde said he would see that we have a place to go, and I believe him"

Then he said the worst thing of all, but they all knew it was the truth.

"Us young'uns have been takin' care of you and everythin' else, and you ain't lifted a hand to help. This Bunk and all the rest of yore people ain't nothin' but plain sorry trash, not a bit like the Stuarts."

Ma rose up then and slapped him so hard across the face that Myra thought he would fall over backward. He ran out the door and headed out through the cotton patch. Myra just knew he was leaving for good, and she was scared. What would they do without him?

"Well, if that's what you're set on doing, I'll tell you right now that I ain't goin' either. I wuz always plannin' to go back to Riddleville as soon as I got y'all all settled again. Anyway, Will Rob can handle things better than me. He's right. Y'all need to stay right here and let Mr. Clyde help you. I told Flossie that I'd be back as soon as I could, so I ain't goin' no farther away from her."

Joe Wiley walked out the door, and Myra prayed he was going to look for Will Rob.

"Just go, all of ya go, take 'em all with ya, and it won't keep me from going back to my people. I hope I never see or hear of another Stuart." Ma kept hollering, "Just go on, just go on all of ya."

Everybody was quiet for a minute and then Annie Lou said, "I wasn't gonna say anything just yet, but I think it's time now. Horace asked me to marry him. I have been thinking about it, and I just decided to say yes. He will come and take me to Glencoe, and we'll marry"

Myra figured Ma was thinking she would be the next one to say that she was leaving, but she didn't have anywhere to go. Besides, somebody had to be there for Dolly and the little boys. Myra looked in the pot of greens and saw nothing left but the pot liquor. She wondered if that was a sign of where they were heading. She looked out the back door and saw Joe Wiley and Will Rob. They were tying up the bantam's feet and putting them in a croker sack. She guessed they were both fixin' to leave and take the bantams with them.

Someone was standing behind her brothers. She got a good look and saw a little boy. He was dressed all in blue, and his eyes were as blue as beads. The other boys didn't seem to be paying him any mind. Myra headed outside to find out about him. He was dressed in fine clothes and sure didn't look like he lived around there. He was gone before she could get out the door. It happened so fast that she knew the boys hadn't seen him. She wondered if what she saw was a shadow and not real, but she saw him plain as day.

After Will Rob and Joe Wiley walked off with the bantams in a sack, Myra just didn't know what to think. She went out and sat on the steps, trying to make some sense of what was happening. She knew she was going to lose things that she had grown to cherish. Mr. Clyde, Miz Sara, her prized canned goods, and the house where she still could almost see and smell Papa had helped her learn to live without him. Knowing that she was a Stuart and had kin in Tennille had been the main thing that kept her going.

As darkness came, she sat alone on the porch steps and wished she could run off somewhere herself. She realized she had company beside her on the steps. Jesse and Arno were sitting on either side of her. She looked at poor little Jesse and knew he didn't stand a chance without her. Nobody had ever paid him any attention except Papa. Sometimes it seemed as if Ma had something against him. She whipped him harder than she did Arno, and she would whip him for the least little thing.

"Myra, tell us a story," said Arno.

Papa used to read stories from the Bible. He could read them so good that you felt as though you were right there with the people. The boys loved the ones about little David killing the giant with his slingshot and strong Samson pulling down the house on the bad people. They liked to hear those over and over. Myra always liked the one about the little baby Moses floating down the river in a basket. She couldn't read good enough to read from the Bible, so she tried to think up a good one to tell.

Before she could decide on a story, she realized there was someone else in the yard. The little boy was standing by the chinaberry tree. Even though it was dark, it seemed as if daylight was all around him. Just as

Myra caught a glimpse of him, he was gone, and she could only see the dark night.

Then the best story to tell came to her. She told a story that Papa had read to them a lot. It was about the Lord telling the prophet Elijah to ask a poor widow woman to feed him. The only food she had for herself and her son was a handful of meal and a jar of oil. Myra figured the oil must be something like cooking grease. The widow woman was gathering up sticks for a fire to make a little cake for her and her son to eat before they died. She must have figured they were going to starve to death. Myra couldn't help thinking the Lord picked a poor one to ask to feed him.

Elijah told her to go on and fix him a little cake and then fix one for herself and her son.

"For thus says the Lord the God of Israel: The jar of meal will not be emptied and the jug of oil will not fail until the day that the Lord sends rain on the earth."

Myra remembered how to say all that by heart just like it said in the Bible. She figured these folks had been a long time without rain, and that is why they didn't have much to eat. Myra could remember some years when the rain had been scarce, and they didn't make much of a garden. Papa's share of the crop would be short in those years, so in the winter they never had enough rations. They always had something to eat, but often when she went to bed it seemed as though her stomach was sticking to her backbone. Myra sure knew how those folks felt.

Myra went on telling the story and said, "The widow woman did just what the Lord told her to do and fixed Elijah something to eat, and there was still plenty for her and for her boy to eat. Just like the Lord said, their meal and oil did not ever run out until there was plenty in the land again."

Myra told the boys that Papa must have liked that story 'cause it made him think about how their barrel of flour never seemed to run out. She wondered why that story came to her to tell. Was it the Lord saying he would take care of them?

"Just before I started the story, boys, did you see a little boy standing out there in the yard?"

"I couldn't see nothin' out there. It wuz too dark."

"Me neither," Jesse agreed with Arno.

The next day she went out and looked for tracks but didn't see any sign. She was starting to wonder if she was goin' crazy.

Myra had gone to bed when her big brothers came home. She wasn't asleep, so she heard them come in and was relieved. She wondered if they had anything to eat. They left without eating dinner, and it was way after suppertime.

The next morning they called her out back to talk.

"I give the bantams to the colored folks. They promised not to eat 'em but would use the eggs."

Myra didn't believe that. She knew as soon as their rations got scarce, those little chickens would hit the frying pan. Will Rob knew this, but it helped to think his pets would be safe.

"Next, we went to talk to Mr. Clyde about settling up. We didn't say nothin 'bout how we feel about going off with Uncle Bunk, 'cause Mr. Clyde can't do nothin 'bout hit. He's been too good to us to worry him. We did ask if all the settlin' up could be done before Uncle Bunk gets back.

"When we get our share, we ain't gonna give it all to Ma. Myra, you make us a list of everythin' we need, and we'll buy that first." Joe Wiley sounded a lot like Papa.

"If y'all planning to leave, you better keep back some of hit fer yoreselves."

"Mr. Clyde's gonna take the last load to the gin tomorrow, and then the next day we all going to Tennille and get our share. He's gonna take all of us in the big Jersey wagon, 'cause he says we all deserve a trip."

"He's gonna let me go with them to the gin tomorrow. I guess he thinks I'm old enough now that we made more cotton than any other cropper in the county." Will Rob still smarted about Mr. Clyde thinking he wasn't man enough to make a crop.

After the boys left the next day, Myra and Annie Lou went up to see Miz Sara. Myra took her most prized crocheted piece to give to Miz Sara. She also took the first piece she had made and asked Miz Sara to try to get it to Miss Caroline. Miz Sara acted real proud and said she would keep her piece forever and would take it to Miss Caroline when she had a chance. Mr. Clyde had already told her about them moving.

"I'll miss y'all, but I'm proud you are going to stay with your kin. Annie Lou, you have shore kept yore Mr. Morris a secret. Clyde told me his mother was a MacTavish. I've heard some about his kin. They are well-thought-of folks. It's a big family, and they own most of the county. His grandpa is a judge. You're doing well for yoreself."

Annie Lou grinned and blushed at the same time. That was the first Myra ever heard the name MacTavish, but it was not going to be the last. Of course, she didn't know that then.

Miz Sara asked Annie Lou if she was getting herself up some wedding clothes. Of course, Annie Lou had nothing except one dress and the clothes she wore in the field.

"You look about the same size that I was when I married Clyde." Then she went to her bedroom for a few minutes and came back with two dresses, the prettiest they had ever seen. One was pale blue and the other was white with lacework all around it.

"Annie Lou, it will make me real proud to have you wear these clothes. I have kept them all these years, hoping to give them to someone I love."

Myra couldn't believe that her sister would own such pretty things, and she knew Annie Lou couldn't believe it either. Then she gave Annie Lou stockings and a petticoat. Annie Lou was the happiest that Myra had ever seen her. She knew her sister could just see herself getting married in that pretty dress and going with Horace to Glencoe to meet his MacTavish kin.

"Myra, honey, you'll never know how much you have meant to me, and I will never forget you. I didn't think I could make it through the summer, but when you started helping me, I started getting better. Little lady, you are going to do well in life."

Myra knew she had better get out of there right then 'cause she was about to cry just like she did with Aunt Mary.

When the big boys came home that evening, they were excited about how much cotton they had made. They said there would be plenty of cash to do all they had planned. Myra asked if Jesse and Arno could go to town with them. She wanted to buy shoes and overalls for them. Besides that, they never got to go anywhere except to the field or to the little colored boy's house.

"Shore," said Joe Wiley, "and we're all going to the café and eat us some ice cream, just like Papa promised."

"Don't forget we're going to see Aunt Mary. I can't wait to do that. She made me promise to bring all of ya the next time we came to town."

As soon as the sun was up the next morning, they started walking up to Mr. Clyde's house. Jesse and Arno didn't know where they were going, but that didn't bother them. They couldn't believe they were going anywhere. They had always been left at home before. Joe Wiley asked Ma if she wanted to go.

"I ain't lost nothin' in Tennille, and I don't never plan to go there again."

Myra wanted to take Dolly and show her to Aunt Mary. She didn't tell the part about Aunt Mary just that she would like to take Dolly to Tennille. Ma wouldn't agree to that. Myra still had concerns about leaving Dolly with Ma. She usually took care of Dolly, but sometimes she just did crazylike things.

The lamps were lit in the house when they got to Mr. Clyde's. They hadn't eaten anything before they left home and didn't expect to eat until after they finished their business and got their money. Myra told everyone to sit down on the steps and wait for Mr. Clyde and Miz Sara to finish their breakfast. Just as they sat down, out came Mr. Clyde with two packs of cinnamon buns that came off the rolling store. He also brought out a big pitcher of milk and cups for all of them. The cinnamon buns were filled with raisins and sweet icing on top. Eating them along with the cool milk did taste good. They never expected anyone would feed a pile of young'uns like them. Mr. Clyde sure must be the finest man left on earth.

Myra saw the rolling store pass their house yesterday, so she knew Miz Sara had bought the cinnamon buns especially for them. The rolling store is a fine thing for country folks. The rolling store man built sides and a roof onto a big jersey wagon. He fills up the inside with all kinds of things that you could only buy at the stores in town. He had a big horse to pull it, and he would come by their house about once a month. They never bought anything off it 'cause there was never any money to spare. Papa said it was worth the price to bring that stuff out to the country folks, but all the same he couldn't afford the prices.

One time they did buy something. When the wagon came and stopped where it always did, Myra and Will Rob ran to it. They just liked to look at the stuff. The rolling store man had stopped in a real sandy place. Will Rob was kind of digging around in the sand with his toes when he uncovered two dimes. He picked them up and ran home to give the money to Papa.

Papa smiled big and said, "I reckon it was meant for you to buy something off that store since the dimes turned up for you right there. Now you two run and catch him before he leaves and buy anything you want."

The man was about ready to leave, but he waited for them to look. Cinnamon buns cost a dime a pack, and there were twelve in each pack.

They figured that was the best and the most for the money. They had never had one before and didn't really know what they were. The two packs were enough for all of them to have plenty. The whole family got their fill of cinnamon buns that afternoon, and they remembered the good taste. Myra figured that Miz Sara must have thought about their breakfast when the store came by yesterday and bought the buns for them. She couldn't let herself think about how sad it was going to be to leave Miz Sara and her kindness.

As soon as they finished eating, they loaded up in the wagon. Everybody got in the body, except for Myra and Will Rob. They liked to sit on the tailgate with their legs hanging off the back, so they could hop off and walk for a while. Myra was hoping she and Will Rob could talk a little while they walked. She wanted to know what he was thinking about doing. She knew Joe Wiley and Annie Lou were leaving for sure.

"Myra, I don't rightly know what I'm gonna do, but I promised Joe Wiley I'd stay and help y'all get moved. I shore don't want to go off to Johnson County. I want to quit farming and try to make a livin' buildin' things. I talked with Mr. Clyde about it, and he said he thought I could do it, but I need to go to some place like Glencoe where there's a boom going on. He says everybody's making money there, and there's lots of building going on"

Myra thought about what Miz Sara had told them about Glencoe and the MacTavishes. Annie Lou was marrying into the family, and that might help things work out for Will Rob. She hoped so, 'cause Will Rob would kill himself working a farm. He wasn't as big as a washing of soap. No matter how much he ate, he stayed skinny as a rail.

Everyone was enjoying the trip and were laughing as they bounced along the road. Mr. Clyde let Jesse and Arno move up to sit on the front seat with him and take turns driving the mule. Both felt really big doing that. Mr. Clyde tied up right in front of the bank. The bank people must have been surprised to see such a bunch of young'uns coming in. Mr. Clyde and Joe Wiley and the bank man sat down at a table. The rest of them gathered around the table.

"I have been hearing about the fine crop you young'uns made. Your pa and I were boys together. I know Martin Stuart is mighty proud of his young'uns."

Then the bank man started showing Joe Wiley a lot of papers. He couldn't read a word on them, but that didn't bother him. He knew if anybody on earth was a good, honest man, it was Mr. Clyde. When they got through talking and figuring, their share turned out to be 437 dollars. That was a lot of money for anybody to make from sharecropping a cotton patch. Papa's dream did come true.

"Now, Mr. Clyde, are you sure you took out for everything that we owed you?" Joe Wiley asked.

"Every penny is yours. You young'uns earned it fair and square." Then he counted out the money and handed it to Joe Wiley and shook his hand.

"Now I want y'all to do whatever you want to do for the rest of the day. Have yoreselves a good time. Meet me back here at the wagon in the middle of the afternoon. It takes about two hours to make the trip home. That'll give us plenty of time to get there before dark."

They hurried back to the wagon to sit down and divide the money the way they had planned. Joe Wiley took twenty dollars and made Will Rob take twenty dollars.

"I ain't gonna take none of the money. Keep my share with what you givin' to Ma."

"No, sir, you don't know what is ahead of y'all, and it's best that you keep this hidden from Ma."

Will Rob saw his point and folded the twenty-dollar bill in a tight little square, put it in a little drawstring pouch and stuck that in his pocket.

"Annie Lou you take twenty dollars and buy some of the things to start yore housekeeping. Papa wouldn't want you going to a new family with nothing."

"Thank you, Joe Wiley. I know I can put it to good use."

"This is for you, Myra. I want you to hide this twenty dollars just like I told Will Rob to do. Ma don't need to know nothin' about it 'specially with that Bunk hangin' round."

"Naw, I don't have no use for no money. You keep it fer when you go off on your own."

"Just like I told Will Rob, y'all don't know what could happen. You need to have it in case you need medicine for some of y'all. I'd just feel better knowin' you had it in case of need."

Joe Wiley was sure acting a lot like Papa 'cause then he gave Arno and Jesse each a quarter and told them they could buy whatever they wanted. With money in their pockets, they all headed to the store. They fitted the little boys out in new shoes, heavy socks, overalls, and caps to cover their heads in the cold weather. Both the big boys bought shoes.

"Myra, you get you some shoes too. We got enough money."

"I don't need 'em, Joe Wiley. Mine are still good enough. You and Will Rob need to buy new overalls. Y'all can't go off wearing those old ones. Yore butts is almost shining through."

"Let's get us a pair, Will Rob. She's right about them being wore out."

Annie Lou bought all kinds of things, and they had never seen her so excited and happy. It took Jesse and Arno forever to make up their minds. You would have thought they had a hundred dollars. It was the first time they had ever had any money of their own to spend. Finally, Arno bought a sack of marbles and a little top. Jesse just kept walking around looking as if he couldn't find what he wanted.

"Make up yore mind now, Jesse. We ain't gonna be in this store all day."

"What I want, Joe Wiley, is to buy snuff for Ma."

"No, that money is for you to buy what you want. We gonna buy her some snuff out of the money we spending on rations."

Myra felt bad to think about how Ma never spoke a kind word to Jesse and whipped him hard for some things that didn't call for a whipping. Still he wanted to buy for her instead of for himself.

He finally bought marbles and a ball. Myra did not buy anything for herself, but she did get shoes for Dolly and a long wool gown to keep her warm in the cold weather. She had worried that she would get the wrong size shoes for Dolly, but Will Rob fixed that. He drew around her feet on a paper and cut the little feet out. They stuck those little feet into the shoes at the store until they found a pair that fit. Myra was happy seeing her brothers and sister get things they wanted, and she didn't care about buying for herself.

"Myra, you gonna hold on to that money so tight the eagle's gonna scream." Joe Wiley loved to pick at her about being stingy, but he knew she would spend it when it was needed. He trusted her to keep the family going.

When the shopping was finished, it was dinnertime. They didn't want to go in on Aunt Mary when she might be eating.

"Myra, wonder where she eats? Does she go home or eat at her store?"

"Hit don't matter, Joe Wiley. We gonna eat before we go to see her. We don't want her to think she's gotta feed us. We'll go back in the store and buy us some good stuff."

"I thought we wuz goin' to the café and eat us some ice cream."

"Do you know how to go about eatin' in a café? I shore don't."

Everyone followed Myra back into the store. After looking around, they bought soda crackers, a wedge of cheese cut from a big round, a jar of sweet pickles, and right on top of that stuff, they put another pack of cinnamon buns.

Joe Wiley paid, and they had started out the door when Mr. Roundtree reached in the drink box and took out a red-colored drink for each of them.

"Y'all gonna need a belly washer to get all that stuff down. No charge."

Every one thanked him, picked up their drinks, and headed to the wagon to eat. They had never had such a good time before. They sat in the wagon, eating all that good stuff and just watching the townspeople going about their business. After they ate, Myra got a rag and spit cleaned Jesse and Arno. She wanted them to look really good when Aunt Mary saw them for the first time.

The Open sign was on the door, so they figured that she was through eating and ready to take customers. Annie Lou read the sign on the store out loud.

PIECE GOODS
DRESSMAKING
ALTERATIONS
Mary Alice Coleman, Proprietor

They opened the door and heard the little bell ring. Aunt Mary came out from the back room, smiling from ear to ear. Right behind her were two men. Myra recognized one of them and knew it was their Uncle Joe Early. She remembered him from the burial. Besides that he looked just like Papa, except he had a mustache. He looked a lot younger, and you would say more rested and trimmed up than Papa ever looked.

Aunt Mary gave everyone a hug and made them feel as if she had just been sitting there waiting for them to come by. The other man was her husband, the Reverend Daniel J. Coleman. He was a real fine-looking man too.

"When I heard y'all were in town today, I hurried and sent word to Joe Early to come. Have y'all had any dinner?"

"Yes'um, we already ate and had aplenty," Annie Lou spoke for all of them.

"Dan J, put the closed sign out and lock the front door. Let's all go in the back room where we can really visit."

The family and the three adults filled the little back room. There weren't enough chairs, so most of them sat on the floor. Uncle Joe Early picked up Jesse and sat him on his lap and pulled Arno over to sit right at his feet. Myra saw him pat their heads a few times just like Papa always did.

"I bet you still have room for some raisin cake." Aunt Mary brought out a big cake that had sugar icing all over it. When she cut into it, there were raisins and walnuts all the way through. She gave each of them a big slice on a little plate. Everybody else ate it right up, but Myra held onto hers for a minute and then started tasting little bits of it. Of all the cakes she had ever tasted, she knew there was no other cake as good as a raisin cake. She decided right then that if she ever got where she could, she would make a raisin cake every Christmas.

"I knew y'all would like raisin cake. It was Martin's favorite cake, and Ma always made it on his birthday."

Aunt Mary went around and said something nice about every one of them and told them how happy she was to know them and how much she loved them.

"I hear y'all made quite a crop for Clyde Bennett. Now let's hear about it." Uncle Joe Early reached over and patted Will Rob on the back.

Joe Wiley told about their crop and the settling up. He showed his uncle the paper Mr. Clyde gave him that showed all the figures and money.

Uncle Joe Early just laughed and said, "That is shore fine, and we are mighty proud of you. You are showing what you're made of. Your papa did a fine job of raising you, young'uns, and I know he would be mighty proud of you."

Next, Joe Wiley told them about Uncle Bunk and everybody except him and Annie Lou moving to Johnson County. He didn't let on how he really felt about it 'cause he didn't want to bother them with troubles. They did not make any comment about the move.

Uncle Joe Early asked a lot of questions about things like how much they had been to school and what they wanted to do when they grew up.

"I got plans already. That's why I ain't goin' with the rest of 'em to Johnson County. I got me a gal, Flossie. I stayed with her and her folks when I worked over in Riddleville. I'm goin' back to marry her and work for her pa. I 'spect I will take over the place when he gets too old to work.

Flossie is the last young'un and wants to stay there with her ma and pa. It's just a little place. One good farmer can run it without any tenants or croppers. They always been real good to me, and I know they will treat me right."

The men nodded their heads as though that sounded good. Will Rob spoke up next, which was not like him. He wanted to tell them his plans.

"I'm goin' to move to Johnson County, but I'll most likely not stay long after they get settled. I don't intend to spend my life farmin'. I'm good at building things, and I know I could make a livin' at that better than farmin'. Folks tell me I need to go live in Glencoe 'cause that's a real growing place. I want to be somewhere like that instead of little ol' country places."

"You're right about Glencoe, boy. I've passed through there a few times. Glencoe's got railroads, cotton gins, lumber mills, and I heard that some farmers were learning to grow tobacco. They say the land there is real good, and that means farmers have good crops and money to spend in town." Uncle Daniel knew all about Glencoe and thought Will Rob had a good plan.

"I'm goin' to Glencoe too. I'm promised to marry a man from Glencoe named Horace Morris. His mother was named Jane MacTavish before she married Horace's pa."

Since Anne Lou had learned about the MacTavishes, she always mentioned that when she told anyone about Horace. It made Myra kind of wonder about his pa, Mr. Morris.

The two men looked at each other when she said that. Since Uncle Daniel knew so much about Glencoe, he spoke first.

"Annie Lou, that must mean that yore future husband's grandpa is Judge Andrew MacTavish. He is one of the best-known and respected men in the state of Georgia. He's the reason that Glencoe is getting ahead of the other towns around."

Myra felt better about Annie Lou going so far off to live without them after she heard Uncle Daniel say good about Horace's family. She had been a little doubtful before since Horace started out trying to cheat them out of their cotton.

"Now, Myra, how about you? What do you plan to do?" Uncle Joe Early looked right at her with Papa's twinkling blue eyes.

At first all she could think to say was can and crochet, but that didn't sound like much. Before she spoke, another thought came to her, and she knew what it was she really wanted to do. "I want to learn to sew and be a dressmaker."

"Well, honey, you got that natural. That's all I ever wanted to do. I just wish you were going to be close by so I could teach you."

Their aunt and uncle told them about what things were like when Papa and them were young'uns. It sounded like a good time. They said Uncle Joe Early was named after his papa, their grandpa. Then Papa had named his first son Joe after his papa and Wiley cause it was the name of their grandma's family. Myra thought about how Papa had still wanted to name his boy for his family, even though they would have nothing to do with him.

"Now Dan J and I have some news to tell too. Of course, Joe Early already knows it. Dan J comes from a place over in Trutlen County called Friendship. Isn't that a lovely place to be from? It's just a little settlement right outside of Soperton. They have a large church membership and are fixin' to build a new church. The congregation has called Dan J to come and be their preacher.

"We are real happy about it because Dan J won't have to travel around to churches, except when he preaches revivals. The church is right by the main road, and that means lots of new people will come there from all around. They are going to have a nice parsonage built right beside the church.

"The only thing that I didn't like about it was moving away when I had just got to meet all of you. Now that I know you are moving, I think it must have been meant to be. Friendship is closer to Johnson County, so maybe we can visit. Annie Lou, you just get Mr. Morris to bring you to see us. It's not too far from Glencoe either."

Myra was real proud for her aunt and uncle. She knew it would be a while before she would see Aunt Mary again, but she did know where to find her. Someday she would get there to see her.

It was getting to be time for them to go to the wagon, so they started saying good-bye. Uncle Joe Early hadn't said much, but he kept the two little boys right with him. Aunt Mary gave everyone a bag of candy, and she gave Myra a bag with lots of crochet thread.

Uncle Daniel asked everyone to stand in a circle and hold hands. Then he prayed a long prayer for them. He prayed to Jesus to watch over them and called out every one of their names, even Dolly and Ma. Then he raised his voice in a song. Aunt Mary and Uncle Joe Early joined right in, and in just a minute all of them were singing too. Papa had taught them every one of the hymns that Uncle Daniel started.

When they finished singing, Uncle Daniel said, "Now, children, don't you ever forget that singing praises to the Lord will raise your spirits. Your papa, Martin, taught you those hymns to help you get through the rough times. You all have already shown the good training you had from him. No matter where you are, you can always make any place a better place to be. That is what your papa would want from you. Always remember that you are God's child, and He loves you, and we love you.

Everyone was getting teary eyed when they started back up the street, but it was a nice kind of sadness.

When they got home, Dolly came running to meet them. Ma was on the porch waiting. This was the first time that so many of her young'uns had ever been away at one time. The two cans of snuff they brought made Ma happy.

Joe Wiley gave Ma the rest of the money. Even taking out for all they bought and kept for themselves, there was still three hundred dollars.

"Ma, this is a lot of money, but you're gonna need every dime of it. Put it in the sock with the money from Will Rob and Myra. Don't use it except to buy rations for the winter. Let Myra make up a list of what y'all need and take her with you to buy things. You need to hold back some of it for things that might come up, like needing medicine or a doctor. Don't you tell Bunk that you got any money. If he asks, tell him I took it all when I left."

Ma said nothing and didn't seem to care one way or the other. Everyone was tired and went to bed early.

The next morning was busy. They didn't know exactly when Uncle Bunk was coming, but they were trying to get everything ready. Miz Sara had given Myra a lot of newspapers and told her to wrap each of the jars in lots of the paper and put them in a croker sack. That way they shouldn't get broken on the trip. Myra wrapped each jar very carefully, because she didn't want to lose a one of them.

The boys took the chickens and Queen Easter over to the colored folks. They had made enough on their share to buy the chickens and the cow. They wanted Solomon, but he was needed to pull the wagon. Myra was worried that he couldn't make it all the way to Johnson County pulling their heavy wagon. She didn't know how old he was, but she knew he had already seen his best days. Papa always loved that ol' mule. That made her think of Papa and laugh. He always told them that you could find something good to say about anybody.

"Just look at ol' Solomon. He ain't much to look at in most ways, but he shore has pretty teeth."

They always laughed, 'cause you just wouldn't think of a mule having pretty teeth. Myra would look at Solomon's teeth sometimes and wonder what made Papa think his teeth were so pretty. She figured mule's teeth must have a different reason to be pretty than people's teeth. That was the first time she had thought about Papa and laughed instead of cried. She felt almost happy to think about him.

Just as they were getting started with the packing up, a fine buggy drove into the lane with Uncle Joe Early at the reins. They couldn't imagine why he was there. He went right in to talk to Ma. Everyone followed so they could listen.

"Ann, I am offering to take Jesse and Arno home with me. I'd really love to have them, and I'll raise them like my own children. I'll see that they go to school and learn how to make a living. I know you would all hate to be without them, but it would make it a lot easier on all of you and would help them. I will see to it that you get to see them sometimes."

Ma didn't say a word and just looked at him for a long time. Myra was hoping Ma would say yes. It would hurt not to be with them every day, but she knew it was best for her little brothers.

When Ma started talking, Myra had never heard her talk so much or say such hurtful things.

"There ain't no way in hell that I'd give you my young'uns. You only want 'em so you can work 'em to death just like pore ol' Martin was worked to death. Martin went to an early grave because you and yore mean ol' pa and fancy-acting sister cheated Martin out of everything. You Stuarts were never nothing but mean to me and my young'uns. You just get out of my house and never come near us again. You better not let my brother catch you here 'cause he knows how y'all treated me and my young'uns."

"I didn't want to upset you. I was only trying to do something to help all of you. I know it would be best for the little boys."

Myra usually just listened and let the grown folks say how things were to be. This time she couldn't help but speak up.

"Ma, please let them go. They can go to school and always have what they need. We can't do that for them."

Ma looked at Myra with such meanness in her eyes. She picked up a piece of stove wood as if she was coming over to hit her.

Joe Wiley grabbed her arm and said, "Ma, don't you ever hit one of us again. You ain't in no shape to know how or when to hit a young'un."

Uncle Joe Early walked out, shaking his head. "If there is any way I can ever help any of you, please come to me. You know where to find me."

He started driving his buggy away, and Jesse and Arno ran behind him for as long as they could see the buggy.

Uncle Joe Early had hardly got out of the lane when Horace drove up in the finest buggy they had ever seen. It had a front and back seat, and Horace told them it was called a surrey and belonged to his grandpa. He needed it to move all of Annie Lou's things. Annie Lou had been packed up every since she said yes, so all that was left to do was put her belongings in the surrey. It looked pitifully small in that big buggy.

Something about this just didn't seem right to Joe Wiley, so he said, "Ain't it a ways to Glencoe from here. How you gonna get there by night?"

Horace knew just what he meant and replied, "We ain't headed to Glencoe yet. I talked to a preacher over in Sandersville, and he's gonna marry us this evening. We gonna spend the night in a roomin' house there, and then head to Glencoe the next day. It will likely take us two days to get there with this heavy wagon."

Everyone lined up to say good-bye. Ma didn't say one word. She didn't seem to even realize that Annie Lou was leaving.

"Now, Horace, you better be good to my sister, or we're all comin' to Glencoe and live with you."

After Joe Wiley said this, everyone else said, "We sho will."

Horace laughed and said, "I never planned to treat her anyway but the best. Now I know I better do that."

They took off in a cloud of dust, and everyone was real proud for Annie Lou. She always wanted to live in town and have nice things. Now she was going to have all her dreams.

There wasn't anything left to do now but wait for Uncle Bunk. Myra didn't want to go back to see Miz Sara. She didn't even want to go see the colored lady. It was just too sad to say good-bye. The next day she went over to the graveyard and sat with Papa for a long time. She told him all that was going on, although she was sure he knew it up there in heaven.

Just as she was telling Papa good-bye, she heard a bird singing. It was singing the sweetest tune that she had ever heard a bird sing. She looked up in the tree where the noise was coming from, but there wasn't a bird in sight. She blinked her eyes and looked again. There wasn't a bird in the tree. It was the little blue boy. She ran over and started climbing up the tree to catch him. He must have jumped down the back and ran, 'cause he was gone in a minute. Myra couldn't figure out why he was always hanging around her and then running off so fast. It was getting just plain aggravating, and she sure wanted to have a word with him before she left these parts.

When she got home, Uncle Bunk and his boy, Izzie, were there. They had brought their big wagon and wanted to get a good early start the next morning.

"Hit's a fer piece to my place, and them wagons gonna be loaded down."

"Where are we headed to in Johnson County?" Will Rob didn't like just knowing he was headed to a county.

"My place is close by a little settlement called Sullivan's Corner. Hit's a right nice place. They's a few stores and a good sight of houses."

Everyone got busy and started loading up the wagons and hoped it wouldn't rain on their stuff that night. They ate cold supper left from dinner since they had to take the stove down. They would sleep in the empty house on pallets.

Myra wondered what they would eat the next day, but she didn't ask. She didn't care for herself, but the little young'uns would need something. Will Rob had the same thought, 'cause after a while he slipped off to the turnip patch and pulled up some nice roots. Turnip roots are better cooked, but it's something to eat when you ain't got no better. They'd have to figure out a way to feed them to Dolly.

While they were loading the wagon, they got a look at their cousin, Izzy. He was about the funniest-looking fellow they had ever seen. He had one eye that looked one way, and the other eye looked the other way. There was something about his nose that wasn't right. It looked as though it had been flattened on to his face. His hair had places all over it that stood up like a porcupine. Of course, the poor thing couldn't help it, but they couldn't help joshing to themselves about him.

Joe Wiley said that was how he got his name, Izzy. When he was born, everybody looked at him and said, "What Izzy?"

"Izzy, you shore got pretty teeth." Will Rob just had to say that, and they almost fell over laughing.

"Thank you, I try to keep 'em clean." Poor ol' Izzy was proud to hear that.

They had loaded the heavy stuff by sundown. Myra didn't notice that Joe Wiley had slipped away until Will Rob said, "Well, Myra, there he goes." She looked up the lane and saw her big brother headed away from them. He was carrying everything he owned in a croker sack. She knew he didn't want to wait and see them leave. It would just be too hurtful to have to tell them good-bye. They watched him until they couldn't see him anymore just like Papa had done. Myra wondered if she would ever see him again. Even if she didn't, she would never forget him and how much he did for them when they needed him most.

～6～

_____

E very muscle in Myra's body ached when she lay down on the pallet to sleep. She was worn out from lifting things onto the wagon, but she lay on the pallet a long time before she could sleep. Her mind was so full of things to think about and wonder about. They had moved to new places many times before, but Papa was always there to get them through the hard times. She didn't know what they might find in Sullivan's Corner. She didn't have any faith in Uncle Bunk, but he was Ma's kin. Maybe he would take care of them. She must have dropped off just about daylight. The next thing she knew, Will Rob was telling her to get up.

The wagon was loaded, so they threw their quilts in the back and waited to hit the road. Since there was nothing for breakfast, Myra dreaded trying to eat the turnip roots on an empty stomach. Will Rob filled a barrel with plenty of water and carried a bucket to give Solomon water along the way.

Just before they were ready to leave, Mr. Clyde came hurrying up. He had Miz Sara's big canning pot under his arm.

"Myra, Sara wanted you to have this. She won't ever need it again, and she knew you would put it to good use."

Myra was thankful to see the pot. Now she could process the jars safely like she had learned from Miz Sara.

"There's a little something in the pot in case y'all get hungry along the way. Now, Will Rob, you be careful not to push that ol' mule too hard. He ain't ever gone this far at one time. You give him water and a little bit of oats every time you stop. Don't feed him too much at one time.

"I shore wish y'all well and a safe journey. If you're ever this way again, be shore to come see us."

_____

He gave each of them a hand to get onto the wagon, turned, and walked away real quickly. Myra couldn't keep the tears out of her eyes no matter how hard she squinted.

When Will Rob climbed on the wagon seat to drive, Uncle Bunk told him, "You get back in the back with the other young'uns. Izzy gotta drive yore wagon. I don't know nothin' 'bout yore handling a mule."

Will Rob didn't like that one bit. He could drive as good as anyone, and now that Papa was gone, he was the only one who knew how to handle Solomon. Myra was scared that he would run off right then, but he hopped on the back of the wagon. They started bouncing down the rutty road headed southeast to Johnson County. Ma and Uncle Bunk were sitting on the seat of his wagon, and they were a little ahead. Myra fixed a quilt in the back for Dolly, Jesse, and Arno. She and Will Rob sat with their feet hanging off the back like they always did.

After they rode for a few hours, the little young'uns started asking for something to eat, so they opened up the canning pot to see what was inside. It was filled to the top. They found three pones of biscuit bread, a panful of fried side meat, and on the bottom was a bunch of little pears. Myra could tell Mr. Clyde made the biscuit bread 'cause it was kind of burned on the bottom. It would still taste good. He had a late pear tree, and he had left the pears on it a long time to get sweet and juicy. He had let them eat all that they wanted off the tree, and those pears were as sweet as sugar.

Just as they opened the pot, Uncle Bunk called out to them, "Y'all got any vittles back there?"

"Shore," Will Rob yelled back. "We got plenty turnip roots."

"Well, bring me some up here. I'm hongry as a hog."

Will Rob hopped off, ran to the front, and gave him the sack of turnips. When he came back, he sliced up some of the pears with Papa's little knife. Myra broke up the bread and put a little piece of meat between it. She was careful to keep half to eat later that evening. Will Rob gave Izzy a share and took the reins while he ate. Ma and Uncle Bunk didn't look back, so they never knew the young'uns were feasting while they were knawing on turnip roots.

"Ain't you gonna give Ma any of these good vittles?"

"Myra, yesterday she would've knocked your head off with that piece of stove wood if it hadn't been for Joe Wiley. I don't care if she has to eat turnip roots for the rest of her life. I don't know how we are gonna do it, but I promise we'll get away from them and have a better life."

Myra knew he meant it, and she also knew that he was not going to desert them, until they did have a better life.

They hadn't been on the road long before they learned that poor ol' Izzy didn't have much under his hat. He didn't talk much and mostly just grinned and laughed. Will Rob sat beside him and helped to handle Solomon. He reminded Izzy to stop and rest the mule often. Bunk's wagon got way ahead of them, but they could follow their ruts in the road. They seemed to be the only folks going to Johnson County.

Myra and Will Rob started singing to pass the time. They tried to teach Izzy the words of some of the songs, but all he did was laugh. Myra told him that his part was to yell out "Hallulah" at the end of every song. He could do that part real well. He was having himself a good time. Myra noticed that he looked at Will Rob with the same look in his eyes that was like Papa looked at Dolly. She figured that at least they had one member of Ma's kin they could count on, even if he did need someone to tell him to come in out of the rain.

They wondered how to tell when they got to Johnson County. Soon the country began to look different. The hard-packed red clay was beginning to turn into sand, and they saw tall pine trees with burrs as big as a syrup bucket. The road was like a washboard, and along the way a few little shacks were back in the fields.

Along about midafternoon, they came to a little crossroad that had a store and a few houses. Uncle Bunk had stopped his wagon, and he and Ma were already in the store. Izzie told them this was a place called Harrison, and they were about halfway to Sullivan's Corner. All the people standing around looked them over but didn't have anything to say. Uncle Bunk didn't seem to know anyone. He and Ma bought snuff in the store, and Will Rob took that time to feed and water Solomon.

Myra really needed to go to the bushes, but she didn't see any place to go that would give her cover. The little boys got out and ran around to play. Of course, the first thing Jesse and Arno did was start chunking those big pine burrs at the others. Uncle Bunk saw them when he came out, and he used the side of his arm to knock both of them over backward. Will Rob tighten his fists, and his eyes got real beady. Myra was glad he said nothing. Uncle Bunk could have knocked him over the same way. The little boys got in the back of the wagon, but neither one of them were crying. They just looked lost. When Papa got on them, they would cry and snub for an hour. Papa never hit them with anything but a keen switch, and that was just when they kept on doing what he had told them to stop doing.

Myra didn't like this place, so she got back in the wagon and was glad when they started up again. If this was just halfway, she knew it would be way after dark when they got to Uncle Bunk's place in Sullivan's Corner. As soon as they got away from the crossing, she jumped off the wagon and ran to find some bushes. The best she could find were brambles and thorny bushes, but she couldn't wait any longer. She squatted down, and it took her so long that she had to really run to catch up with the wagon. As soon as she got on the wagon she felt as though she needed to go right back, 'cause she was feeling that ol' knot in her insides that came the day Papa passed on.

"Will Rob, you need to start taking Jesse and Arno to the bushes more. They can't hold themselves as long as I can."

"Heck, Myra, you hadn't even noticed that they been peeing off the side of the wagon all the way, and I have too." Myra figured that was one thing that boys could do better than her.

Nothing much happened for the rest of the evening. They just kept riding along. Will Rob asked Izzie what Uncle Bunk planted for his crop.

"He don't plant nothin'. We just sells things."

They didn't know how he made a living doing that, but they guessed they would find out. Myra spent a lot of the time thinking. She thought about how there used to be nine Stuart's living together, and now there would just be five. She had quit counting Ma as one of them. She also thought about Annie Lou and wondered what it was like to be married and living in Glencoe. Myra was glad her sister wasn't making this trip with them, 'cause she couldn't have taken it.

Will Rob had started talking about Glencoe like it was the promise land. Myra hoped he would get to go there someday, and maybe she just might go there herself.

Just before sundown, they finished up the rations from Miz Sara's pot. Now everything about Miz Sara was gone from them, except the canning pot. It was scary going in the dark, and they lost sight of the front wagon. Soon they saw it up ahead waiting for them. Uncle Bunk brought out a lantern and told Will Rob to walk ahead and shine it for them to follow. When the moon came up it was big and bright, so they didn't have any trouble seeing the road ahead. They drove like that for two or three more hours. It was hard to say how long.

It must have been midnight when they passed by a settled area that had a big store, two little stores, a church, a schoolhouse, and four houses on the same part of the road. Everything was dark, as though the people had all gone to bed. That was Sullivan's Corner, and Myra was surprised to see that it was bigger than she had expected. They drove right through and down the road less than a mile.

Then Izzy said, "There's Ma watching for us."

What they came to really surprised them. They had expected a tenant shack, probably worse than they had ever lived in. This was a big, two-story house with a front porch that wrapped all around the sides of it. They couldn't see much of it in the dark, but Uncle Bunk was right when he said he had plenty of room for them.

"Y'all get down. I know you done plumb wore out. I been mighty proud ever since Bunk told me that y'all wuz comin' to live wid us." Izzy's ma came right out to the wagons and took Dolly in her arms.

"I drove good, Ma, and Will Rob hep me."

Izzy was laughing and talking at the same time. Myra could tell that he really loved his ma.

"You young'uns come on in by the lamp and let me get a look at you. I'm yore Aint Nannie Bessie."

Their new aunt was a sight to see. She was so fat that she looked like a barrel with feet and hands sticking out. She had more chins than you could count and her arms just had fat dripping off them. She had tried to pull her hair back in a ball, but there was more of it stringing out than there was in the ball. They could tell she dipped snuff 'cause it was all in the cracks of her mouth. In a minute they knew for sure when she started spitting into a can.

"They's hoecake in the warming oven that I kept fer ya. If'en yore hongry, hep yoreself."

"No thanks, we more tired than hungry," Myra and Will Rob said almost at the same time; and it was the truth.

"Well, lemme just get busy finding y'all places to sleep. They's a plenty room in the upstairs part. If'en I can just find enuf covers."

"We got plenty of quilts in the wagon." Will Rob hurried out and came back loaded down with their soft, thick quilts.

Dolly and the little boys had already been asleep, so they carried them up the stairs to where they were going to sleep. It seemed they didn't use the upstairs at all, and there wasn't anything up there. They didn't stop to look around and just fell onto the pallets and went to sleep.

Myra did think a little bit about Aunt Nannie Bessie before she dropped off to sleep. Their new aunt was a sight to see, but there was something about her that gave Myra a good feeling. She reminded her of the ol' mama cat she had seen at Miz Grace's house. She remembered how the cat sat under the steps and licked her kittens.

Myra had also seen a school in Sullivan's Corner, and she hoped the boys would be able to go there.

The next morning they woke up early. It had turned cold during the night, and the wind was blowing right through the room where they were sleeping. Myra opened her eyes and saw that more had come in than the wind. Leaves were blowing all over the floor, and cobwebs were hanging everywhere. The chickens had been in there too, and you could see and smell their droppings. She saw some of them sitting in a tree by the open window, so they just walked right in. Everything was a mess, and aside from that, the floor sagged so bad she thought it might go right down to the bottom rooms. She put on her shoes, wrapped the quilt around her to keep warm, and headed down the stairs. Downstairs didn't look much better. She had never seen so much mess in a house before. She decided they must keep everything they got their hands on.

Uncle Bunk and Izzy were sitting outside on the steps sopping biscuit bread in syrup. Aunt Nannie Bessie told her to get some too. Myra took a bite and knew the bread wasn't nearly as good as her biscuits, but it did taste good with the syrup. The rest of the family started coming down the stairs, and their aunt gave every one a plate of syrup and bread. There was a table, but it had so much stuff on it that there was nowhere to sit a plate. Everyone just sat anywhere they could. As soon as they finished eating, Bunk told them to all dress up warmly 'cause they were going to be out in the field all day picking scrub cotton. Myra knew all the cotton picking had been done a long time ago, so she didn't know what they were going to do.

They loaded up the wagon and drove to the other side of Sullivan's Corner. The cotton patch looked as though it had been picked clean.

"I made a good bargain with this man that y'all would pick what was left on halves. Now y'all get to work. If'en y'all gonna et offen me, ya gotta work fer yore keep. Pick 'til sundown. Then walk on back home. Me and Izzy got trading to do and need the wagon."

The bitter cold wind kept them shivering. Just as they expected, there just was almost no cotton left on the stalks. Myra remembered how their plants had been loaded with white bolls, and she couldn't imagine why they were even bothering with this.

About dinnertime a man rode up on a mule and looked over what they had done.

"Y'all might as well go on home. What you've picked ain't worth nothing to me or to you."

"No, sir, we were told to stay 'til sundown, and that's what we'll do. We'll do the best we can, but there shore ain't much here."

Myra knew Will Rob was remembering how Papa always told them to keep their word and do what they had promised. They kept trying but found little cotton scattered over the field. By sundown, one sack was half filled, so they gave up and walked back to the house.

As they walked up the lane, they got their first good look at the place. Will Rob said it had been a house on one of those big farms that had been worked by a bunch of slaves before the big war. The back side of it had burned and was just sitting there, falling down with vines growing all over it. Big trees hanging with moss were all around the yard. Myra could close her eyes and picture how it used to look before the Yankees came and ruined everything.

Uncle Bunk was sitting on the porch, leaning back against the wall with a jug of moonshine by his side. He had already drunk so much that he could hardly talk.

"Did he say how much y'all made today? I'm goin' by there tomorrow and git it."

"I doubt we made anything. That was a foolish thing to do, try to pick cotton that had already been picked clean."

"Boy, don't you sass me. You just got too big for yore britches over there with that ol' man lettin' ya think ya wuz runnin' the place. I can make ya have respect fer yore elders."

He got up to come at Will Rob. Myra was scared he would really hurt her brother, but Aunt Nannie Bessie came out right then.

"Now, Bunk, you're tired and sleepy and need yore supper. Put ya head on this pillow and rest."

He did, and in just a minute he was snoring loudly.

"Young'uns, ya just have to learn to stay clear of Bunk when he's been drinkin'. He don't mean no harm, but he can act real mean when he's been into a jug."

The next morning Uncle Bunk was still sprawled out asleep on the floor in front of the fireplace. They tiptoed around him 'cause they knew he wouldn't be easy to be around when he woke up.

"Aunt Nannie Bessie, what do you need for us to do today?" Myra thought there would be work to do just like there was always work to do in other places.

"They ain't nothin' to do. We'll just set here and wait fer Bunk to sleep it off and then fix him somethin' to eat."

They didn't know what to do with themselves if there wasn't any work to do. Idleness was something they had never learned. They decided to bring in their stuff from the wagon and try to clean up as best they could.

When Myra unpacked the canned goods, Nannie Bessie was really surprised to see so much food.

"Where'd ya get all them jars of vittles?"

"We grew it in our garden, and then I canned it in these jars. It'll keep all winter. What do y'all do to have rations last through the winter?"

"We ain't never stocked up much 'cause we can walk down to the store and get what we need. We ain't never planted no garden. We eats mostly biscuit bread, fried salt meat, and whatever game Izzy kills. Them maters shore look good. Sometimes I get a cravin' fer maters."

Of course, their family wasn't used to eating like that, and they were already tired of biscuit bread. Biscuit bread ain't much. It is bread that can be stirred up quick when there ain't much else. You just mix up flour, water, and soda and cook it in a pan on top of the stove. Biscuits are made up with buttermilk and grease, then patted out into fat biscuits and baked in a hot oven. Myra knew Will Rob and the boys were ready for a good supper.

"Nannie, if you want, I'll cook some of my canned vittles fer supper, and I'll make us some biscuits too."

"Ooh, honey, that would be so good. I ain't never been much on cookin'. Yore grandma wuz a good cook when she had somethin to cook, and yore ma used to be too."

Ma did nothing but sit in the chair and rock when she was awake. At least, Myra didn't have to worry about Dolly anymore. Nannie Bessie kept the baby right with her all the time and talked and played with her. Jesse and Arno seemed to be all right. They spent most of their time climbing the big trees.

Myra could tell right away that Nannie Bessie hadn't had much of a life and was happy to have them for company. She talked and played with Izzie just like she did Dolly and always called him "my baby boy." There was a lot about them that Myra couldn't figure out, but she would find out in time.

The first thing they did was sweep the upstairs, get all the leaves out, and clean up the chicken droppings. They were afraid to sing like they usually did when they worked. They didn't want to take the chance of waking up Bunk.

Will Rob went to the store and brought back nails and hinges to fix the windows. Myra didn't want him to spend any of his twenty dollars, but he said he used some of the five dollars he got from selling the stock to the colored folks. He got the windows fixed where they could close them up real tight to keep out the wind and the chickens. Will Rob said he could fix this old place up into a good sturdy home, if it belonged to him. They had already learned that Bunk wasn't a sharecropper. He rented the place by the year from the owner, who did not even live close by. There was a lot of land, but it was just grown up in trees.

After cleaning the upstairs, they went into the part that had been burned out to see if some of the stuff from the kitchen and fireplace room could be put there. A big section could be used so they asked Nannie Bessie if they could move some things out so there would be enough room for all of them to get around the fireplace. She seemed as happy about this as she did about Myra cooking supper. She helped them move out everything that didn't need to be in the main house.

Will Rob said he found a lot of things that he could fix up and sell. Some of it was broken furniture, some was rusty farming tools, and some were things they didn't know about. They cleared the house as much as they could, and then swept and scrubbed the floors. Myra unpacked their table wear and the big oil lamp. Nannie went on and on about how she loved pretty things but had never had any.

As soon as the kitchen was clean enough to cook in, Myra started to put on supper. She wanted to make a really good meal for all of them. Now that Queen Easter was sold, there wasn't any milk. The chickens ran all over the place, so when they laid, you couldn't always find the eggs. Myra knew they had to do something about getting milk and eggs.

Will Rob said he could use wood from the burned-out part and make a pen for the chickens. Then he would crop their wings so they couldn't fly out. They could have eggs and maybe get a hen to set and raise some fryers. Myra sure wished for Queen Easter, but she was back home, with the colored folks enjoying her good, rich milk.

"That store in Sullivan's Corner had lots in it, and the people were all real friendly. Let's go down there before you start supper."

Will Rob and Myra walked down to the biggest store in the little settlement. A pretty young girl was sitting on the front steps playing with jacks like the girls at school used to do.

"You're the new girl that moved in with the Blocks, ain't ya? I'm Annie Powell. My papa runs this store, and we live in back of it."

"Howdy, I'm Myra Stuart and this here's my brother, Will Rob. We come to see about buying some milk."

Annie's pa met them at the door and said, "How can I help you, young folks?"

"Sir, we need to buy some milk fer our little sister to drink."

"Sorry, I don't handle milk. Everybody around here has a cow, so there's no call for it."

He must have seen the disappointed look on Myra's face and gave the milk situation a little more thought.

"My wife don't always need all we get from our cow. Sometimes she feeds it to the pigs. Lemme ask her if she's got any extra."

He took their bucket and went through a door into the back room. A few minutes later he came back with a bucket of sweet milk. They paid him a dime for the milk, and then bought baking soda and a little sugar. They would have to be saving and not drink the milk like they used to do. Most of it had to be saved for Dolly.

Before they left, Annie and her ma came into the store from the back rooms. Myra remembered Aunt Mary's rooms behind her little store and wished she could go back and see their rooms.

"Ask her, Ma, before they leave." Annie followed them to the door.

"We would sure be proud to have your family visit with us in our church tomorrow. We have preaching every other Sunday, and tomorrow is our day to have the preacher with us. On the Sundays that we don't have preaching, we have Bible study. We have mighty good singing, and we always welcome newcomers.

"I know Annie would love to have you go with her, Myra. There aren't any others girls her age around here."

When she said this, Annie just smiled at Myra, and she couldn't help but smile back. She'd never had a chance to make friends with anyone outside of her family. It seemed real nice to have someone invite her to go to their church with them.

"Our church is a Baptist church," Annie said.

Will Rob chimed in for the first time and said, "Oh, we are all Baptists. Our uncle is the preacher of a big Baptist church at Friendship in Trutlen County."

That was good news. If Will Rob set his head for something, they usually did it somehow.

When they got home, Nannie had already set out jars of okra and tomatoes and made a fire in the cook stove. Nannie was smiling and looking forward to a feast. Myra made a big pot of okra and tomatoes and thickened it up to make good gravy. Nannie didn't have a biscuit pan, so Myra used the top of the lard can and filled it with fat biscuits. She opened a jar of blackberries, sweetened them good, and rolled out rich dough to put on top of the cobbler. The oven was hot enough to brown everything just right.

Bunk had gone off again, and Nannie said she sure hoped he wouldn't get more liquor. Soon they were all sitting around the table eating the first good meal they had since packing up to move. Myra gave Dolly and the little boys a cup of milk, but the rest just drank water.

Izzie ate and ate. Every time he cleaned up his plate, he would say, "Want somma t'eat."

They knew he meant he wanted something more to eat, and they were glad to see him enjoying it. Nannie put up a plate for Bunk, and she cleaned up the kitchen.

"I'd give anything to learn to cook as good as you, Myra. When I was comin' on, my people didn't have much of anything. We just et whatever we could find. I run off with Bunk when I wuz 'bout yore age, and I just never learned nothin'. Yore grandma could cook when she had something to cook. I believe I could have learned it."

"I can teach you, Nannie. It ain't hard." Myra felt a wave of tenderness coming over her for this aunt whom she had known only two days. "Where are yore folks now?"

"Lord, I don't know. Me and Bunk and his folks moved around so much. I lost track of even which way they lived from here. I wonder about them sometimes."

"When we wuz down at the store, Miz Powell asked about us going to preachin' at their church tomorrow. Do ya think we can?"

"Shore, you young'uns need to meet some of the good folks around here. They can tell ya had good raisin' and come from good folks. It shows. That's why she asked ya. Now when you come home, I want you to tell me all what the preacher said. I love to hear about the Good Lord and his baby boy, Jesus."

This surprised and delighted Myra. Things weren't what she had hoped for, but she was beginning to believe they could make a good life here.

Will Rob spent the rest of the day penning up the chickens. Izzie held them for him to crop their wings, and he acted as if he was doing a real important job. They all went out and laughed at the chickens walking around inside the pen with nowhere to go. Myra sent the boys to get broom straw to make nests for the chickens.

"When you get the broom straw, bring back enough to make some brooms. I need a new one, and maybe I could sell them to the people in Sullivan's Corner.

When they rounded up the chickens, they found four roosters and six hens. That was way more roosters than needed, so they decided that one of them was going in the pot. Right after supper, Will Rob caught the rooster and put him in a croker sack. This rooster was too big for Will Rob to wring his neck like he usually did. Izzy held him down, and Will Rob chopped his head off with the axe. Jesse, Arno, and Izzy were hollering in the yard and enjoying watching the rooster flop around with no head. Myra didn't want to watch, but she did want to boil him up good. Nannie picked and cleaned him. Their plan was for Nannie to put the rooster on to boil early the next morning and cook him until he was good and tender. When they came home from preaching, Myra would fill that pot with dumplings.

Myra had to start getting everyone ready for church the next morning. She had washed and ironed their clothes after the trip to Tennille, but everything needed pressing and all the shoes needed cleaning up. Myra decided to take Jesse and Arno to church, even if she would have to pinch them to make them be still. They needed to hear some preaching and praying too.

Nannie boiled a big pot of water, and Will Rob mixed the hot water with water from the well and filled the washtub. He put it in the kitchen and told everybody to stay out until the person washing hollered, "I'm through."

Myra washed first and then put Dolly in the tub. Will Rob came in next and then he washed Arno and then Jesse. Everyone had to use the same water, so the only fair way was for the dirtiest to wash last. Of course, that was Jesse. Everyone was excited when they went to bed. They were as happy as they could be, all things considered.

Just as they got under the covers, they heard Bunk coming in. He was stumbling over things, so they knew he was drunk. He was swearing and cussing at Nannie. They couldn't hear her speak, but they knew she was giving him his supper. He was quiet for a few minutes and then he started ripping and rearing again. Nannie hollered, and they knew he must have hit her. Will Rob jumped up and started down the stairs.

"No, Will Rob, you will only make it worse. Nannie knows how to handle him."

"She has lived with him this long, and she is still living, but it's hard for me to take."

"Anything you do will just make it worse for Nannie."

Things quieted down in a while, but they found they had a new bedfellow. Izzie had come up the stairs and brought his quilt to sleep with them. He must have wanted to be out of the fussing. He slept upstairs for the rest of the time they lived there.

The next morning when Myra started getting ready for church, Nannie came in like nothing had happened the night before. Bunk was sleeping off his drunkeness. She helped Jesse and Arno get ready while Myra dressed. Just as Myra finished dressing, Nannie took the brush and started brushing her hair. She seemed to have a real way with hair and pulled it back from her face and fastened it with her comb. Myra got the comb for Christmas the year before they moved to Mr. Clyde's place, and she only wore it on special times.

"Myra, you are the prettiest girl in these parts. Yore hair is black as coal, and yore skin is as smooth as silk. Don't you let any of these ol' sorry boys mess with ya."

"Don't say that, Nannie. I know I'm as ugly as homemade soap. I won't never even think about no ol' boy. Boys ain't never been nothin' but mean to me, except fer my brothers."

"Baby gal, I know better. Ya just better be careful. A ol' sorry boy can turn yore head and get ya in a hep of trouble."

"What do you mean by that? It don't matter 'cause I shore ain't having none around me."

"You just be sure ya don't let no ol' sorry feller look ya right in the eye 'cause that will be the beginning of yore troubles."

Myra didn't know the cause, but she knew babies came to you somehow. For a long time after that, she thought if you let a fellow look you right in the eye, you were going to get a baby. She had enough young'uns to tend now, so she was sure going to keep her head down.

When they got to the church, Annie was waiting on the steps. She was wearing a pretty print dress and a long coat. Myra and the boys wore coats too, but theirs weren't pretty and new looking like Annie's. This didn't bother Myra 'cause Annie just smiled and made them feel welcome. She didn't seem to notice that Myra's old coat must have belonged to one of her brothers before it belonged to her.

The service started with singing. The piano made the singing sound so good. They knew a lot of the songs, and their row sang louder than the rest of the church. The preacher came on and preached about an hour. He talked about Jesus and how the time of his birthday was coming soon. Myra didn't get a lot of what he was saying. He talked real loud and fast and said "J-e-e-uz." He shook his fists a lot too, but nobody got the spirit like they used to at the tent meetings.

After the preaching, he asked for announcements. Annie's pa got up and told about how the church would be having a program and a tree again this Christmas. He said that next week they would give out the parts for the program and start practicing every Sunday afternoon until time for the program.

"I hope you try out for Mary. You look just like her," Annie whispered. Myra didn't know what "try out" meant, but she would try to do whatever Annie wanted.

After the announcements, there was a little more singing, and several men were called on to pray. One of them thanked the Lord for sending the fine Stuart children into their midst. Myra had already thanked Him herself.

When the service ended, a lot of people told them to come back next Sunday. Myra couldn't believe her ears when folks told her how nice Jesse and Arno had acted. They didn't know that she told them they wouldn't get any chicken and dumplings if they didn't behave.

When they got near the house, they saw smoke coming out of the stovepipe and could smell the rooster cooking. Myra hurried in and made the dumplings. Nannie was smiling big when she opened up the oven to show that it was full of sweet taters. Bunk had brought home a sackful last night. Myra was starting to make up a pan of corn bread when Will Rob came in with the first egg. She put it in the corn bread batter and popped it in the oven. Bunk came in behind Will Rob and sat down at the table, waiting for his dinner.

"Boy, been lookin' at what ya done to them chickens. That's good. I can eat me a egg ever day. They's lotta things ya can do around this place. Me and ya and Izzy gonna go off and cut firewood to sell and make us some money."

Thinking about having eggs to eat seemed to make Uncle Bunk think better of Will Rob. Myra was glad. She knew her brother would feel better if he could start making a little money again.

Nannie had cooked the rooster until it was falling off the bones. They took most of the meat out and put it on another plate so Myra could fill the broth with dumplings. She had never made so many dumplings in her life. The table was filled with food, and it looked like a feast. Everyone ate until they couldn't hold anymore. Myra asked Will Rob about killing another rooster for Christmas.

"I reckon we can kill 'em all but one. One is all ya need to do the job."

When Bunk said that, he winked at Will Rob who turned red as the rooster's comb.

After they cleaned up the kitchen, Myra decided to take a little walk. The little boys were playing on the porch, and the others were taking naps. Myra didn't think about Ma much anymore. She did nothing but sit in the rocker and come to the table and eat a little. She didn't bother nobody, and nobody bothered her. Myra didn't know what Ma thought about all day in the rocking chair. At least she didn't have to worry about Dolly now. Nannie had just taken her over. Dolly had started talking a lot, and she started saying "Nannie" right away. They had stopped calling her Aunt Nannie Bessie. That was just too much to say, and she liked Nannie better.

Myra headed down to Sullivan's Corner, and there wasn't a soul around. It looked as though everyone was asleep there too.

"Myra, come around to the back."

She walked behind the store and saw Annie sitting in a swing that was hung from a big tree. It was a swing just like Miz Grace had on her front porch in Tennille. They sat together in the swing, and Annie taught her some little songs and a clapping game about their mamas hanging out clothes. This was the most fun Myra had ever had with someone outside her family.

"Oh, Myra, I'm so glad you came here. I love to talk with you."

"Me too."

"Did you have ya a feller back in Washington County?"

"No, and I ain't never gonna have one. I shore ain't gonna get messed up with young'uns 'fore my time. If ya let some ol' sorry feller look you right in the eye, that's what will mess you up with young'uns." Myra was surprised that her friend didn't know this, especially since she lived here with folks coming in the store all the time.

"I ain't ever been sure how young'uns come about, but I figgered boys had something to do with it. I will shore be careful from now on."

"Are you going to start to school tomorrow?"

"No, I done finished all the learnin' I can learn. I'm gonna make the boys go."

"I wuz hopin' you'd be going. Our teacher is a man named Mr. Walter Smith. He is real hard and don't mind using the stick on the bad boys. He makes you work, but he really teaches ya good."

After hearing this, Myra knew that come tomorrow, Jesse and Arno would be in school. Mr. Walter Smith was just what they needed. She was having such a good time that she never wanted to leave.

"I gotta go home now. I might be needed. I shore thank ya fer letting me sit in the swing and play with ya."

"Myra, I have been dreaming about having a good friend like you. Let's always be best friends."

"Me too." That was all Myra could say, but her heart was happier than it had been in a long time.

As she walked home, she started thinking about how it is right that the good people in yore life are strung out instead of being with you all at the same time. First she had Papa and lost him. Then she had Miz Sara and Aunt Mary and lost them. Now she has Annie and Nannie. The Good Lord must have planned it that way.

When she got home, Nannie was waiting to hear all about the preaching. Myra told her about the Christmas program.

"I'd shore like to go to that program and take the boys to it. Reckon it would be right fer us to go?"

"Shore, I want ya young'uns to do all there is to do. There ain't much to do around here, but y'all seen to find more things to do than most folks do."

"I like bein' with Annie. She asked me to be her best friend. She seems almost like a sister to me. I love Annie Lou, but me and her just never did seem to see things the same way. I know one thing fer shore. Mr. Jesse and Mr. Arno are goin' to school tomorrow morning."

"You sound just like a little ma. One of these days you'll have a houseful of young'uns of yore own, and ya'll be a good ma to 'em."

Nannie had started talking to Myra a lot, and she seemed to like telling about things that had happened to her. That evening, she told about how her and Bunk's other babies had died right after they were born.

"I wuz so happy when Izzy was born and lived. He wuz the prettiest and smartest little baby that ya ever saw, and I played with him and rocked him and sang to him all the time.

"Right after he started walking, he got real sick and had chills and fever for three days. I wuz so scared that he was gonna die. Bunk went fer the doctor, and he told us what we had to do fer him, and we done it all. He started to get better in about a week, but then we seen that he couldn't do some of the things that he used to do He had to learn to walk all over again and didn't smile or pay attention to nothin'.

"As he got older, we could see that he just didn't have as much sense as other young'uns his age. He was a good boy and did what he could. We figgered the high fever must've done somethin' to his head and killed some of hit. I'm just thankful to the Lord that he spared Izzy and let us keep him, even if he is like he is."

She looked so sad that Myra went over and curled up in her big lap like she used to do with Papa when she was little. They just sat there quietly for a long time.

Ma would sit and listen to what was going on around her. She would talk a little, but that was just when she needed something brought to her.

"Nannie, I shore pray Ma will get better. You reckon she ever will?"

"She's still grieving over yore papa. She might be better in time."

"We all still hurt over Papa. It seems like to me that the best way she could remember him is to help his young'uns out some."

"She's actin' just like yore grandma did after her man passed. She stayed here with me and Bunk, and we had a worse time with her. She'd wander off in the woods at night and get lost. She always said she wuz out looking for toothbrushes. Ya know, them twigs off 'en sweet gum trees is good fer cleaning yore teeth. A lotta old women liked to dip them in their snuff and chew on 'em. Yore grandma musta really liked to do that. She was always lookin' fer them trees in the woods. We couldn't keep her in the house, 'til finally she wandered off and fell in an old well and drowned."

Myra was shocked to hear that. She had never known anything about it or even that she had a grandma.

"Did they get her out of the well?"

"Yea, they had a hard time, but finally they lowered Izzy down to put a rope on her. I was shore worried crazy about him doing that. She wuz already dead, and I didn't want him takin' such a chance. They pulled her up, but she was way too far dead to help. We buried her out there in the little clearing. That is where my babies are all buried too."

Jesse and Arno were surprised and not too happy the next morning when Myra told them that they had to go to school. She got them ready, and Arno wrote down their names and birthdays as Papa always did when they started a new school.

"I filled this bucket with some good dinner fer y'all. Now they ain't no reason why you can't behave yoreself and try to learn as much as you can."

"You better do what Myra says. If I hear of y'all getting a switchin' at school, you gonna get another one from me when ya get home." Will Rob was trying to sound just like Papa.

-7-

Myra loved seeing her little brothers walk to school carrying their dinner pail. The meal she was able to fix for them was as good as anybody's, and she was thankful they did not have to be ashamed for the other young'uns to see their dinner. At night when they did their lessons, she worked right along with them. She was trying to learn to read and write. She could tell that Arno was learning, but she wasn't too sure about Jesse. No word came about them getting a switching from Mr. Smith. Will Rob's talk must have done them some good.

Will Rob went off every day with Bunk and Izzy to cut wood. He didn't seem to mind. They always had money to buy things from the store for Myra to cook. Everyone loved her cooking. One day they brought home a can that had a picture of a fish on the front. When Bunk opened the can, Myra knew from the smell that it was some kind of fish.

"That's whatcha call sammones. Hit comes from sommers way off in them cans. Ya ken eat it right out'en the can. That's how me and Izzy eat it when we off a working."

Bunk's description didn't sound too appealing to Myra, so she decided to find a way to cook the canned fish. She stewed it in a pan with chopped onion and a little milk. They ate it over grits and thought it was the best thing they had ever tasted. Bunk brought salmon often and asked Myra to cook "her stuff."

Nannie and Myra kept busy fixing up things around the house and trying to keep it clean and straight. When they had spare time, they made brush brooms. At the end of the week, Myra took the brooms to Miz Powell and asked if she could sell them in the store. Myra didn't think the folks around there would take the time to make their own brooms. Miz Powell thought that was a good idea and bought the first three for a dime each. Those extra dimes would buy milk for Dolly and the boys. Will Rob told her that Miz Powell probably sold them for a quarter apiece. Myra didn't care, as long as she got her dimes.

The crochet thread was used up, so now she just unraveled and worked up another piece. Nannie loved to sit and watch her crochet. Several times, Myra tried to teach her how to make the stitches, but she got real nervous and couldn't learn.

Annie was in school all week, and Myra missed her. Sometimes she thought about what it would be like to sit in the schoolhouse with Annie and eat their dinner together. That time had passed for her. She just couldn't catch up on all she needed to learn.

When Saturday finally came, Annie came to the house and asked Myra to come home with her. Annie had her own room in back of the store. She had her own bed and everything. This surprised Myra, and she figured that must be the way it is when there ain't but one young'un in a family, especially a family that has a store. They laughed and talked and told each other things that they wouldn't tell anyone else. Annie just walked right into the store and got them a soda pop from the drink box.

There was no preaching the next Sunday. The preacher served two churches, and each one had him every other Sunday. This was the Sunday for Bible study, and Myra liked those stories better than the preaching. The church was divided up with a section for the little young'uns, the grown folks, and what they called "the young people." Myra and Will Rob were with the young people. The teacher was a young fellow not much older than them.

The first meeting for the Christmas program was that afternoon. Miz Powell was in charge of handing out the parts. Myra learned that "trying out" meant the person sat in the place of the part in the program that they wanted to play. The preacher read each part from the Bible, and you did not have to speak your part. Several older ladies sat in the Mary part. Miz Powell couldn't make up her mind right away. Myra thought none of them seemed just right.

"Mama, Myra wants to try out for Mary."

Myra wanted to run right out of the church. She would never have said such a thing. Everybody was looking at her, and she was shaking all over.

"Go on up and sit in the chair."

"We want to see you."

"Go ahead up there."

Everybody in the church seemed to be urging her to try out. There didn't seem to be any way out of this, so she walked down the aisle to the front of the church.

Miz Powell handed her the shawl to put around her head and told her to sit by the manger and put the shawl around her head. When she sat down in the manger, her knees were knocking so hard that she knew the whole church could hear.

While the preacher read the part, she sat very still and clutched the shawl around her shoulders. Then everyone in the pews started clapping.

"We have our Mary," Miz Powel said. "Hallulah."

She threw up her hands as if she was rejoicing. The other ladies had all been Mary at some time or another, so they didn't mind. The rest of the parts were given out. Joseph went to Tom Crawford, who was the teacher of the young people. Annie got to be the Angel, and that was the part she wanted. One of Annie's dolls would be the baby Jesus, since nobody in Sullivan's Corner had a little baby the right age. The rest of the parts were shepherds, wise men, and animals. Will Rob would be one of the shepherds. Jesse and Arno were going to be sheep and had to come down the aisles on all fours. There would be a lot of singing before and after the program. Practices would be every Sunday afternoon for the month before Christmas. Myra had never done anything like this, and she loved every minute of being Mary. She thought a lot about how Mary must have felt when the Lord asked her to be the mother of his very own son.

Papa always got real excited about Christmas, and the family had a celebration of the Lord's birthday every year that Myra could remember. They didn't always get presents, but they always had a good time together. She was going to make sure the little boys and Dolly had a good Christmas this year. Nannie told her that none of her folks had ever paid any mind to Christmas. Some years she didn't even know when it was, but she thought it would be a good thing to celebrate the birthday of the little baby Jesus.

The next weeks were filled with practicing and finding ways to make the first Christmas without Papa a happy time. Will Rob found scrap wood that he used to make a little dancing man for Dolly. Papa used to make them, and Will Rob remembered how he did it. The little man's legs and arms were hinges, and a string is hooked to them. When the string is pulled, the little man dances. He made Jesse and Arno each a bow and arrow with string and some branches. Myra told him she hoped they wouldn't try to shoot her. She worked on her crocheting and was making an ear wrap to give to Annie. She had to think of something to make for Nannie.

Myra and Izzy brought pine boughs and holly branches from the woods. They put these up and down the stair railings and on the front porch over the door.

"If this don't beat all. Ya young'uns can shore fix things up." Nannie said this every time they talked about Christmas. Izzy got so excited that he would run round and round the house laughing.

Will Rob shut up the rooster they were planning to kill for Christmas dinner. They fattened him with extra food. Myra had saved up bread scraps and grits to make dressing. There were plenty of eggs now, so she could make a syrup cake.

"If this don't beat all. I never knowed folks carried on like this fer Christmas." Nannie was as excited as Izzy, but she didn't run around the house.

Soon there was only a week until the church program on Christmas Eve. Myra begged Nannie to go with them.

"No, sweet baby, I can't go. I ain't got nothing fit'en to wear. Y'all jest have to tell me all about it. Izzy can't go neither. He wouldn't behave himself fer that long. When folks don't know him, it scares 'em when he gets to laughin'.

"Please, Nannie, I know these good people would be glad to have you there."

"Ya jest ain't seen the things I've seen."

Myra knew her aunt didn't have anything to wear and was really afraid that Izzy would cause trouble. She knew there was more to it than that. Nannie was afraid to leave the house and be around people. Somehow she hoped to help her get over this, 'cause she was as good as anybody.

School had let out for the holidays, and everyone was at home when Horace Morris came riding up in his buggy. Will Rob went out to meet him.

"Come on in, Horace. We're shore proud to see ya. What brings ya way over here?"

"My grandpa sent me over to Wrightsville on some business. When Annie Lou heard how close it would be to Sullivan's Corner. She wouldn't have nothin' but fer me to come by to see y'all. She has been real worried about how y'all getting along. I stopped at the store and asked how to find you."

"We doin' right well. We got a good place to live and ways to make a little money. The boys are goin' to school. You can see Dolly's growin' like a weed."

Myra was thinking how glad she was that she had put on a pot of soup that morning. She had plenty to offer him for dinner.

"Horace, we got plenty of hot soup and corn pone on the stove. We'd be proud fer you to eat with us."

"I am hungry. I need to get back on the road as soon as I can. Annie Lou will kill me if I ain't back in time fer the tree at North Connolly on Christmas Eve. Come help me, Will Rob. I need to unload some things Annie Lou sent you."

He brought in a big bag of oranges, a can of hard candy, bag of big raisins with the seeds in them, and a sack tied with string for each of them.

"Now you ain't to open the sacks till Christmas. That's from Santa Claus. Here's a letter that Annie Lou wrote to all of you. Now I'll eat a bite and then head out."

During the meal Will Rob asked Horace a lot of questions about Glencoe, and everything he heard made him determined to go there when he could.

Myra was beginning to believe there really was a Santa Claus, and that he must live in Glencoe. After Horace left, they all gathered around for Arno to read the letter.

To my beloved family,

There is so much to tell you that I don't know where to begin. First, I want to tell you how much I miss all of you and think about you every day.

Things couldn't be better for me. The MacTavish family has been so nice to me. Glencoe is the most up-to-date town you could ever find. I wish all of you could be here with me. I hope you will like what I am sending you and will think of your sister on Christmas Day.

With love to all of you,
Annie Lou

They were so happy to hear from Annie Lou and to know she was in a good place. Myra put the letter in her pocket and intended to learn every word by heart. As soon as Horace left, the boys wanted to get into their sacks.

"No, this is from Santy and you can't have hit 'til Christmas morning."

Myra piled everything in the corner and put a chair in front of it.

"That goes for you too, Will Rob. If I see that chair moved one bit, I'll be on to you like white on rice."

"Myra, you talkin' like you the Santy."

"You better watch yore step, boy, or you ain't gettin' nothing."

Both of them were feeling happy and enjoying joshing with each other like old times.

"Is Santy gonna come to see me too, Ma?"

"Now, Izzie, you know he ain't gonna leave a good boy like you out," Myra spoke up before Nannie could speak, and she vowed to herself that Izzie would have his first visit from Santy.

"I swanney. I never heared of such. Y'all young'uns just carry on over ever thing."

Myra knew including Izzy in the Christmas presents made Nannie happy. There was no question about Izzy being happy. He started running around and around the house and laughing loud enough to be heard at the crossroads.

Bunk had been drinking again and was not home when Horace came. Myra was glad he was gone. She didn't want Horace to have anything to tell Annie Lou about them, except good things. Ma hadn't said a word while Horace was there. Myra thought she would want to know about Annie Lou, since she was always her pick of the young'uns.

After Horace left, she asked, "Does Annie Lou and that feller have any young'uns yet?"

Myra started to try to explain that she hadn't been married but two months, but she didn't even bother and just said, "No, not yet."

The next day was spent cooking and cleaning house. They would be busy on Christmas Eve getting ready for the program. Myra had one more problem. She had promised Izzy that Santy would come, and she had to find a present for him. Will Rob did not have any wood left to make anything for Izzy. All of Myra's crochet thread had been used on the presents for Nannie and Annie. She couldn't have thought of anything to make for him anyway. She did have a little of the broom money. There was the twenty-dollar bill that Joe Wiley made her keep, but she was holding on to that.

She headed down to the store with three dimes and two pennies in her pocket. Powell's Store didn't have anything that seemed right for Izzy. Miz Powell told her to go down the street to the Brantley's store, and they might have something. When she walked in, she saw just the right gift for Izzy. It was a knitted hat that would pull down and cover up his ears. It was red, and she knew he would love it. It cost fifty cents, and she needed eighteen cents more.

"Mr. Brantley, is there any way that you'd let me buy that hat if I give you thirty-two cents now and finish paying for it when I sell two more brooms?"

Never would she have had nerve to ask such a thing, except for needing it for Izzy. He just stood looking at her for a minute, and Myra knew she shouldn't have asked.

"No, I don't sell on credit, but my store needs dusting real bad. I will pay you the rest that you need if you can get that done for me before I close in about an hour."

If there was one thing Myra could do, it was to clean. She got busy and dusted everything in the store. She even dusted off all the cans on the shelf. She gave him the money when she finished, and he wrapped the hat up in paper and handed it to her. As she hurried back home, she felt a funny feeling again. This time it wasn't that old bad feeling like she got after Papa left them. This feeling was like little bubbles inside that made her want to laugh right out loud.

There was a lot of whispering going on between Nannie, Will Rob, and Myra. Nannie wanted to know how Santa Claus was going to come. They told her to wait and see, but he would come for sure.

On Christmas Eve they left early for the church to get into their costumes. Every pew in the church was quickly filled with everybody who lived anywhere nearby and a bunch of little young'uns that Myra had never seen there before. The pews were filled right up to the front. In the front corner was a huge Christmas tree. It was decorated with all kinds of shiny things and had candles on it, but they weren't lit.

When the preacher opened the service, everyone in the program was standing in the back of the church. After a few songs and prayers, he started reading from the Bible. It was the same part that Papa always read to them on Christmas. It started out telling how all the world was going to have to pay taxes and had to go to their own home places. Joseph had to take his pregnant wife and go to Bethlehem. Myra knew every word by heart, and oh, how she wished Papa could see his little girl being Mary.

When the preacher got to the part about them looking for a place to stay and having to stay in the stable, Tom Crawford and Myra came in and sat down. It went on, and every time the preacher got to a part, the ones that he was talking about came in. Will Rob was the first shepherd, and he looked every bit the part. Jesse and Arno came crawling in on all fours, and there was cotton all around their face to make them look like sheep. They did real good, except nobody had told Jesse that the sheep were not supposed to bah, and he thought they should.

All the way coming down the aisle, Jesse kept saying, "*Bah, bah, bah.*"

Myra thought for sure they would take him out of the program, but most folks, even the preacher, couldn't help laughing.

After they all came in and gathered around Tom Crawford and Myra looking down at the doll that was supposed to be their baby, everybody sang "Silent Night." Someone had lit the candles on the Christmas tree, and it was the prettiest thing that Myra had ever seen. She looked at the back of the church, and standing just outside the door were Nannie and Izzy. Then she saw someone else standing right behind them. She knew who he was, but she didn't know how he got there all the way from Washington County. She saw his blue suit, and his pretty blue eyes were looking right at her. As quickly as she blinked her eye, he was gone, and Izzy and Nannie were standing there alone.

After the program, the preacher went up to the Christmas tree and gave a big stick of peppermint candy to everybody in the church—not just the young'uns, but everybody. She knew Nannie and Izzy had already gone home, but this time she could find out for sure about the blue boy. He was standing right with them, so they would know.

It was getting late when they got home, and everyone was ready for bed. Before they went upstairs, Myra told them to get their longest sock and put it over the stair rails. Izzy got his and hung it with the others.

"Now the quicker you get to sleep, the quicker Santy will come. When you wake up in the morning, yore socks will be filled up."

Will Rob said the same thing that Papa used to say when they were little.

They hurried up the stairs to go to sleep. Every one of them believed there was a fat man in a red suit on his way to their house right then.

As soon as Myra thought they were asleep, she put their little gifts in their socks and filled the rest with oranges, candy, and raisins.

"Well, if this don't beat all. I never knew what ya wuz suppose to do on Christmas, but I know Izzy is going to have a fit over hit."

Nannie kept saying that over and over. If she hadn't seen Myra fill the socks, she surely would have thought Santa had really visited their house.

Bunk had come home while they were at church. He was not drunk, and sat and watched what they were doing. Myra knew that was Nannie's best Christmas present.

Before they went to bed Myra said, "Nannie, I saw you and Izzy at church, and I wuz glad."

"I didn't want to make no bother, but I just had to see my baby girl sitting there being the ma of the baby Jesus."

"It made me happy to see you. There was a little boy standing right behind you and Izzy. Do you know him? I hadn't ever seen him before." Myra tried to make this sound real ordinary.

"Myra, there wasn't nobody there but me and Izzy."

"Are ya shore? I saw him there with y'all."

"There wasn't nobody there but me and Izzy. Besides, Izzy would have tried to talk to him, if he had been there."

Myra knew that was true. Izzy always said howdy to everybody he saw, whether he knew them or not. Somehow she had to find out who he was and why nobody ever saw him but her. He was there! She knew that for sure.

Every night, Will Rob went out to the shed to check on Solomon and give him a little bit of oats. When he went out that night, he was laughing and was saying he had to give a little extra for his Christmas present. In just a few minutes he came back in, looking white as a sheet.

"Myra, he's dead. I found Solomon just lying there dead."

Myra knew he had been crying, and she couldn't hold back the tears. They all loved that ol' mule.

"You young'uns don't need to cry for that ol' mule. He lived his time and had more love shown to him than most folks even do. He don't have to haul a heavy load every again. He has gone on to his reward."

When Nannie said this, the sadness they had felt just lifted right off.

"Well, if Solomon goes to mule heaven, maybe Papa will get to see him there. He can show off his pretty teeth." Will Rob was laughing now instead of crying.

The next morning everybody got up early to get their Santa Claus, and you have never seen folks so excited. Izzie just ran around the house laughing. He put his hat on, and Myra never saw him again without his red hat on. When they opened the little sacks from Annie Lou, they knew she had been thinking about them a lot. Myra's sack had two balls of crochet thread. Dolly had a little doll, and Jesse and Arno got marbles. Will Rob's bag was heavier than the others. He opened it and found a small hammer that was just right to use when he made little things. There was also a bag of little nails.

Their dinner filled up the table, and they ate on it for the rest of the week. With all things considered, Myra had to think that her family was making out all right.

After dinner, Will Rob hitched up Bunk's mule to the wagon and hauled Solomon's body off. He said he took it as far back in the woods as he could. Now one more Stuart was gone. Myra wondered who would be next, or maybe they would all go together to some good place like Glencoe.

~8~

_____

After Christmas passed, Myra knew that blessed season had done all of them a heap of good. This wasn't the family she had started out with, but she was starting to feel like they were a family and had to stick together.

The weather turned freezing cold and stayed that way all through the month of January. They stayed in the house by the fire to keep warm and went outside only to do what had to be done and hurried back inside to warm by the fire. The good wood that Will Rob and Izzy had cut was stacked up right by the door. Most nights they didn't even try to sleep upstairs. Everyone rolled up in quilts by the fire. Nannie sat up by the fire to keep it going and watched for sparks that might set the house on fire. It didn't seem to bother her to get so little sleep. The cook stove was going all day, and big pots of Myra's soup and stews simmered on top. The canned goods were going fast, but that is why she had canned.

To help pass the time, they told stories. Everybody liked scary stories about haints and such, and they all tried to outdo each other in making up a scary story. One night, Will Rob came running into the house and bolted the door behind him. He was white as a ghost. They knew something had scared the daylight out of him. When he told what had happened, they knew why. He vowed it was the truth.

He had left right after dinner to go over to the place of Miss Sally and Miss Mamie Porter. They were two old maids who lived about a mile on the other side of Sullivan's Corner. One day at church they asked him about coming by their place once a week to break up wood for their stove and do any chores that needed to be done. He was glad to do it. Papa had always told them to try to help old folks whenever they could.

Everyone was ready to hear a good one. The howling wind was making the house creek and groan when he started telling his story.

"After I chopped the wood into little sticks, the sisters kept finding more things fer me to do. It wuz gettin' late, and they asked me to stay and take supper with them. Miss Mamie had fried a chicken, so I stayed.

"By the time I finished eatin' and headed home, it was already dark as pitch, and no moon. I started walkin' down the road, but since it wuz so cold, I took a shortcut through that settlement where them colored folks live. The wind was blowin' and howlin' somthin' fierce. In going through the settlement I had to cut through a little buryin' ground where there was some mounds of dirt piled up to show the graves. I saw something shining all around one of the graves and couldn't figure out what it might be, so I stopped to look. Somebody had taken bottles, the kind that syrup comes in and laid them all around the grave. I guess they figured this marked it good and looked good too.

"Just as I passed through the graveyard, I heared somethin' a comin' behind me. I could hear the steps crackin' on the leaves. I didn't look back, but every time I walked faster, the footsteps walked faster. Then I started to run, and I could hear the thing behind me runnin' too. I started to holler, and the wind started up again and made an awful howling noise.

"I figgered I couldn't outrun whatever it was, so I better try to turn and maybe hide from it. I got under some brush. Then I felt somethin' all over me like I wuz smotherin'. I thought it wuz gonna kill me fer shore. The wind just got louder and louder. Then just as quick as it started, the thing was gone. The wind died down, and a great big moon came out from behind the clouds.

"It wuz light as day, and I couldn't see nothin' around that looked like what had been on me. The bushes weren't tore up, and I couldn't find tracks or signs of where somethin' had been. I lit out and run home as fast as I could."

They had all been sitting there, hanging on his every word. If anybody had said "Boo," they would have all messed up their britches.

"Boy, you put a good one on us this time. You will have to tell that one again."

"No, Nannie, it really happened. I swear it did."

"Will Rob, that was a good, scary story, but you know Papa told you that you was never supposed to swear to anything that wasn't the gospel truth." Myra had been as scared as the others, but now she knew it was just a tale.

"I wouldn't swear, if it wasn't the gospel truth"

"Will Rob, how did you get those scratches all over you?" Arno pointed to his face.

Deep scratches were all over his face and arms. Nannie said it looked as though he had been scratched by some kind of claw. They never talked about that story again, and none of them ever went close to that graveyard again. When Will Rob went to help the Porter sister, he always left with plenty of time to get home before dark, and he walked right down the middle of the main road.

Another big thing happened to Myra this time ever year. She counted off nineteen days after Christmas to January thirteen. That was her birthday, the day she was born. This year was 1910 and she turned fourteen years old. Papa always mentioned it to her on that day, so she knew that she was a year older. Now she had to keep up with it every year. It was good that it came right after Christmas so she didn't have too many days to count.

A new problem was bothering her. She had only one decent dress to wear to church. And it was starting to get tight on her. In fact, it was so tight in the top that she could hardly pull it on. She wasn't getting fat, but for some reason her bosoms were starting to get really big and round. She tried to tie them down with rags, but they kept popping out. She had missed church for the last few Sundays because she couldn't keep the buttons from popping open. She was afraid that her bosoms would just pop right out in front of everybody. She hated to miss church and spending time with Annie, but she couldn't take a chance of the congregation seeing her big, ugly bosoms. She didn't know what to do. There was no way she could get a new dress.

One day, near the end of January when only Myra, Nannie, and Dolly were home, someone knocked on the door. Myra went to the door, and there was Miz Powell, Annie's ma. She had never seen her outside of the store except at church.

She came in, and after she had warmed by the fire she said, "Myra, we have been worried about you and wonder why you haven't been at church with your brothers. I hope you haven't been sick or nothing like that."

"No, ma'am, I've just been busy what with the cold weather and all."

That wasn't much of an excuse, but she couldn't tell her the real reason. She was wearing one of Will Rob's old shirts, but even that was too tight on her.

Miz Powell talked to Nannie about the cold weather, and she played with Dolly a little. Myra was beginning to wonder why she had come.

Miz Powell never left the store during the time it was open. Finally, she talked to Myra.

"Myra, Miss Mamie and Miss Sally were telling me that they have a bunch of really nice dresses made out of good material that they can't use anymore. You know, I do dressmaking and alterations. They said I could have these to fix and try to sell. I can't go over there right now, but I wondered if you'd go and pick them up for me. Maybe if the little boys went, you could bring them back in one trip. I will let you pick out any that you want and fix them to fit you to pay you for your trouble."

"Yes, ma'am, I'd shore be glad to do that for you. We'll go Saturday morning when they don't go to school."

"That's soon enough. Now I must get back to the store. *Bur-r-r*, I hate to go out in this cold."

The day was Tuesday, and Myra couldn't wait until Saturday. The next morning, she set out for the Porter sisters' house. She would make as many trips as it took. She had just left the house when Izzie came running to catch up with her. He was wearing his red hat and wanted to go with her. She was glad to have him to help carry the load of dresses, and she was a little scared to go right up to their house and knock.

She had seen the sisters in church, and Will Rob said they were real nice to him. Still, it didn't seem right for her to go right into their house. They both looked old, and neither had ever married. Will Rob heard that their papa left them a house and enough money to keep them all their days. They stayed dressed up all the time and wore lots of white powder and lip rouge on their face. They pulled their hair back in a ball and wore lots of pins and combs. Myra figured in their day they must have been real pretty, so she wondered why they never married.

She knocked, and Miss Mamie came to the door.

"Ma'am, I'm Myra Stuart, this here's Izzy. We come to get them dresses fer Miz Powell."

"You come right in. Clarice told me to expect you. I do appreciate you taking the time to help us out like this."

The first thing Myra noticed when she came inside was the good smell of the house. It was kind of a mix of smells like the peppermint sticks they got at Christmas and fresh flowers in the summer. There was a nice fire burning in a little pot-bellied stove, and they warmed up fast when they sat beside it. Miss Mamie kept putting little sticks of wood in the stove. Now Myra understood why they wanted Will Rob to cut their wood up into little sticks. Besides fitting right into their stove, the sticks were easy for them to carry. Myra figured they had thought that up pretty smart. They seemed very glad to have company, even it was just Myra and Izzy.

Miss Sally came out from the kitchen carrying a little pot, four cups, and a plate of teacakes on a platter.

"Me and Sister always have a cup of cocoa when we have been out in the cold. Will you have some with us?"

Myra didn't know what she was fixing to have. If it tasted as good as it smelled, she knew she wanted some of it. Miss Sally filled the cups with what looked like coffee. The first sip was so hot it burned Myra's tongue, but it was so good that she didn't care if it burned all the skin off. She and Izzy drank two cups and ate all the teacakes on the plate. Izzy made her proud. He sat in that fancy chair and drank from those little cups as if he had been doing it every day of his life.

"We thank ya fer giving us this good stuff. We shore enjoyed it, didn't we, Izzy?"

Izzy just grinned and laughed his laugh.

"Papa always said that if I had ever found a man that I loved half as much as I love chocolate, I would have married him for sure."

Now Myra knew how good cocoa was and also why Miss Sally had never married. She kind of doubted that was the only reason.

After they finished the cocoa, Miss Mamie left the room and brought back two big bundles of dresses, a coat, and three sweaters. Myra was anxious to leave and get the clothes to Miz Powell.

When she got up to leave, the sisters just kept on talking. Sometimes they were just talking to each other, and they would argue about when or where something happened. Neither one of them ever admitted to being wrong. Finally, they were able to break away and start walking home. There was almost more clothes than the two of them could carry. When they got to the store, Myra took the clothes inside, and Izzy walked home. Miz Powell sorted out six dresses, the sweaters, and the coat.

"Myra, I want you to try these. Those ladies are tall and used to be a lot stouter than they are now. I can let the dresses out in the top, take in the waist, put in a deep hem, and they will be just right for you.

"Now the coat fits fine except for the length. I will have to cut it off."

"Ma'am, I shore thank you for these clothes. Won't it take too much of yore time to fix them right for me? I know you need yore time in the store."

"It's not gonna take much of my time, Myra. I'm gonna teach you how to do it. As good as you crochet, I know you can learn to sew. You can help me with the other dresses too."

Nothing would have made Myra any happier than to hear that. Her dream was coming true. She remembered telling Aunt Mary that what she really wanted to do most was learn to be a dressmaker. Now that was going to happen. Myra had no doubts that she could learn to sew really good and maybe even make dresses.

"Now I want you to come down here every day right after dinner. The first thing you will learn is how to hem. Then I will show you how to take in the dresses on my sewing machine. I will be able to help you about an hour every day. That is all I can take off from the store. I know you will learn fast and will be a help to me."

Myra hurried home to tell Nannie. She had started telling her about everything that happened to her. She told her about every dress that she was getting, and her aunt was as excited as if they were her own. Myra did wish there was some way she could fix up one for Nannie, but she was just too big.

"Nannie, why are my bosoms growin' so big and ugly?"

She could ask her aunt anything and not feel shamed. Nannie didn't know much, but she was always glad to listen.

"Honey, you are just starting to shape out, and pretty soon you are going to have the prettiest little shape in this part of the country. Now is when you really have to start watching out for them ol' sorry boys. They all gonna be after you, but you don't let them mess you up. Ya so pretty, and some fine gentleman with a good place is going to come by and that is who you want.

"You look just like your ma did the first time I ever saw her. You wouldn't know it now that she is so wore out and everything, but she was the prettiest thing I had ever seen. I 'member when we first went to Washington County and your pa saw her. He would have married her no matter what. That is how it will be with you too."

"Ya just puttin' me on. I know I'm ugly as homemade soap. I will be careful about them ol' sorry boys. I ain't seen no boys around here that amounts to much."

The next day, Miz Powell showed her how to hem, and in no time she could make her needle whip in and out as good as Miz Powell. She learned to carefully rip out the seams. She didn't like this as much, but it was something that had to be done. She started out sewing on scraps with the machine. After a few days, she could pedal the machine and keep the material moving under the needle as smooth as could be. Miz Powell said she had never seen anyone who took to sewing like Myra.

She could tell that Miz Powell really enjoyed teaching her. Annie had never liked sewing and didn't want to sit down and try to learn. Soon, Myra was taking home hemming or basting every evening. She loved every minute of it. Every time she had the needle in her hand or sat at the machine, she was having the best time of her life.

Her days were busy. First thing every morning, she helped Nannie clean and put dinner on to cook. Then she hurried to the store to meet Miz Powell while the store was closed for dinner.

Nannie was doing a lot of the cleaning now. In fact, she had got so particular about the house that you would never have believed that it was in such a mess when they came. They were having a lot of good eating. The chickens were laying enough eggs to have plenty for anything Myra wanted to cook and still have eggs for breakfast. Izzie brought in lots of squirrels and rabbits. She had learned to fry squirrel where it tasted almost like chicken. The rabbits were used for stews or dumplings.

The canned stuff was beginning to run short, but it wouldn't be long before they could plant a spring garden. There was plenty of space near the house. Will Rob would break it up soon. He planned to keep it fertilized from the dried chicken droppings. They were trying to decide what to plant and figure out how to get the seed. Bunk stayed drunk more than he stayed sober, but when he made a little money, he was good about bringing home things to cook. He liked side meat and canned salmon, so that was mostly what he brought home. It tasted pretty good, but they were getting ready to have some fresh vegetables.

Myra had kept all the scraps that she cut from the dresses. One day, Miz Powell saw her trying to put them into some kind of pattern and asked what she was doing.

"I am trying to figgger out a way to make a dress for Dolly.

"Myra, run home and get her. I will measure her and see what we can do."

She ran home and washed Dolly's face and combed her hair. She was proud to show off her little sister. Dolly was almost three years old now and could talk as good as any of them. Her head was full of black curls, and she was always laughing and smiling. They had done a good job raising her without any thanks to Ma. Of course, Nannie was like a ma to her.

When they got back, Miz Powell had cut off a big piece from one of the skirts. It was a pretty light blue piece with little white checks in it.

"We've got enough scraps to make her several little dresses"

"Yes'um, I am ready to learn. I can't believe I am going to make a whol' dress from scratch even if it tis just a little one."

Miz Powell showed her the places to measure to make the dress fit right. Then she got out brown paper like those she wrapped parcels in and started to draw off a pattern to match the measurements. Myra watched while she pinned the pattern down on the cloth. It was easy then to cut around the pieces and baste the parts of the dress together.

All this time, Dolly had been sitting on the floor, playing with the leftover scraps. She didn't know what they were doing, but she liked being there.

The little dress was basted in no time. Myra had practiced enough on the machine to stitch around it all by herself.

She finished the hemming at home. The fire was hot enough to heat the iron, so she pressed the little dress and felt so proud to know she had made the dress with almost no help. It wasn't anything fancy. It was made round at the neck with strips of cloth to tie to make it fit. It came way down below her knees with no waist. The sleeves were long and set in. When Myra tried it on Dolly, she pranced around like a little show horse. The shoes they bought for her in Tennille still fit. It was good they bought them a little big. Now that she had her dress, Myra decided to start taking her to church. She did wish she could figure out a way to make a dress for Nannie. About the only way to do it would be to use material from more than one dress, but that would look as though she was wearing a quilt.

During the next weeks, Myra finished her dresses and had used scraps to make several for Dolly. She sewed every afternoon and worked on dresses that Miz Powell was making for folks.

The Porter sisters gave Will Rob a suit of clothes that had belonged to their dead brother. It had a coat, vest, and pants. They gave him a shirt, a bow tie, and a hat too. Miz Powell helped Myra cut down the suit to fit him. He dressed up in the outfit every Sunday, and he did think he was something. He always had a funny smell. The suit had been packed up so long, and the smell never did leave. He had stopped growing, so he kept wearing that suit for a long time. A few years later, he would get married in that suit.

The next Sunday when they went to church, Myra looked down the row at her big brother in his new suit, Dolly in her pretty, new blue dress,

Jesse and Arno in old clothes but clean and pressed. She was in a pretty new dress and coat, and she thought of Papa.

"Papa, you were right. We can find a way to make things better."

When the spring weather started, they got busy on the garden. Will Rob made a deal with the Porter sisters to get the seeds. They would buy the seeds, and Will Rob would share the vegetables with them. Both sides thought this was a fair deal. Soon they were eating freshly dug taters, beans, squash, cabbage, and onions from the garden. Two of the hens had set, and just before Easter, eight little biddies hatched out. Everyone loved to watch the biddies walk around the pens right behind their ma. Somehow the baby chicks seemed to know just which hen was their ma. They loved the biddies, but they were going to love them fried and on their plates even more. Every day Will Rob took a big basket of fresh vegetables to the Porter sisters. He said he was fattening them up some, because they had looked real bony.

There was big doings at the church on Easter Sunday. Everyone dressed in their very best, and the Stuart family looked as good as anybody. Nannie made a bouquet of wildflowers for Myra and Dolly to wear and pinned flowers on the boys' shirts. The church was packed with people, and some were standing on the sides. Myra had given up trying to get Nannie to go with them. She always wanted to hear all about the preaching when they got home. The preaching and singing lasted about two hours that day. No one minded sitting that long, 'cause it was such a happy day to know Jesus had come out of that dark tomb. Myra couldn't help wondering what it would be like if Papa could come out too.

Every family brought a bunch of hard-boiled eggs, and after the service ended, some of the ladies slipped off and hit them around in the grass and bushes. Then all the little young'uns went out to find the eggs. This was the first Easter egg hunt they had ever seen, and everybody was having a good time. Will Rob carried Dolly around to hunt, and she would squeal every time she saw an egg. Jesse found more than anybody, and he won a prize. It was a little book with pictures of Jesus in it. Myra wished Arno had been the one to win it, because he never got much. He would have to be the one to read the book anyway.

After the egg hunt, they went to tables set up behind the church, covered with food that people had brought. Myra brought their share, and she knew it would be as tasty as anything on the table. She had cooked a big pot of green beans and taters from the garden, a bunch of teacakes, corn bread with cracklings in it, and cabbage slaw. She had learned to make the slaw by watching Miz Powell. She chopped up the cabbage and some onions real small and then she mixed up sugar and vinegar to pour over it. She had bought a nickel's worth of vinegar from the big jar in the store. The slaw tasted real good with other things. She didn't have any meat to bring. She was ashamed to bring squirrel or rabbit. There was plenty of chicken and pork meat brought by the others. Her pots were some of the first to be emptied, so she knew what she brought was good. The boys ate until she was ashamed of them. She tasted a dish that she had never eaten before and knew she would make this for her family. It was called tater salad. She thought it was made just like slaw, except eggs were in it. She had plenty of taters and eggs.

After filling their plates, Annie and Myra went over to a ridge of little trees behind the church. They were having a good time just talking and laughing until two boys came over and asked to eat with them. Myra had seen both of them around, and they came to church most of the time. One was named Alvin Atkins, and the other one was named Dick Edingfield. She was all ready to tell them to "git." She sure didn't want to sit with them. She didn't have time to say anything before Annie spoke.

"Just have a seat. You are more than welcome to eat with us."

Alvin sat down by her and when Dick sat by Myra, she moved over just as far as she could. Annie started talking and giggling like she had never done before. Annie seemed to have forgotten what Myra had told her about letting boys look you right in the eye. When the boys left to get more lemonade, she figured she had better remind her.

"Why did you let them ol' boys sit with us?"

"Myra, I've had my eye on Alvin for a long time. He is a fine-looking boy and from a good family."

That did it for Myra, and she got up and went to sit with her brothers. Later, she saw Annie and Alvin walking down the road together.

She felt really funny about how Annie had acted, and she didn't want to see her for a while. She would finish up the sewing and head home before school let out. One day, she couldn't finish in time and ran right into her. She tried to pretend that she didn't see her and started running home. Annie ran right behind her.

"Myra, please wait. I know you see me."

There was no way out. Myra had to stop and talk to her.

"Why won't you talk to me anymore? I know you slip out of church ahead of me just so you won't have to speak."

"It ain't me. It's you that only wants that ol' Alvin fer a friend."

"Myra, don't be like that. I like Alvin a different way that I do you. You are my best friend. You should have stayed with us. Dick told us that he wished you had stayed. He thinks you are the prettiest girl in these parts."

"Well, you just tell him to go suck a rotten egg, and you can suck one with him. I don't care about no sorry ol' boy, and he is about the sorriest one I've seen. I don't ever need to sit with some ol' boy."

Myra couldn't believe that she said such hateful and ugly things to her friend. She knew Annie's feelings were hurt. In a few days they got back together, but things were different between them after that. They never talked about Alvin again, but Myra saw her walking home from school with him every day.

Right after Easter a man from the church named J. Q. Bailey came up to Will Rob and asked if they were interested in chopping cotton for him. Myra wasn't a bit interested, but they were beginning to need some way to make money. It seemed as though everybody who needed a broom had bought one. Firewood wasn't selling because folks only stocked up on it during the cold weather. She had the twenty-dollar bill that Joe Wiley gave her, but she was saving it for something real important, like medicine for Dolly. Mr. Bailey had a pretty good stand of cotton growing, so they could count on picking for him too. They worked for about three weeks and made enough to get some staples that were running low.

She also bought a ball of yellow crochet thread. She wanted to make a little vest to wear with one of her dresses. Now that she had pretty clothes, she was starting to care about how she looked. She washed her hair in rainwater and wore it down long sometimes. One day, Will Rob started teasing her about trying to catch a feller. She got so mad that she threw him in the dirt and tried to beat the tar out of him. He just kept laughing and held her arms so she couldn't hit him. She didn't know why everybody thought she needed a feller.

The hot summer days came, and they started taking it easy. The summer garden was growing good, and Myra was canning everything she could find. Jesse and Arno picked every blackberry from the bushes around them. Mr. Bailey let them pick his peaches on halves. She had lots to put in her jars. Butter beans were her favorite, so she canned more of those than anything. She was glad to have plenty of tomatoes to put up. There were so many things she could cook with tomatoes. Everybody pitched in and helped pick, shell, and wash jars. Myra did all the processing. She didn't trust anyone else to do this. Every time she used the big canning pot, she thought of Miz Sara.

The school breaking up was a big event that they enjoyed. There was a cake walk to raise money to help pay the teacher. Myra made a cake to take as their part. She never knew until then that all the parents chipped in to pay the teacher. They had let Jesse and Arno go for free, so she was real glad she could at least take a cake. The cake walk was a lot of fun. They wound up the Victoria, and everybody walked around until the music stopped. If it stopped on your number, you won a cake. It cost a nickel to walk, and she let the little boys walk one time. There was a big burnt sugar cake to win when they walked, but they didn't win. It was exciting to watch and see who won cakes.

After the cake walk, there was a spelling bee. All the pupils in certain grades stood up, and Mr. Smith called out words. When you missed a word you had to sit down. Jesse and Arno stood up with about ten other young'uns around their age. When Mr. Smith got through calling out the words, Arno was still standing. Myra was so proud of him. He won a ribbon to wear on his shirt. She had hoped to be with Annie, but as usual, she was hanging around with that ol' Alvin.

When the weather got real hot, they started going down to a little creek and going in the water. None of them could swim, so they just waded where they could stand up. A lot of other young'uns came there too, and there was always a lot of laughing and carrying on. It was a good time for all of them. The girls had to be real careful when they went to the creek 'cause the boys were bad about swimming buck-naked if they thought no girls were gonna be there. Will Rob always went first and checked it out before Myra went down there. She knew her brother didn't ever do that. He had always been real shy about somebody seeing him naked, even when he was a little fellow.

Bunk had stopped trying to go out and find ways to make money. He lay around a lot and what he ate came right back up. He would break out in awful sweats. Myra asked Nannie if she thought he had some kind of sickness.

"Baby girl, he's just 'bout drunk himself to death with that ol' rot gut whiskey. He'll be all right if'en he could get it outta his system."

Myra felt sorry for him even though he had done so many bad things. Sometimes he would shake so hard that she thought his eyes would pop out.

Nannie was more worried about him than she showed. She even sent Izzy to the bootlegger to buy whiskey for him. Myra thought that was the worst thing to do, but Nannie explained that when a fellow has drank as long as Bunk, sometimes they just had to have it. One morning, after he had hollered all night, she said the only thing left to do was send for Preacher Mose. She sent Izzie off to get him. Myra thought the only reason a preacher might be needed was to preach Bunk's funeral.

Izzie didn't come back until late that evening, and Preacher Mose was with him. The preacher looked more like a scarecrow than a man. He was tall and bony, and his eyes were sunk way down in his head. He walked right into the room and looked down at Bunk.

"Brother Bunk, Satan's power is strangling you. He is sapping up every ounce of your flesh, but I won't let that happen. I will save you for the Lord God Jehovah."

Bunk reached out and took his hand. He pulled out a bunch of roots and asked Nannie to boil them in the kettle until you could almost cut it with a knife. When the roots started boiling, there was an awful smell. They were coughing and gagging so bad that they had to stay in the yard. Preacher Mose wanted to keep a fire going in the cook stove, even though it was the hottest days of summer. He wrapped Bunk up in a quilt and started feeding him the root stuff when it was ready. This went on for more than a week, and you never heard such praying. Sometimes Preacher Mose would talk in what Nannie said was the unknown tongue, sometimes he would get the spirit and start jumping and shouting and sometimes he would fall over in a faint. It scared them, so they stayed in the yard or upstairs as much as they could. Myra never went in the room except to take them more of the root stuff. She didn't know what it was, but it must have given them nourishment. Neither of them ate one bite for the entire time.

Myra didn't know how long this could go on without one of them dying. One morning she got up and everything was quiet. She went to the porch and found Bunk sitting on the steps, eating a cold biscuit. He looked white as a sheet. His beard was all grown out shaggy, and he had lost a lot of weight.

He looked at her and said, "Myra, the Lord God Jehovah has saved me from the depths of hell. His mercy is everlasting. I am free of the devil and full of the spirit of the Lord God Jehovah. It came to me last night through the hands of Preacher Mose."

"I shore am glad to see you better, Uncle Bunk. Where's Preacher Mose?"

"He left as soon as I took the Lord God Jehovah's hand and let him into my heart. Now you go wake up the others and bring them down here. I want to give 'em my blessing."

Everyone was still half asleep when they came down to the porch. Bunk prayed over them for a long time. Myra was afraid Will Rob would start to giggle, and she knew she would if he did. Seeing Bunk praying was about the last thing they ever expected to see.

"Dearly beloved, a miracle has happened to me. Preacher Mose helped me find the way and showed me how the devil kept me drinkin' and sinnin'. I'm a changed man, and I'm giving my life over to the Lord God Jehovah. My life will never be right until I go back to Brewster and make up fer what I done there."

"Oh no, Bunk. You know how those folks in Brewster told you to never come back for what ya and ya pa done there. They'll put ya back in the jail or worse they might hang ya this time."

"I've got to go back, Sister Nannie Bessie. That's the will of the Lord God Jehovah, and I must follow his will."

At the time, it didn't bother Myra and Will Rob. They just thought Bunk was planning to go over there by himself to make up for something he had done.

After listening to him for a while, they realized that he was talking about moving back there to live and taking all of them. Myra didn't like that a bit. Sullivan's Corner was the best place they had ever lived, and the people were starting to feel like family. This Brewster place was way over in Laurens County, and that's no place she wanted to go. Will Rob started right in saying that he wasn't going, but she knew he would not let them leave without him. They had no idea of what Bunk could have done to the folks in Brewster, but whatever it was, he seemed to feel as though he had to go and make amends.

Bunk wasn't in condition to even think about taking a trip for a long time. He sat on the porch and slept a lot for the rest of the summer. They fed him good, nourishing food, and he was beginning to get his color back and gain some weight. When he was awake, he spent most of his time praying and asking for forgiveness for all his wrongdoings.

He wanted someone to read the Bible to him, but the only one who could read good enough was Arno. Myra knew he would hate to have to sit there and read for such a long time. She started opening up the Bible and just told Bunk some of the stories that Papa used to tell. He didn't know the difference, so when she ran out of stories, she just started making up things that she thought might have happened way back then. Bunk was happy as long as you said "the Lord God Jehovah" often enough

Myra, Will Rob, and Izzy started picking cotton for Mr. Bailey in mid-September. After talking about it, they decided to send Arno and Jesse to school. They figured Izzy could make up for what they would have picked. This was a good crop, and Mr. Bailey paid them a penny for every pound they picked. Arno could figure it up and said that a hundred pounds of cotton would give them a dollar. Since Myra and Will Rob had always picked more than a hundred pounds a day, this meant they would bring home more money than they had ever made. A bunch of colored people were picking with them, and they all had a good time singing and laughing. Everyone sat together to eat dinner, and after a while they started swapping food. They began to try to outdo each other in what they brought, and that made for some fine eats. Myra felt real happy that she had put up plenty of canned goods for winter and the cotton picking would give enough money to buy their staple goods. She could buy shoes for the boys and Dolly without going into her twenty-dollar bill.

One evening on the way home from the cotton patch, they stopped at Miz Powell's store to get milk. Miz Powell met them at the door with something in her hand.

"I am glad to see you all. You got some mail."

The Powell's store was also the place where folks in Sullivan's Corner sent and got mail. You brought your letter there and paid a penny to put a stamp on it. Once a week, Mr. Powell went to Wrightsville and took all the letters people were sending, and he brought back the letters they were getting. Myra didn't know what happened after the letters got to Wrightsville, but somehow they got to the right folks. She had seen people getting letters, but she never thought about getting one herself. They took it, but didn't open it up until they got home. It was written on one piece of paper and looked about as if Jesse had written it. Some words were hard to make out, but Arno read it to them as best he could.

Howdy,

    This is being rit by yore new sister, Flossie Stuart. We gonna have us a young'un come spring. Joe Wiley wants to know how y'all are faring and to tell ya that we livin over here in Ailey. That's in Mongome Coty and ain't too fer from Glencoe. We seed Annie Lou when we come thro there. You can rite to us care of Kickliter's Store. Joe Wiley worry to hear how you doin'.

From, yore brother, Joe Wiley and his wife, Flossie

They had no idea how or why their brother went to a place called Ailey. They were glad to hear from him and hoped him well. Arno would write a letter back to Joe Wiley.

Bunk and Izzie left to go to Brewster one morning before anyone was awake. Nannie was real upset about them going, and she acted as if something bad was sure to happen to them. She begged Bunk not to take Izzy with him, but Bunk said the boy needed to be a part of the atoning. Myra had never seen her so upset.

"Nannie, what did Bunk do that was so bad when y'all lived there?"

"Hit wuz all caused by his pa. Bunk and his pa wuz drinkin' bad, and one night they wuz comin' home real late in the mule and wagon. It wuz dark as pitch, and right outside Brewster his pa made Bunk get out and walk with the lantern. They were both so drunk that they could hardly stand up, and Bunk dropped the lantern and set all the pine straw on fire. They wuz too drunk to even try to fight the fire. The woods wuz real dry, and it spread fast. That fire burned out several families with their houses, barns, stock, and everything. The mule went wild when hit saw the fire and ran off with the wagon. They come walkin' in home, and your grandma and me didn't know what had gone on. All we knowed wuz the mule and wagon wuz gone, and they wuz real sooty and smokey smelling. It wuz so late when they got home, and we had already been asleep. If we had looked out, we could have seed the smoke from the fire.

"The next morning, here come the sheriff and took Bunk and his pa and locked them up. He charged 'em with starting the fire and for what it caused. We didn't know what to do. We figured they'd most likely hang 'em. After they had been in jail for a few weeks, they came walkin' in home one evenin'. The judge had set them loose. What they done wuzn't somethin' you could hang fer. He didn't want to keep them locked up fer the county would just have to feed 'em.

"The way they left it wuz that all the Blocks had to be cleared out of Laurens County before the next day's sundown. The people around there had never liked us livin' close to 'em, so I guess they wuz just glad to get rid of us. I didn't know what we wuz gonna do. We didn't even have a wagon. Your grandpa Block was a real tricky kind of fellow, and he had ways of getting people to do things for him. He went off the next morning and come back pretty quick with a mule and wagon. We never knowed how he got it. We packed up and headed south along the river.

"We pulled up in Sullivan's Corner about dinner the next day. We stayed in the wagon, while your grandpa Block asked about someplace we could camp at for a few days. Somebody told him about this old house out of town that nobody lived in. We went on out to it, and we been here ever since. After a while a man came by and said that we could rent it from his pa and use the land anyway we wanted. His pa had moved off and didn't plan to come back. He charged us thirty dollars a year, and somehow we have come up with the money every year 'till now. Bunk could always find some way to make up the money when it come due. I guess we come out all right. I never thought Bunk give what happened back there any thought, but I guess getting' saved put it in his head."

"Wuz Ma with y'all when this happened?"

"No, she done run off with yore pa. She never knowed nothin' about hit. I never seed her agin until when y'all come here. First, yore grandpa took a fever and died, and then yore grandma died, but we just kept on a staying here."

"How did Bunk know where to find us after Papa died?"

"Him and Izzy had gone off tradin' stuff up near where y'all wuz, and he heared some fellers talking about yore pa dying and leaving y'all such a good crop growing."

That solved one puzzlement for Myra. She thought it was probably good that Bunk wanted to make up for what he did, but she knew for sure that she didn't want to go there to live. She wouldn't worry about that yet. Maybe they would run him off again.

When Bunk came back, he was real excited. He couldn't find anybody that had lived in any of the burned-out places, and nobody else seemed to care about it anymore. Then he had really big news.

"They's a new lumber mill there in Brewster. They's hiring and paying good wages. Sounded like me, Will Rob, and even Izzy could get hired on. The feller that owns hit all is puttin' up some pretty good houses fer the hands. They take the rent right outten yore pay. They's a store there that lets you buy fer nothin' and takes it outten yore pay too."

From the way he talked, they would be going and soon would have lots of money to buy things from the store. Myra still didn't want to go, but she knew Will Rob liked the idea of working at the lumber mill.

The next day, Bunk and Will Rob took off for Brewster to try to get hired on. They didn't come back for more than a week. They came back happy that they had been hired and had started right to work. The houses would be ready in spring, so they couldn't move to Brewster until then. They went back the next day and said they would try to get back when they could. There was still a little money left from the cotton picking. Will Rob told Myra to use that to buy what she needed, and they would bring home more money when they came back.

Will Rob was learning to do the sawing, and he thought that was a good trade to follow. He said Bunk just mainly helped load and unload the wagons. Myra was relieved to know they could stay in Sullivan's Corner for a while longer. She couldn't imagine how they would ever move all the stuff in the house.

She had Arno write a letter to Annie Lou and to Joe Wiley. They just wrote them that they were moving to Brewster and would let them know when they got settled there. She didn't want to worry them, so she told Arno to write that they were doing good and Will Rob was learning to do the sawing. They addressed the letter to Joe Wiley as Flossie had told them. Myra thought she would send Annie Lou's letter "in care of Judge MacTavish." She should get it for sure since the MacTavishes were so well known in Glencoe.

Myra was really lonely after Will Rob left. She started thinking about what their life would be like when they left Sullivan's Corner. That ol' sick feeling came back in her stomach every time she thought about moving. She wished Ma was where she could talk to her, and that she would be like she used to be just before Papa died. Nannie seemed happy about moving to Brewster, so Myra didn't want to let on that she was worried.

Bunk's Lord God Jehovah seemed to be taking good care of him. Somehow Myra didn't feel like asking him to take care of her and her brothers and little sister. She felt more like talking to the little baby Jesus, but he was too little to do anything for them. She knew he grew up and helped folks to get well and all that, but she always thought about the little baby more than she did the grown man with the beard.

She was most lonesome in the time between supper and dark. She always went out and sat on the steps and thought about how much she, Papa, and Will Rob enjoyed that time of day.

One night when she was sitting on the steps, she realized someone was sitting beside her. At first she thought it was Arno, because he was always real quiet. She looked out of the corner of her eye and saw a soft light. It looked like a lantern does when someone is coming from way off. When her eyes got used to the light, she knew it wasn't Arno. It was the little boy. His blue pants and shirt were the same color as his blue eyes. He reached over and put his arm around her. Without a word being said, she knew that her family was going to be fine and would all be together again someday. She had tried to catch him for so long, and now here he was sitting right beside her. He was gone as quick as he came, and Arno did come out and sit down beside her.

-9-

Leaving Sullivan's Corner gave Myra mixed feelings. She was sad to leave the good home she had found and all the people who had been so good to her. Yet, something seemed to tell her that it was time for a change. She had a feeling there was something even better waiting for her.

Will Rob and Bunk came home for a day several weeks after they went to Brewster. They were able to catch a ride with a man that was going through Wrightsville and pass back through the next day. During that time, Myra and Will Rob talked over their plans for Christmas. They were determined to make their last Christmas in Sullivan's Corner a happy time.

"Dolly and the boys really need shoes. I've got the money, but none of the stores in Sullivan's Corner carry shoes."

"I can get 'em some in Dublin. Every Saturday after we get paid off, the boss man lets one of the wagon drivers load up the back of a wagon with as many fellows as want to go and take 'em over to Dublin. They say it's some kinda big place. It cost a quarter to ride, so I ain't never done it, but I been a wantin' to. I figger there'll shorely be stores in Dublin that sell shoes"

"We can draw around their feet just like we did when we bought Dolly shoes in Tennille. You can take the drawings to Dublin with you."

Myra could tell her brother liked the idea of knowing he would have money coming in every week. He was excited about going to Dublin. Will Rob liked to see new places.

Will Rob and Bunk did not get home until late Christmas Eve. They had to catch rides all the way and had been on the road all day. Myra was relieved to see them. Christmas wouldn't have been much without them.

Will Rob hurried upstairs to show Myra the things he had brought. Three pairs of shoes were in boxes, and he had a sack filled with other things. He used scrap pieces of lumber to make a doll bed for Dolly. He bought Arno a little book to read and a wooden soldier for Jesse. Izzie was hard to buy for, since he already had his hat. Will Rob found a little pouch for him to keep things in, like money, if he should ever have any.

Bunk surprised them by bringing home a big bag of oranges and a can of hard candy. He had a sack under his arm that he presented to Nannie.

"I'm just like Santy. Nannie Bessie, you just look in this here sack and see what else I brung us."

Nannie's eyes were beaming when she opened the sack and brought out a big piece of pork meat. This was sure a different Bunk from last Christmas.

As they walked to the church, Will Rob told her how Bunk had changed. He hadn't had a drop of liquor the whole time they had been in Brewster, and he didn't stay around anyone who even cussed or took the Lord's name in vain. Getting saved had surely helped him.

The Christmas program was the same as last year, except a few of the people were different. When they tried out, no one went up to sit as Mary. Myra thought she shouldn't try out since she had the part last year.

Everyone said, "That part is for Myra."

There had to be a new Joseph. Tom Crawford had moved away. Myra almost refused to be in the program when they picked the new Joseph. It was Dick Edenfield, the boy she had avoided since that day he had tried to sit by her. Having to stand by him just took all the joy from her. All the way through every practice and even in the program, he grinned at her like a mule eating briers. When the Christmas program was over, he came over to her before she could get out the door.

"Miss Myra, it's shore been a pleasure to be in the program with ya. I hope ya don't mind my sayin', but you just as pretty as the one you played."

"That ain't so."

"Well, you is to me. Tomorrow I'm coming by yore house and bring ya a Christmas present."

"I'll give ya a Christmas present rite now." Then she kicked him in the shin as hard as she could and ran out of the church.

He didn't show up the next day with a Christmas present. She hoped he had learned better than to hang around grinning at her.

In the weeks before Christmas she had been busy. Now that she could sew on Miz Powell's machine, she made a lot of things. She made little clothes for the doll that Annie Lou had sent to Dolly last Christmas. She took one of the shirts that came from the Porter sisters' dead brother and made it over for Will Rob. Then she ripped up an old dress to make an apron for Nannie and crocheted all around it.

Christmas morning, they had a good time opening presents. Will Rob shyly brought out a sack and handed it to Myra. She opened it and was delighted to find a new pair of shoes. She had not had a new pair since before Papa died. Her feet had stopped growing, but her old shoes were nothing but shreds.

"Oh, Will Rob, you oughtn't spent yore money on me, but I shore am proud. These are like the ones that Annie wears. They just fit. How'd ya do that?"

"Shoot, Myra, ya wuz sound asleep when I drawed around yore foot."

"You never."

"Then how ya think I got 'em to be such a fit?"

She never knew if he was kidding, but she didn't doubt that he had done just that. They hadn't heard from Annie Lou since last Christmas and that worried them. They hoped it meant she was too busy enjoying her life in Glencoe to think about them.

Ma was beginning to act a little more pert. She would sit with them, and sometimes she asked about things. She asked over and over about Annie Lou. Myra told her every time, but it didn't seem to make any difference. They still hoped that she would get back to acting like her old self. Myra remembered how she used to laugh and joke with Papa. Christmas Day, she seemed a lot better and even joined in singing the Christmas songs like they did with Papa. She played with Dolly and helped dress the doll.

Myra and Will Rob had a little time to talk before he left the next day. She was wondering about a lot of things.

"What's it gonna be like over there in Brewster?"

"It's all right, but I ain't gonna stay there much longer. Bunk drives the wagon to the railroad spur to load the logs. He's pretty good at it. He can probably work on there fer a long time, and even Izzy can get work doing something. 'Course, I'm one of the sawyers."

"What's a sawyer?"

"Those are the only fellers trusted with the saws."

"So why you wanna leave that good work?"

"Hit's all right fer now, but I wouldn't wanna do it ferever. Everybody talks about Glencoe, and I figger that is the best place fer me to make somethin' of myself.

"Besides, them houses they building ain't big as this front porch. Y'all can fit in better if I'm gone."

"I ain't though to ask but where have you and Bunk been stayin' since they ain't got no houses built."

"They put up a shack of a place they calls "the bunkhouse." All the fellows bed down in there. We all put our rations together and they's one old man who cooks up some stews and such, but usually it ain't fittin' to eat. In the mornin' he cooks grits and eggs, and that's pretty good."

"What we gonna do if you leave us?"

"Hit won't be fer long. I want you and Dolly to go on with them to Brewster fer a while. When I leave, I'm taking Arno and Jesse to stay with Joe Wiley. He ain't far from Glencoe. I know he can use 'em in the field. After I get work and get us a place, I'll bring you all there."

That sounded good to Myra. Still, she had her doubts of it ever happening. She did have another plan that might work out.

"If that place in Brewster is so small, what're we gonna do with our housekeeping stuff?"

"See if ya can sell it to somebody before ya leave."

"They ain't nothing nobody would want enough to pay fer. I betcha Joe Wiley would be proud of it if he had a way to get it."

"Let's get word to him and see. Arno can write a letter. We know where to send it."

All of a sudden, Myra had a better feeling about what was ahead for her. She didn't even feel sad when Will Rob and Bunk walked off to the crossroads to catch a ride. The day was warm and sunny, so that seemed a good sign.

Arno wrote the letter, and she took it to Mr. Powell just before he left for Wrightsville. He said it would go off on the train that day.

After Christmas, there was a spell of really nice weather. Every day the sunshine was warm enough to keep the house open, and they didn't need a fire. Myra's birthday came again, and she was now fifteen years old. Nannie said she was already living with Bunk and had one baby to die by the time she was that age. Myra had to be thankful that was not her life.

While they were sitting on the porch enjoying the sunshine, they saw a wagon coming up the lane. As soon as it got close enough, she could see it was Joe Wiley. Myra jumped off the porch and ran down the road to meet him. She hadn't cried in a long time, but this time she couldn't hold back the happy tears.

"Oh, Brother, I wuz so scared you wouldn't get our letter. How'd you get that wagon, and where is Flossie? I shore want to welcome her to the family."

"Yore letter was a godsend to us. We got a pretty decent house to live in, but we ain't got a thing but a worn-out mattress to sleep on the floor. Flossie's cooking on a one-eyed, pot-bellied stove. Hit'd be a long time 'fore we could scrap together enough to get what we need to live decent.

"Mr. Peterson brung me the letter from the store, and he read hit to me. Right off, he said fer me to take the big wagon and come get the stuff."

"He must be a boss man like Mr. Clyde."

"He's just as good a man. Flossie's brother took everything from her pa's place"

"Well, she can do better cookin' now. We got a fittin' stove and oven. We ain't never needed it here 'cause Nannie has a good stove. I reckon Flossie couldn't come 'cause of the baby."

"Yea, she wanted to come, but she's as big as the side of the barn now. Hit's gonna be here next month, she says"

Myra got busy and cooked a good supper. Izzy killed two of the fryers 'cause she wanted Joe Wiley to have plenty. She used the bony pieces to make dumplings and fried the rest. She really put out a spread for her big brother. She made tater salad, corn bread, and opened jars of butter beans, squash, and peaches. It looked like Christmas dinner all over again. Ma seemed proud to see him too and kept asking if he was going to stay this time. Myra could tell he felt real sorry for Ma.

After supper, they went on the porch to talk just like old times. Myra was anxious to know all about how he ended up in Ailey.

"I'm planning on takin' the boys back with me. They can help out, and it will be good to have them where I can keep a hand on 'em. We got room in the house. Flossie loves company."

"That'll be fer the best, since we goin' over there to Brewster. The way Will Rob tells it, it wouldn't be much of a place fer them. I hate fer Arno to have to stop school, but he knows about as much as he needs, I reckon."

"Mr. Peterson is a good man. He owns a lot of land and businesses all around Ailey. He has brung in a man from off in Carolina to learn us to grow tobackey. It ain't like cotton. You have to be real 'ticular with hit, but hit will bring a good price every year. Mr. Peterson pays me a set wage every month. I ain't gotta wait to settle up or nothin'."

"Sounds like you got yoreself a good place, but how in the world did you get there? I thought you wuz gonna work Flossie's pa's place."

"That's what I planned, but the ol' man took sick with the consumption and died the first winter. Right after we got him buried, her ma got hit too and died. Then their oldest boy come from where he stayed up near Macon. He had a paper that said everything was left to him. He put me and Flossie out, and we had to leave with nothing but our clothes. I couldn't believe hit, her being his sister and all. There weren't nothin' I could do, and I didn't know where to turn.

"The only thing I could think of was to go back and see if Mr. Clyde could use me. We had to walk most of the way. Now I hate to be the one to tell you this, Myra. When we got up to their place, some other folks wuz livin' there. They told me Miz Sara died not long after we left. Their girl came and got him, and he moved off to where she lives. They sold the place right off."

Myra's eyes ran over with tears when she heard that. Her sweet Miz Sara was gone from this earth, and she couldn't even be with her at the end. She had a good cry, and Joe Wiley was wiping his eyes too. Myra was still snubbing when he went on with his story.

"I headed back to town and wuz hopin' I could find Uncle Joe Early. I walked down the street in Tennille and saw Aunt Mary's store all closed up. I wuz tryin' to keep up a front fer Flossie, but I was at the end of my rope. When I walked back up by the bank, who should come walkin' out but Uncle Joe Early. He acted awful proud to see me and wouldn't have nothing but fer me and Flossie to go home with him. We stayed there a few days, and they treated us like we wuz kin folks.

"He wuz tryin' all the time to find a good place fer me. He had rented out most of his land 'cause he wuz runin' to be the sheriff. One day he come in and told me the banker had told him about this Mr. Peterson and how he was starting to grow tobackey in Georgia fer the first time. He said that would be a good thing fer me to get into.

"He put right in to find out more and sent something called a wire to the man. He sent one right back and said fer us to come on the train and he would meet us in Glencoe. Uncle Joe Early paid fer our tickets and took us to Sandersville to get on the train and put some extra bills in my pocket.

"When I tried to thank him, he said that Martin would've done the same fer his boy. It wuz somethin' riding that train. Flossie wuz scared at first, but soon she shore liked hit better than walkin'. We got to Glencoe late that same evening.

"Mr. Peterson wuz right there to meet us just like he said. Now that Glencoe is an up-to-date place just like Annie Lou said. After we had been there a month or so, I rode back to Glencoe with Mr. Peterson and went to see her. She and Horace got a new house out from town in a church settlement. She's gonna have a baby sometime in the summer and is staying in bed all the time. She ain't changed much. She's still thinks she's Miss Uppity now that she's in the MacTavish family. In Glencoe that name means somethin'."

"Aw, don't say that. I'm proud to hear she is doing good and gonna have a baby. Now we will have two new ones in our family."

"Myra, there's something else I been thinking 'bout. When I go back and take the boys, I'm gonna take Ma too."

"Are your shore? You know how Ma can get."

"I think Flossie would be glad to have a woman around with her now with the baby coming and all. The change might help Ma. 'Sides, I'm the oldest boy, and hit is my place to take care of her."

Myra was surprised at this, but she was glad. If the house in Brewster was as small as Will Rob said, having Ma gone would help. She still had hopes of getting to Glencoe someday herself, and then she could help with Ma.

The next morning they loaded up the wagon, and Ma, Arno, and Jesse took off to live with Joe Wiley. They put as much on the wagon as it would hold. Myra divided up the canned goods and sent them. They tied up the chicken's feet, and he took them too. She was glad to give the food, because she knew how much the boys could eat.

Myra prayed the good weather would hold until they got to Joe Wiley's place. They would have to stop at a settlement and spend the night in the wagon. Myra sent plenty of heavy quilts to keep them warm.

"You tell Flossie to be shore to save my jars."

"I'm plannin' on plantin' a big garden. I hope we're close enough so I can keep you in vegetables."

"If we are, I'll teach Flossie how to can."

As they drove down the lane, Myra didn't feel sad like she thought she would. She had a feeling that her life was working out.

Now it was just Nannie, Izzie, Dolly, and Myra. She had never been in such a quiet house before. They got busy and started packing up, so they would be ready when Bunk came for them.

Nannie had to decide what to take and what to throw away. Myra talked her into keeping only what she would use since Will Rob told her the house was so small. Nannie did seem happy about moving, getting a new house, and knowing that Bunk was sober and was working every day. Myra hoped and prayed that Nannie was going to have a better life. She loved her aunt and would hate to leave her when the time came. It did seem that Nannie was better off than she was when they came to live with her.

Now it was time to start saying farewell to the townspeople who had taken them in and made them feel welcome. First, Myra went to school to tell Mr. Smith that the boys were gone. He bragged on Arno and told how important it was for her to keep Arno in school. She couldn't do anything about that now, but maybe the time would come when he could get a chance to better himself. She knew he was the smartest in the family.

Annie promised that she would write and always keep in touch. Myra didn't much believe that, since all she talked about was Alvin.

"Alvin's working in a store in Wrightsville now that he's finished with school. He's learning to run a store and plans to own his own store someday."

"I doubt that he will own as much as a changing of clothes, much less a store."

"Oh, Myra, don't say such about Alvin. He likes you." Annie's eyes were shiny with tears, but they didn't spill out.

After that, they only saw each other in passing. Myra thought that was just as well, because it would be easier to leave her first friend when she was mad.

They didn't hear anything from Bunk or Will Rob until about the middle of March. One evening they heard a lot of racket and saw the biggest contraption they had ever seen pulling up in the lane. Will Rob was driving it.

"Brother, what have you come home in?"

"This here's a two-mule wagon. We use it to haul the logs. The boss man let us borrow it to get us moved. Ya can put lots more stuff in hit, and hit goes a lot faster."

"It's a shame we ain't still got Solomon. We could've hitched him up to it too. Then we would have a three-mule wagon." Both had a good laugh at the thought.

She was relieved to see him. She had begun to wonder if he had already left for Glencoe. She should've known that he wouldn't leave until they got settled. He seemed relieved when she told him about Joe Wiley coming and taking the boys and Ma home with him.

It didn't take long to get everything loaded up. Bunk had sold the mule and wagon when he started the job in Brewster. There wasn't any place to keep a mule, so he had to sell it. They slept in the house that night and were ready to start moving at daylight the next morning.

Myra couldn't help thinking about the day they moved from Washington County and how worried she felt. This time she had faith that something was ahead for her, and it was going to be for the best.

Brewster wasn't really a town. The lumber mill was in the center, and everything was built around it. There was a store, but it was part of the mill too. The houses had been built in a line across from the mill. Will Rob was right when he said the houses were small. All the houses were just alike and had bright tin roofs. Down the road were three bigger houses that belonged to the boss men. Even with Ma and the boys gone, it would be hard for the rest to fit in the little house. There was just one room and a little shed room on the back. They would have to cook, eat, and part of them sleep in the front room. The shed room wasn't big enough for Myra, Will Rob, and Dolly to stretch out on quilts. It would be cramped, but they would have to get by. For the first time, she was looking forward to Will Rob moving out.

The houses didn't have their own toilets or wells. One well served all the little houses. Myra hoped it was deep enough to keep them in water through the summer.

The toilets were built at the edge of the woods. There was one for women and one for men. The women's toilet had four holes and was always in use. A big wasp nest hung right by the door, so you had to hurry in and close the door quickly. Myra didn't like sitting in there with people that she hardly knew, so most of the time she went to the bushes. Nannie couldn't walk to the toilet. She had to use the slop jar, and they kept it emptied for her. Her ankles had started to swell up real bad. Sometimes she had spells and hurt somethin' awful. She'd take a dose of soda, and that usually helped. Myra worried about her.

None of the houses had porches, and Myra missed that most of all. The steps were built to the front door, and people were walking to and fro right in front of your door.

Will Rob left about three o'clock one morning to walk to Dublin to catch the train that went right to Glencoe. The train went through a lot of little towns along the way, but he would get there in about half a day. The train left the station at eight o'clock sharp. He took the suit that came from the Porter sisters' dead brother and changed into it before he got on the train.

A few weeks after Will Rob left, Bunk came in with a piece of mail that had been sent to the store. Myra found a woman at the store who could read it to her.

Dear Myra,

I hope this message reaches you. Your sister, Annie Lou, is not doing well at all. We had hopes of having a baby in the early summer. It was born way too soon and did not live. This has been very hard on her. She stays inside and cries most of the time. I know she is sad but she ought to be getting over it by now. One reason she's so sad is that she misses her family.

Is there any way you can come to Glencoe and stay with her for a while? That would be the best medicine she could have. Bring Dolly with you. I have thought about this a lot, and I would like to keep her and raise her as our own. Annie Lou might not be able to have more children and her little sister will fill her heart in this way.

If you are willing to do this, I will wire a train ticket to Dublin for you. Please send a letter right back and tell me the day you can come. As soon as I hear from you, I will wire the ticket. You could be here in two weeks.

Your brother-in-law,
Horace V. Morris

When Myra heard the letter being read, she knew that she had to go. Annie Lou was more like Ma than any of the rest of them. Myra knew all too well how this could end up. She didn't even think about herself and what it could mean to her. She just knew that she had to get to her sister as fast as she could. She got paper at the store and gave the girl a quarter to write and send the letter back to Horace the same day. She told him she would be at the depot in Dublin to get her ticket in three weeks from that day. She didn't know how she would get to Dublin, but she could work on that later.

In the short time left, she tried to get Nannie settled in the new place. Giving up Dolly would be hard for Nannie, but she was happy that her baby would have a better chance and be brought up by her kin.

Being cooped up in the tiny house made Dolly fret and cry more than usual. She only went outside when someone could walk down the street with her and hold her hand. She didn't understand why she couldn't run and play as she did at the house in Sullivan's Corner. It would be better for all when Myra and Dolly left for Glencoe.

The dream of going to Glencoe was coming true, and Myra was thankful that she didn't have to stay in Brewster. Folks living in the houses didn't act like the people she had known before. Will Rob called them low class. She didn't know how you judge that. She figured if folks such as Aunt Mary, Miz Sara, Miz Powell, and the Porter sisters were high class, then these folks could be called low class. It wasn't who they were. It was how they acted. They talked loud, fussed a lot, and even the women did a lot of cussing. Papa wouldn't have ever stood for that. Nannie didn't seem to mind at all. In fact, she shocked Myra by going out of the house, talking to people.

Finding a way to get to Dublin was a problem. She went to the store every day and asked everyone she saw if they knew a way she could get to Dublin. Nobody offered any help, and she was getting desperate.

"I'm just gonna march right up to that mill office and ask if me and Dolly can ride on one of them wagons carrying the lumber."

"No, no, you ain't gonna do that. They wouldn't dare let you—a slip of a girl and a baby. They'd think we wuz all crazy for shore. Sides that, Bunk and Izzy just might get fired."

"There just ain't any way. I could walk it, but Dolly couldn't."

"Yeah, there's another way."

"I don't know where else to turn."

"They's wagons and mules in the mill barn. I've seen some of these folks usin' 'em. I betcha they let ya hire 'em."

"Who's gonna ask 'em and where we gonna get the money?"

"Bunk will ask 'em fer ya, and they won't turn him down. I've put aside a little money from what Bunk gimme while we wuz still in Sullivan's Corner. Ya just stop worryin' 'cause Nannie will take care of her baby girls."

If Nannie was willing to do all that, Myra knew she really wanted them to go to Glencoe. That seemed strange, since she would miss them both so much. Then one night in a dream, Myra saw Nannie standing in the door watching her walk away.

"Myra, there's a fine gentleman waiting for ya somewhere. You're gonna have a good life."

She woke up knowing that Nannie loved her enough to do anything to help her. If she was going to find a better life, Brewster was not a fit place for her to live. Everything just seemed to be happening as though it was the right thing to do.

During the next weeks, Myra tried to tell Dolly about where they were going. She didn't understand any of it. She didn't even remember Annie Lou, but she laughed when Myra asked if she wanted to go to see Will Rob. It was hard to keep from getting real scared. Myra had never been anywhere by herself. She had no idea of what she was supposed to do. She had only seen a train once before, and that was a long time ago when they lived near Davisboro. It scared all of them. She still remembered how it sounded and smelled. If this was what she had to do to get to Glencoe, then she would just stop worrying and do it.

Nannie tried to keep up a good front, but her heart was breaking. She hardly let Dolly out of her sight. It was like she was trying to get every minute of her baby that she could. When Myra thought about how Nannie had become like a real ma to her little sister, she wondered if she was doing the right thing.

"Now don't ya worry about how Dolly will take to this. This baby has already seen more changes in her little life than most folks ever do. She's used to it, and hits the right thing fer the both of ya."

The night before they were to leave, Myra packed up as much of their clothes as she could put in two croker sacks. She was carrying the big canning pot too. She knew she would need it again someday. The big pot, two heavy croker sacks, and Dolly would be hard to manage.

None of them slept a wink that night. Bunk walked with them to the barn to get the mule and wagon. He didn't say anything, but for the first time Myra felt as if he was really her uncle. They left about two hours before daylight. Izzie was driving the mule. Nannie sat by him and held the lantern. They didn't seem to be making much time, and Myra started worrying that they wouldn't make it to Dublin in time to catch the train. It was just five miles, but sometimes they didn't even seem to be moving. Izzy didn't know how to get the mule to go the way Will Rob did. They rode and rode and had just gotten a little past Brewster when they heard a lot of noise and saw lights behind them. A horn blew and an automobile came right up beside them. Myra had heard about automobiles, but she had never seen one before. A man stuck his head out the window.

"What in the hell are you all doing out here in the middle of the night?"

"Sir, we headed to Dublin to catch the train."

"Why you doing that?"

"My sister is sick and needs me."

"Well, you aren't going to get there at this rate. Besides, it's not safe for you to be out here by yourself in the dark of night."

"There ain't no other way, sir. My auntie and cousin are taking me and my little sister."

"I'm Dr. Beddingfield from Dublin. I just delivered twin babies to a woman a few miles back, and I'm on my way home. Little girl, you and the baby get in my car and I will take you to the train station.

"Ma'am, you and that boy turn around and go on back home."

This happened so fast that all they could do was hug and say a quick good-bye. The doctor put the two sacks and the pot in his car. They climbed in the seat beside him.

After riding in the mule wagon with the old mule barely moving, this seemed like flying. Dr. Beddingfield did not have much to say, and in a minute Dolly was fast asleep. It did feel nice to be sitting on soft seats and not worry about the mule stumbling or anything.

Myra dropped off for a bit and had a dream. The little blue boy was in the dream, and he looked at her as if to say, "Didn't you know that I would take care of you?"

When they got to Dublin, the town seemed to be asleep, except for the bright lights of the depot. Dr. Beddingfield asked if they were hungry.

"We got a little somethin' in the sack, but I'm saving hit fer later in the day."

"Come on in with me. There's a little café in the depot that is already open. I could use some breakfast and coffee."

As soon as they sat down at a little table, a lady put a cup of hot coffee in front of the doctor. That made Myra think he must come there a lot since she knew just what he wanted.

"Bring us all a bowl of hot oats and bring a glass of milk for these girls."

Myra had no idea what she was about to eat. The only oats she knew about was what mules ate. It was a bowl full of something that looked a little like grits. The doctor put sugar and milk on his, so Myra put it on theirs too. It did taste good. Dolly just pure loved it. They didn't talk any until they finished up their bowls of oats.

"Now, young lady, do you have your ticket already bought?"

"My brother-in-law said he wuz sending it through the wire."

She was puzzled about how the tickets would be folded up and sent through those little wires, but it must be the truth.

Dr. Beddingfield made a funny face as though he wondered about that. Then he went over to a man behind a wire cage and talked for a minute. He came back with her ticket.

"This ain't but one ticket. Horace said fer Dolly to come with me."

"She doesn't need a ticket. Little children under a certain age get to ride for free. The railroad is good about that. Now I have to get on to my office. You will be fine from here on to Glencoe. The station manager said he would see that you got on the train and tell the conductor to look out for you until you get to Glencoe. I wish you a pleasant journey and good fortune in your future."

"I shore thank you fer all ya done. We wouldn't got here if it hadn't of been fer you. I have some money. Can I pay you fer yo trouble and our breakfast?"

He smiled for the first time since they had met him. "No pay is needed. It has been my pleasure."

Myra thought that was the nicest thing she had ever heard anybody say. They didn't have to wait long before the train came roaring in. She remembered the smell, and for the rest of her life, the smell of a train gave her the same happy feeling that she had that morning.

When the train was ready to leave, the conductor helped her get the sacks, pot, and Dolly up the steps and find a seat. When they started moving, she thought if the automobile was flying, this train was double flying. The trees and things beside the tracks went by so fast that they all ran together. They looked out the window and waved to the people they passed. Some of them waved back. The train stopped at several towns on the way. The biggest one was called Swainsboro. Myra had never heard of it before. When they reached the town, the conductor walked through and called out, "Swainsboro, Swainsboro. All going to Swainsboro get off now." That relieved one worry. She would know when they got to Glencoe.

Myra didn't have a way of knowing the time, but her stomach was starting to feel like dinnertime. Just as she started to take out the biscuits and fried meat to feed Dolly, the conductor came through the car calling out.

"Next stop will be Glencoe, Glencoe, Sweet Glencoe, the town of the future."

That made everyone laugh, and most of the people started getting their things together. It looked as though almost everyone was going to Glencoe.

The conductor put down the steps, and they got off the train. Myra looked up and down the tracks, but she didn't see hide nor hair of Horace. Before she had time to start worrying, she heard a familiar voice calling.

"Myra, Myra, I will be there in a minute."

Will Rob was running down the side of the track. He had been standing on the wrong side from where they got off. They hugged and laughed and then hugged some more.

"Horace asked me to meet ya. I wuz gonna be down here to see ya get off the train, anyway. I borrowed my boss man's wagon to take y'all out to North Connolly where they live."

He led them to a long, fancy-looking wagon with a big black horse hitched to it. There was writing painted on both sides of the wagon. Will Rob saw her puzzled look.

"That says Hutchinson's Funeral Parlor. That's where I work."

They climbed onto the wagon, and it gave almost as smooth a ride as Dr. Beddingfield's car. Their mouths were going a mile a minute trying to catch up on all that had happened since they last saw each other.

"It's workin' out, Myra, just like I planned. I ain't had nothin' but good luck ever since I set foot here.

"When I got here, I started asking around to find Annie Lou. Right off, a man offered to take me out there in his buggy. It seems like when folks hear you might be some kin to the MacTavish folks, they are glad to help ya."

"Now tell me about Annie Lou's sickness."

"The best way to put it is that she is acting a lot like Ma. She ain't been herself at all since I have been here. It worries me. I don't think Horace will put up with her craziness the way Pa put up with Ma."

"She ain't crazy. Don't say that."

"You know what I mean. I want to help her if I can. I'm the one who told Horace to write fer you to come. If anybody can help her, it'd be you."

"I hope it ain't too late. How did you come to get this job?"

"I just walked right up to Mr. Hutchinson at the funeral home and told him that I made coffins and would like to make a deal with him. He put me right to work. I make the coffins and drive this wagon to take the bodies to the graveyard. This is a big business here. Glencoe has a big graveyard right in the middle of town."

"You mean to tell me that you are riding me in the coffin wagon."

"Yep, and there's the graveyard right over there. Horace's grandpa gave the land fer hit."

They were driving down the main street, and there were stores of all kinds. Will Rob pointed out two stores that were owned by the MacTavish brothers. As they passed one store, a young man was standing in front. He was dressed up as if he was going to church. Myra couldn't help looking at him, and he looked back and smiled a big smile. He had on a derby hat, and he tipped it to her. It gave her a funny feeling, as if she was laughing all inside. She remembered Nannie's warning about looking fellows in the eye, but he was so far away that maybe it didn't hurt. Will Rob did not notice, and she was glad. She didn't want him to start teasing her about having a feller.

As they drove along, she couldn't stop looking at the people. The streets were full of folks going about their business. They all looked dressed up and "up to date" just like Annie Lou wrote in her letter.

"I know this is the right place to be. There's plenty of work for somebody like me that wants to work, and the wages are good."

"Where do you stay and take yore meals?"

"I get a little room fer free at the funeral home. I have to stay there at night in case there is a body to be picked up. I take my meals at the boardin' house. Even with payin' fer my eats, I still put a little back."

"It's hard to believe I've finally got to Glencoe. Remember how we have talked about coming since we first heard of the place?"

"Yea, it's all I hoped it'd be. Most all the families living here are named Mac-something or other, like MacTavish, MacIntosh, MacNatt, and such.

That's because they come from people who came from a place across the water called Scotland.

"Now there's a lot of people moving into Glencoe from Johnson and Washington counties, just like us. The town is run by the people with the Mac names. I heard from a feller that Glencoe grew and got so well off because all those Scots knew how to make money and how to keep it."

Just before they got to Annie Lou's place, they passed through a little community called Armity. It was just a little group of houses and a church.

"The folks who live out here came from Washington or Johnson County just like us. I should be able to rent a little place here fer us to live. It is close enough to walk to Glencoe."

"That sounds good to me, and maybe I can find some way to make a little money."

When they drove up, Horace was on the porch and came out to meet them.

"Annie Lou doesn't know about you coming. I didn't want to tell her ahead in case something happened to keep you from coming. Come on in, and we'll give her a surprise."

They walked through the house, and Annie Lou's bedroom door was closed.

"Annie Lou, here is some folks who want to speak to you."

"Just tell them I'm sorry, but I'm not up to any company."

"I think you are going to want to see these folks."

When they walked into the room, she jumped up from the bed and grabbed Myra so hard that it hurt. They hugged and hugged and hugged some more.

"I am so glad ya came. The Good Lord only knows how much I have missed you. I can't get over Dolly. She shore ain't a baby no more. She's the prettiest little thing."

Dolly didn't really remember her, but she loved all the attention she was getting. Nannie was right that Dolly would be just fine.

"Myra, you look real different. You're all grown up now."

Myra blushed and had that same feeling that she had when the man had tipped his hat to her. She knew she was in the right place.

"Horace, show me to the kitchen. We didn't eat no dinner, and I'm ready to cook us a good supper."

The kitchen was a room all to itself. There was a stove, icebox, long table and chairs, and a lot of shelves to keep things on. There was even a special place to keep water and to wash the dishes. Myra looked on the shelves and saw plenty of food. Horace went out to the smokehouse and brought back a big smoked shoulder. He told her to use as much of it as she thought they would eat. She hadn't ever been able to do that.

She cooked a pile of the meat, scrambled a dozen eggs, cooked a big pot of grits, made a pan of biscuits, and a big pan of gravy from the ham fat. The shelves were full of all kinds of canned goods.

"Did Annie Lou can all this stuff. How did she learn?"

"Noo, she don't even open 'em up to cook. My ma always makes a big garden, and she brought all this stuff over here. She was hoping Annie Lou would start cooking a little more. Use any that you need. Ma's got plenty more if you ever need it."

Myra spied a jar of what she thought were peaches, but it turned out to be apples. She put this in a pan with a little sugar and thickened it up with flour. That would be something sweet to eat with the rest of the supper. Horace set a big pitcher of buttermilk on the table.

"Annie Lou hardly eats a thing. I doubt that she will even taste this, but I am shore hungry. This kitchen ain't ever had such good smells in it."

"She does look awful peaked. I'll fatten her up."

The fattening up started as soon as Annie Lou sat at the table. She put away a supper that night and said it tasted better than anything she had since leaving home. She laughed and talked as if nothing was wrong. Myra could tell that she had done the right thing to come and help her sister.

Will Rob had to leave to get back to Glencoe before dark. Myra walked to the wagon with him, and they had a little private talk as they always did.

"I think I'm going to turn Dolly over to her. What she needs is something to keep her busy and get her mind on somethin' besides herself."

"That's what she needs. You always did the work, and she just sat back and got the best of whatever there wuz. Are you gonna leave Dolly here with them when you leave?"

"I'll wait and see how it goes. I'm not real sure if Horace will want her around after he sees how aggravatin' she can be at times. If I don't have to worry with her, maybe I can find me some kinda work with my sewing and make a little money."

"I think ya might could. If not with sewing, they's other things. Some girl works at the boarding house filling up the bowls and clearing the table."

"I would do somethin' like that, and I could cook too."

"We'll see. It's gonna all work out now that you're here with me. I gotta go, but I'll be back soon."

She had to laugh to see him driving away in the funeral wagon. It seemed like a good job for him, but she knew he would find something better.

The sisters spent the next few days catching up on all that had happened during the time they had been apart. Myra had never sat and talked with Annie Lou like this before. She was surprised that her sister listened and seemed to care about her.

Annie Lou's life sounded just right for her. She certainly had plenty of anything that she needed or wanted. Horace's folks were all real good to her. She said the men tended to drink a little, but that was just their way.

Horace still wasn't much to look at, and he had a kind of grumpy way about him. Myra could see why Will Rob thought he wouldn't put up with Annie Lou the way Papa had put up with Ma. This made Myra even more thankful that she was there to help.

Having Dolly around was the best help. Annie Lou had always loved her, and now she just doted on her. She loved taking care of her little sister, and Horace seemed to enjoy her too. Dolly crawled on his lap at every chance. This was the first time she had ever been around a grown man that could seem like a papa to her.

After a few weeks, Annie Lou was better than she had ever been. Myra started thinking about what she wanted to do next. Will Rob came and told her that he had arranged to rent a little house in Armity.

"A feller started eatin' at the boarding house, and I heard that his wife had died. I overheard him saying that he had a house that he didn't want to live in right now but he wasn't ready to sell. So I just went up to him and asked about renting hit. We made a deal fer me to rent hit and all the furniture. I figger he want's to hang on to hit till he finds somebody else to marry."

"That sounds just right fer us, but won't hit cost a lot?"

"You don't worry 'bout that. I can pay the rent with what I make at the funeral parlor. It will be a little tight, but I will save money on my eatin' and my wash."

"I can shore do all that fer ya and do it better besides. You know, we've always known how to make do with very little."

"Ya gonna like livin' in Armity, Myra. It's a little settlement with good folks. A lot of 'em has told me they knew Papa and Uncle Joe Early back when they lived in Washington County. I promise ya these ain't folks like them in Brewster.

"I'm gonna keep on workin' at the funeral parlor, but I'm plannin' to start buildin' cabinets in folks' houses. There's a big call fer that, and I can do it when there ain't nobody dead."

"I hope to find a way to help out too."

"When we get settled, I'll bring Ma and the boys back to live with us. I went to see 'em before you came. Flossie had the baby before I went."

"You didn't tell me that. What is it? What's it's name?"

"They's been so much goin' on that I didn't get around to it. Hit's a boy, and everythin' about him is fine. They named him Wade Martin fer Pa and Flossie's pa, but they done started callin' him Bud."

"That's more good fer our family. If you go there again, I'll go with ya."

"I'm goin' as soon as I can. Flossie and Ma ain't getting along. Ma tries to run everything, and Flossie had done got used to doin' things her way. I 'spect Joe Wiley hears a lot of quarreling."

"That sounds like Ma is better. Even if she is bossin', that's better than how she just sat and didn't say or do nothin'.'."

"She is better. Joe Wiley said she did all the cookin' and cleanin' while Flossie was laid up with the baby. That was good, but now I think it might be time to give her a change."

"When can we bring 'em back and move into the house?"

"The man ain't out of it yet, but hit shouldn't be much longer."

Myra was ready to get her brothers and Ma with her and start taking care of her family. She hadn't decided what to do about leaving Dolly with Annie Lou. It was lookin' more and more like that was the best thing to do for her.

The weather was turning springlike, and Myra saw what a pretty place she had come to live. Horace's ma loved flowers, and her yard was already filled with blooms of all kinds.

Horace came home one night with the news that the church at North Connolly was having a pie supper. It was to be the next Friday night, and he wanted them to go. At first, Annie begged not to go and said she couldn't make a good-enough pie. Myra thought it would do her good, so she offered to make the pie. Horace was happy to have encouragement.

"The way this works is you make two pies. One is for eating and one is far selling to make money for the church."

"That's fine. I can make two pies. I'll make apple and custard."

In the days in between, Horace and Annie Lou did a lot of whispering and grinning. Myra got suspicious, but since she had never been to a pie supper, she didn't know what might be going on.

The day of the supper, they insisted that she get out her best dress and fix up real nice. She figured it was so they wouldn't be ashamed of her. She washed and ironed one of her prettiest dresses. She washed her hair and put it up in a braid. She wore some beads that the Porter sisters had given her. Annie Lou dressed Dolly up like a little doll in one of the dresses she bought her from a store in Glencoe. Myra felt real proud as they set off for the church.

Buggies and even a few automobiles were all around the church. This was going to be a big to-do. Tables were filled with pies. Horace put one pie on a table and the other pie on another table. He picked up a piece of paper, wrote something on it, and put it under one of the pies.

A man stood up and said they would start the supper with the auction for the pies brought by the unmarried young ladies.

"I know all you single fellers don't want to wait any longer to enjoy the company of the young ladies who baked these pies."

"Horace, you didn't tell me nothin' about no auction. I'm leavin' here right now. Y'all can eat all the pie ya want. I'll walk home."

Before Horace could speak, she looked across the church and saw the young man who had tipped his hat to her. He seemed to be looking right at her too. She tried to stop looking, but her eyes just seem to be locked on him. Then he started walking toward them.

"Well, look what the cat drug in. What're you doing here?" Horace said with a laugh.

"I always go where there's pretty girls and good food. Welcome to Glencoe, Miss Myra. I'm James MacTavish, Horace's uncle."

Myra didn't know what to say back to him. Something funny was going on inside her. Her heart was beating so hard that she knew everybody could see it through her dress. He took a seat with the other fellows who were going to buy pies.

A lot of pies were sold before they put up Myra's. The man held her pie and said, "This delicious-looking custard pie was baked by Miss Myra Stuart, who is the sister to our dear Annie Lou Morris."

Almost before he got the words out, she heard someone say, "I bid three dollars."

She didn't need to turn her head to know that it was James MacTavish. None of the other pies had brought more than a dollar, so she knew he would get her pie.

"Sold to James MacTavish, and thank you for the fine contribution to our church."

Myra had to walk over and meet him at the eating table. Her legs were shaking to pieces. They sat down across from each other at the table, and James took out his knife and cut the pie into pieces. He picked up his piece and ate it in about two bites and then took another piece. Myra nibbled on one piece and tried to think of something to say, but all she could do was keep looking at him. She didn't know if he was what is called a handsome man, but he sure was pleasing to look at. He was dressed so neatly and smelled like something good that grows in the woods in the springtime. She had never been around a man that smelled good. He wasn't a real big man in height. He looked like a grown man, but there was still something about him that looked boyish, especially when he smiled. She knew if what Nannie told her about looking men in the eye was true, she was in big trouble. He didn't say much except to tell her how much he was enjoying the pie.

"You must really like pie to pay so much for one."

He looked her right in the eye for what seemed like a long time. Then his face lit up in a smile. Even his eyes twinkled.

"Miss Myra, I've been looking forward to meeting you ever since the first day I saw you. The money is going to help the church, so I'm glad to give it. This is the best pie I have ever eaten, but the company is even better."

She didn't want the time to end, but when the pies were all eaten, everyone started leaving. James talked so nicely and thanked her for her company. It made her think of the way Dr. Beddingfield had said that taking her to Dublin had been his pleasure.

He walked her over to Annie Lou and Horace. Myra was ready to tell him good night.

"Horace, I'm coming out here to church Sunday and eat dinner with Jane. How about all of us taking a ride in my buggy before I go back to Glencoe. I'd like to show Miss Myra some of the pretty places around here."

"That's good. We'll most likely eat at Ma's. We eat there most every Sunday."

Myra didn't say a word all the way home. She figured they would set in to teasing about having a feller, but neither one of them said a word about it. She had always thought that a feller was the last thing she would ever want, but now she wasn't so sure.

~10~

After getting home from the pie supper, Myra went straight to bed. She didn't want to give Annie Lou or Horace a chance to talk about James, and she wanted time to pass quickly so it would be Sunday. Sleep just wouldn't come. Every time she closed her eyes, she saw James. She went back over everything he had said. Was it really true that he wanted to take her for a buggy ride, or did she just dream it? He invited Annie Lou and Horace to go along, but she knew he only wanted to take her. These feelings were strange and made her feel different than the Myra she knew.

She was thankful to be busy all day Saturday. She washed and ironed clothes for everyone and cooked some dishes to take to Horace's ma's house the next day. This would be Annie Lou's first time to bring food, and that would be a big surprise for everyone.

A big revival would be starting tomorrow at North Connolly Church. That meant a lot of extra people would be in church, and a lot of them would eat with Miz Morris. Horace's uncle Samuel was going to be one of the preachers. He and his wife, Molly, would stay with the Morrises for the week. Annie Lou had grown to love Aunt Molly and Uncle Samuel, and was excited to see them. From the way Annie Lou talked about them, Myra looked forward to meeting them.

She discovered that it was easy to cook when you had plenty of things to cook with. Miz Powell had told her how to make a pound cake, and since she had plenty of butter and eggs, she decided to bake a cake. This was her first time to make the cake. It took a whole dozen eggs and a pound of butter. That was the reason she hadn't tried it until now. Folks would take all kinds of good things to eat at Miz Morris's, so she wanted to think up something different. She ended up making tater salad and a big pot of chicken and rice. She was hoping James would eat some of her food, especially the cake.

The next morning, she dressed and brushed her hair out long in back with one braid across her head. She crushed some sweet shrubs from Miz Morris's garden and put down inside her dress. She remembered how good James smelled and hoped he would notice the sweet smell on her.

The church was almost full when they walked in. In no time there was not a seat left, and the men were giving their seats up to women and were standing around the sides. She tried to look for James but couldn't see him anywhere. All through the preaching, she told herself that he was somewhere that she couldn't see. The preaching and singing went on about two hours. Preacher Samuel was a real fiery preacher, and he really brought out the people on the altar call. She knew a lot of people would get saved that week. She didn't expect to be one of them since she couldn't keep her mind on the preaching and off James MacTavish.

When the service ended, at least half of the people got baskets of food out of their cars and buggies and headed over to the Morris's house. James was nowhere in sight. She had to squint her eyes up real tight to keep from crying. Her stomach had the same bad feeling that she felt for so long after Papa died.

Long tables were put up under a grove of trees and covered with food. Everyone filled their plate and most went to sit on blankets on the ground. Myra fixed a plate, but she didn't feel like eating a bite. She figured James decided that he didn't want to waste time on an ignorant country girl.

"Myra, come sit with Jane and me. I haven't had a chance to get acquainted with you since you have been here."

Miz Morris and Molly were sitting in rockers on the front porch of the house. Molly was just as pretty and sweet as Annie Lou had said. Everybody came over to speak to her, and she seemed to enjoy laughing and talking to everyone.

"I thought James said he was coming out today."

Jane, Horace's ma, asked Molly just what Myra wanted to know. She was eager to hear the answer.

"Oh, Jane, you know how James is. He doesn't know one day what he is going to do the next."

Miz Morris shook her head and said, "That boy just can't settle down. He is smart as a whip, and everybody loves him. He needs to find a good girl and get married like Malcolm did."

"The problem is that Mama and Olieta have spoiled him all his life, and Papa lets him do whatever he wants. He is having too good a time to think about settling down."

Myra knew she shouldn't have been listening to their family business, but what she heard made her feel even worse. She wanted to leave and go back to Annie Lou's house, but she didn't want the sisters to think she didn't like their company. All of a sudden a buggy came flying up the lane with dust stirred up all around it. James got out, brushed off his clothes, and came over to where they were sitting.

"Howdy do everybody? I'm sorry to be late and miss the preachin'. I couldn't get away from the house until now. Olieta had a bad nervous spell early this morning and needed me to stay with her."

He didn't seem to recognize Myra at all and headed to the tables to fix his plate of food. Myra sat there wondering what she should do if he had forgotten about her.

"What do you think was the matter with Leit?"

"You know what was wrong, Jane. Leit always pitches her spells when she wants to stop James from doing something. He must've had a reason to really want to come out here if he was willing to leave her."

Myra put those words in the back of her mind to think about later.

James came back with a plate piled high with food. A big wedge of Myra's pound cake was right on top. He was balancing his plate and two cups of iced tea.

"Miss Myra, will you do me the honor of sitting in the swing with me and enjoy another cup of cold tea while I eat my dinner."

Before she could open her mouth Molly said, "Of course, she will, James. She needs a break from us old folks who need a nap after dinner. She made the most delicious pound cake I think I have ever eaten."

"I know she's a good cook, and she's about the prettiest thing I have ever seen too."

Myra turned red as a beet. Molly and Jane seemed happy to hear him say that.

They sat in a swing hanging under a big oak tree. Myra had always loved to sit in a swing. James pushed his feet and made the swing move back and forth.

"I love to sit in a swing, especially first thing in the morning. If I ever have me a house of my own, I'm gonna have a big front porch and a swing on both ends."

"I just been thinkin' about how I never wanted to live in another house that didn't have a porch. I love to sit in a swing in the morning and late in the evening."

"Miss Myra, you're somethin' else!"

He started eating his food, and she had never seen anybody eat as fast as James. He ate everything and the big wedge of cake in no time. They sat swinging and enjoying the cool breeze and warm sunshine for a while.

"I promised you a ride. Are you ready to go?"

"What about Annie Lou and Horace? If we go, we'll have to take my little sister, Dolly. Is that all right?"

He walked over and talked with them for a few minutes, and then walked back over to the swing without them.

"They said they're sleepy and Dolly needs a nap. They want us to go without them. Is that fine with you?"

She didn't need to answer. She started walking with him to his buggy. James had a really fine buggy that was made with good wood and trimmed with lots of leather."

"How you like my mare. She's not very big, but she makes up for it by being smart. That is more important for a buggy mare."

"What's her name?"

"June Bug, get up here June. We takin' Miss Myra for a ride."

She just broke out laughing at that. She had never heard of a horse or mule with such a funny name.

"My papa always named our stock after people in the Bible."

"June Bug is in the Bible."

"Can you tell me where? I'd like to look it up."

"I ain't shore, but it's in there somewhere. If it ain't it ought to be."

He cracked his whip and said, "Get up here, June." She started prancing with her tail held up in the air. Myra decided that she couldn't be named anything better than June Bug. James really knew how to handle her. He would crack his whip, but he never struck her. She just seemed proud to be carrying them along on a smooth ride. As they rode, James pointed out several places that he thought were real pretty. They ended up at a little creek.

"I just love this place. Ain't the trees hanging over the water pretty? Me and you are going to come here and have us a picnic."

They sat by the creek and talked. For the second time in her life, Myra found someone outside of her family that she did not have trouble talking with. He looked at her and listened while she told him how sad she had felt for so long, but how she was really getting to feel happy about the way things are going for her family.

"Soon I will be moving to Armity with my ma and brothers. I'll be glad to have most of my family all living together again."

"I'm glad too. Armity is much closer to Glencoe. That makes it easier for me to come to see you, if you'll let me."

He grinned and winked at her. She didn't know how to answer that, but she knew he didn't need an answer.

"I better be getting you back home. Ol' Horace might be coming after me with a shotgun if I keep you out too long."

Myra knew she was in really big trouble now. She had done more than just look James in the eye. She had opened up her heart to him, and it felt good. When they got back to Horace's house, he tied up the buggy and walked her to the porch.

"Thank you for the buggy ride. I saw some pretty places, and I liked riding with June."

He started down the steps and then turned around and said, "Miss Myra, if you will allow me, I will come by every evening next week and walk you over to the revival."

Nothing could have made her feel any happier than she did at that moment. She would say yes but she didn't want to sound like she had never had a fellow ask her that before.

"I certainly plan to go and hear Preacher Samuel, and it would be nice of you to walk me over there."

When she went into the house, Annie Lou gave her a sour look and said, "Myra, you better watch your step. That James is the best catch around here, but he might not be the best for you. He can charm the honey from the bees, I've heard."

"You don't need to worry about me. I enjoyed myself today, but he ain't gonna keep comin' back to see a country girl as ignorant as a stick."

Every evening throughout the next week, Myra was dressed and sitting in the swing waiting when James drove up in his buggy. When he came on the porch, he always said the same thing.

"Good evening, Miss Myra, you look prettier every time I see you."

Hearing him say things like that was making her feel pretty. He never sat down but offered his arm, and they started walking to the church. He wore a different shirt every night, and the collar was always starched so stiff that it didn't have a wrinkle in it. She wondered who did his washing and ironing. The church was just a short distance from the house, but they always walked slowly enough to make the walk last longer. They talked and laughed and just seemed to fit right together.

When they got to the church, the only empty benches were on the back row. Myra was always glad when some latecomers had to squeeze in beside them because then she could feel James's shoulder pushed up against her. She felt ashamed and knew that must bring on even worse things than just looking a fellow in the eye.

If the Lord Jesus himself had been preaching, she wouldn't have heard a word he said. She was just looking forward to the last hymn, so they could walk home and sit in the swing. They talked a lot about things they liked, and some of the things James said really made her laugh.

"Have you ever seen a goldfish? Man, they're pretty things. When I have a house and yard, I'm gonna dig a pond and fill it with goldfish."

"No such, I ain't ever seen any. I ain't never even heard of 'em."

"I'm gonna prove it to you. Colonel Dolby has a pond full of goldfish. I'll take you to Glencoe to see them."

"I'll have to see 'em to believe it."

He didn't usually talk about his family, except for Miz Morris and Molly. One night he started telling about his brother. He said Malcolm had married a nice woman named Olla and moved into a new house, and they had a baby boy. Myra couldn't tell if he thought that was good or bad.

The revival ended on Friday night, but there was to be a big sing and dinner on the ground the next Sunday. That Friday night when they sat in the swing, James put his arm around her shoulder and pulled her over close to him. Quick as a wink, she moved over to the far side of the swing. She knew this could lead to more trouble than just looking him in the eye.

"I'm sorry if I offended you, Miss Myra. I've just enjoyed your company so much this week, and I hate for it to end. I can't say that it won't happen again though, but I will be sure that you know my feelings by then."

When he left, he did not say anything about coming back on Sunday, but she felt sure that he would.

She was sitting on the bench with Annie Lou, Horace, Dolly and Will Rob at the Sunday service. The first hymn was being sung when most folks turned around to look at some people coming down the aisle.

An old man with a long beard and two women were walking up to an empty bench on the front. The women were small and had their faces powdered like the Porter sisters. Their hair was pulled back so tight they couldn't have smiled if they had wanted to. They walked down the aisle with their noses stuck up in the air, and took a seat. Right behind them was James, with his hat in his hand. He looked so serious and not a bit like her James. All through the singing, she hoped he would look around and at least smile at her, but he looked straight ahead the whole time. The service was so long that she had to slip out to take Dolly to the toilet. Annie Lou followed her outside.

"That's James's ma, pa, and old-maid sister, Olieta. They usually go to church in Glencoe, but I guess they came here today because of Uncle Samuel preachin'. They've all been good to me, except fer Olieta. She thinks she's better than anybody that's not one of the old Mac families in Glencoe."

Myra remembered hearing how Olieta petted and did everything for James. She knew she didn't stand a chance with him.

"I'm turning sick on my stomach. I need to walk on back to the house."

Annie Lou didn't argue. She knew how her sister was feeling.

After the service ended, Will Rob came to the house to see about her. He didn't know anything about James, so he thought she was really sick. He didn't ask much because he thought it was some kind of girl sickness.

"You better be well by tomorrow morning. I been waitin' to tell you that we're goin' to Joe Wiley's. You be ready to leave at daylight. We'll spend the night, and the next day, we'll bring the boys and Ma to the house in Armity."

"If you're gone, what're they gonna do if somebody dies?"

"They'll just have to wait. After all, they gonna be dead fer a long time. It ain't like they're in a hurry."

Myra had to laugh at her brother. She was thankful that anytime she felt low, Will Rob was always there for her.

Early the next morning, Will Rob came driving up on a plain old wagon with a mule pulling it.

"Where is your fancy coffin wagon? You don't think I'm gonna lower myself to ride in that ol' piece of junk after what I've got used to ridin' in, do you?"

"Suit yourself. You're welcome to walk along behind. You've done that plenty of times. I had to rent this from the livery stable, and it was the cheapest they had. I just hope this ol' mule won't die on us."

She climbed in, and they took off. They reached Joe Wiley's house about dinnertime. There wasn't much to see in between the places, just fields of cotton and corn, a few big framed houses, and a lot of tenant houses.

Everyone was real glad to see each other, especially Ma. She hugged Myra for the first time in her life. She wanted to know all about Annie Lou, but she didn't even ask about Dolly. It seemed as though she has forgotten that she ever had a baby girl. That was probably for the best, because it had already been decided that Dolly would live with Annie Lou and Horace. They really loved her and could give her the best home. Dolly had started acting as though she had lived with them all her life.

Their first nephew, Bud, was a fine fat baby, and he seemed real strong for his age. Flossie was already pregnant with another one, but they seemed happy about it. The boys went to look at the tobacco patch, and Ma went to the porch with the snuff they had brought her. That gave Myra time to get better acquainted with her new sister.

"Flossie, if it suits ya, we gonna take Ma and the boys back with us. We gonna have a house that's big enough fer 'em."

"Honey, it's more than fine with me. I've had all I can take of her fer a while. I hate to talk about ya ma, but nothin' I do suits her. We'll try to take her back after a while. You take Arno on with you but not Jesse."

"I wuz hopin' to sent them both back to school. Arno needs it more than Jesse. Why do you want to keep him? Is he that much help?"

"No, they help a little, but Joe Wiley can get along without 'em. Jesse asked us if he could stay here, and we want him.

"I most likely shouldn't say this to ya, Myra, but yore ma is downright mean to Jesse. She whips him fer the least little thing, and she whips him way too hard if Joe Wiley ain't around to stop her. One time Joe Wiley had to wring a piece of stove wood out of her hand to keep her from knocking his brains out."

"If he wants to stay, let him stay. I know what you're talkin' about. Ma has always been harder on him than any of the rest of us. He does get in a lot of mischief, but that is just how he is. Joe Wiley could always keep him straight."

Myra knew exactly what Flossie was talking about. She remembered how Joe Wiley had saved her from being hit with stove wood by Ma. There had always been something about Jesse that Ma just did not like. Staying with Joe Wiley was the best thing for him right now.

Flossie had used their housekeeping stuff to fix up the little house right nice. They had a big garden, and Flossie cooked a good vegetable dinner. Joe Wiley asked Myra to make the biscuits and show Flossie how to make them like she did.

While they were eating, he told them about growing the tobacco.

"Hit don't look like much of a crop, but this little bit will bring a big price. After dinner, I'll show you the barn where we'll cure it in about another month. They's a lot of work in that, and you have to stay at the barn and keep the fire goin' night and day. They's a feller from Carolina staying here to oversee all that.

"This year we ain't growin' much 'cause we just learnin'. Mr. Peterson says hit will be a real money crop. He must know."

"Does he live around here?" Will Rob still couldn't understand why the man was paying his brother to grow a crop that wasn't going to make much money that year.

"No, he stays over in Ailey and comes over here about once a week. Carl, the Carolina man, stays up the road and tells me everythin' to do. What I like is that he pays me off every month. We ain't never run out of vittles."

Later that evening, the boys went fishing and brought back a big mess of bream and little catfish. They cleaned the fish, and Flossie fried them for supper.

"Flossie, honey, them fish smell so good. I'm gonna have to nail up the door to keep the folks up the road from comin' in and tryin' to eat with us."

Everybody laughed, and Joe Wiley was proud. It was so good to be together, just eating, talking, and laughing. Myra really took to Flossie and knew her brother had a wife who would be a help to him.

The next morning they loaded up the wagon. Joe Wiley gave them a pile of vegetables, two dozen eggs, three fryers, a hen, and a rooster to take home. Now they could raise chickens again.

Myra didn't ask Flossie to give the empty jars back. It was too late for putting up anything that summer, and she could buy more for next year. They took off headed for the fourth place they had live since Papa died.

Myra decided to set her mind on making a good home for them in Armity and stop thinking about Mr. James MacTavish. She decided that either he didn't like it when she wouldn't sit close to him, or he got tired of her country ways. Whichever it was, she didn't even care. If that was how he felt, he could just keep right on following along behind his ma and his pa and his old-maid sister with his hat in his hand, looking like a dying calf in a hailstorm.

When they drove up to the house, she was surprised to see a man sitting on the porch. Will Rob told her that was Mr. Flanders, the man who owned the house. He opened it up and showed them through. It was the best house they had ever lived in. There were two good-sized rooms, a little shed room, and a porch on the front and on the back. There wasn't a lot of furniture but enough to get by with it. Everything was clean and neat as a pin. He said they could stay there for twelve dollars a month until he wanted it back. He also told them that he wanted everything to be kept as good as they had found it. Well, he didn't need to worry about that, because if there was anything the Stuarts knew, it was how to take care of what little they had. Will Rob counted out twelve dollars for him, and Mr. Flanders left.

"Will Rob, how're you gonna pay him that much every month?"

"Myra, I wanted to give us a good place. It will be tight, but I am gonna start doing some extra carpentry work. Besides, I will save on a lot on things that you can do for me now. Things that I wuz having to pay to get done, like washing and ironing."

That set Myra's mind to thinking up a plan. She wanted a way to earn money and help him out with the expenses.

"Who does yore washing now?"

"They's people who put signs in front of their house saying they take in laundry."

That was the first that she had heard of washing and ironing called laundry. It didn't sound right to her, but if that is what they call it here, then she'd call it laundry too. She sure did have a lot to learn.

"Since I have to wash fer us anyway, how 'bout me doin' that to make a little money? I saw two washpots and a clothesline in the back."

"All I've ever seen doin' that is the colored folks, but I reckon you could try. I ain't gonna let you put a sign in the yard, though. I'll ask around to the single fellers that work in the mill or on the railroad. Their clothes get real dirty."

First they had to fix up a pen for the chickens. Then they got busy moving into the house. There was a little patch where a garden had been, so they would plant a few late vegetables. Ma seemed real pleased to be there and took a seat in a rocker on the front porch. Several houses were close to their house, so someone was always coming by. She started right out speaking to them and passing the time of day. In a few days, several ladies had stopped by to sit with her for a while.

The next morning Myra cooked breakfast and asked Will Rob if he would be home for dinner. He said that he might not have time, so they decided that Arno would walk into Glencoe every day and take dinner to him. They were thinking about Arno as much as dinner for Will Rob.

There wasn't much for Arno to do, and they thought this would break up his day. It would be good for him to get into Glencoe and see different things. That is what they did every day. When Myra needed something from the store, she gave Arno a list to buy and bring back. She warned him that he was not to ever go into the MacTavish store to buy anything. If she wasn't good enough for James, her money wasn't going to him. She knew this might bankrupt his store, since she usually spent at least ten cents at the time.

After a few days, Will Rob came home with good news about the laundry business.

"I saw Mr. Flanders today and asked him about using the washpots. He said it was fine with him and asked if you could do his laundry. He said he wanted his shirts starched and put up on hangers. I told him that you do mine like that, and you do it better than anybody. I told him to have it ready tomorrow, and I will bring it to you."

"How much can we charge?"

"Most folks charge by the basket. I think the best is to charge a dime fer a shirt or pants and a nickel fer a suit of underwear and socks."

"How we gonna keep up with all that and count up them nickels and dimes."

Arno had been listening and spoke up. "I'll take care of all that and deliver and collect."

Now they were in business. Will Rob found some little wheels and made a wagon for Arno to use to pick up and deliver the clothes. He put two poles on it with a rope in between, so the starched things could hang up. Word spread about Myra's good "laundry," and soon she had all the work that she could do. Some weeks she made as much as five dollars. There were a lot of single men working in Glencoe, and they all seemed to want to wear starched shirts. She started giving Arno a nickel every time he made the trip to take back the clean clothes. He never came right home because he liked to look around the stores and think about what he was going to buy when he had saved up enough.

Some bad news came their way after they had been in Armity about a month.

"Myra, I ran into a feller that just moved to Glencoe from Brewster, and he gave me some real bad news. Nannie died just a few days after you left. He said Bunk came in and just found her sittin' in the chair dead."

"Oh no, my pore Nannie. I worried 'bout her. I knew she wasn't feelin' right when we left. I hope it wasn't tryin' to take us to Dublin that caused it." Myra's heart was broken again, and she had to have a hard cry before she could say more.

"Nah, that wouldn't have nothin' to do with it. Maybe it was the heart dropsy that got her too. At least, she didn't have to suffer."

"Did he say anythin' about Izzy?"

"The fellow said that both of 'em seemed to be doing all right. Izzy has a little job at the mill sweepin' up the sawdust. Bunk got so much religion and both of them go around to revivals. He said he thought Bunk was even preachin' some."

"Did the feller know where Bunk buried Nannie?"

"He didn't say, and I didn't think to ask."

"I hope he took her back to Sullivan's Corner and buried her beside her dead babies."

Myra would never forget Nannie. They got together right at a time when both of them needed a good friend, and they helped each other. She wasn't a drop of kin to Myra, but she would always seem like family. It was hard to think of the Bunk that they used to know being a preacher. She remembered hearing Preacher Samuel say the Lord works in mysterious ways. She was thankful Nannie went to her death knowing that Bunk was straightened out from drinking and from all the other evil ways he had.

Their days were in a routine. Will Rob worked every day. Arno went to town to take the clean clothes, get the dirty clothes, and take dinner to Will Rob. Myra started the washpot boiling early every morning and had the clothes on the line before time to start dinner. She heated the irons while she cooked dinner, and by two o'clock she had everything ironed. She didn't like this as good as sewing, but it gave her something to do and helped out with expenses. No matter what happened, it seemed they made the best of what they had. She hoped Papa could see that they were doing as he taught them.

Late one evening, about the first of August, Myra was sitting on the porch. She had finished a big load of the laundry and was resting and cooling off. She hadn't changed clothes and was hot and sweaty. She saw a buggy coming and recognized it right away. She ran in the house, smoothed down her hair, and tied on a clean apron. She didn't know what he wanted, but there he was.

She heard Ma call, "Myra, you come on out here and talk to this fellow."

She came out and there was James sitting in the swing, talking to Ma as though he had known her forever.

He grinned and said, "So you got you a house with a porch and a swing."

Myra just nodded her head.

Then he turned to Ma and said, "Miz Stuart, I got to know Miss Myra when she was living with Annie Lou and Horace. You might not know it, but I am Horace's mother's brother. I want to ask your permission to start calling on Miss Myra."

Ma didn't even seem to notice that he asked to call on her daughter. She just said, "Now that would make you Horace's uncle. How can that be when you are younger than him?"

James broke out laughing and replied, "I'm just one year older than Horace. His mother is one of the oldest in my family, and I am the youngest, except for my sister, Grace. In fact, Grace and Horace are the same age. Horace is just one of those fellows who has looked old all his life. It's probably because he has lost most of his hair. I am twenty-three years old, Miz Stuart, and Horace is just twenty-two. The main thing that I want to talk to you about is calling on Miss Myra."

Ma finally answered him by saying, "Well, her pa is the one you should talk to, but he has passed on. I can't rightly say myself. Maybe you had better ask Will Rob when he comes in."

That didn't help much, so Myra piped in and said, "I think the answer to this is the same as the answer that Joe Wiley gave to Horace about calling on Annie Lou. I am the one to ask, and I say yes."

"How about me coming back tomorrow after supper and enjoying that fine swing with you?"

"That will be just fine."

James told them good evening and left. She knew this might not be best for her, and she might get hurt again, but she wanted to be with him enough to take a chance.

Now she would have to tell Will Rob since he would see James coming to see her. She just hoped he wouldn't start teasing her.

After supper she told Will Rob all about James's coming and how they had spent time together during the revival at North Connolly. He didn't tease her, but he sure didn't seem happy about it.

"I don't know about him, Myra. I have heard things that don't sound good."

"Tell me what have you heard?"

"Things that you shouldn't even know about."

"You just don't want me to do nothin' except what you tell me. Just because all you want to do is work and then sit on the porch and smoke yore pipe don't meant I want to do that. I want to enjoy life a little. I like James. He has been mighty nice to me, and I don't want you to ever say another word against him."

She had never talked mean to Will Rob before, and she was sorry as soon as she said it.

"You do what ya want. I ain't yore boss or yore pa. You just don't come whining to me when you get in trouble."

Myra didn't say anything back to him, but she vowed right there that he wouldn't ever know any trouble she had from James.

The next evening she hurried with supper and had the kitchen cleaned up in plenty of time to fix herself up and wait for James. It was good that she did because he and June came driving up even earlier than she expected him. She had saved some tea from supper because she remembered how much he seemed to like it. Will Rob brought home a little piece of ice every night. It cost a nickel, but the iced tea was worth the cost. In fact, they were having enough extra money now to enjoy a lot of good things.

When James came on the porch, he said, "Miss Myra, I sure have missed being with you, and I thank you for letting me come back."

Myra had already decided that she was going to get a few things straight with Mr. James MacTavish before she let him keep coming to see her.

"I shouldn't let you in my yard after the way you didn't even speak to me that last Sunday at North Connolly."

If cold water had been poured on him, he wouldn't have looked any more pitiful. For a minute she thought he was going to cry.

"I am so sorry about that. I tried to get a chance to talk to you, but by the time I could get away from my folks, you had already gone home. I planned to come alone that day, but before I left home, Olieta put in that she wanted to go. Then Ma and Pa decided they would go with us, and I just couldn't find no way out of it."

She could believe that, and maybe if she had stayed longer, they could have gotten together for a little time. She still wasn't ready to let him sweet-talk his way back.

"You've shore been slow in coming back. You must not have been too sorry."

The way he looked this time made her think for sure that he was going to cry. He took out his handkerchief, blew his nose, and squirmed around in the swing.

"Now let me try to explain some things to you. First of all, I want you to know that I think more highly of you than I have ever thought about a girl in my life. After that last time we were together, I went home and started thinking about you and me. Mainly, I thought about me and how I really am not worth a lady like you. I've done some things that I'm not proud of, and I know you can do much better than me. I decided that no matter how much I wanted to be with you the, best thing I could do was leave you alone. So I stayed away, and I tell you it just about killed me.

"When I couldn't stand it any longer, I went by my brother, Malcolm's house. He has a nice wife and a little baby boy named Tom. They said I looked awful, and I told them I felt worse. Then I just spilled it all out to them and ended up saying that I'm just not the kind of man that should be with a smart, pretty lady like you. Olla spoke up then and said that maybe I ain't been and maybe I ain't now, but there ain't no reason why I can't start being that kind of man. When Olla said that, I felt like the sun had finally come out after a month of rain. I told myself that I could be that kind of man. I ain't mean, and I shore ain't dumb. In fact, for a lady like Miss Myra, I could be the best damn man in Aberdeen County—now you got to excuse me for saying that. You see I have a lot of work to do in changing, but will you be patient with me?"

"James, I don't ever want to hear any more talk about you not being worth me. I think you're a fine man."

She felt as though the sun just came out for her too. James put his arm around her shoulder and pulled her over close to him. This time she stayed there and felt as though that was where she always wanted to be. They sat like that for a long time without saying anything. Neither of them needed to say more. One thing that she did think about and say thanks for was Olla. She wouldn't ever forget her for what she said to James that made him come back to her. Maybe someday she could do something as nice for Olla in return.

Just before dark, Will Rob came out on the porch, and she thought, *If he calls "bedtime" on me, I am going to leave the soda out of the biscuits all next week.* He didn't say anything, but James knew it was time to go. She walked to the buggy with him. They both got real tickled, because just as they walked up, June Bug lost her manners and put out as bad a stink as they had ever smelled. Myra tried to ignore it, but she couldn't help giggling.

"Now, June, you done embarrassed me again. Don't you stand there grinning at me. I'm going to stop feeding you before I take you anywhere."

He saw she was laughing and that made him laugh all the more. She wasn't embarrassed. She had walked behind mules her whole life, and she knew what they did. June was a lot fancier than Solomon, but the smell was the same.

"How about me taking you to North Connolly to church Sunday? We can eat dinner at Jane's. She always cooks plenty to feed as many people as might show up at her house to eat after church. You can visit with Annie Lou, because they are always over at Jane's for dinner after church. Then I want to take you into Glencoe and show you those goldfish in that pond at the Dolby's house."

"I'll be ready for church, but I won't believe it about those fish until I see for myself."

He went off shaking his head and laughing. Myra couldn't stop laughing either.

She didn't know how she could pass the time until Sunday. She went back over every thing that James and had said or done. For so long she had felt as if she didn't fit anywhere and was always trying to find where she belonged. Now she knew where she belonged and where she wanted to be for the rest of her life.

Will Rob was mad and grumpy all the rest of the week. He didn't say anything directly to her and left every time she came close to him. She didn't know why he had it in for James so bad. She was sorry that she talked ugly to Will Rob, but then he shouldn't have said the things that he did. She would have tried to talk to him about it, but she did not want to hear him say anything else against James. Of course, Ma didn't care one way or the other. She forgot who James was from one time to the next. Maybe she could get a chance to talk to Annie Lou on Sunday. Nannie would understand, if only she could talk to her. Now she wished she hadn't said those ugly things against Alvin Atkins. If Annie felt the same way about Alvin that Myra was feeling about James, she knew that she hurt her friend's feelings real bad. She wished she could write to her and tell her that she was sorry. She didn't dare say all that for Arno to write.

Sunday morning, James drove up just in time for them get to church. His starched white shirt was already sticking to his back in the heat.

August is what is called dog days and is the very hottest time in South Georgia. At least she didn't have to work in the fields this year. She did the washing early in the morning. It was a hottest time of day when she did the ironing, but then she could sit on the porch and cool off for the rest of the afternoon.

James helped her up into the buggy and said, "Now, June, you remember what I told you. If you don't behave, you ain't getting' any supper either."

When James helped her up into the buggy, she felt like the princess in the stories Miss Caroline used to read. She was glad the pews would be packed tight, because she liked sitting so close to James. As usual, there was some fat woman sitting on the other side of her, sweating and fanning. It was so hot by the time church ended that it was a wonder they didn't all float away on the sweat. When they stepped out the church door, the cool breeze felt refreshing. A lot of people stopped to speak to James and ask about his ma, pa, and Olieta. He really had a way of talking and getting along with people. Several people asked him about things they needed from his store. She thought he must have a lot of trade since everybody liked him so much.

They walked over to Miz Morris's house with Annie Lou, Horace, and Dolly. Dolly was dressed up like a little doll, and she was getting to be just as prissy as Annie Lou. Miz Morris made her feel real welcome and made her acquainted with the other folks when they went to the table. There must have been a dozen grown people and about as many children eating there, but the food just kept on coming out of the kitchen.

James's sister, Grace, her husband, and baby were there. Grace didn't look a bit like James and sure wasn't as friendly as Miz Morris or Molly. Myra always thought babies were pretty but Grace's baby girl, Louise, was rather scrawny and cried and whined most of the time. Myra tried to start a conversation with Grace and talked about the baby, but Grace wouldn't have anything to do with her.

After dinner she did get a few minutes alone with Annie Lou when they took Dolly to the toilet. She told her what Will Rob had said and how he had been acting.

"Will Rob is just jealous. He wants you to always be there to do things for him. It's high time he found him a gal."

"It just don't seem right fer him not to like James."

"From what I hear, Myra, James will be a handful, but maybe he will be worth it."

"Tell me why Grace acts so unfriendly towards me."

"I ain't been around her much, but she won't be your problem. Olieta is who you need to watch out for. She is more jealous of you than Will Rob is of James."

That didn't bother Myra. She knew she could handle her old timey brother and James's scrawny old-maid sister.

They left in the buggy not long after dinner and headed for Glencoe. James drove right up to a big two-story brick house. A man and woman were sitting on a side porch.

"Howdy do, Colonel Dolby and Miz Dolby? I have a young lady here who just moved to Aberdeen County, and she hasn't ever seen any pretty fish like you have in yore pond. Is it all right if I go in the backyard and show them to her?"

"Help yourself, James. Then bring your guest back by and let us meet her."

James opened the gate, and they walked into a backyard that looked like how the garden in the Bible that Papa told them about must've looked. There were flowers and bushes everywhere and a swing under an arbor covered with a flowering vine. She had never smelled so many good smells at the same time.

The fishpond was right in the middle. It was cemented all around and shaped like a half-moon. At first, all she could see were the lilies floating on top, but soon she saw the fish. They were as gold as a wedding ring and just sparkled in the sun. She couldn't stop looking at them.

"We're gonna have us a pond like this someday."

She couldn't help noticing that he said "we" instead of "I." Sitting on the side of the pond was what looked like a real little colored boy, but he was made out of concrete and painted up to look real. He had a fishing pole and line in his hand. She had to laugh and think that he looked just like the little boys Jesse and Arno used to play with. They walked around to the side porch to thank the Dolbys.

"Colonel Dolby, Miz Dolby, I want to make you acquainted with Miss Myra Stuart. She just moved here from Washington County. Thank you for letting us look at the fish."

"Glad to meet you, young lady. I hope you are enjoying our town. Now, James, you come on back anytime. We are always glad to see you."

"Won't y'all stay and have some lemonade with us?"

"Thank you, ma'am, but I will need to get Miss Myra home soon."

Myra knew Will Rob was wrong about James. Everybody thought so well of him, even the colonel. She had never heard of a colonel before, but she knew it must mean somebody important.

James headed right down the main street of Glencoe and stopped in front of a drugstore. He said he was going in to get something for them that he knew she would enjoy. She was surprised the store was open on Sunday, but later she found out that people called when they needed medicine, and the druggist opened the store for them. James just happened to catch them open. He came out with two glasses that had ice and some kind of brown liquid in it. It looked kind of bubbly and had foam on top. She was scared to taste it because she was afraid it might be whiskey, but then she realized that drugstores wouldn't sell whiskey.

"This is a cola. It was made up by a druggist, and people liked it so much that now it's sold all over. A lot of people think it cures stomachaches and other things, but I just like the way it tastes."

She turned it up and took a little sip. Then she took a big sip. Yes, sir, this was good stuff.

"What did you say this is called?"

"You just call it a cola. Some times folks call it soda water."

"This is my first cola, and I have to say I am enjoying it."

After that, she bought a cola every time she went to Glencoe. It wasn't long before you could buy cola everywhere. Later it was put in bottles, and she could pay a deposit and take a bottle of cola home to Ma, who got to love cola even better than her snuff.

On the way back to Armity, they stopped by a little creek. She found that James really loved little creeks and couldn't pass one without stopping. He helped her out of the buggy and spread a blanket on the bank for them to sit.

"Miss Myra, did you enjoy the day?"

"I was just trying to think of how to tell you how much I enjoyed it."

"Well, let me show you how much I enjoyed it."

He lifted her head, and she thought he was going to try to kiss her. She knew that wasn't a proper thing to do, but she didn't want to stop him.

"You are so pretty and sweet. I could put my two hands around your waist." Then he took her hand and held it for the rest of the time.

They didn't say much riding home in the buggy, but they didn't seem to need to say any words. When they got back to Armity, she felt as if she had been off in another world, where everything was beautiful and all the people drank colas. Will Rob and Ma were sitting on the front porch, so they said good-bye at the steps.

"I will be back early Wednesday evening and take you over to see Malcolm's new baby boy."

"I'd like that. I want to meet Olla. I know I'm gonna have a good friend in her."

James left, and she started to sit down on the porch. Will Rob got up and left before she could sit down. She had to get him and James together. She knew they would get along, if Will Rob wouldn't act so old-timey.

Wednesday evening, she fixed supper early for Ma and the boys and left it on the stove for them to eat. She was too excited to even think about being hungry. At the last minute, she thought she better eat a bite so that her stomach wouldn't start growling and embarrass her. That would be even more embarrassing than what June did. She took a piece of corn bread and tried to eat it so fast that she choked.

When James drove up she was still coughing and trying to get her breath. He ran up the steps like he was scared.

"Are you all right?"

"Yea, I just strangled on a piece of corn bread."

"You scared me to death. I don't know what I would do if somethin' happened to you."

"That ain't nothin' to worry about me. I ain't never been sick in my life."

She wanted to thank him for caring about her, but she couldn't think of the right words to say. She followed him to the buggy, and they drove away. It seemed like no time before James stopped the buggy right off the main street of Glencoe.

"Are you hungry?"

"I had a little somethin' that was enough fer me."

"Well, I didn't get a chance to eat, and I'm hungry for a hamburger. Have you ever had one?"

"Is it some kinda ham?"

"Nooo, I'm gonna go in here to Johnny Higgins and get us some. He makes the best hamburgers in the world."

The smell of onions and meat cooking made her start to feel hungry. James came back with a sack and two colas. He put the sack down between them and told her to help herself. She reached in and brought out something round and wrapped up in a paper. She opened it up and found a round biscuit cut in half with a piece of meat between it. There were onions and something red and something yellow smeared on the bread. She took a bite and then a swallow of cola. She had never had such a good taste in her life.

"Do you like it?"

All she could do was nod her head because her mouth was so full.

"Miss Myra, you make me feel just like Santa Claus every time I do anything for you. I love hamburgers, and I'm so glad you do. We will eat these together every chance we get." James had bought two apiece, and she had no trouble finishing both.

Malcolm and Olla were sitting on the porch waiting when they drove up. Olla was nursing the baby, and she just kept right on until the baby went to sleep. Tom was just a few months old, but already Myra thought he looked better than Grace's baby. She loved Olla the minute she set eyes on her and loved her for the rest of their lives. They sat and talked as though they had known each other forever. Malcolm didn't talk nearly as much as James, but Olla made up for it.

After a while, Malcolm asked, "Did Olieta see ya'll drive by?"

James stammered a bit when he said, "No, we didn't come that way."

"James, you rascal, you came the back way so that you wouldn't have to pass the house. How are you going to pacify Olieta?"

This was the first time that she ever saw a sign of temper in James. His eyes got real beady and his face turned red.

"I ain't a bit worried about her. She don't run my life, even if she thinks that I need her to. I do as I please, and courting Miss Myra is what I please."

"Good for you, James. If we all tried to please Olieta, there wouldn't be any MacTavishes left in a few years, because all she wants all of us to do is just stay home with her."

After hearing all this, Myra felt like another big burden had been lifted off her shoulders.

They left in time to get back to Armity before dark. James was real concerned about keeping everything between them real proper. She knew it was hard for him. She was beginning to realize that he wasn't used to having to do that. He told her good night at the steps and that he would see her the next Sunday afternoon.

"You're not comin' in time fer preaching?"

"No, I can't make it 'til after dinner. Samuel is preaching at the Glencoe Baptist Church, and I have to take Ma, Pa, and Olieta. Then we are taking dinner with my brother George."

She understood that he had to be with his family. She knew he wasn't ready to take her where they were going to be, and she wondered if he ever would be.

When she walked up on the porch, Will Rob told her to sit down and talk with him. She knew what was coming, and she had already made up her mind that she wasn't going to put up with him saying one bad thing about James.

"Myra, are you getting serious about him?"

"I just might be."

"Well, if you are, there is nothing I can do about it, but I am going to make sure that you know what you might be getting into. I have asked around Glencoe about him. Everybody likes him, but they all say that he is just a "good-time fellow." He drinks a lot and likes to hang around that juke joint out on the Loop Road where those Chalker gals stay."

Annie Lou had already told her that all the MacTavishes tended to drink, but he had never even smelled like whiskey around her. She did want to know more about the Chalker gals.

"Who are the Chalker gals?"

"What I have heard is they are three sisters who hang around that juke and go out with men."

She shrugged her shoulders and said, "What's wrong with that?"

Her brother looked at her for a long time and then he said, "Myra, you know as good as I do, but you just don't want to admit it to yourself."

She couldn't think of another word to say, and she flounced into the house. She was mad, but she didn't know if she should be mad with Will Rob or James. She settled on the Chalker gals. If they weren't doing things like this, then she wouldn't have to deal with it. Her stomach was really churning, and she didn't know how to handle these feelings.

Then she remembered what James said Olla told him about changing and being the best man in Aberdeen County. She believed in James, but she couldn't stand not knowing and wondering. She decided to do what she had always done when she wanted to know about something. She would ask him. As she lay in her bed, she started to think about things in the past. Thoughts of the blue boy came to her and wondered where he was now. How would he take to James?

₌11₌

After being with James, Myra always had a hard time falling asleep. There was so much to think about, and she went back over ever minute and remembered every thing that he had said or done. Usually, she had such a happy feeling when she drifted off to sleep. Tonight the talk with Will Rob seemed to have blotted out the good times and happy thoughts. She kept trying to convince herself that James had not done anything to make her feel this way. It was only things that Will Rob had heard, and after all, Will Rob was just like an old settin' hen. He tried to protect her even when she didn't need protecting.

She finally fell asleep only to have a bad dream wake her. In the dream, she saw James driving in his buggy, and then she saw his buggy tied up at some strange house. The knot came back in her stomach, and she had to run to throw up in the slop jar. She knew she had to get over this feeling, and to do that, she had to hear James's side of the story. He would be back on Sunday, but she couldn't wait that long.

The next morning, when Arno started to deliver the clean shirts, she told him to wait for her. As they walked along, she took that chance to have a talk with Arno.

"While I'm in town today, I'm gonna see about gettin' you in the Glencoe school when it starts back. I figger Glencoe will have a better school than you've ever been in."

"Myra, I ain't going back to school no more."

This surprised her. He never objected to anything, and she knew he wanted to learn more.

"Why don't you want to go back to school? Is hit 'cause of the laundry?"

"No, I know I've learned all I can learn in any school. I want to get out in the world and learn about other places and things."

"Where could you go better than rite here in Glencoe?"

"Anywhere that I want to go. I might go all the way to New York City. I'm gonna make somethin' out of Arno Stuart that is a lot better than a farmer or a laundry boy or a carpenter. I will make all of you proud of me."

She had to laugh, but he was almost thirteen years old and could take off on his own. She knew better than to try to talk him out of this.

"I know how you feel, Arno, but please let me know before you go, so I can help you."

"Myra, you better quit helping us and think about helping yourself. I will be just fine, and Jesse will be fine too."

When Arno said that, she looked at him in a different way. Her little brother was growing up, and he understood far more than she had realized.

When they got to town, Arno made the deliveries, and Myra went straight to James's store. She felt a burst of pride when she saw the name on the window.

GLENCOE EMPORIUM
B. James MacTavish, Proprietor

When she walked in the door, she saw James sitting on the edge of the counter. A made-up looking girl was standing real close to him, and they were talking and laughing together. He looked up and saw her.

"Myra."

He looked surprised to see her. She turned around and ran out as fast as she could and started running down the road toward Armity. She hadn't gotten very far when she heard James running right behind and calling her. She was out of breath by then, so he caught up and grabbed her.

"Myra, what in the name of God are you running from?"

"Will Rob said . . . he told me . . ." She was sobbing and snubbing so hard that the words wouldn't come out.

"I don't know what you're tryin' to say."

She was crying so hard that she couldn't do anything but sob and try to get her breath. He put his arms around her and petted her like he would a baby.

"There there now, don't cry. There ain't nothin' can be this bad. Let's go on back to town and get us a cold cola. Then we'll talk about whatever scared you so."

James took her hand, and they walked back to the store. She didn't even think about what the people who saw them might be thinking. They sat down on the little back steps behind the store after he locked the front door. He had left it standing wide open when he ran out. He went across to the drugstore and bought the drinks for them. While he was gone, she had time to think about what she had to ask him and to get up courage to do it. She had to know so she could get rid of the feeling that she was scared to trust him.

As they drank the colas, she told him all that Will Rob had said. He listened to every word. Her worst fear was that he would say he didn't care and to tend to her own business, but he didn't act that way at all.

"Myra, I was planning to tell you this in a few more weeks, but I think you need to hear it now. I know that I love you, and you mean more to me than anyone ever has in my life. I want to ask you to be my wife."

Her heart nearly jumped out of her chest when she heard this. Right then, she didn't care about anything else but knowing that he loved her. She did know the other things would always stand between them. He knew that too.

"Now about that other junk. First of all, Will Rob had no right to say things like that to you. He should have talked to me about it. That is what I would have done, if you had been my sister. There are a lot of things that are better left unsaid, and this is sure some of them. I am going to talk to you about this now, but I never want you to bring it up again."

She nodded her head, and he continued to talk.

"Sure I was talking and joking with the woman in my store this morning. She don't mean a thing to me. I am a businessman. People only trade with businessmen they like and enjoy being around, so that is why I do good business. Yes, I do enjoy having a little nip of good whiskey in the evening after work, but I am not a drunkard. There ain't a thing wrong with having a little drink with your friends. As far as women go, I will be the first to say that I have always loved to be around pretty women. I like to be friendly and enjoy myself. There is not a thing wrong with that, as far as I can see. I have done some things before I met you that I probably shouldn't have done. Remember, I have already told you about that, and I also told you that I was going to become the best man I could for you.

I know that I love you, and I promise that I will always do the best that I can for you. I need you to believe in me, and I want you to promise me that you will put these things out of your mind so that we can have a good life together. I am not going to ask you for an answer today, because I know you are upset. Now come on into the store. I've wanted to show it to you. I better open back up, or Malcolm will get all my trade."

She looked right into his face for the first time, and they both broke out laughing—just because they were happy. Then James held her face up and kissed both of her eyes as if to dry the tears away.

When James opened the front door, there were two old men standing at the door trying to get in.

"Come in, Mr. MacDilby and Preacher Hicks. I'm sorry I had to close up for a few minutes, but it was an emergency."

"James, you are not going to be in business long if you keep closing up at the least little thing. You need to get you a clerk."

"I know that, Preacher Hicks, and I am working on it. Now what can I do for you gentlemen today?"

Mr. MacDilby needed a new lamp chimney, and Preacher Hicks bought writing paper. As Myra looked around James's store, she saw a lot of different things on the shelves. She had never seen a store exactly like this. There were a few groceries, but mostly just junky stuff and candy and crackers. He had a lot of thread, buttons, ribbons, and some material. There were pots, pans, and a lot of kitchen things. He had two big rolls of something that she had never seen before. It was a smooth kind of material, but it wasn't cloth. One bolt was white with yellow flowers on it, and the other was a red and white checked. James saw her looking at it and feeling it.

"Myra, is that the first oilcloth that you've ever seen?"

She didn't like him thinking that she was so country and backward, so she said, "Oh no. I have always seen oilcloth in stores."

James looked real serious and said, "If you will accept it, I would like to give you enough of it to make yourself a dress. Which pattern do you want?"

"I like the flowered best."

He rolled out a big piece and handed it to her. She held it for a minute and then started to laugh. James grinned for a second and then burst out laughing.

"Now, Myra, don't you try to put on airs with me ever again. I knew you didn't know what it was, because this is the first that has ever been for sale in Glencoe. It is used for table cloths. You don't have to wash it, because you can just wipe it right off. Now I'm going to put this in a sack for you to take home and enjoy."

She looked around more and saw bedcovers, framed pictures of Jesus, reading books, and even Bibles.

"I ain't trying to put on airs. But I ain't never seen a store like this before."

"Well, Myra I want to sell things that make people's life a little brighter. They have to buy food and things from the feed store or the hardware store. Most of the things in my store are not what they need but what they want. I just feel like everybody should have a chance to buy something just because they want it."

"Well, that's good as long as they buy what they need first and don't need to hang onto the money."

She didn't understand what James meant, and she knew he did not understand what she had said. She did know that she needed to find Arno and head home. She had a lot to think about. Then she decided to say something that she had been trying to get up enough courage to say.

"James, I'm going to cook dinner next Sunday and ask Annie Lou and Horace to eat with us. Could you come and eat dinner with us after church?"

She had been thinking that getting Will Rob and James together might be a good idea, because anybody who talked to James always seemed to like him.

"You know, I will. I'll be there with bells on."

Arno was standing outside the store when she walked out. On the walk back to Armity, she tried to make plans. She had to get word to Annie Lou, clean the house until it shone, and cook the best dinner that she had ever cooked. Just before they reached Armity, they passed the house of some colored folks. Myra noticed a pen of fat hens in the yard. An old lady was throwing scraps to them.

"Howdy do? You shore got some fine hens there. I'd like to buy one if ya willin' to sell one."

"I'll sell ya one fer fifty cents, but I ain't gonna kill hit or clean hit."

"That's fine. I like to do that myself anyway. My brother will come get hit Saturday morning."

She would start saving up bread to make dressing. Their garden still had plenty of tomatoes, okra, and probably some late peas. She would make custard for a sweet and have plenty of ice and tea. That would make a really good dinner.

Thoughts about James wanting to marry her would have to wait until she got everything set for dinner on Sunday. One thought did keep running through her mind and that was James saying that she meant more to him than anyone ever had in his life. She knew Pa loved her, but he loved all of them. Her brothers and sisters loved her, but someday all of them would love someone else more. That is the way it is meant to be, and now she would have someone who loved her most of all. She didn't have to ask herself if she loved James. She knew she had loved him since the day she met him, and she would love him until the day she died. She hoped she could get Will Rob to like him. She didn't worry about Joe Wiley or any of the others, because they would think he was fine if she loved him.

When she got home, she went to look over the garden and was disappointed at what she saw. There was plenty okra and enough small tomatoes to make a dish of okra and tomatoes, but the peas were a real disappointment. There wouldn't have been a cupful after shelling. Then she realized the hens weren't laying enough to save up to make custard. She would be doing good to have enough to put in the dressing. She had milk, but that wouldn't help if she didn't have eggs. She'd have to think of another sweet. There had been times when she didn't have near as much as she had in her kitchen right now, and she always managed to put a meal on the table for the family. She couldn't even imagine James sitting down to a dinner of biscuits and flour-water gravy or stewed blackberries.

Arno had run off to play as soon as they got home. Just before she went into the house to stir up a little quick dinner, he came running up, howling, and had a big knot on his head. She took him inside and put a cold rag on it, and he started telling what had happened. Arno didn't usually talk much, but he was really running on about this.

"I was just walking down the road, and them colored boys started chunkin' at me, and one of 'em hit me right on the head with a pear."

She was holding the rag to the knot on his head, but her ears had picked up on the word pear.

"Where are these pears?"

"They's a bunch of old trees in the field down the road, and they's pears on all of 'em. I think it must be where an old house burned down"

She forgot about fixing dinner and headed down the road. She found the trees were loaded and lots were on the ground. The pears weren't very big and most had bad places on them. She picked up one, bit into it and found it sweet and juicy. After peeling and cutting out the bad places, they would be fine. A pear cobbler would make a good sweet. She filled her apron full and sent Arno back to the house to get a basket and the laundry wagon. They picked up two bushels and decided they could go back for more later.

She cooked up a big pot of pears, added sugar, and thickened it with flour. Will Rob came in for supper just as the biscuits were ready. They split the biscuits, put the stewed pears on top, and poured sweet milk over it. That made a fine meal. Will Rob really enjoyed it and ate two platefuls. While he was enjoying his supper and seemed in a good mood, she told him about the Sunday dinner she was planning. She was ready to hear him fuss about James, but he surprised her.

"Is there anything you need me to do?"

"Could you get word to Annie Lou that I want them to come? Early Sunday morning, you could go to the crossroads and get a block of ice."

"I have to go to a burying at North Connolly tomorrow, so I will stop and see her. Is ice all you need?"

Since the peas were all gone, she had tried to think of something else to cook. She thought about the beans she had picked, snapped, and helped Miz Morris put up last summer. She knew she had worked enough to ask for one jar.

"Ask Annie Lou to send me a jar of them snap beans that I helped with when I was staying with her. I know she ain't cooked all that Miz Morris gave her."

"OK."

She felt relieved that her brother had been so willing to help, but then maybe he was just looking forward to a good dinner.

The hen and dressing could be cooked early in the morning and be done before James got there. She'd have the vegetables simmering on the stove and the pear cobbler and biscuits ready to pop in the oven. She didn't want to be in the kitchen, looking all sweaty with flour all over her, so she wanted to have everything ready ahead of the company.

She had watched Miz Morris put up peaches with vinegar, sugar, and spices to make pickles. She decided to try this with the pears and make just enough for them to eat that day. The pickled pears would set the dressing off real good.

When James got there, she would be clean and neat and wearing a pretty dress. The table would be covered with the oilcloth, and all the dishes would be set out. It would be a dinner like they had never seen.

Will Rob came in that evening and said that Annie Lou, Horace, and Dolly would be there on Sunday, and they would have a surprise. He opened up a sack and brought out two jars of beans, two jars of corn, two jars of soup mix, and two jars of cucumber pickles. She was happy but really surprised.

"I just can't believe Annie Lou was willing to send all this. We both know how selfish and stingy she's always been. I'm proud that she's changed."

"Ha, it wuz not her that was so givin'. Horace's ma wuz there when I went by and asked about the beans. She told me to come home with her, and she would get the beans. Then she gave me all of this."

"Did they seem surprised to hear that James wuz comin' to our house to eat Sunday dinner?"

"Heck no, they all seemed to know all about it already."

She cooked, cleaned, and had everything perfect in plenty of time on Sunday morning. The table looked really pretty with the new oilcloth and a bouquet of sunflowers on it. She wore her favorite dress, the one with little lavender flowers on it. James had always bragged on her when she wore that dress. She had washed and brushed her hair until it shone like coal, and she pulled it back with her combs. Ma was even fixed up, and she seemed excited to be having company.

Arno and Will Rob had just left to get the ice when James drove up. He was dressed fit to kill. His hair was brushed back and oiled, and he smelled better than ever. He was grinning from ear to ear and sat on the porch with Ma and kept her laughing and talking. Ma used to act like this with Pa, but they hadn't heard her enjoying herself like this in a long time.

Just as Will Rob and Arno came back with the ice, they heard a motor coming and a horn blowing, and dust was flying everywhere. Annie Lou, Horace, and Dolly came driving up in an automobile. It didn't look too different from a buggy, except that it didn't have a horse. Horace kept blowing the horn until everyone came running out. They were so proud, and everyone was proud for them. James and Will Rob had to look over every bit of it and asked all kinds of questions. Horace told them they had come the six miles from North Connolly in fifteen minutes, and that meant the car could go twenty miles in an hour. James was almost licking his lips, and she knew he really wished he had a car.

Everybody was talking and laughing and in such a happy mood when they went in to eat. It was a fine meal. Myra loved seeing James eat what she had cooked. There was plenty of everything, and everyone ate until they couldn't hold anymore.

Just as they were finishing the pear cobbler, James said there was something that he wanted to say before leaving the table. Myra didn't know what to expect when he reached over and took hold of her hand before he started talking.

"I know all of you know what a fine lady Myra is becoming, and I am the luckiest man in the world to have met her. I want you all to know that she means more to me than anything in the world, and I plan to make her my wife. I will do everything in my power to make her happy and give her everything she needs and wants. I've got a good business started, and my pa's going to give me enough land to build a good house for us. I don't guess there is any need to ask permission from any of you, 'cause as you all know, Myra makes up her own mind."

Everybody laughed at that and hugged Myra and shook James's hand. She hadn't said a word through all this. She had never really said yes, but James knew without her saying. The women got busy cleaning up the kitchen, and the men folks all went out to the back to smoke. She noticed that Arno had joined them and had gotten him a little pipe from somewhere. She never knew what James and Will Rob talked about that day, but from that day on, Will Rob never said a discouraging or critical thing about James for the rest of his life.

Later, everyone, except Ma, went for a ride in the new car. She wouldn't get in it, because she was afraid she would fall out and the wheels would roll over her. As they rolled down the road in the car, Myra had a comfortable feeling about her family. Annie Lou had a good life, and she and Horace had made Dolly a real part of their family. Arno seems to know what he wanted to do and how to do it. Joe Wiley was set up good and taking care of Jesse. She could feel free to leave and marry James with good conscience. Things just seemed to happen at the right time.

After everybody left or drifted off to take a nap, James wanted to ride to the creek. He always liked to sit by the water. He spread a blanket, and they settled down to sit on the creek bank. Then he brought out a piece of paper and handed it to her. She didn't know what it was, but it had Aberdeen County at the top of it and her name and James's name were on it. There was a gold seal at the bottom.

"This will show you just how much I want to marry you. I had to drive all the way to Campbell to get our marriage license."

"I didn't know what it wuz. I don't know if you know this, but I can't read much."

"You don't worry about that. I'll read it to you. It says that the State of Georgia has given Brian James MacTavish and Frances Elmyra Stuart a license to marry."

"I wondered why you asked about my whole name the other night. I ain't never been called anythin' but Myra. Why did you have to go to Campbell? I know you don't like it there."

"Ya have to go to the courthouse in the county seat to get a license. See, when they made Aberdeen County, they made Campbell the county seat 'stead of Glencoe—which it ought a been. That's why I don't want nothin' to do with Campbell.

"Now this is all legal, and all we have left to do is decide on a day and find us a preacher."

"I have to get my things ready, but that won't take long."

"Well, how about next Sunday afternoon? I want to go to Preacher Foster over by Cobb's Creek. I'd get Samuel, but he and Molly have moved too far off in Emanuel County."

She still had not said yes, but everything seemed to be all set. When James took her home, she was glad to find Ma and Will Rob sitting on the porch.

"Me and James will be marrying next Sunday, and I'll be leavin' to live with him."

"Where are y'all gonna live 'til the house gets built?"

She was surprised when Ma asked that. She had not even thought about where they would live. She only knew that she would be with James, and her name would be Myra MacTavish.

"Is there anything that you need that I can do for you?"

"Thank you, Will Rob, I think it is time fer me to use the twenty-dollar bill that Joe Wiley gave me after settling up. I do want to buy a few things."

"Myra, I don't want ya to hold back on nothing on our account. We got a good place to live, and Will Rob is making enough fer us to live good."

She was worried some about Ma being able to take care of things. She had done all the cleaning, washing, and cooking for a long time.

"Now don't you go thinking that I can't manage without you. Remember, I took care of you before you could take care of yoreself. You like to run the house, but I can do just as good as you."

Myra didn't mind her saying that. She knew Ma had always come through when there wasn't anybody else around to do what needed to be done."

"I think a lot of James. He comes from good stock, and I know yore pa would be glad to give ya hand to him."

This surprised Myra even more, and she reached over and hugged Ma. They were both thinking of Papa and cried together.

Myra went inside and got the twenty-dollar bill from the hiding place where she had kept it for so long. She started thinking about things that she wanted to buy. She did want to be married in a new dress and to have a pretty petticoat that she could use to sleep in. Even though she wouldn't need housekeeping things for a while, she did want to buy a few. She remembered Joe Wiley saying that Papa wouldn't want Annie Lou going into her marriage with nothing.

Since she had been going to church regularly, she had learned to love the Lord, but she hadn't spent much time praying except in church. Right then, she felt as though she wanted to thank Him for putting two good men in her life as He did. For a long time, she felt as if He hadn't done her right when He took Papa at the time they needed him so much. If that hadn't happened, she would never have come to Glencoe and met James.

She sat and thought about this until darkness filled the room. She looked out the window before she lit the lamp and saw a buggy coming past the house. She knew it was James's buggy, but she had no idea where he had been and why he was passing back by their house. He didn't stop but drove right past. She watched him pass and realized there was someone else sitting in the buggy with him. She knew who he was. She hadn't seen him in a long time, but there he was in his blue suit.

-12-

Thoughts of James, wondering what it would be like to be married, and seeing the blue boy again filled Myra's mind. Usually she had a hard time getting to sleep when her mind was so full of thoughts. This night was different. As soon as her head hit the pillow, she was sound asleep and didn't stir until she smelled coffee. She slept right through the roosters crowing at daybreak. Never in her entire life had she stayed in bed so long. She hopped up and hurried to fix breakfast for the boys before Will Rob left for work.

Ma and the boys were already sitting at the table, sopping syrup with biscuits, and drinking coffee. Ma was dressed for the day, and the food looked and smelled good. All three laughed and shook their fingers at her for staying in bed so late.

"Myra, I thought I would get started on being the ma again this morning. You're gonna be busy getting ready to start yore married life, so you better rest up when you can."

Myra felt ashamed, but she knew there was no reason to be. She dropped her eyes without answering, filled a plate, and found she was really hungry. She knew Ma was trying to show that things would be fine without her.

She had planned to go to Glencoe to see about getting a dress made and buying a few things. It would be nice to ask Ma to go with her, but that was too much to expect. She would let well enough alone and just be thankful that Ma was talking and acting as if she was going to be their ma again.

When Arno left to deliver the clothes, she joined him. He went to each customer's house to deliver the clean clothes. This gave her a chance to tell everyone that she was going out of the laundry business. She did hate for the folks to be left with a load of dirty clothes, but that couldn't be helped. Her laundry business had brought in some money, and she even enjoyed it. It was hard work, but she got a lot of pleasure from seeing the clean, starched, fresh clothes. She knew that James would never want her to do any work outside of their home. He didn't believe in that, and he would feel like people thought he couldn't take care of her. She was already learning that she would have to change a lot of her ways because of his pride. She would do whatever it took to make him a good wife and keep him happy. If he was happy, she would be happy too.

After they delivered the clothes, she and Arno split up. She walked to a little house at the end of the street where she remembered seeing a sign. It was a two-room house with a big front porch. There wasn't much yard. In fact, you stepped right onto the porch from the street. She knew what the little sign by the front door said—Dressmaking and Alterations.

The door was standing open so there was no need to knock. She could see a lady sitting at a sewing machine and concentrating on her work so much that she didn't notice Myra. After waiting a few minutes, Myra called out.

"Ma'am, I'd like to talk to ya about making me a dress."

"Come on in. I'll be finished with this sleeve in a minute, and then I can talk with you."

The lady kept right on sewing and didn't even look up for a long time. Myra understood that the lady had to keeping sewing until she got to a stopping place.

"I'm Miz Steptoe. I'm a widow woman just tryin' to make a livin'. Now what can I do fer ya?"

"I'm Myra Stuart from out in Armity. I know how it is to be trying to finish up. I sew, but I ain't got a machine that I can use."

"Well, what kind of a dress do you want?"

"I want it to be real nice, made from pretty light-colored material, maybe voile." She hoped she wouldn't have to tell Miz Steptoe why she wanted the dress.

"I can do that for you. Let's go behind that curtain for me to take yore measurements."

She took the measurements and wrote them down.

"You are a fine filled-out young woman."

Myra turned red as a beet when she heard that and didn't know what to say.

"I know some of these Glencoe fellows are going to take notice of you, if they haven't already. Now tell me how you want the dress made."

"I know in my mind just how I want it, and I'll try to tell ya. I want a full skirt, with a set in bodice and little buttons all down the front and set-in sleeves. I want a lacy petticoat too."

Miz Steptoe figured in the little book, and then handed Myra a slip of paper showing how much material was needed to make the dress and the petticoat.

"I'll make them both for you for a dollar and a half. You have to furnish all the material and notions."

She didn't know how much Miz Powell charged, but that sounded like a fair price for the work it would take. Notions was a new word to her, but she figured it must mean buttons, thread, and such.

"Ma'am, I'll go and buy what I need and be back by dinner."

She walked up and down the main streets of Glencoe looking for a dry goods store. She made sure not to pass James's store, because she didn't want him to see her. He had material in his store, and she was afraid he would want to give it to her. She didn't think it was fitting for him to do that before they wed. She stopped in front of a good-sized store that she had never seen before. "Rosenberg's" was written in gold letters on both of the big windows.

She went inside, and a little Jew lady met her at the door.

"Welcome to Rosenberg's. I'm Mrs. Rosenberg. How can I help you?"

"I need to buy me some material and notions to make a dress and petticoat. Here's how much I need."

Mrs. Rosenberg took the slip of paper and walked right to a bolt of the prettiest voile that Myra had ever seen. It was white with little light yellow patterns worked into it. She could just see it made up into the dress she had planned. Mrs. Rosenberg measured off the material for the dress, and some soft muslin for the petticoat. Myra started looking at the buttons on a rack.

"Now this looks like a wedding dress to me, so let's see what else you might need."

They picked out lace to go on the dress and petticoat, a pair of silk stockings and garters to hold them up. The only stockings Myra had ever owned were the wool ones she wore in winter. She was thankful to have Miz Rosenberg's help and bought everything that she suggested.

She could tell that Mrs. Rosenberg knew what you need to wear to get married, even if she was a Jew. By that, she didn't mean there was anything wrong with Jews. She just didn't know anything about them. In fact, she'd never heard about them until she came to Glencoe and heard people talking about all the new "Jew stores." She knew they were the people in the Bible, and they had different ways. This was the first time she ever met one face to face, but she decided right then that if they were all like Miz Rosenberg, she would think a lot of them.

The total of everything came to four dollars and seventy-five cents. Mrs. Rosenberg wrapped and handed the parcels to her with her eyes twinkling.

"Since this is a wedding dress, I have a gift for you." She reached under the counter and picked out a pretty lace handkerchief. Myra had always loved the way the Porter sisters pinned a lace handkerchief to their dresses.

"I shore thank ya, ma'am. This is about the prettiest handkerchief I've ever seen."

"I want to give you this to wish you happiness, good luck, and many children. Now would you tell me who this fortunate young man is?"

"His name's James MacTavish."

"James MacTavish, James MacTavish, my, my, he is quite a dashing young man. I know you will be very happy."

A big lump came in Myra's throat. It was a good lump not like the lump she got when she thought of Papa. She wanted to say more, but all she could think to say was thank you. She knew Miz Rosenberg for the rest of her life and shopped in her store many times. They became good friends, but she never saw her anywhere except in the store.

Miz Steptoe was still sewing as hard as she was when Myra left. She had to wait for her to finish again. Finally, she looked up but did not stop sewing.

"Did you get everything?"

"I went to Miz Rosenberg's store, and she sold me everything that you wrote on the paper."

"Good. Just put the parcels on the table and come back Tuesday about three o'clock for a fitting."

"Ma'am, will the dress be ready by Sunday? That's when I need it."

"Of course, it will be ready just before dinnertime on Thursday."

Myra had given Miz Rosenberg the twenty-dollar bill and had the exact amount ready to give to Miz Steptoe.

"Don't pay me now. Wait 'til you see if the dress is right."

"Oh, I'm sure it will be."

She left and walked around looking in the stores to find some pieces of cooking ware or plates and things like she remembered Annie Lou buying that day in Tennille. She was standing and looking in a store window when she felt a hand on her shoulder. She looked around and there was Mr. James MacTavish himself grinning at her.

"Hey, honey, I am surprised to see you in town. What're you doin' here?"

"I just want to buy some things fer our house when we get one."

She didn't want to tell him anything else. The dress would be a surprise for him. She was glad to see him and could tell he was happy to see her.

"That's sweet of you. If you buy anything, I hope it will be some big glasses for tea. I like a lot of ice in my tea, and the glasses we have at Ma's just don't hold enough.

"I have to get on back to the store. I just ran out long enough to go to the bank. Seems I gonna need some money next Sunday. Come by the store before you leave town."

"I won't have time. I have to get back home to cook dinner."

She looked in all the stores until she found the biggest drinking glasses. The glasses were a nickel apiece, and she bought six of them. Buying something that James would enjoy made her so happy that she couldn't keep from giggling out loud. She completely forgot about going home to fix dinner or even to eat. She didn't buy anything else. Her money was going fast, and she wanted to hold on to what was left. She might think of something else that she needed before Sunday.

James had not told her where they would live, and she was beginning to wonder. Since Molly had moved to Emanuel County, maybe her house would be empty for them to live in for a while. She decided to walk by and see if anyone was living there. Before she got close to the house, she saw his youngest sister, Grace, walking up the front walk. The house was big enough for two couples, but she knew Grace wouldn't want her to live in the same house. There was no need to worry. James would take care of where they lived. She would just wait and see.

She hardly remembered what went on for the rest of that week. She went to Glencoe to have the dress fitted and to pick it up. Ma seemed to want to spend a lot of time with her. She didn't talk much, but she kept looking as if she had something she wanted to say. Myra knew she wanted to tell her some things about being married, but that was just not her way.

Myra didn't know much, but she had figured out a few things. She would just learn as she went along. She did know that James knew a lot more than she did.

One evening, Will Rob came in carrying a box that at first she thought was a baby coffin. He sat down a pretty chest that he had made for her to pack her things in and take when she left. It was made from oak wood and smoothed and polished until it was smooth as silk. Will Rob had put it together so good that you could hardly see the nails, and he had carved a fancy design all around the edge.

"I'm shore proud of this, Brother. I hated to carry my stuff off in a croker sack like I come to Glencoe with. Now I got this pretty chest. I do thank ya fer all yore hard work on it."

It was hard to say anymore. She knew how much he hated to see her leave home. They had been through a lot together, and she couldn't remember a time when it wasn't the two of them together in anything that came along. She hoped things would turn his way soon, and he would find somebody that he wanted to marry. It would to be hard for him because he had to take care of Ma and Arno.

When she got up early Sunday morning, her things were already packed in the little chest, and her clothes were laid out and ready to put on. James drove up a little after nine o'clock. They headed over to Cobb's Creek, which was between Armity and North Connolly, but off to a side road.

"Preacher Foster is expecting us about eleven o'clock. I drove over yesterday and talked to him."

"How can he marry us during preaching time?"

"It's the fifth Sunday. Not many churches have preaching on fifth Sunday. That's why I picked today."

Before they got to the preacher's house, James pulled over under a shade tree as though he wanted to talk for a minute. Her heart skipped a few beats, because she was afraid he had changed his mind.

"Miss Myra, I just want to get one more look at you and tell you how happy I am that you are going to be my wife. You are the prettiest thing that I have ever seen. That dress looks so good on you, and the pretty lace handkerchief just sets it off. I could put my two hands around your waist. I won't ever look at you without remembering how you look on this day."

"I'm happy too, James. You are a fine-looking man to me."

"Hell, Myra, me and you are the best-lookin' pair in the entire state of Georgia."

James couldn't be serious for too long. He laughed out loud after saying that and cracked the whip for June to start moving.

She had never felt pretty before, but all at once she put back her shoulders, held her head up, and stuck her bosoms out. If she was pretty enough to be Miz James MacTavish, then she was the prettiest girl in Aberdeen County at least. She knew James had his pick of them all, and he had chosen her, Elmyra Stuart, the daughter of a tenant farmer from Washington County.

They started to drive along, and she had one more thing to ask James.

"I saw you drive past the house again last Sunday evening. Who was the little boy sittin' in the buggy with ya?"

"Honey, you must have been dreaming. I did not pass your place again. I drove straight down the road back to Glencoe. I shore didn't have any little boy riding with me."

She didn't say anymore, but she knew that she was not dreaming. James definitely came past her house and the little blue boy was in his buggy. Even if it was a dream or such, she was always glad to see the little boy and know that he was still around.

They drove into the yard of a big white-washed house. Several people were sitting on the porch, and they all started clapping when the buggy stopped. Myra was so nervous and shy, but James hopped down and lifted her right out of the buggy. James shook hands all around and introduced her to the folks. They all hugged her and said how pretty she looked.

They went into the parlor of the house, and Preacher Foster had them stand together in front of the windows. Miz Foster gave Myra a big bouquet of daisies to hold. Preacher Foster read some scriptures first. These were scriptures that Myra had never heard and were all about love. Then he started talking right to James.

"Brian James MacTavish, do you take Frances Elmyra Stuart to be your lawful wedded wife. Will you forsake all others, love and honor her for so long as you both shall live?"

James took her hand and looked right into her eyes and said loudly, "I do."

"Frances Elmyra Stuart, do you take Brian James MacTavish to be your lawful wedded husband. Will you forsake all others, love, honor, and obey him for so long as you both shall live?"

Myra said, "I do," but it was so low that she could not even hear it. The preacher must have heard something, because he went on with the service.

"Now by the authority vested in me by the State of Georgia and as a minister of the Lord God, I now pronounce you man and wife. What God has joined together, let no man put asunder."

Myra was married, but she was confused about why he said, "Let no man put in thunder." She thought it meant for them to stay out of storms. Later she learned that it meant a husband and wife should always be one. From this day on, it would be her and James together in everything.

When Preacher Foster told James that he could salute his bride, she was caught off guard when he gave her a big kiss right on the mouth.

Everyone laughed, clapped, and congratulated them again. James paid the preacher, and Mr. and Mrs. Brian James MacTavish got in the buggy and took off. James stopped at the same shade tree, which surprised her.

"Before we go any farther, I want to really kiss my bride."

He kissed her and kept right on kissing. He sure did seem to like kissing, and she guessed this was part of being married. When he finally pulled the reins for June to start going, she wondered where they were heading. Now it was the time to ask.

"James, where are we gonna live now that we are married?"

"First, we're goin' to Malcolm's. They are expectin' us for dinner. We're gonna stay at Pa's for right now. They got plenty of room. You'll like it there. It's close to town and to Malcolm's. I know you like to be with Olla. It'll just be 'til we get our own house built."

It would be nice to be close to Olla, but she didn't know about the rest. Anyway, she would soon find out. She had done the best that she could in a lot of new places in the past few years, so she figured she could do it again. James would be there to make it easier this time.

Malcolm and Olla were sitting on the porch waiting for them. Olla was nursing Tom, and Myra realized she had never seen her when she wasn't nursing the baby. Malcolm slapped James on the back, and Olla hugged and kissed Myra.

"You son of a gun, you really did it. I'm proud of ya."

"Myra, me and you are gonna be just like sisters. I've wished fer a sister like you ever since I've been here. Now y'all come on in and set down at the table. We're ready to eat."

Myra felt so happy and proud to be married to James, and she liked the thought of being like a sister to Olla. She hadn't thought about eating, but she was excited to sit down for dinner with her new family.

Right away, she saw that Olla was not much of a cook. She served a piece of beef that she had cooked with gravy. Myra had never eaten beef before, and she found it tough and hard to chew. It did have a good taste, and she though if she ever had some to cook, she would cook it all day if it took that long to make it tender. There was rice and gravy, but that didn't have much taste. She made her dinner on baked sweet tater and butter. Nobody could mess that up.

She had her first taste of store-bought light bread. She had seen it in the stores in Glencoe, but she always thought it cost too much. James and Malcolm both seemed to love it and ate most of the loaf. They drank milk and dipped the bread into the milk. James filled up on bread and milk. He didn't like Olla's cooking either. She couldn't wait to have her own kitchen and cook three good meals a day for him, but he would probably still want to buy light bread.

Right after dinner, James and Malcolm went to Glencoe to buy cigarettes. She was glad to have the chance to talk with Olla.

"Myra, you gonna have to learn that James likes to go off with Malcolm and leave us behind. Both of 'em gets tired of stayin' at home too long and like to go off together. It don't bother me and don't let it bother you. We know they'll always come back."

"Oh, I don't mind that one bit. I always liked to go off with my brothers."

"Myra, it ain't quite like that, but you'll get used to it. I did."

Myra didn't like the sound of this, so she changed the subject to find out more about Olla. She knew Olla had come from real religious folks because she wore long dresses that came nearly to her ankles and wore her hair long and pulled back in a ball. She looked like the ladies who helped carry on tent revivals. Those ladies seemed to think about nothing but the "Lord God Jehovah" just like Bunk did, but Olla liked to laugh and talk about all kinds of things.

"Are yore folks here in Glencoe?"

"Oh no, I was born and raised in Montgomery County, close to Kibbee. All my people are there."

"I ain't never heard of either place, but they sounds like a far piece off. How did you get all the way to here?"

"Malcolm come through buyin' timber fer his pa. He come in a store I wuz in, and we hit up to talkin'. We wuz havin' a camp meeting nearby, and he met me there that night. We hit it off. The next time he come through, he asked my pa if he could marry me. We married the next day, and I come back to Glencoe with him. I didn't know his pa was so well-off 'til I got here. We stayed with them 'til our house wuz built."

Myra didn't ask what that was like. She had always been one to want to make up her own mind. She knew when she married James, she married his folks too.

Myra went through everything that had happened in her life since Papa died and told how she had come to Glencoe to help Annie Lou. One part of the story really surprised Olla.

"I know Brother Bunk Block. Is yore uncle married to Sister Rachel and goes around spreading the gospel in travelin' tent revivals? He's got a pore boy what ain't right."

Myra knew that was him. Ever since he got healed, all he talked about was "the Lord God Jehovah. She was surprised to hear he was married again and preaching.

"Yes, that's him. The boy is my cousin, Izzy. He's not bright, but he's a good boy."

"Yea, Brother Bunk tells about his boy in his sermons. He says the Lord placed this burden on him, but he still sings the Lord's praises and serves Him. He tells about how he was healed from the demons in his body. He and Sister Rachel have healed a lot of folks."

Myra didn't have much faith in what Olla was telling her. If he could heal, she wondered why he didn't heal Izzy.

"They come near Glencoe every few months, so I'll watch out for 'em and let you know if I hear about them preachin' around here. Won't that be somethin' if I can take you to a revival where he's preachin'. Myra, are ya saved?"

Myra didn't answer, since she had never known what that meant. If it was like Annie Lou getting the spirit, it didn't amount to much. She didn't really care about seeing Bunk again, but she did want to see how Izzy was fairing. She owed that to Nannie.

Olla was so much fun to be with. She didn't seem to care about cleaning up the kitchen and just wanted to talk, laugh, and nurse Tom.

"Does Tom always nurse most of the time?"

"That's the only way to keep him from squalling. You'll see when ya start having 'em."

Myra hadn't thought about having her own babies, but she knew babies came to married folks. When she did have babies she thought she could do a right good job of raising them.

James and Malcolm came back just before sundown, and James was ready to leave and go to his pa's house. Before they left, Olla took her aside.

"Don't you worry about them, Myra. If I can take them, then you can too."

Myra didn't comment and just followed James to the buggy. The MacTavishes' house was a little piece up the road, but she was wishing it would take a long time to get there.

They pulled up right into the barn, and she sat in the buggy while James fed June and put her in the stall. James did not say a word on the ride or walking up to the house. The house was already shut up, but she could see lamplight through the windows. They had glass windows with curtains on them. She had never lived in a house like that, except for the time she stayed with Annie Lou. They walked right in and saw his ma, pa, and sister, Olieta, sitting up close to the fire. It didn't feel cold enough for a fire, but they had a nice one burning in their big fireplace. They didn't get up but just turned around to look at them. James finally spoke.

"This is Myra. We got married this morning."

He was talking in a little shaky voice that she had never heard before. None of them made any move toward her, but she had enough manners to know that you should do something when you are made acquainted.

She walked over to them and said, "I am pleased to meet you."

Miz MacTavish put out her hand but just kind of touched Myra's fingers.

Judge MacTavish (she had heard Annie Lou call him that) said, "Well, take her on to the back and let her put her stuff up."

Olieta didn't say or do anything. She just started looking back into the fire. James took her to the room that had been just for him. It was big enough and had a comfortable-looking bed with a spread on it, two chairs, a little table, and a chest to put clothes in. She saw that James had some clothes hanging on a hook behind the door. It was so clean and neat that it looked as if nobody ever stayed there.

"Myra, find a place to put yore things. Just push my stuff to the back. I'm goin' back to talk to Ma and Pa a bit. This did come as a surprise to them."

She just left her clothes in the little chest. She wasn't sure how long she would be staying there.

Since the door was open, she could hear them talking. The first voice she heard was Olieta.

"Where in God's name did you find that thing? I can't see why you thought you had to marry her and bring her here."

"I didn't marry her for you, Leita. I married her for me, because I love her more than anything on earth."

His voice still sounded low and shaky and nothing like she had ever heard from him. Leita sounded so mad when she spoke again that she sounded ready to kill Myra.

"Well, if you were trying to find a wife, you could have stood on the street corner blindfolded and picked out one better than that. She is some of that Washington County trash that is trying to take over Glencoe. She has no place in the MacTavish family."

"Son, we just want what is best for you. You have a place in this community as a MacTavish, and you need a wife that will be a help to you. You know, your pa can get you out of this if you want him to."

His ma sounded sad. James yelled out then and said awful things.

"God dammit it to hell. You all try to run my life, and I am tired of it. Myra is finer than any of you because she has a good heart. She is the only wife I will ever want, and if she doesn't suit you, then we will just pull out and make it on our own."

Myra's heart stopped then, because she thought about Papa and how he had lost his family over Ma. She would not let that happen because she knew they loved him and he loved them. She was about ready to slip out the back door and leave when she heard Judge MacTavish start to talk. He didn't raise his voice, but every word was easy to hear.

"James is a man and a smart man. If this girl suits him, then she suits us. She is a fine-looking young woman and should make him a good wife. This family needs some new bloodlines. Just look at how all the young'uns are starting to look so scrawny. She will give him a fine family, I know. Now I don't want to hear another word about it. You will take her in and make her part of this family."

"Well, after we had to take in Olla, I thought we had done enough."

"Olieta, that is enough. You keep your mouth shut unless you have something good to say. Talk like that has kept you sitting by our fire when you should have a home and family of your own."

She heard Olieta running down the hall and sobbing loudly. Even though Myra thought Olieta got what she deserved, she wouldn't hold anything against her. That was not her way, but she knew this wouldn't be the end of it between Olieta and her. James came into the room in a few minutes and seemed his old self. He was smiling and joking.

"They've already ate supper, but Ma said for us to go in the kitchen and help ourself. She don't fire up the stove for supper, but there is always plenty to eat."

Miz MacTavish was in the kitchen and gave Myra a weak smile. That was probably the best she could do, but at least she was trying.

She set out a pitcher of milk and some light bread and said, "I'm sorry I haven't got better for you. This is all James eats for supper, anyway."

"This is fine, ma'am. I ain't much hungry."

James did just like he had at dinner and ate several slices of bread dipped in the milk. Before going to their room, James showed her how to get to the toilet and drew a bucket of water to put in the pitcher in their room. He lit the lamp and then went back to check on June. Myra bathed off, slipped off her dress, and got into the big feather bed.

When James came back, he blew out the lamp, slipped off his clothes, and got into bed beside her. They lay still for a minute but not for long. In a short time, she knew a lot about being married. She learned real quick that looking a fellow right in the eye didn't have a thing to do with anything.

~13~

The smell and feel of James beside her and the soft featherbed put her into the sound sleep of her childhood. She awoke to the crowing of roosters. She sat up and could see the first light starting to show. James wasn't in the room, but she could hear him talking somewhere nearby. The good smell of coffee was coming from the kitchen.

She looked out the window for the roosters and didn't see any. The ones she heard were from houses down the road. After dressing quickly, she headed to the kitchen to help with breakfast. The voices of Olieta and James stopped her outside the door.

"Leita, there ain't no need in you carrying on like this. Myra will be a big help to you and Ma with the cooking and cleaning. She wants to work, and she's a fine cook."

"Well, she won't cook in my kitchen. This kitchen is not big enough for me to stay far enough away from her."

The kitchen was the biggest one Myra had ever seen, so she couldn't understand what Olieta meant by that.

"Well, just suit yourself, but you are only making it harder on you and Ma."

That was the last they said, and after waiting a few minutes, Myra walked into the kitchen. James grinned from ear to ear when he saw her.

"Come on in and eat breakfast with me. I just can't stay in the bed after sunup, and I wake up hungry."

He was eating light bread and wrapping it around slices of ham. She started to eat the same thing, but she knew quickly that she would rather have a good biscuit than store-bought light bread. The MacTavishes seem to have everything they wanted, but they sure didn't eat as good as the Stuarts! James finished up and asked her to walk with him to the buggy.

"I won't be back home 'til supper. I can't close the store during dinner 'cause that's when a lot of folks come in. I just grab a bite in town."

"What do you want me to do all day while you're gone?"

"Ma will most likely need you to help her with something, and you can go to see Olla."

She didn't look forward to spending the day with his ma and sister, and she would miss him. Her eyes filled with tears, and he pulled her close in his arms.

"Honey, I will shore miss you, and I'll think about you all day. I want you all fixed up pretty and waitin' fer me tonight. Now I gotta go make us some money."

He gave her a kiss and cracked the rein for June to take off.

She hated to go back into the house, but there was nothing else to do. Miz MacTavish and Judge MacTavish were eating breakfast at the kitchen table.

"Good morning," Myra mumbled. Both of them looked up and nodded to her.

Olieta was standing by the stove and made an ugly grunt noise and looked at her as though she was full of maggots. Myra decided right then and there that she would stand up to her sister-in-law. She was as good as anyone, even a MacTavish. Actually, she was a MacTavish.

Judge MacTavish pulled out a chair beside him, and she plopped herself down at the table.

"Miz MacTavish, I like to keep myself busy, and I know how to do most everything. Can I do somethin' to help with the house today?"

"Do you mind ironing?"

"No'um, I love to iron and smell the fresh-washed clothes."

"James and the judge go through a pile of shirts, and it's hard for Olieta to stay ahead of them."

"I love to iron shirts best of all. When I ironed fer my brothers, I put 'em up on hangers." She almost told her mother-in-law about her laundry business but decided that was somethin' best kept to herself.

"There's plenty of wood to keep the stove going to heat up the irons. I appreciate you helping out like this."

"Since the stove will be goin' all mornin' anyway, how about me cookin' a pot of somethin' fer dinner and make up some biscuits?"

Miz MacTavish seemed to think for a minute and then said, "You know that is a mighty good idea. Go in the pantry and see what there is, and I will try to find anything else that you need."

Myra cut her eyes over to see how Olieta had taken all that, but she wasn't anywhere to be seen.

The pantry was lined with jars of about anything she might need. A big side of ham was hanging from the rafter and a croker sack was filled with dried peas in the shell. One shelf was full of sweet taters, onions, and Irish taters. She looked in the barrels and found flour, rice, sugar, and lard. There was as much food in that pantry as in most stores.

She put the irons on to heat and then started to work on dinner. She had a happy morning in the kitchen all by herself. Every once in a while, she heard talking from the front rooms. She would iron awhile and then tend to the cooking. When she was ironing James's shirts, she could sniff his good smell. It felt good to know she was taking care of him. When she finished with the ironing, she went to ask Miz MacTavish what to do with the shirts.

"I'll come back and put them in the right rooms." She walked back to the kitchen with Myra.

"Oh, these look so nice. I don't see any little wrinkles, even around the collars. James will love his shirts. You probably know how particular he is."

"Yes'um, I know he likes his shirts starched stiff. I've always been proud of my ironing."

"My, somethin' does smell good." For the first time, she had a smile when she looked at Myra.

As Myra was finishing up dinner and putting it on the table, there was a little knock at the back door. She opened the door to see Olla holding Tom. He was completely wrapped up in a shawl, so Myra knew he was nursing.

"I just hadda come to check on ya. How has it been here with them by yoreself?"

"I've been fine. I've been busy ironin' and cookin' dinner."

"Ya ain't sayin' Olieta's lettin' ya cook in her kitchen!"

"Olieta didn't have nothin' to do with it. This has been between me and Miz MacTavish. And they's something else, Miss Old Maid Olieta is fixin' to learn I'm James's wife, not her!"

Olla looked in all the pots, Myra could tell she wished she was eating with them. If it had been her house, she would have insisted that Olla stay and eat, but that might not be a good idea. She had heard enough to know Olla and Olieta weren't on good terms.

"There's plenty fer ya to have some. I'll fix ya a plate to take home. I want ya to try feedin' Tom some sweet taters. Mash 'em up real good, and maybe it will hold him longer before he has to nurse. That's how we fed the babies in my family."

Olla took the plate and left without seeing the others. Myra walked to the front room to tell them to come to dinner. Judge MacTavish had just come home and was sitting with them. Olieta jumped up and started walking down the hall to the bedrooms.

"I am too sick to eat a bite. Just smelling that mess she was cooking has turned my stomach."

"Suit yoreself." Myra looked her straight in the eye and turned to walk to the kitchen. The judge and Miz MacTavish followed her.

Just as they sat down at the table, James came rushing through the back door.

"I said to myself, 'Why would a married man like me let a store keep him away from eatin' dinner with his bride.' *Ummm*, whatever we're havin' shore smells good."

"Myra, cooked it all, James, and she did a big ironing besides. You gonna love your shirts." Miz MacTavish seemed as happy with the morning as Myra.

Nobody said anything about Olieta not being at the table. The table was filled with stewed tomatoes, rice, fried side meat, big fluffy biscuits, and sweet tater custard. They all seemed to enjoy every bite, and James didn't even ask for light bread. She could tell he was proud of her, and that made her even happier.

"Honey, that dinner was shore worth coming home for. I just couldn't stay away from you all day. Come and walk me to the buggy."

They walked out with his arm around her. He gave her another big hug and kiss and hurried back to open the store.

The kitchen was empty when she came back, so she cleaned up the kitchen and even mopped the floor. She thought back to the first time she had cooked dinner and cleaned up Miz Sara's kitchen. Instead of crying from those thoughts, she giggled and had a happy feeling.

The house was quiet, so she realized that everybody was taking a nap. The bedroom doors were closed. She tiptoed close to Olieta's room and could hear her snoring worse than a mule. Olla would get a laugh about that, so she decided to go to visit her.

It was a surprise to find Olla outside sweeping the yard. She seemed really excited and couldn't wait to tell her about Tom.

"Ya shore told me a good thing to do. I mashed up that tater and fed him. He pure loved it. Afterward, I figgered I'd still have to nurse him to get him to sleep. He fell right asleep 'fore I could even get it in his mouth. That wuz right after I left ya, and he's slept ever since."

"I'm glad. I know that's a help to ya. Didn't ya know that somethin' solid would fill him up more and last longer than nursin'?"

"I had wondered about that but just didn't know when wuz the time to do it."

"Nobody ever told me either, but I figgered when a baby got some teeth, it was time to feed 'em more. That's when I started feedin' my baby sister, Dolly."

The leaves were ankle deep all over the yard. Olla hadn't got much done so Myra pitched in to help. The work went faster when one raked and one piled up the leaves. As they worked, they talked and joked. Myra told her about hearing Olieta snore like a mule. Olla started mocking and sounded just like her.

"You just wait 'til summer when ya have to sit on the porch with her. She sits up ramrod straight in the chair, and every once in a while, she'll lift up one hip. Then ya better hold yore nose, 'cause what she let's out is worse than a mule."

They laughed until the tears ran down their cheeks.

When they finished raking, they moved the piles of leaves far away from the house, drew buckets of water, and burned the leaves. They stood and watched until the last ember stopped burning, and then covered the spot with sand.

Olla threw up her hands and said, "Lord, help me. I plum forgot about Tom."

They ran inside and found him still sleeping as soundly as when they left him. Myra knew this was the first time the poor little fellow had ever been really filled up. Olla was such a frail and skinny little thing that Myra doubted her milk could be very rich.

"I'm proud as I can be of him sleepin' like this. What else can I feed him?"

"Crumble up biscuit or corn bread in buttermilk."

"All I got is the store-bought bread. Will that do? I ain't never knowed how to bake bread."

"Well, startin' tomorrow you will. As soon as I can get away from the house, I will be down here to show you how to make biscuits."

Myra hadn't thought about how long she had been away. Being with Olla almost seemed like being with Annie, and Myra enjoyed every minute. From the way the shadows were looking, she knew she had better head back to the MacTavishes' and see if they wanted help with supper or anything else.

She hurried back and found Olieta sitting on the front porch, all wrapped up because the air was a little coldish. As she walked up the steps, Olieta let out a loud grunt.

"It is about time you drug your sorry self back. I guess you're just used to walking off and not letting anybody know where you are or what you're up to."

"I've just been down to Olla's. I didn't tell anybody 'cause y'all wuz all sleepin' when I left. Is somethin' wrong?"

"Not long after you left, some puny-looking ol' boy came up to the door looking for you. I could tell there was something not right about him, but I didn't know where to tell him to find you. I'm not about to get mixed up in your messing. That's why I'm sittin' out here in the cold. I'm waiting for James so I can give him the straight story."

"I don't know what there is to tell, but I sure wish you knew more about who was lookin' fer me." Myra was a little worried.

Miz MacTavish didn't need help with supper. There was plenty left over from the big dinner. She seemed to be pleased when Myra told her about helping Olla and about Tom sleeping after he ate the sweet tater.

"You are right about feeding him more. You go on and help Olla all that you can. She sure needs some help. I think she didn't have much raising."

There was talking on the front porch, and she walked out to see James and Will Rob talking to Olieta. Then she knew it had been Will Rob who came looking for her, so she knew he needed her for something.

"Hit's Arno, Myra. He ain't come home yet. Most of his clothes are gone. I've looked all over town, and I don't know where he could be. Ma's 'bout to go crazy. Myra, I was hopin' you'd have some idea where he might've went to."

"I ain't seen him, but I do know that he kept talkin' to me about wantin' to go places and see things."

"The first place I thought to look fer him wuz here with you, but when I couldn't find ya, I went to ask James if he'd seen him. We hunted all over town and couldn't find him."

"Myra, you say he talked about going off someplace? Did he have any money?" James seemed to think that was important.

"No, he didn't—no, wait a minute, he did have all the nickels I paid him fer deliverin' the clothes."

"Get in the buggy. We didn't check at the depot."

The three of them got in, and James drove real fast to get there before the depot closed for the night.

"Lynwood, did a slight-built, blond-headed boy about—how old is he, Myra?"

"He's almost thirteen."

"Well, did a boy like that come in here today?"

"Yea, the boy that used to bring the laundry to town in the wagon. I sold him a ticket on the first train out this morning. He paid fer it all in nickels."

"Where was that train goin'?"

"It would end up in Augusta, but it goes through Swainsboro and Louisville, but he was gonna have to change to another train in Louisville to get where he wanted."

"Where was that?"

"Sandersville."

"That's close to Tennille. Arno went home. I bet he tried to find Uncle Joe Early. I feel better to know where he is." Myra thought that was the best thing that Arno could have done if he had to run off.

"There isn't anything more we can do tonight. Let's go home. Will Rob, can I take you home?"

"Nah, I feel like walkin' home. I ain't too ready to tell that to Ma. I shore am thankful to ya fer yore help."

"Don't mention it. I'm glad to do what I can. After all, y'all are my family now too. I am hoping to get me an automobile before much longer. When I do, we'll go over there and look for him."

They rode home in the buggy, and Myra felt contented knowing that James was there to help her.

"James, I shore thank ya fer helpin' us find out about Arno. I think he's gonna be all right with Uncle Joe Early, but I shore will miss him."

"Myra, I'm your husband, and I will always be there when you need me."

She and Will Rob had always done the best they could, but James knew how to get things done.

They sat down to eat the leftovers, and she found out right then that Mr. James MacTavish thought he was too good to eat cold supper. He pushed the plate aside and brought out the light bread and milk. There wasn't anything she could do about it now, but she vowed to herself that as soon as she had her own kitchen, he would never have to eat a cold supper.

After James went to sleep, she lay there thinking over her first day of married life. She had learned a lot about being a MacTavish. She could make James a good wife and be a help to him. She knew that she did care for him, and she knew he cared as much about her. He really liked kissing, hugging, and all that other stuff. She didn't mind it too much, but she never had been one to do a lot of hugging and all, even to the little young'uns in her family. She thought about Arno and wished she had hugged him a little. Nobody ever seemed to pay him any attention, and maybe that is what he ran off to try to find. She hoped he would, and every night she would ask the Lord to watch over him.

The next morning at daybreak, Myra popped out of bed. She had hoped to beat James up, because she wanted to get to the kitchen first and have breakfast ready. She beat the rooster but not James. He was already standing by the washstand in his underdrawers. He was shaving and cussing because he kept cutting himself. Myra had to laugh. It was a funny sight, but he didn't seem to think it was anything to laugh about.

She dressed and headed to the kitchen, but Olieta was already there and had coffee on and ham frying.

"Good mornin', is there anything I can do to help with breakfast?"

"Huh, the best thing for you to do is stay out of my way. I'm not putting up with your tricks today like I did yesterday."

"What tricks? What're ya talkin' about?"

"You just keep out of my way for the rest of the time you're here. That won't be much longer. James will get enough of you before you can say jack shit, and you will be gone just like all the others."

Myra felt a sob coming, but she stifled it quickly. Olieta was not going to get the best of her. She felt like laughing in her face. For someone who thought she was so high and mighty, she sure had a filthy mouth.

James came into the kitchen, and as soon as Olieta saw him, she changed her tune and was all sweet-talking to him. James ate quickly, and Myra almost choked on every bite. She walked to the buggy with him without saying a word. He knew there was something wrong, but he didn't seem to want to hear about it.

Instead he said, "Myra, you and Olieta are just going to have to get along better. You are worrying me and Ma, and I want you to quit it."

She hadn't said a word to him about his sister, so she knew that Olieta must have told him something about her. When he drove off, she went behind the barn and let the tears come out. She hadn't felt this lonely or sad in a long time. After she got her cry out, she knew that she had to make the best of things and make a place in the family somehow.

She walked back to the kitchen with her head held high. Olieta stood blocking the door.

"Just git. This is my kitchen and it's going to be my house when Ma and Pa are gone. I don't want you in my kitchen or my house. I am a MacTavish, and you will never be one."

Myra had heard enough and wasn't taking any more. She bowed up and was ready for the fight that had to come.

"Yes, I am a MacTavish, and I will be one long after your old bony toes are sticking up. I don't want to be in yore house, and I won't be much longer. I've got news for you. When I leave this house, James will be leaving with me, and we just might not ever come back."

She turned and walked out. She didn't know where Miz MacTavish or Judge MacTavish was, so she knew the best thing to do was get away for a while. She headed down to Olla's and got there just as Malcolm was starting to leave for his store. Olla knew there was something wrong, but she waited until he was gone to ask. Myra told her the whole story.

"Myra, I could strangle her for treatin' you like that, but she's been just as mean and ugly to me. Just be thankful that the rest of the family is not like that. Grace is a little like Olieta, but Ada, Jane, Molly, and the others are fine folks. I don't know what to tell you, except that you can't win against Olieta. She always finds how to get her way."

Myra knew the best way to put this out of her mind was to get busy and help Olla. After cleaning up the house, they started the cooking lessons. Biscuits came first. Myra couldn't see how something that came so easy to her was so hard for Olla. The only cooking she knew how to do was fry meat, which she usually burned to a crisp. Myra could help her learn to make some things, but Olla just wasn't cut out to be a good cook.

Since there wasn't anything more to talk about, they started singing as they worked. Olla loved all the gospel songs, and their voices sounded pretty good together.

"You know, Myra, I hope Brother Block comes close by here soon, and we'll just make James and Malcolm take us. I hope hits a revival that goes on all week, and one night they's dinner on the ground."

"Well, you listen out fer that. I don't know nothin' about such." Myra didn't care about the meeting, but she would love to see Izzy again.

For dinner, they ate Olla's biscuits with syrup. Myra broke up one in buttermilk and fed to Tom. He didn't seem to know the difference in a good biscuit and Olla's.

After dinner, Olla was sweeping off the front porch, and she yelled to Myra.

"Myra, come quick. Something must be bad wrong up at the MacTavish." Myra came out just in time to see James's buggy fly past with Malcolm sitting beside him. Olla grabbed Tom, and they followed the buggy. Near the house they could hear awful screaming and crazy noises. Grace was sitting on the porch with her ma and pa.

"That is old Dr. Youmans buggy. He delivered Tom, so I know him."

"What's wrong?" Myra knew it was bad if the doctor was there.

"You ought to know. You caused it."

"Now, Grace, there is no need for that. Girls, Olieta has had a bad nervous spell. It is the worst one she has ever had. James is in there trying to help her to get ahold of herself. He usually is the only one who can calm her. There isn't anything you can do, so why don't you all just take the baby on back home and wait."

Myra thought that was the best thing to do too. She was shaking all over as they walked back down the road. She hadn't really done anything to Olieta, but she had said angry words to her.

"Lord, Olla, I ain't been in the family but three days, and already I've got myself in a mess."

"Don't you worry. She deserved every word that you said and more. She'll be all right. I've seen her pull these spells but not quite this bad. She's gonna keep on 'til she comes between you and James. Don't you let her."

"How did you keep her from comin' between you and Malcolm?"

"Hit wasn't hard fer me. She don't dote on Malcolm like she does James."

"There goes the doctor leavin'. I'm goin' back up to the house. It's my home too."

She walked back up the road to the house and met Malcolm coming down the steps.

"How is she?"

"She's settled down some. The doctor gave her some nerve medicine, and she went to sleep. I'm drivin' James's buggy back to town. She wants him right by her bed."

Myra knew Miss Olieta's scheme, but there wasn't anything she could do about it right then. She would find a way to beat her at her own game. No way would she let Olieta come between her and James.

Miz MacTavish and Grace were in the kitchen cooking a little dinner, but it was really getting closer to suppertime. She went in and asked if she could do anything.

Miz MacTavish looked up and said, "Myra, when Leita gets better, I want you to promise me that you won't aggravate her anymore. Her nerves are just not in any shape to take a lot of quarreling."

"Miz MacTavish, I don't even know what happened."

Neither of them said anything else to her, so after standing there for a while, she went back out to the porch.

Olieta did get better, or at least she got over that spell. From that day on, Myra tried to keep her mouth shut around Olieta, no matter what she said. She tried to explain what happened to James, but he seemed to think Olieta should be taken care of over everything else.

"She means a lot to me and always will. She's always taken care of me ever since I was a baby. You just got to understand the sad things that have happened in her life and try to help her all you can.

"You don't know this, but Olieta was a twin. Ovieda was her sister, and they say they were born just a minute apart. The twin sisters were so close and pure worshipped each other. While they were still girls, Ovieda took the fever and died real sudden. That broke Olieta's heart, and she has just needed special care ever since."

Myra didn't say her thoughts to him, but to her way of thinking, bad things happened to a lot of people, and they had still managed to go on living and not take it out on others. Olieta and Ma seemed a lot alike in that way. Maybe some people just don't have the get-up-and-go like others. Somehow she would find a way to live under the same roof with her, until they got their own place. A few days later, she asked James about the plans for building their house.

"Pa's already marked off the land for me and promised to give me the lumber to build it. It'll be spring before they can start working on it because of the cold weather. Now don't keep nagging me about it."

He saw Myra's look of disappointment and changed his mood. He grabbed her hand and said, "Come on and let's go look at our place."

Their land was about a quarter of a mile from the MacTavish house and down the road toward town. Malcolm's house was in the same direction, but it was closer to the MacTavish house. His sister Ada lived about the same distance down the road in the other direction. She was glad to be that close to Olla and farther away from Olieta. As they walked down the road, James was laughing and talking like his old self.

"I want you to start thinking about what you want in the house."

"Oh, I know that I want a big kitchen and a pantry with plenty of room to store my canned goods. I want enough room to eat in the kitchen . . ."

"You planning on doing a lot of canning, aren't you?"

"Looks like there will be plenty of space fer me to grow a big garden. I'll want chickens and a cow. There ain't no need in buying milk and eggs. 'Sides, the fresher, the better."

"Now, Myra, you ain't making no farmer out of me." He laughed and slapped his sides.

"You don't need to worry. I will take care of everything. I've always done it."

It was a pretty place and about three acres. There were a lot of big trees that she wanted to keep to shade the porch.

James took a stick and drew all the rooms off in the dirt. He wanted five rooms with a front and back porch. That sounded wonderful, and she could just picture them sitting on the porch after supper every evening. He even showed her where he wanted to put the well and the toilet. It didn't seem real that she would have such a nice home of her very own. She would make it a good home, and they would be happy. If she could just keep thinking about the new house, she could stay out of trouble for the rest of the time that she had to live in the same house with Leita.

Things did settle down between them. Christmas was coming, and she found that all the MacTavishes put a lot into it. They had been going to church in Glencoe, but she asked James if they could go to North Connolly for their Christmas program. She wanted to see Annie Lou, and she hoped Dolly would be in the program.

"Yep, we can do that. We'll leave early enough to go by and see yore ma and Will Rob on the way. Go to Miz Rosenberg's and buy some of that thread for yore sewin' and make up some Christmas presents. Just tell her to put it on my bill."

She had been trying to think of what she could give for presents. Now she would have gifts to give and work to keep her busy. Since the quarrel, she had let Olieta do all the cooking and ironing. It was hard on her to just sit around with nothing to do.

The next day she rode into Glencoe with James and went to Rosenberg's. Miz Rosenberg met her at the door.

"Come in, little lady. Congratulations to you and James. You walked off with the prized catch of Glencoe."

Myra felt so proud to know that Miz Rosenberg remembered her. From that moment on, there was a bond between them.

"Thank you, ma'am. James is lettin' me buy some crochet thread from ya. I'm gonna make Christmas presents. He said he will come by and pay ya."

"That's fine. You pick out what you want."

It took her awhile to decide, because she loved every color. Finally, she decided on some dark shades of green, blue, and red.

"You made some good choices. Since it is winter, those dark colors will look lovely. Are there any babies that you plan to give a gift?"

"Oh, yes'sum. I did forget about Tom."

"I just got in this light blue thread. Isn't it soft? It's just right for a baby. It comes in pink too."

"Oh, that is so pretty, but I hadn't ever made anything fer a baby. They don't use scarves."

"You could make a little blanket, but what I'd make is a sweater or cap. The directions are on the back of the thread."

Myra didn't want to tell her that she couldn't read. There were some pictures, so she knew she could figure it out. First, she'd make the cap and see how that went.

"I do want this, and I want a roll of the pink. I can make a cap fer my little sister."

She couldn't wait to get back to the store and show James what she had bought. She looked in the front window before she went inside, and the sick feeling came back. The same girl who had been in the store before was sitting on the edge of the counter. She and James were talking and laughing. He had told her about being a businessman and the girl being a customer, but it still just didn't seem right. She didn't want to walk in on them, so she walked back down the street and watched until she was gone.

She decided that she would not say anything about it. Maybe there wasn't anything wrong with what she saw, but she didn't like it a bit. James did look a little sheepish when she walked in.

A man and woman were standing at the counter with several purchases, and James kept right on waiting on them.

"I'm busy right now, Myra. When I finish up, I'll drive you home. I hope you got what you need."

"I did. You don't need to close up to drive me home. I feel like walking, and it's not very cold."

He just nodded his head to show it was all right with him. She did notice that the man and woman were buying a lot more than the girl, and he didn't seem to be nearly as friendly with them. In fact, come to think of it, the girl didn't buy anything as far as she could see.

The weather turned real cold, and she spent a lot of time working on her crocheting while she sat by Olla's fire. They had begun to feel as close as sisters to each other. When she offered to help at the MacTavishes', Olieta would not let her do a thing.

She tried to keep her promise to get along with her sister-in-law, but sometimes she had to say something back when Olieta said mean things right to her face. Whenever this happened, Olieta would meet James at the door and tell him how "that ol' gal of yours" was worrying her into a nervous breakdown.

James didn't say much to Myra about it. What troubled her most of all was that she knew exactly which side he was taking. Some nights he was real late getting home, and often she could smell the sweet little drops he used to cover up when he had been drinking. He never seemed to be drunk, like she remembered Bunk. Usually, he was in a good and playful mood, but she still didn't like it.

On the Sunday before Christmas, North Connolly would have preaching, a program, a big dinner, and Christmas tree. They invited Olla and Malcolm to go with them. Nothing was said about James's ma and pa or Olieta going, and she was really thankful for that. She worked in Olla's kitchen to make a syrup cake, apple tarts, and a big chicken pie to take for the dinner. Every year people came from all around, because it was really done up right.

James was late closing the store the Saturday night before the program at North Connolly, and again he came in with the sweet clove smell that was supposed to cover up the smell of whiskey. It didn't really help because when she smelled cloves, she knew he had been drinking whiskey. Olla didn't seem to mind when Malcolm drank and keep telling her that all the MacTavish men seemed to like their liquor. It still scared Myra, because she remembered the shape that Bunk got in. When James finally walked in, he was in a real happy mood and told her about all the sales he had made that day, because people were buying for Christmas.

Just when she was getting ready to let him have it for being so late and for drinking, he let her know what a good man he could be. He opened a big sack and brought out snuff and stick candy he had bought for Ma. He pulled out a little bow tie for Will Rob and candy for Dolly. The last thing was a little small sack for her.

"Open it. I want you to wear it to church tomorrow."

Myra opened the sack and pulled out a clasp for holding her hair. It was shiny white and had little bits of sparkly stones all across it.

"Oh, James, I've looked at this in Miz Rosenberg's showcase. I never could have dreamed to own it. How did you know how much I loved this?"

"I have my ways. Now that ain't no cheap thing. It's made out of ivory, and that comes from elephants."

Myra never knew when he was kidding. Elephant or no elephant, it was the prettiest thing she had ever owned.

He pulled her hair back and fastened it on, and then he said, "Myra, I never thought that anything could make your hair any prettier, but this just sets it off."

She was so full of feelings then that she just broke down and cried.

"What's wrong, darlin'? I thought you would be happy with your present."

"Nothing ain't wrong. Everything's right. You are the best husband in the world, and I love you so much." That shocked them both because she had never said those words before.

The day at North Connolly was really fine. It was so good to see Annie Lou, Dolly, and James's sister, Jane, again. She couldn't believe how much Dolly had grown. Horace held her on his lap all through church and acted like her real pa. Myra gave Annie Lou a green scarf and she put it around her neck as if she was proud of it. The pink cap just fit Dolly and looked pretty on her dark hair.

Ma and Will Rob were glad to see them, but neither one had much to say. She hated to leave them alone while she went off to have a good time. She knew Ma didn't care about doing anything, but Will Rob needed to get out with people and maybe meet someone.

During Christmas Day, most of the MacTavish family came by the house. Two colored women had come in and helped cook food, and the table was spread full all day. Every time some of the family came, they filled a plate and ate. The food was good, but Myra knew she could have cooked some of it better if Olieta had let her help. She met two more of James's sisters, Hannah and Callie. She liked them just fine, and they weren't a bit like Olieta.

When she gave out her scarves, Olla and Miz MacTavish were real proud. They bragged on her work, and both thought Tom looked so nice in his blue cap. Olieta didn't so much as nod when Myra gave her the red scarf. Actually, she picked out the prettiest one for her just for spite.

Myra knew that Olieta was just laying low and ready to jump on her at any time. When she saw Myra wearing the hair clasp from James, she mumbled something about seeing the same one on one of those Chalker gals. Myra knew what that meant. Then she got to saying things under her breath, just loud enough to be heard.

"He's about had his fill. I can see the signs. She won't be around for long.

"There's better out there, and he knows it.

"Trash—trash—throw out the trash.

"MacTavish, that's what I am. MacTavish, and that's what she will never be."

About the middle of January, Myra had been shut up in the house and had been listening to Olieta too long. One morning she decided to talk to James about moving someplace now instead of waiting for their house to be built. Before she hardly got started, James pitched a fit.

"I have had all I am going to take about you and Olieta fussing. Dammit to hell, I got where I pure hate to come home. If it ain't you telling me what she's done, it's her telling me what you've done or said.

"I got more important things to do with my time than listen to y'all acting like two old setting hens. I asked you to be patient with her, but that just ain't in you. I ask you—no, I am telling you. You have got to stop causing trouble like this. Leita has been here all her life, and you have just moved in. You have to treat her better."

Then he stormed out of the house and headed into town.

This was the time Myra knew she had to stand up for herself. She wasn't about to hang back and take that kind of treatment when she knew she had done nothing wrong. It was taking a chance, but she knew she had to put James's love to the test.

"If Olieta wants me out of her house that is just where I am going. Thank God I do have a place to go to."

She put a few of her things in a little bag and left through the back door before anyone knew she was gone. She wanted to stop at Olla's, but it would be best if she did not know anything. She headed toward Armity. It was a cold day, but she was walking so fast that she didn't feel the cold. She made a wide circle, so she didn't have to walk through town. She was trying to get as much distance between her and Olieta as fast as she could.

It took over an hour to get to Ma's house. She walked in and just sat down by the fire. Ma didn't ask why she was there, and Myra didn't tell her. They just sat there looking into the fire and rocking until time for dinner. She went to the kitchen to see what she could find for them to eat. There was such a knot in her stomach that she couldn't eat a bite, but she wanted to get something for Ma. When she walked into the kitchen, she could see how her brother was taking care of Ma. He left a plate of dried peas and corn bread sitting on the back of the stove, and he had poured a glass of buttermilk. He was trying to make sure Ma had something to eat.

From this, Myra knew Ma was going back to when she did nothing but sit and stare. She felt bad that he had to take care of her by himself. It also made her even madder to think that Olieta was so selfish and only thought about herself. Myra knew she would never take care of her ma or pa like this—even if she was a high-class MacTavish.

She brought the dinner out, and Ma ate without saying a word. Myra only drank a glass of buttermilk. They just kept sitting and rocking until middle of the afternoon when Will Rob came home. He was shocked to see her and wanted to know why she was there. She wasn't going to lie to him, so she told him what had happened. He didn't have much to say, but his eyes got real beady like they always did when he was mad. He started trying to make her feel better by acting like old times.

"Myra, I am so hungry fer sammons and grits like you used to make in Sullivan's Corner. Can you still make that?"

"Shore, if I have the sammons"

"Let's walk to the store at the crossroads and buy a can. It'll taste good on this chilly night."

They took off together, and it felt good just being with him and knowing how much he wanted to help her. Even the little crossroads store seemed welcoming to her.

"Myra, have you ever done a punchboard?"

"I ain't never heard of such."

"This store's got one, and I really like to do it. Here's a nickel fer you to take a punch."

He turned to a big board filled with circles to be punched out to find your number. She punched and got the number 342, and her luck was good. She won a little chalk horse.

"You are lucky. That's the best thing I've ever seen anyone win. Most folks just win a piece of candy or nothing."

"Maybe this is the beginnin' of better luck fer me."

He bought the can of salmon, a few other things, and a cola for each of them.

"The way you're spendin' money must mean you're doin' real well with yore carpentry."

"I'm makin' cabinets, and I have all the work I can do. I've quit the funeral parlor and only make a coffin now and then. You just can't keep on goin' to funerals almost every day."

They walked back home talking about old times and laughing about some of the things they did as young'uns.

"Do you know anything about Jesse and Joe Wiley?"

"I heard from a feller that they had another baby. It's a boy, and they call him Peachey. I reckon it's got a better name, but that wuz all the feller knew. I'm 'bout ready to bring Jesse back to live with us. I'd like fer him to learn to do somethin' besides work in the fields. He could help out with Ma."

"What could you get fer him to do? You know he ain't near as smart as Arno. I shore think about Arno and wish I knew how he's getting along."

"Knowing Arno, I 'spect he's doin' just fine. I reckon I could let Jesse work with me, but I don't know if he's smart enough to really do carpentry."

"Learnin' to grow the tobackey might just be the best fer him. You know how Ma always treated him. I know Flossie is good to him."

When they got to the house, James's buggy was parked in front. He was inside sitting by the fire with Ma. Myra didn't know what to expect when she walked inside, but he grinned at her.

"Well, Miss Myra, you decided to show out a little, didn't you. Are you ready to go home now?"

"I am home. I've always tried to do the best that I could no matter what was going on around me, but if yore sister don't want me in that house, then I ain't gonna stay there one more day. I will just stay here 'til you decide if you want to get us another place. If you want to stay there under Olieta's coattail, then I'll just stay on here."

He was surprised to hear her speak up like that. She looked around and saw that Ma and Will Rob had gone back into the kitchen. James looked at her with the saddest eyes, and when he started to speak, his voice broke.

"Myra, if it has been that bad for you, I don't want you to stay there another day. I will not spend another day or night without you. How about cooking some supper for all of us, and I will make up some plans during that time."

Will Rob had started a fire in the stove, so she went into the kitchen and fixed the salmon, grits, and hot biscuits. She chopped up a lot of onion in the salmon because James would like that. They sat down to eat, and in no time, James had Ma and Will Rob smiling and laughing. He really enjoyed the salmon and asked why she hadn't cooked it for him before.

"James, you know good and well that Olieta wouldn't let onions stink up the MacTavish kitchen."

James laughed and shook his head at that. She cleaned up the kitchen while James kept sitting at the table. Ma and Will Rob went back by the fire. When she finished up, he asked her to sit down with him.

"Well, Miz Mac, how does this sound to you? We will go to Malcolm's and bunk up with them tonight. Tomorrow I am going to buy us a bedstead and mattress, and we will put it up at their house. I will start looking for us a place in town. Olieta is still my sister, and I care a lot about her. I don't want bad feelings between you and her, but I promise you that you do not have to live with her anymore."

Those were the sweetest words she had ever heard. She hadn't unpacked her bag, so they went right to the buggy and started driving back to Glencoe in the pitch-black dark.

"Don't worry about driving in the dark. June knows the way back, and anyway, mares can see in the dark just like cats."

She never knew when he was kidding, but they made it back to Olla's just fine. Nobody talked about why they were going to stay there, but everybody knew. Olla fixed a pallet on the floor, and that was the best bed Myra had since she had been married. She gave Olla the little horse to keep for Tom when he got older.

-14-

J ames kept his word and bought a bed, mattress, and linens the next day. They set it up in Olla's little shed room. With the bed, their clothes and the two of them, the room was so cramped they could hardly turn around. James wasn't used to getting around in such tight spots, so he kept bumping into things. She laughed at him, but she had to keep it quiet because he wouldn't have liked that one bit. Olla and Malcolm seemed glad to have them, but it really bothered James to be there.

Everything seemed fine to Myra until one morning when she woke up with the sickest feeling. She started throwing up before she could make it outside. She thought it might be from the pork she had eaten the night before, but the sickness kept on. For the next few weeks she couldn't keep anything down until late in the evening. She had to force herself to get out of bed in the morning, and she was hardly eating at all. This was different from the knot in her stomach after Papa died. She was happy to be at Olla's, so she didn't know what could be wrong. Every night when James came home, she hoped he would tell her that he had found a place for them to live. There just didn't seem to be anything that suited him. He wanted to live right in town, and people were already living in every house.

He started coming home later and later and always smelling of cloves. Of course, Malcolm usually stayed out with him, and when they did get home they were laughing and cutting the fool. She was getting pretty tired of that, especially since she was feeling sick most of the time. She hadn't told James anything about the sickness. One night when he came home, she just broke out crying.

"What in the hell is the matter with you, girl?"

"James, you don't know it but Myra has been sick as a dog ever since she has been here. I am getting real worried about her. I think she needs to go to the doctor."

It wasn't like Olla to speak up, but she did this time. James went cold sober when he heard what she had to say.

"Myra, why ain't you said something to me about this? I know I ain't been acting right, but I just feel so damn bad about not finding us a place. Let me put you to bed, and first thing in the morning, you are going to the doctor."

The next morning James left her sleeping and went to town. When she woke up a little later, Olla and Miz MacTavish were standing over her. Miz MacTavish spoke in a very kind and gentle way and asked several questions.

"How are you feeling, dear?

"Olla says this has gone on for several weeks, but James said he hasn't noticed a thing."

It didn't surprise her to hear that James had not noticed her being sick. He was not home enough to see anything.

"I'd be all right if I could just get over this sick feelin' I have when I first get up."

"Myra, do you remember the last time you had your monthly?"

She hadn't thought about that, but she knew exactly why Miz MacTavish was asking.

"I know that hit was right after Christmas."

"You'll get over the sickness in a few weeks. You just need to take it easy and take care of yourself. James stopped by the house this morning because he was so worried about you. I told him to come back later and take you to see Dr. Youmans. I'll go now so you can rest."

"Now, Myra, I should have 'spected the same thing. I don't know why I didn't, 'specially when I think I'm in the same shape again. You know, the MacTavishes don't waste no time in having big families."

"Olla, you always can make me laugh and feel better."

Even though Myra knew she was pregnant, she felt as though it was someone else and not her. She had spent most of her life taking care of the little young'uns in her family, but this was going to be her very own. She had never thought about wanting a baby. When she was little, she had never even owned a doll. She was always too busy helping Papa to make playhouses like most little girls did. She knew how to take care of young'uns—as far as keeping them fed and in clean clothes—but she didn't know how to do the other stuff, like rocking them to sleep and talking baby talk like some folks did. She would do the best she could and hope to learn as she went along.

"You better get up and dress. Miz MacTavish said James was coming to take you to the doctor."

The thought of going to the doctor scared her more than anything. She had never been sick in her life. The only times a doctor had ever come to their house was the time the mule kicked Jesse and when Papa died. Then she remembered the good Dr. Beddingfield who had given her and Dolly the ride to Dublin. She wouldn't be scared of Dr. Youmans because doctors must be real special to help people like they did.

James drove up about the time she finished dressing. They rode to town without saying much. He went right into the doctor's office with her and did all the talking. The doctor didn't do much. He listened to her heart, poked around on her belly, and asked embarrassing questions about her last monthly.

"Congratulations, James, you are going to be a pa in late August or early September. This little lady is strong and well. You take care of her, and she will give you a fine son or daughter."

James pumped the doctor's hand and grinned from ear to ear. He hugged and kissed her, right in front of the doctor. This didn't even bother Myra, since the doctor must already know they did that. He helped her out to the buggy like she was made of glass. He was talking and laughing so much that she would have sworn he had been drinking, but she knew he hadn't had a drop. He wanted to stop and tell his ma and pa what the doctor said, even though they knew already. She was glad to stop and tell them and didn't even think about what Olieta might say.

Judge MacTavish had not said much to her since that first night, but he seemed pleased.

"You just watch, Flora Ann, this little gal is going to give us some fine, nice-looking, smart grandchildren. I think it's time to name one Andrew."

"Or her name could be Flora. Now I don't want y'all staying cramped up down there at Malcolm's. Besides that, I know Myra will be doing too much work if she stays down there. I want you back here, so that I can take care of her. I promise you that you won't have anything to upset you, Myra. I won't allow it."

"Andrew, you get those men working on their house. I want this new grandbaby to be born in its own home. You go get your things and come on back here until then."

James looked at Myra, and she nodded. As they headed to Malcolm's, she had one thing to get straight.

"You know how hard it is fer me and Olieta to get along. How's yore ma gonna keep her from botherin' me?"

"You won't have a minute of trouble out of her. There ain't nothing Olieta loves more than MacTavish babies. She will take good care of you."

"That's hard to believe, but I'm willin' to give hit a try."

To her surprise, everything was just as James and his ma had promised. Olieta was kind and helpful to her. James was wonderful. Every evening he brought home something special for her to eat. Miz MacTavish would hardly let her lift a hand to do a thing. She did continue ironing James's clothes. He wore a clean, starched, and pressed shirt every day. She liked the way he looked in a freshly ironed shirt and enjoyed doing this for him.

By the first of April she had gotten over morning sickness and was starting to fill out all over her body. She couldn't fasten her clothes, so she started wearing some of James's old shirts over her clothes. As she got bigger and bigger, she worried about what she would wear.

One day James's sister Hannah came to visit. She was just a year older than James and was so pretty and sweet. She had a little baby boy named Lewis and a little girl who was just walking named Lottie. This was the first time Myra had been with her and she liked her right away and loved her sweet little children. Hannah had help for the problem.

"Myra, you're gettin' to where you need some waiting clothes. I have some big dresses with drawstrings in the waist that I wore when I was waitin' on these two. I want them back but you're welcome to borrow them."

"That would shore help me. When I get much bigger I won't have nothin' I can get in."

"I would've brought them today if I had just thought."

Hannah and her husband lived out on the loop road. He had business in town that day, so he brought Hannah and her children to visit. She didn't come to town very often, so Myra wondered how long it would be before she got the clothes.

"I will send them to you by the mailman."

Myra had never thought of anyone sending her something by the mailman, but he did stop at the MacTavishes every day or so and leave off letters.

She thought James would be happy about the clothes, but he seemed peeved.

"Why didn't you tell me about needing those dresses? My wife shore don't have to borrow clothes to wear."

"It's just that I won't need them very long, and it seems a waste to buy when I have some offered to me."

"No matter, I'll get you some."

James was so full of pride and put that ahead of everything. He didn't make any mention of when she would get clothes of her own. In about a week the clothes came, and she started wearing them. He never said another word about it, so he must have forgotten.

When the clothes came, she showed them to Miz MacTavish and told her how kind Hannah was to send them.

"Oh yes, she has a heart of gold and always did. I worry so about her. Every winter she gets a bad case of consumption and just can't get over it. Lord, I don't know what would become of those two babies if something happened to her."

"She is so pretty and sweet, and I'll pray that she stays well."

Hearing this about Hannah made her feel so sad. That evening, James told her more that caused her to worry.

"Will Rob came by the store today and said yore ma has got a lot worse. When he ain't there, she goes out of the house and gets lost. She says she's lookin' for yore pa. Several times, he's had to get help in finding her."

Myra felt helpless. There was no way, in her condition, she could help her brother. She didn't know what to do or say. Then James showed her what a good heart he had.

"He asked me if I could go to Ailey and get Jesse. He could be there during the day and keep an eye on her. I can't get away right now, but I got a feller named Tom Crawford to take my buggy and go get him tomorrow."

"James, you do the kindest things fer me. I can't help them, but Jesse will. He needs to come back anyway."

She remembered a fellow named Tom Crawford had been in the Christmas program at Sullivan's Corner with her. She started to ask James if this fellow had come from Johnson County, but she had learned that

James got real peeved any time she talked about any fellow outside of the family. She didn't know why he would feel that way. She would never want any other fellow but James.

"On Sunday, could you take me to see Ma?"

"I'll see about it. Let me talk to Ma."

She didn't like that he felt he had to ask his ma, but she knew better than to say more. He left the room for a few minutes to talk to his ma.

"Ma says you don't have no business riding that far in a buggy in yore condition."

She was all ready to say that she should be the one to decide that, but again, he showed why she just couldn't stay mad with him.

"Honey, I know you want to see your ma, but we just can't take a chance on anything that might hurt you or our little baby. I want that baby more than I have ever wanted anything except you."

The days passed fast and soon it was the middle of the summer. Myra felt as big as the side of the barn, and her feet and hands were swelling up something awful. Dr. Youmans came by a few times, but he didn't think there was anything to worry about. She was more than ready to get this baby born. Every day she walked down to watch their house being built. She couldn't believe her eyes. It was so big that all the houses she had lived in before could fit inside it. A big crew was working on it, and everything was being done just right and with the best materials. Who would have ever believed that Myra Stuart would live in such a grand house?

Right after the fourth of July, James told her the house was ready for them to move in. She was so happy that she thought her heart would burst wide open. James knew some folks who had lost their place and had to move out. He bought a chest, stove, ice box, table, and four chairs from them. Myra felt sorry for them, but it wouldn't help if they didn't buy their stuff. After the furniture was moved into the house, James moved their bed from the MacTavishes. Right behind James was a black man driving a wagon with Olieta sitting right beside him. She brought one of the best rocking chairs from their house and a big basket for the baby to sleep in. The colored man unloaded two big boxes that held all the kitchen stuff they would need and two oil lamps. Myra had never seen any of it before, so she knew someone had bought it for them. Somehow, she just knew it was Olieta. Now they were set to start housekeeping on their own.

"Sister, we shore thank you for all this. I never knew we'd need so much."

"Well, I wanted a good chair to rock the baby in when I come down here, and it needed a place to sleep. I don't guess Myra has thought of that."

There she goes, Myra thought. *She just can't keep from getting back at me.* She was proud of all the stuff, especially the rocking chair. She would let Olieta get away with those words.

The next morning after James left, she started putting things away in the kitchen. Until she could get some shelves, she would just have to set things on the floor. She was working away when someone knocked at the back door. Will Rob was at the door.

"What are you doin' here? Come to see my new house?"

"I've brought a load of the best oak lumber I could find to build yore kitchen cabinets."

"You gonna build me some cabinets?"

"Yep, that husband of yours wants me to start today and be finished before my niece gets here. He's payin' me good money too."

Myra's first thought was how did he know it was a niece. Maybe he just thought it was time for one, since Joe Wiley had two boys.

"You tell me how you want them to be and where to put them. James said fer me to build just what you wanted no matter what it cost."

"Lord, Brother, I never thought I would ever have a place like this."

Will Rob's eyes filled up with tears and he said, "Myra, I think our papa is still looking out for us."

"Well, how is Ma? Is it a help to have Jesse?"

"She just gets worse all the time. She ain't never in her right mind. Jesse is some help, but he's gotten to be a handful. He's a lot bigger than me now, and he thinks he can come and go as he pleases."

"You tell Mr. Jesse Stuart that as soon as the baby is born I will come out there and whip his tail good. I've done it plenty of times before, and I can do it again."

The next few weeks were some of the happiest of her life. Will Rob came every day, and she watched her cabinets take shape. Every day she cooked a big pot of vegetables and corn bread. They ate all they wanted, and there was plenty to send home for Ma and Jesse. The blackberries were ripe, so she made a cobbler almost every day. They laughed and talked about the old days and had such a good time. She felt sad that he had to give up everything for Ma. If he had a wife and family, he would sure be good to them.

By the first of September the cabinets were finished. Will Rob also built two big wardrobes in the bedrooms to store their clothes and other things. Myra love her home more each day and every night gave thanks to God for her home, good husband, and baby. She prayed that she would never have to leave this house for the rest of her life. Almost every year of her life she had lived in a different place, and she wanted to live in this house forever.

She hoped each day would be the day for the birth. Her feet were swollen almost double, and she felt as though she had to pee all the time, but only a drop came out. It seemed as if this would go on forever. Miz MacTavish and Olieta took turns sitting with her while James was at the store. For once Myra was glad to have their help.

Late in the evening on the day of September fifth, she started having hard stomach cramps. This hurt like nothing had ever hurt before. Olieta was in the sitting room, and she did not want to say anything to her. She walked out on the porch just as some little colored girls were coming down the road.

"Girls, come over here to the porch. I need ya to do somethin' fer me."

"Yes'sum." They all hollered and ran over to her. They were not used to being called over by a white woman, so they were uneasy.

"Will you run up to Miz Olla's and tell her that I need her to come down here quick. I'll give you a syrup biscuit when you get back."

They took off and raced down the road. In no time, Olla came up the road, dragging Tom by the hand. She was expecting her baby any day, but she hadn't had trouble like Myra. She said it was because this was her second.

When the girls ran onto the porch, Myra was sitting in a big puddle of water. She wasn't able to get their biscuit.

"Go in the house and tell Miss Olieta that I said to take biscuits out of the warming closet, poke a hole in 'em and fill it with syrup."

Olieta was standing at the screen, so she heard every word and saw the puddle of water.

"You girls, wait here. I'll bring the biscuits to you. Then you git on home."

Myra thought the puddles must be all the pee that she had trouble passing. It just all came out at one time. Olita knew the cause. Before Olla got in the yard, Olieta yelled to her.

"Get in here and stay with Myra. The baby's fixing to come. I have to send for James and Dr. Youmans. I'm going to Ada's. I think one of her boys is home."

"Look at her, Myra. Have you ever seen her move at anything but a snail trot? There goes Olieta running up the road."

Olla seemed to know what to do. She got Myra into bed, stirred up the fire in the stove to boil water, and laid out linens. Myra remembered the night Dolly was born and how long it took before they heard her cry. She couldn't stand this pain for that long.

The little colored girl's ma came to help, and Miz MacTavish came right behind her.

"Rosa, thank you for coming. You know a lot about this, and it might be hard since it is her first."

"Lawd, have mercy. This here gonna be over soon and Rosa know how to help Miz Myra."

James finally got there. You would have thought he was the one that was hurting. He was carrying on so that Olla told him to sit on the porch. He said Dr. Youmans was out in the county, but his wife would send him as soon as he got back.

Myra didn't remember much about what happened after that. She knew she was hurting and hollered out some. Miz MacTavish and Rosa were helping her when the doctor arrived. Just when she thought she would die if it didn't end, she heard the doctor say, "Here it comes." Then she heard a cry, and she must have blacked out.

When she woke, it was daylight. James was sitting in the rocking chair by the bed, and he was holding the baby in a pretty pink shawl. He came over and put the baby beside her.

"It is about time you woke up. This little girl is getting hungry."

He laid the baby beside her and right then, she started to nurse. Myra felt a warm, soft feeling that she had never felt before. The baby looked a lot like James and was so sweet looking.

"Just look at her. Ain't she the prettiest thing you have ever seen? Her head is as round as a little apple. I am going to be the best pa there is to her."

"I want you to name her, James. Have you thought of a name?"

"I've always known what I wanted to name a girl if I ever had one. Idella, that's the prettiest name in the world, and she's the prettiest little baby girl in the world."

"I like that too. Can her middle name be Frances? That's my other name, and I always liked it better than Elmyra.

"Then, that is her name, Idella Frances MacTavish."

He kissed her on the forehead and kept rubbing her little round head.

"Idella, today is your birthday, September sixth."

Olieta came in and brought a bowl of broth. She took the baby and sat in the chair, rocking her. She looked pleasant and happy for the first time since Myra had known her. She rocked and sang and cooed to Idella, and Myra knew that her sister-in-law really had a heart filled with love for this baby.

Dr. Youmans insisted that Myra stay flat on her back for six weeks after the birth. There was no way that she was going to do that. She wanted to get right up and take care of her baby girl, the new house, and James. She tried, but she quickly found that she wouldn't be in shape to do that for a while. The doctor said she was torn up quite a bit because the baby had come feet first. She gave in and agreed for Miz MacTavish and Olieta to stay and help during the day.

After two weeks, she asked James if he would get one of Rosa's girls to stay with her during the day. She was getting tired of Olieta, and she knew Olieta was getting tired of her. He brought back a girl who looked about twelve. Myra was sure the girl knew as much about taking care of a baby and getting things done in the house as she had known at twelve. And that was plenty! Her name was Geneva, and she was a big help. James gave her some coins at the end of every week. He never said how much, but Myra knew he was always generous with folks that didn't have much, especially the colored. Olieta and Miz MacTavish came every afternoon, but all they did was hold the baby.

There was no more trouble with James staying out late or drinking. He couldn't wait to get home. He loved to sit and watch Idella nursing, and then he would rock her to sleep. Myra never dreamed he would have been such a proud papa. Some of the family got tired of hearing him brag about his pretty baby girl.

Will Rob came by to see the baby. He said that Ma sure did want to see her. Myra asked James about taking the baby for her to see, and he said that they would as soon as she was able. The weather turned cold and the days short, and time started to fly. Idella started to smile and hold her head up just before Christmas. When she smiled at James, you would have thought he had won a new mare. Myra begged to go to Ma's at Christmas, but James said riding in the buggy in the cold wouldn't be good for Idella. He sent them some things from his store.

They had a happy Christmas in their new house with their new little girl. Most of the family came by during that time to see the baby. On the night before Christmas, James was late coming home. He kept the store open as late as people wanted to shop and was always happy when he made lots of sales.

Christmas Eve, Myra heard a terrible racket and saw James and his nephew, Matthew, pulling something up the steps. She had never heard so much laughing and bumping. She knew they had had a few of what James called "nips." When they finally got in, she saw it wasn't the "nips" causing the bumping. James rolled in the biggest baby buggy that she had ever seen. It was leather with wire wheels and had a cover that could be put up for shade or rolled down for sun. He was proud as a peacock.

"James, what in the world does the baby need that for?"

She was about to fuss at him for wasting money, but she didn't have the heart since he was so proud. James didn't ever answer her. He took Idella over and put her in the buggy.

"Idella, this is your first Christmas present. It's from your daddy. As soon as the weather is warm enough, you are going to ride in it to town every evening. I want everybody in Glencoe to see how pretty you are, Miss Idella Frances MacTavish."

Idella gave him one of those big grins that just lit up her face every time she saw her daddy. Then James reached in his pocket and pulled out a roll of money. He kept on talking to Idella.

"Look at all your daddy made this week. He was so busy that the only thing he took time off to do was buy your buggy. He didn't have time to get your sweet ma anything, but I am going to give her this to buy herself whatever she wants."

Then he peeled off five dollar bills and gave them to Myra. He couldn't have bought anything that she wanted as much as this money. A few days before, she had walked by Miz Steptoe the dressmaker's house and saw a sign on the porch.

For Sale
Sewing Machine
$5

Ever since then, she had been trying to get up enough nerve to ask James if she could buy it. If she had a machine, she could keep Idella in pretty clothes. If Miz Steptoe hadn't sold it, she could buy it for her Christmas present.

Matthew stayed all night and slept on a pallet by the fireplace. He and James stayed up a long time after she went to bed. They sounded as if they were having a good time together. She could hear them go outside every now and then. She knew they had a bottle out there somewhere. Matthew was not any older than Will Rob, but he was a MacTavish, and the MacTavish men like to celebrate Christmas by having their "nips." It sure wasn't the way she would want it to be, but so far, no harm had come from it for James. He seemed to think this was just a way to have a good time.

About a month after Idella was born, Olla had a baby girl. They named her Emma, and she was a long, scrawny-looking little thing just as Tom had been. Of course, Olla was proud and thought she was just as pretty as Idella. They spent a lot of time together with the babies. Many nights they cooked supper together and all had a good time sitting around the table eating and talking. Idella was a good baby. She hardly ever cried, but then she never had any reason to cry. She was always being held and rocked by someone. Geneva kept working for her and was a big help with the washing and the kitchen.

One day in early February, she was nursing the baby by the fire when there was a knock at the door. A fellow whom she had never seen before was there. He spoke quickly before she could be scared.

"Miz MacTavish, my name is Avery Benton and I live by your ma and brothers out in Armity. Will Rob sent me to get you, because yore ma is real bad off, and he don't know how much longer she will last."

"Oh my Lord, no. What happened?"

"You know she wuz bad about getting' loose from them and runnin' off lookin' fer yore pa. Yesterday while Will Rob wuz at work, she slipped off and went into the woods. It wuz real cold and sleetin' some. Jesse looked and looked fer her. It took all mornin' to find her. She had fell and was cold as ice and soaked to the bone. He got her to the house and sit her by a big fire to warm up. My wife saw him bringin' her back, and she sent my boy to town to get Will Rob. When he got home, he sent Jesse fer the doctor. The doctor said she had broke some rib bones and would take the pleurisy from that. He said there ain't nothin' can be done to help her."

"Thank you fer getting me the message. Tell my brother that I will be out there as soon as I can."

She knew this was bad, and all she thought about was getting to her ma and brothers as soon as she could. She sent Geneva to the store to tell James. She started getting their things ready to go when James came home. If he hurried, he could take her and get back by dark. She hoped he would stay with her, but she knew he would need to come back. She was working and crying when James came in. He took her in his arms, and he sounded so sad as if he was about to cry.

"This is just awful. Jesse should have been watching her better."

"Don't blame poor little Jesse. He did the best he could. I am ready, so can we get started."

"Get started to where?"

"Armity." She sounded huffy, because he knew where they were going, and she didn't want to waste any time.

"We ain't going nowhere tonight. There is no way that you're taking my baby out in an open buggy in cold weather like this."

When she stopped to think, she knew he was right.

"We can leave her with Olla, and you can just take me. You don't have to stay."

"No, that's too much for Olla to do. Two babies and Tom would be too much. We'll get Ma and Olieta to keep her. Wrap her up good and let's go."

When they stopped to leave Idella with her grandma and aunt, both women started carrying on. They said Myra's place was at home with the baby, and James was a fool to even think of such as thing. As usual, James let them sway his thinking, and they turned around and went back home.

All night she sat in the rocking chair by the fire and cried. She had always been with her family when they needed her. She didn't know what she was going to do, but she knew that somehow she would get to them tomorrow. She prayed it wouldn't be too late. She didn't sleep a wink, and sometime in the night she heard a mournful sound right outside the house. She finally looked out, and in the moonlight she could see a big owl in the chinaberry tree. He was hooting and kept it up all night. She remembered a long time back in Sullivan's Corner when they heard an owl hooting down the road from Bunk's house. Nannie told her that meant there would be a death soon. Sure enough, the next day, an old woman in a house close by died. Of course, she had been ailing for a long time. Whether she believed that or not, it was a sad sound.

Just before daylight James came in to see about her.

"Myra, come on back to bed. The fire has gone out, and this room is freezing. Idella will need to nurse soon."

"As soon as it's daylight, I'm going to my ma. I'll go if I have to walk."

"What about yore baby?"

"I'm leavin' her with Olla. She can take care of her better than yore ma and Olieta. Besides, she's got plenty of milk and can nurse her. Can they do that?"

"Come on to bed and nurse her. It will soon be daylight, and we'll leave then. Can Olla really nurse her?"

"Of course, she's done it before, and I've nursed Emma."

"I am so damned mad at myself for not buying me a car before now. We wouldn't have had all this ruckus if I had bought me a car."

When they got to the house, she knew it was too late. She saw Horace's car and heard Annie Lou and Dolly crying in the house. Will Rob had started building the coffin, and Ma was laid out on the bed. Myra cried because she had not been able to see her one more time, and she cried because she had not been able to bring Idella for her to see. James and Horace went to Ailey in the car and brought Joe Wiley, Flossie, and their two boys to the house.

They buried her the next day in a little graveyard in a field just past Armity. It was a cold windy day, and there wasn't anybody at the grave but the family. Ma hadn't ever had any religion, but Will Rob got a preacher to say a few words over her. Myra looked around and thought her family was a sad-looking sight. They had lost Papa and now Ma. She wondered what Will Rob and Jesse would do. Jesse and Ma had not ever got along, but he sure was taking it hard. She went over to try to talk to him.

"Myra, it just ain't right fer Ma to be lying here in this field and Papa to be lying up there in Washington County just under a mound of dirt. Someday I'm gonna bring them to bury in the big cemetery in the middle of Glencoe. I'll buy a big tombstone to mark their graves."

"That would be a fine thing to do, Jesse. I hope you can do that someday."

When they went back to the house, Will Rob told her that he had decided to give up the house and just get a room in town. Jesse wanted to go back to Joe Wiley's house, so that would all work out. She was ready to pack up and go home to Idella, and James was anxious to get back.

Before they got home, she was going to have her say to Mr. James MacTavish.

"James, never again will I let you and yore folks keep me from goin' to my folks when they need me."

"We'll just wait and see about that."

"There ain't nothin' to wait and see. I mean what I say."

As they drove away from Ma's house for the last time, she looked back and caught a glimpse of a little boy sitting on the steps. It was way too small for Jesse, and even in the early dark she could see his blue suit. Where had he been all this time, and why is he here now?

-15-

Not a word was spoken on the ride back to Glencoe. Myra looked out into the shadows of the late evening, and James kept his eyes on the dark road. She could not see a speck of brightness anywhere. James was aggravated with her, but he was taking it out on poor ol' June. Every time she jerked or stumbled a little on the rutty road, he would pop her with the whip and cuss at her. She had never seen him use the whip on her before. He cussed her for being slow and stupid. He was mad at June because she wasn't a car.

When they stopped at Olla's to pick up Idella, they could hear her crying. All three young'uns were squalling. Myra knew this was the time of day when young'uns were tired and hungry, and all they knew to do was cry. James was even more disgusted when he saw Idella on a pallet in the corner of the room. Olla was feeding Tom, and she would get to the babies next. James didn't say anything, but Myra knew he was upset that *his* baby wasn't being tended. Olla tried to get them to stay and eat supper, but James was in a hurry to get home to his cold house and no supper. Myra told him to go on ahead because she was going to sit by the warm fire and feed Idella. He stormed out, and she felt really ashamed of how he was acting.

She needed to talk to someone, and Olla was the only one that really cared and understood.

"I just feel so lonely without Ma. Since I married, I ain't seen her much, but I knew she was there."

"I know, you miss her and always will. I've heard that when you lose yore ma, you've lost yore best friend on earth. This makes me want to see my ma, and I'm gonna make Malcolm take me when the weather warms up. They ain't nothin' you can do now but try and get over hit."

"There is somethin' I can do about Jesse. He was so lost at the burying. He don't have nobody to care what happens to him."

"I thought you said he wuz going home with yore other brother."

"He is. They'll treat him as good as they can, but they have such a hard time, and all he will ever do is work like a mule for the rest of his life. I have to find someway to help him."

"That still might be best fer him. Me and you lived that life as young'uns. Not many get to live like we're livin' now. If what you're thinkin' is to ask James about takin' him in, I shore wouldn't want you to do that."

"I never know with James. He can be so selfish and turn right around and be good to folks. I've got to try to help Jesse."

"I would at least wait awhile before asking him. Now you better get on home to James. He's mad enough already."

She hated to leave the warm room and cozy feeling that she had sitting by the fire with Olla. What Olla said was the truth, but she still didn't like to hear it.

As she started down the road, she could see smoke coming out of the chimney, and she knew James had started a fire. She hoped that meant he was over his mad spell, because she needed to talk to him about Jesse. When she walked in, he grabbed Idella and started rocking and talking to her. He had made a nice fire in the cook stove, so she went in to see what could be scraped together for supper. She was surprised to feel hungry and knew James was ready to eat. She had to fix somethin' that was quick. She made a hoecake of biscuit bread and used the few eggs she had to make egg gravy. She had never fed James such a scrappy supper before, but it was the best she could do. He must have been hungry because he ate it without saying a word. James had rocked Idella to sleep and put her in bed. She was dead on her feet, but she was not going to bed until she had her say about Jesse.

"James, I know you're tired, and I am too, but I want to talk to you about Jesse. I'm so worried about him."

"Well, make it quick. I've had all of this day I can take."

"I think hit's only fittin' that I take Jesse in and take care of him. Annie Lou already is takin' care of Dolly."

James looked at her as though she had asked him to take in a bunch of Yankee soldiers. His face turned red as a beet, and his eyes were looking bullets at her.

"Don't you even mention that to me. No way, I mean no way on earth would I let that aggravating boy come here. I didn't marry you to take yore family in."

"What do you mean? My family has never taken anything from you. Jesse is just a boy and an orphan boy at that."

They were both mad and argued on until James got up to go in the bedroom. Myra had never yelled at him, but she was doing it now.

"James, you oughta be ashamed of yoreself. Any decent man would want to take in a pore orphaned boy like Jesse."

"I will never stay in the house with Jesse Stuart. There is just something about him that rubs me the wrong way every time I see him. He talks too much and acts too big for his britches. You just forget that, and don't mention it to me ever again."

She didn't get a chance to say anything more before the bedroom door slammed.

She did not sleep a wink that night. She'd cry for a while and then get mad. She had no choice but to do what James wanted. Jesse would have to make it somehow without her help. Young'uns did seem to have a way of growing up no matter how hard they had to live. He was almost grown now, so maybe he could find a better place for himself on his own. She wondered about Arno, but she did not feel the worry for him that she did for Jesse. Arno had always been able to make people like him, even if he did not do much talking.

The next morning James left without breakfast, so she knew he was still pouting. He was acting just like a young'un. He had been spoiled rotten by his ma and Olieta. She cooked a good dinner in case he came home, but she didn't see him again until way after dark that night. When he came up the step, he was the drunkest that she had ever seen him. This went on for most of the rest of the winter. She thought she might die of being so lonesome and sad. The only thing that kept her going was hoping to buy the sewing machine, as soon as she could get to town.

In the middle of March the weather warmed up, and the days were sunny. Myra was ready to get out of the house, and she was anxious to see if the machine was still for sale. She fried some of the apple pies that James loved, wrapped up Idella, and put her in the buggy and headed to town. James liked surprises, and she hoped he could take time to eat the pies and enjoy being with her and Idella.

When she reached the store, she held the door back to roll the buggy into the store and got the shock of her life. The same old gal that she had seen sitting on the counter before was sitting there again. She and James were laughing and both eating hamburgers out of a sack. She could tell from his red face that James had already had a nip or two, even though it wasn't even noon. This time she knew there was more going on between them than business. She was so mad and knew she had to get out of there before she called the gal the name that fit her and called James even worse.

She snatched the baby buggy out of the door and started to head home. No, she was not going to let him make her run home without checking on buying the sewing machine. She turned around and pushed Idella up the street to Miz Steptoe's house. Not only was her sign gone, she was gone too. The house was completely empty. A lady came out from the house next door when she saw Myra staring at the house.

"Where is Miz Steptoe? I came to buy the machine she had fer sale."

"She's been gone since before Christmas. She got the rheumatism so bad that she couldn't sew or even take care of her house. She moved over to Terrytown to stay with her brother."

"Do you know what she did with the machine?"

"I don't exactly know about the machine, but they sold everything in the house before she left."

This was the last hurt Myra could take. She cried and cried as if she had never cried before. She cried for Pa. She cried for Ma. She cried for Arno and Jesse. She even cried for poor June because James had whipped her for not being a car. Most of all she cried for Myra, because she knew she didn't have a thing left now. She was still crying when she started down the street and ran right into James.

"Myra, you shouldn't have run out like that and not let me explain. Why are you way down here?"

She didn't say a word to him but hurried on down the street. When she got to the corner and turned, she caught a glimpse of James standing in front of Miz Steptoe's old house talking to the neighbor woman. She knew she had shamed him in front of the lady, but she didn't care a bit. He had shamed himself even worse.

She almost ran home and just crawled into the bed with Idella. She felt like pulling the covers over her and just staying there forever. After a while she let her mind go back to the days when all her folks were in Washington County and working together to help Papa. Just to cheer up a little, she started humming a hymn that Papa had taught her. She remembered what Uncle Daniel had told them about lifting your spirit by singing praises to the Lord.

Somehow this did seem to help a bit. Maybe she could find a way to be a better wife and helper to James. Maybe then he would have more patience with her. Papa said she had a brightness. If she did, now was the time to use it. If she made herself better, could she guide James into living right?

She jumped out of bed and was ready to find what she could do to make their life brighter.

To her surprise, she saw a truck pulling up to the front, and on the side was painted Hunter Furniture Company. She opened the door and saw two men lifting out a sewing machine. She figured they had come to the wrong place and was about to tell them so.

"Miz Mac, yore fine husband has bought you a brand-new sewing machine. Where do you want us to put it?"

She couldn't answer; she was so taken back. They brought it into the front room, and she told them that was fine. All she could do was sit and look at it and wonder how James knew how much she wanted the machine. She'd never mentioned it to him.

The machine was inside a fine wood cabinet, and you had to open it up and pull out the machine. When the machine wasn't out, it looked like a table. There were two draws on either side of it and space between to put your chair and work the treadle.

James had known just what to do to get her out of her sadness. She knew that no matter what she thought about him at times, he loved her and wanted her to be happy.

About that time Olla came in with her two little ones. She was as excited as if the machine belonged to her.

"Tomorrow I'm going to town and get material and thread and make Idella, Emma, and Tom aprons just alike."

"Then the next day, we will take them to Glencoe and show them off. What made James think about buying you a machine, do you reckon?"

"That's just how he is. I don't know if James will be home fer supper, but in case he is, I need to get started on cookin' a good one. Come in the kitchen and sit with me."

While Olla was sitting in the kitchen, she told her all about the day, even to the part about hiding under the covers most of the afternoon. After she finished, Olla waited a few minutes as if she was getting her mind made up as to what to say.

"Myra, you married James because of what he was. You knew full well that he was not going to change his ways, because that is just not him. He don't ever mean to hurt ya, and he tries to make it up. He ain't able to handle being around sickness, death, or sadness of any kind. He don't know how to act around that kind of thing, so he runs off and drinks or does something to take his mind off of the trouble.

"Now as to yore folks. It ain't as though he don't like them. He's just plain jealous of them or anybody that you care about besides him. He ain't jealous of Idella because she's part of him. He has always been petted and had his way, and he wants the same thing from you. That ol' gal don't mean a thing to him, and I doubt there is any more between them than what you saw today. He likes sorry gals like that because they play up to him and make him feel good. That is what you need to do too."

Again what Olla was telling was the gospel truth, and Myra knew she meant it to help. That still didn't make it easy to hear, except for the part about the ol' gal not meaning anything to him.

"I just can't be that way for him. It just ain't in me. Papa and I always worked along beside each other and knew our feelings without having to say. I work hard and make a good home for James. That oughta be enough. I wish he could see that and quit acting like a spoiled young'un. All the kissin', huggin', and sweet talk that James wants don't wash and iron the clothes, clean the house, or cook our meals."

"Myra, I'm not going to say any more, but you had better try to learn how to make over him or he is going to find someone that will."

She headed out the door with her young'uns, and Myra was left feeling as if she was lost on a foggy night. In her heart she knew what Olla said would make things better for them, but how was she going to do it?

She didn't have time to think anymore because she heard James coming up the steps. He stood in the door grinning from ear to ear. She ran right into his arms, and they hugged and kissed, and she didn't even think about cooking supper. Later, they went in for her to show him the machine.

"James, this is the finest thing I've ever had. You're a mighty good husband to buy hit fer me. I don't know how to thank you."

"Just seeing you happy is thanks enough."

"Now I can keep Idella dressed in pretty clothes."

"You keep the baby dressed pretty, but don't you forget about making dresses for my pretty wife too."

They were so happy together that evening that she never did finish cooking supper. Some things changed after that. James still drank and stayed out later that he should. She was busy making their home bright and hoping that would change him for good. She sewed every day and loved every minute she sat at the machine. James let her have a cow and chickens but still teased her about trying to make a farmer out of him. They had plenty of milk, butter, eggs, and chicken. Most of the year, her garden gave them all the vegetables they could eat. In the winter their table was filled with the foods she had canned. James let her buy all the jars that she needed, and she still used Miz Sara's big canning pot. Olieta made remarks about her making James' house look like the ones in Armity. Myra didn't pay any mind to that. She noticed that Olieta never refused when Myra filled their pantry with canned goods or took them freshly churned butter.

The year passed quickly, and they were happy. On December 2, almost nine months from the day that James bought the sewing machine, they had another baby girl. She was just as pretty as Idella, and she was the spitting image of James. Myra knew he wanted a boy to name after him, but he was just as happy to have another baby girl. He wanted to name her James anyway. Myra told him that was no name for a girl, but it could be her middle name, so they settled on that. He picked Laura for the first name, and she would be called Laura James. James was proud as a peacock of his two little girls. Olla always laughed at him and said James acted as if he was the only man around that had made any babies. Laura James was a fat and good baby, and she was much easier to tend to than Idella had been. Myra thought it helped that Miz MacTavish and Olieta did not hold her all the time like they did Idella. They came to see her almost every afternoon, but they still showed more attention to Idella.

Olieta still said things that got Myra's dander up. She knew it would be best to let the spiteful things Olieta said run off like water on a duck's back, but that was hard to do. Olieta dearly loved to get her into an argument, so she could tell James. She covered her nose with a handkerchief every time she walked in their yard. She said the chicken yard stink made her "deathly" sick, but that didn't keep her from eating more than her share of the eggs.

While she nursed Laura James, Myra enjoyed pulling the rocker close to the window. One day in late January, she saw Will Rob and someone else coming down the road. She knew it was him even from a long way off, but she couldn't make out who was with him. When he got closer, she saw a woman walking with him. She went out to the porch to greet them and got a better look at the woman. She was not much bigger than a young'un and looked as thin as a snake.

"Well, Brother, I shore am glad to see you and show ya yore new niece."

"Myra, I want to see the baby, but first I want you to meet yore new sister-in-law. This here's Angie."

She couldn't believe her ears, and all she could think to say was, "I'm glad to meet ya, but I shore am surprised. I didn't even know Will Rob wuz courting.'"

"Well, I ain't been fer long. We just met a few weeks ago."

"How did all this come about?"

"I'd come to Glencoe with my ma and pa from where we live in Higgston. We come to buy things we can't get there. I wuz lookin' in the window at Rosenberg's, and I saw Will Rob in there buyin' shoes. When he came out, we got to talking and then walked around town together. Before I had to go to the wagon to ride home, he asked if he could catch the bus and come out there to see me. That wuz fine by me.

"He came the next Saturday, and the next, and the next. The last time he asked me to come to Glencoe the next week and marry him. I told him he had to ask my pa. Well, he did and Pa said we had to get married there in Higgston, so he'd know we wuz proper married before I went off to Glencoe with him. We married that evenin' with the Justice of the Peace. We spent our first night in the house with Ma and Pa. Hit wuz funny 'cause my little brother had to sleep in the room with us."

Will Rob turned beet red as he always did when he was embarrassed. She knew that Angie had told more than he wanted her to tell.

"That is somethin' to tell yore grandyoung'uns about. I'm happy fer ya. Where are y'all stayin'?"

"We moved right into the room that Will Rob already lived in. The landlady lets us have kitchen privileges. I like it 'cause hit's right off the main street, and I can go to town anytime I want. I always love to go to Glencoe. Don't you, Myra?"

Myra had hoped her brother would find someone to be with and have a good life. Angie wasn't much to look at. A puff of wind would blow her away. Will Rob seemed pleased with his new wife, and she seemed to think a right smart of him. Angie made herself right at home and kept talking fast and loud. Myra asked them to stay for supper, but they needed to start back to Glencoe before dark.

"I am proud to have you fer a sister-in law, and I know that Will Rob will make you a good husband. I hope ya come back soon."

"After meetin' you, Myra, I don't feel nearly as lonesome fer my folks. I hadn't ever been away from them before. When you come to Glencoe, come and visit with me. If I ain't home, I'm probably walkin' around the main street. I've been in yore husband's store. He's got some pretty things but nothin' I need."

"As soon as the baby is old enough to take out in the buggy, I will come to see you."

Myra kept that promise and stopped to see Angie every time she went to town. She did this until the day she died. Angie never changed much, and the older she got, the skinnier she became. She continued to talk too much, but she made Will Rob a good wife.

Annie Lou, Horace, and Dolly came to see the MacTavishes during Christmas, and Myra was really glad to see them. She was surprised to learn that Annie Lou had finally gotten pregnant and they were hoping to have a baby around May. Annie Lou didn't pay Idella and Laura James much attention, but then she never did pay attention to anything that wasn't hers. She had met Angie and wanted to run her down, but Myra wouldn't let her get into that. She did say that she thought Will Rob could have done better than a "dumb ol' girl from Higgston." Myra had to laugh because she wondered what her sister thought she was when Horace first saw her. Dolly was going to school now and just as prissy as Annie Lou. She wondered if they would keep on spoiling and petting her when they had their own baby.

Even if she didn't see eye-to-eye with Annie Lou on most things, she loved her and hoped and prayed that she would have a fine, healthy baby this time. She didn't see her again until the baby was born. Horace's pa came to tell the MacTavishes about the baby. Myra happened to be there when he came and heard all about it. The baby was a girl and had come more than a month before they were expecting it. They didn't have much hope for her living because she didn't weigh but three pounds. Mr. Morris said he had never seen anything so little, and they were trying to keep her warm and get a little nourishment into her. Horace and Annie Lou were real upset and worried that even if she lived, she would never be right. They were all talking about the baby as though she wasn't even living, and that didn't seem right to Myra.

"Mr. Morris, what did they name her?"

"Rachel."

"How old is she now?"

"She's a week or two, I think."

It just broke Myra's heart to think about her sister's little baby dying. She hoped that since Rachel had made it this far, she might live.

That night she told James about it and asked him to take her to see them.

"Yea, we will go next Sunday. We need to see what we can do to help them."

She saw a side of him that she had never seen before. He went over and picked up Laura James and Idella in his arms, and she could tell from the way he was sniffing that he was trying not to cry. She hadn't ever thought that James was one to pray, but she knew he was giving thanks for his two healthy little babies.

They went to North Connolly every Sunday until they knew Rachel was going to make it. She was never healthy and always small for her age, but she was a good girl and a blessing to Annie Lou.

Just after they knew that Rachel was strong and seemed to be thriving, sadness came. James's sister, Hannah, died. It wasn't unexpected because she had been sick with the consumption all winter. They had thought when she made it to spring that she would get better, but there just wasn't any better for her. Myra had only met her a few times, but she always thought she was the prettiest and sweetest of all the sisters. James took it real hard. They were close in age and had grown up together. He even offered to take in her two little children, Lewis and Lottie. Their daddy would have all he could do just trying to keep his farm going. They lived way out in the country, and he didn't have any family to help. Myra would have been willing to take the young'uns even if James wouldn't take in Jesse. She loved those little children because she had loved their mother. It turned out that another sister, Lizzie, could make a good home for them. She lived nearby, so everyone could help with them. They grew up with all the MacTavish young'uns and were in and out of Myra's house until they grew up. The years were moving on now, and there had been a lot of changes. Myra's life was good. She had her girls, a house to keep, sewing, her garden, and she and James were getting along better. He still drank and loved to cut the fool and be around people who enjoyed that. She couldn't change him, and she couldn't help getting on to him about it. That made him mad as fire, but most of the time he would come back and want to make up. He did love his little girls and wanted them to have everything they needed.

In the early summer of Laura James' second year, Myra was beginning to feel as though her life was settled, and she was happy. She loved taking care of her home and two little girls. She had already seen signs that another one was on the way, but she hadn't told anyone yet. She kept busy sewing and keeping up with the garden, cow, and chickens. She was just about keeping the MacTavishes in fresh food. They always had plenty of food, but after she started sharing her homegrown things with them, she could tell they really enjoyed it, expecially Judge MacTavish. Leita still acted as if Myra was embrassing the family with her "Washington County backwards ways."

Even Miss Olieta was getting to look forward to Myra coming in every morning with fresh churned butter and buttermilk.

Nobody but Myra seemed to be noticing it, but she thought Judge MacTavish was starting to age and look real worn-out. He was sixty-eight years old on his last birthday, and she thought that meant his time was near. He never had much to say to her and was real stern with everyone, but she would never forget how he stood up for her the first night that James brought her home. The summer heat seemed to be hard on him, and he kept moving from place to place trying to find a breeze. She mentioned to James how worried she was about his pa. He didn't want to hear or think about it. She knew this was his way of covering up his worry.

When she told him about the new baby coming, he said he was glad. He didn't carry on like he did with the other two.

"I hope this one will be a boy. I know you will be happy to have a son."

"It don't matter to me one way or the other. I just hope it's as healthy as these girls."

All through the fall and Christmastime, she could tell Judge MacTavish was going down. The doctor came several times when he had spells of indigestion. Dr. Youmans gave him some kind of medicine in a bottle that he would take a swig of every time he started hurting. He couldn't eat hardly anything that didn't cause him to take a swig of the medicine. The one thing that didn't seem to bother him was Myra's buttermilk and fresh-baked corn bread. She started taking it to him several times a day. One of his young'uns was with him day and night. Grace had another little girl named Fern who was just about the same age as Idella. During those days she got to know Grace a little better and decided she was easy to be with when Leita wasn't around. James's oldest brother, George, and his wife, Sophie, were there a lot too. They had a houseful of young'uns already. Their boy, Matthew, was nearly grown, and they had a big girl named Juanita, and two younger girls, Doris and Betty Jane, who were close to the age of Myra's girls and Olla's young'uns. Some days they would put them all down on a pallet to play together. Olieta always enjoyed seeing this, but she was usually right beside her pa. James kept saying he thought his pa was just tired and would be better in the spring.

That Christmas was the first time they put out Santa Claus for the girls. Idella was big enough to remember, and she believed anything that her papa told her. He made a big to-do about Santa Claus coming and bringing her lots of presents. The night before Christmas, he had them set out sewing machine drawers and told them the next morning they would find the drawers full of things from Santa Claus. As soon as they were asleep, he brought in two big sacks. Myra couldn't believe her eyes. There was more in those sacks than her whole family had ever got for Christmas in their life. He had a wax doll for Idella and a stuffed rag doll for Laura James. There was a ball, a picture book, and a new cap for each of them, and bags of candy, nuts, and raisins. The machine drawers were running over. James was so excited to give his girls such a good Christmas. He never stopped doing this, even in the years when they did not have much to do with. After he finished filling the drawers, he told her that he had stopped at Lizzie's on the way home and left off a sack for her to give to Lewis and Lottie. He had a real soft spot for those two little motherless young'uns, and so did Myra.

The next day she cooked a big hen, dressing, vegetables, pies, and cake; and they packed it up and took it up to the MacTavishes'. She watched the judge, but she didn't see him eat a bite. His eyes were sunk way back in his head, and she thought he looked as green as grass.

Every night she prayed that they wouldn't lose the judge. While she was praying she could hear an old owl hooting off in the woods. She knew God would do what was right to Him, so prayers weren't always answered.

On the morning of January 9, they woke up to hear Malcolm banging on the door and telling James to get to his pa quick. He grabbed his pants and ran out in the cold without any kind of coat. She wanted to go, but she couldn't take the girls out until she got them dressed. She saw Olla and her young'uns heading up the walk to the house, so she just wrapped a quilt around the girls and ran up there. As soon as she got in the yard, she knew the judge was gone. She could hear Leita, Grace, and Miz MacTavish crying and carrying on. She walked into the house and saw him covered up with a sheet. She pulled it back and thought he looked as though he had gone to sleep. Later she found out that was what had happened. Miz MacTavish just found him dead when she woke up. They never knew exactly what had killed him, but they knew he had something wrong with his insides. She looked for James and finally found him out in the lot with the mule. He was sitting on the cold, nasty ground with his head in his hands, and she had never heard such hard sobs coming out of anyone. She didn't know what to say or do, so she sat down. In a few minutes he looked up and told her to take the girls back home out of the cold.

The funeral was held in the First Baptist Church of Glencoe, and the church was overflowing with people. Some were even waiting out in the yard. Of course, all of the family was there and all the old-time people of Glencoe. As Will Rob would have said, "All of the Mac people were there." He was buried in the cemetery in the middle of town. James acted as though he was playacting all the way through the burying. Everybody wanted to shake his hand and say how much they thought of his pa. She felt so sorry for James when he had to walk away from the mound of dirt and leave his pa in the cold ground. She knew how he felt, but she also knew that James had a hurt that wouldn't go away anytime soon, and he couldn't work it away like she had always had to do.

The main thing that seemed to keep him going was getting a big tombstone that he thought was fitting for his pa. He went to a lot of places to look and often talked with his ma about getting it set in place as soon as he could.

Myra didn't have much chance to think about herself during this time, but she was getting bigger and bigger and closer to her time. The first week in March she knew that she had better get ready, and she was right. On March fourteen their first boy was born. He was a fine little fellow and a bigger baby than the girls had been. He was well filled out and strong. She was filled with love for him the minute he was put in her arms. It just seemed he was there to help her. He didn't look like the girls. She knew that Idella was just like James. As much as she hated to say it, Laura James looked a lot like Olieta, and Olieta was a fine-looking woman. Nobody said anything, but she knew that Stephen was the first one to really take after her. He looked a lot like Jesse as a baby. She thought James would want to name him, but he told her it was her turn to name the baby. She knew he was proud of his son, but he was still too upset over losing his pa to really get into thinking about a name. She thought about naming him James, but somehow that just didn't seem to suit him. She wanted him to have a really fine name, and she picked Stephen Andrew.

The first outing they took Stephen on was to the cemetery to see the tombstone that James had finally put up for his pa. It was a big marble stone and at the top in big letters was written MacTavish. His name and dates of his birth and death were under that. There was an emblem that showed he was a veteran of the Confederate States of America army. At the very bottom was written,

Though our loss is great
We trust tis your eternal gain.

She knew James had picked that verse out from somewhere. It sounded just like the right thing to say, and she hoped James did feel that way. Maybe that feeling will help him get over some of the hurt. As they started walking away from the grave, James reached over and took Stephen from her.

"Come to me, Son. All of us MacTavish men have to be strong and smart like your old grandpa."

-16-

After finishing the business of the tombstone, James was more down in the dumps than ever. He went to the store every day but never talked about how his business had been or told stories about the people who came by like he used to do. Most nights he stopped on his way home to have a few little nips. This put Myra in a really bad humor, and they fussed over the least little thing. He didn't even pay attention to the young'uns, and they didn't know how to take this and kept out of his way. She was thankful that Stephen was such a good baby and never cried. She made sure to nurse him in plenty of time, so he was not hungry when James came home. It worried her, but she knew how he was feeling. She knew time would help, but the hurt would always be there.

Compared to how little her family got by on, the MacTavishes seemed like rich folks to Myra. She was surprised when James told her that he was hoping his ma could get a pension for being a widow of a Civil War veteran. His pa had served in the Savannah Artillery, and the family was proud of that. There were still plenty of old Civil War soldiers around, and they always got recognized and honored everywhere they went. James would have to take her to the courthouse in Campbell to sign up, and he hated to be a part of anything that was going on in Campbell.

One Monday morning he stayed home from the store and drove his ma and Leita down to Campbell. He seemed relieved when he got home and was more like his old self.

"We made the trip just fine. I was kinda worried about taking Ma and Leita so far in the buggy, but it was a nice day. It wasn't no trouble to get Ma signed up. She had Pa's papers, but they didn't even ask to see them. I appreciated them treating her so good. I just didn't expect that in Campbell, but they all knew who Pa was."

"So is she gonna be gettin' some money?"

"Oh yea, she will draw five dollars a month for the rest of her life. With that and what they can get from renting land and Leita taking in a few piano pupils, they can keep up the taxes and get what they need."

Myra wanted to know more, but she knew better than to ask why they needed to worry about money when they had owned so much land and his pa had been a judge.

The next day after James left for work, she headed to Olla's to talk it over. Olla was behind her house chopping with her hoe as if her life depended on it.

"What in the world are ya choppin' up? You act like you're fightin' the Yankees."

"This ol' vine's startin' to sprout back up. I hoped the winter had killed it, but I see it sprouting up everywhere. I'm tryin' to get rid of hit before it gets going like last summer. You remember it nearly took over the house with us in it."

Myra laughed until the tears were rolling down her cheeks. Last summer Olla had ridden the bus to Baxley to see her sister. She brought back a root from a vine she saw growing on the side of the road. She thought it was real pretty and would cover the ground in a place in her yard that wasn't good for anything. Well, it did grow, and by the end of that summer it was covering everything around it. It covered the ground, went up into the trees, covered the wash shed; they had to chop it every day to keep it from climbing the well.

"You just chop on, but I'm bettin' in a few years the whol' state of Georgia will be covered with yore vine."

Olla wouldn't put down her hoe, so Myra started helping pull it up and talked as they worked. Olla didn't know any more than she did, but she was just as puzzled.

"I know who will know, and that's Angie Stuart."

Every since Angie and Will Rob had been married, they had lived in rooms in a house on the main street, right down from the stores. Angie sat on the porch most of the time and talked to everyone who passed. She spent a lot of time walking around town and always talked to the folks in the stores. Every time Myra went to see her, she loved to tell about everything happening in Glencoe. In other words, Angie was nosey, and she liked to talk. She didn't do it in a bad way. She just didn't have anything else to do. She and Will Rob had a baby girl named Doreen. She was a sweet little thing, and Angie carried her on her hip when she walked to town. James would laugh and tell Myra about seeing Angie on her "route" that day.

After dinner, she took off for Glencoe to see Angie. When Myra asked what she had heard about the MacTavishes, she was only too glad to tell all she knew.

"Folks all over town are talkin' about the MacTavish and how they would get along with the judge gone. They say his judge's pay will stop. Right now, they are what ya call "land pore." Their land ain't worth the taxes due on hit."

"How can that be? Judge MacTavish had plenty and gave all that land to build the depot and graveyard. Not long ago he gave land to build a home for old folks."

"They say fer the last few years all he had wuz the money from being a judge. His oldest boy, George, is gonna run fer that. Some folks tried to get James to run fer hit. They say he's a lot smarter than George. He wouldn't do it 'cause he though George wuz due hit."

Myra would have liked for James to be a judge and wondered why he never mentioned it to her. He probably thought she would have tried to talk him into it.

"I still don't see why they are so hard up when he gave all that land away."

"Like I said, the land wasn't worth the taxes. The reason so much of his money is gone was the way his young'uns have done. He set George up in business over and over again, but he's never been nothin' but a drunk and lost everything he ever had. James and Malcolm have run their business pretty good, but both of then cost him money their whole lives.

"One story I heard is about Judge MacTavish having to dig a new well at the schoolhouse one time when they wuz boys. James and Malcolm were the ones the teacher always made go draw the water and bring it to the schoolhouse. They got tired of this and wanted to find a way to get around doing it. One day they saw a bloated-up dead calf in a field near the schoolhouse. They got the idea that if they threw the calf in the well, it would mess up the water, and they wouldn't have to carry water anymore. They wuz right. Not only did it mess up the water, but before they knew what was wrong, a lot of the young'uns and the teacher got sick from hit. They wuz a big commotion, and the school board had to hire somebody to clean out the well. When they found the dead calf, they knew somebody had to have thrown it in the well. The sides were too high fer hit to have stumbled in.

"Judge MacTavish was on the board, and he was raising sand about it. It seems that Mr. James and Mr. Malcolm hadn't been as smart as they thought. Both of them had to brag to their buddies about what they had done. Well, like always, the ones they told turned around and told some others, and they told some others, and they told some others. Finally, it got to a little girl who was the teacher's pet, and she went right to the teacher with it. The judge really lost face over that, and he had to have a new well dug and settle up with the folks of some of the ones who got sick.

"Nobody ever knew what kind of whipping or anything that James and Malcolm got, but it was just things like that going on all the time. After they grew up, they got into scrapes about women. Judge MacTavish always paid their way out. Folks think some of the husbands of the girls cost him money too, especially Grace's husband, Lonzy Watson.

"Anyway, now that the old man is gone, all the family is on its own, and the only one of the young'uns that was left anything in the will was Olieta. All she gets is the homeplace after her ma is gone."

The more that Angie talked, the faster she talked, and the more her eyes blinked. She sure did love to tell tales. None of this bothered Myra one bit. She didn't want James to be getting anything from his pa. She knew they would make it better if they worked for what they got. She was glad that Miz MacTavish would have enough to live on for the rest of her life. From all Angie had told her, she figured the folks in Glencoe sure had a big time talking about the MacTavishes' business.

That evening she told James that she heard about the calf in the well. He burst out laughing and told her the same story that Angie had heard. He thought it was funny and said he and Malcolm had some big times when they were growing up. He told her a few more scrapes they had gotten into. She didn't say it to him, but she knew if her young'uns did such things, when she got through with them, they wouldn't think it was funny.

When the weather started to warm up, Myra was ready to break up a place for the garden and to let the young'uns play outside. James had been so sad all winter, and this had been hard on her. Sometimes she felt as if James thought marrying her had caused all the sorrow for the MacTavishes. She fought to keep her head up and tried to think about things she remembered from the Bible or had heard at preaching. Sometimes, she thought about the little blue boy and wondered if he would ever come back. Her own little boy was healthy and growing fast, and it always made her feel better just to hold him.

The garden was coming up by the middle of April, and she was looking forward to having fresh vegetables to cook. She wanted to stew the fresh taters real soft to feed to Stephen. James always liked fresh garden peas with taters and dumplings. Maybe soon he would feel good enough to enjoy supper with them. Most of the time he got home way after dark and did not want any of the supper that she always saved for him. She knew he was eating somewhere, but she was afraid he was drinking more than eating.

Olla told her that Malcolm was doing the same thing, and often they were out together. Olla kept saying that she thought Malcolm had a woman, but Myra would not listen to that. She couldn't let herself even think this about Malcolm and certainly not James.

One night she was waiting up for him after the girls were in bed. Stephen was starting to smile real big and stretch his arms up to her. She wanted James to see this, so she was holding him in her arms when she heard James staggering into the house. When he came in the house, he kept bumping into things and cussing.

"There's my man. Give him here, Myra."

As much as she had wanted James to pay Stephen some attention, she was not about to hand her baby boy over to be dropped on the floor.

"You ain't in no shape to get close to this baby."

At first, she thought he was going to hit her, but then he sat down on the floor and started blubbering about what a sorry sot he was and not fit to be a MacTavish or have MacTavish young'uns.

She put Stephen to bed and then started trying to get James up and into bed. She was starting to feel sorry for him, until she realized the good smell that he had about him. He smelled just like the cheap perfume they sold in one of the new stores that had just opened in Glencoe. She knew how it smelled because one time she and Olla had opened a bottle and smelled. They knew that only sorry women wasted their money on such.

She had him by the shoulders, and she just let him drop to the floor hard. There was no way he could smell like that, unless he had been real close to whoever was wearing it. She thought her heart would break but knew she had to find a way past this.

James got up the next morning as if nothing had happened. He acted better than he had in a long time. She could still smell the scent on him, and she let him know it and how she thought it got there. He turned red as a beet and started stammering about women coming in the store and staying so long. He went to the basin and washed himself off all over, but it was too late to change her thoughts.

The next three years passed along with good times and bad times. James kept on drinking, and many times she knew he had been doing what he should not do. There would be other times when he acted like he loved her as much as that first day they married. She never knew what to expect from him. Some days she would have to feed them from the canned goods or garden, and other days he would come in with a big sack of groceries. One night he was in a real good mood when he came home.

"Myra, I've brought plenty fer supper, so you don't have to cook. This is a can of somethin' called pork and bean."

That sounded good to her, especially when he brought out a big jar of pickles to eat with the pork. He opened up the can and dumped out the beans. Then he started looking in the can for the pork. The pork turned out to be one little glob of fat in the middle of the beans. James never liked it when the laugh was on him, but she did have a good laugh and enjoyed the beans and pickles. Neither of them touched the pork. In times like that, she knew he loved her and wanted to make their life better.

For the first time since she left Brewster, she was giving some thought to Uncle Bunk. She kept trying to remember some of the scriptures he said by heart and wished she knew more. She had never been able to get comfort from the Lord God Jehovah that he always prayed to, because that just seemed like a pa who did nothing but whip his children. She and James didn't go to church much anymore. In fact, she hadn't been since before his pa died. His ma and Leita would get him to take them to the First Baptist in Glencoe every once in a while, but with the young'uns, she just couldn't feel at home there with all those up-to-date folks.

Samuel and Molly were in Emanuel County serving a church and never came near enough for them to go to one of his revivals. Horace's pa had bought a sawmill way over on the coast of Georgia, and he and Annie Lou moved there. After they left, Myra and James never went to North Connolly anymore. She thought about the blue boy a lot and wondered why he had stopped showing up. She needed something to help her keep going through the hard times.

A boy did come to help her. She could see the main road from her front porch and enjoyed sitting there and watching the cars, wagons, and buggies go past. There was getting to be a lot of cars passing by, and even a bus went by going somewhere. One day she saw the bus slowing down on the main road and saw someone sitting on top. The bus stopped, and a man climbed off, grabbed a croker sack, put a red hat on his head, and headed right to her house. Before he got halfway there, she left the young'uns on the porch and ran to him.

"Lord, Izzy, where did you come from?"

"Right off the top of that bus. I can't buy no ticket, but the driver lets me ride on top for nothing."

She had to laugh about him riding on top of the bus. She was so glad to see him, and he laughed and jumped around just like always.

He kept hugging her and saying, "Myra, Myra, Myra."

Finally, he settled down enough that she could ask him what he had been doing and how he had found her.

"I been goin' round ever place with Pa. I give testimonies at the tent meetin's."

"What kind of testimonies do ya give?"

"Pa tells me to tell folks how I been saved from the devil's grasp to bring my story to them."

Bunk had made him go over and over that until he could say it by heart. She knew Izzy had never been in the devil's grasp.

"After I give my testimony, we gets a love offerin' and most times we go to somebody's house to eat.

"I asked about you ever time we came close to Glencoe. We wuz in Terrytown, and a feller told me that his sister wuz married to Will Rob, and he knowed where 'bouts you lived. I run off from Pa and come over here on that bus. They wuz some folks on the bus that told the driver right where to put me off at yore place."

Myra could hardly believe that Izzy had been able to find her. They talked and talked about Nannie and the old times. He played with the young'uns as if he was one of them. He kept saying, "Myra, you a rich woman now."

Thinking back to how it had been when they all lived together, it must look that way. Back then she had a good feeling about herself, and now she was scared she had lost it forever.

She went to the kitchen to start supper before Izzy started saying, "Want some-teat." She was praying James would be sober when he got home so Izzy wouldn't see him in the shape they used to see Bunk. She didn't know how to explain Izzy's being there to James. He always hated for any of her folks to come.

James came in sober as a judge and acted as though he was happy to have Izzy. He laughed and laughed about him riding on top of the bus and told him that he was smart to take his hat off so it wouldn't blow off in the wind. Izzy just beamed when he heard James say he was smart, and he worshipped James from then on.

Later that night when the two of them were on the porch, Izzy told her he didn't want to go back to Bunk and keep on going to the tent meetings.

"I know hit's the Lord's work, but hit makes me feel shamed when I have to do that. I want to stay here with you. I'll work fer James."

She wanted to help him, but she knew for sure that James wouldn't be willing to take him in. James seemed to enjoy him and laughed a lot at some of the things he said. She felt bad when he acted like a little child, because he was a full-grown man and was almost as old as James. She knew he couldn't help it, but James would lead him into something that made him act silly and then James got a good laugh out of it. Izzy didn't mind at all. In fact, he seemed to love James better than anybody.

After a few days, James did ask when she thought Izzy was going to leave. She had to tell him what Izzy said about not going back to Bunk, but she made it plain to him that she wasn't expecting him to stay on with them. James thought for a few minutes and then came up with an idea that she should have thought up herself.

"What about Will Rob? He could use him as a helper, and he wouldn't have to pay him much of anything."

That sounded good, but there was still the problem of where he was going to stay, since Will Rob and Angie just had a room with kitchen privileges. James said he would work on it.

The next morning Izzy packed his things in the croker sack and left for town with James. She wondered all day what was happening, and she was fearful that James would just tell him to go someplace else and not come back to their house. This was another time when she misjudged what a really good and kind man she had married. James came home by himself and grinning from ear to ear.

"I got ol' Izzy fixed up, and that boy is tickled to death. I took him to Will Rob first, and he was glad to give him a little job to do. Will Rob took him over to Miz Perkins, who runs a boarding house for the railroad men. She has a little storeroom that has enough space for a cot. She said he could sleep there, and she would give him his meals. In return, he could chop up her stove wood, build her fire every morning, and clean up the kitchen every night. She said that as long as he behaved himself, he could stay there. The first thing Miz Perkins did was fix him a plate of biscuits and syrup. When we left him, he was sitting on the steps and sopping away."

She felt so relieved that he had a place where he could help out and have a home. She didn't see Izzy much after that. He came to the house a few times, but she could tell he didn't need her and that was good. He stayed in Glencoe for a few years, and then he just disappeared. Some said that he climbed back on top of a bus and went to his pa.

She worried about the way James was acting, but she kept hoping and praying he would get over whatever was bothering him. He was drinking more and more, and staying out. Angie told her that he was losing business in the store to a new ten-cent store that had come to town. Olla told her that Malcolm said some days James just put the Closed sign on the door and left for most of the day. He sure wasn't coming home, so she didn't know where he might have gone. She had some notions about it, but she couldn't let herself think like that. She stayed busy trying to keep her growing young'uns in clothes and food.

Almost before she knew it another year passed. One day in the early spring, she had just started hanging out a big wash when she saw a shiny black automobile driving up to the front walk.

The young'uns started hollering, "It's Papa, it's Papa."

They ran and climbed onto the running boards, and James started blowing the horn. She didn't know what to think, and she wasn't about to run out there like a young'un.

Idella came to the backyard and said, "Mama, come out and see Papa's new car. We all going for a ride in it."

She didn't know why, but her blood ran cold, and she said, "I've got wash to finish and no time for a fool who doesn't have any more sense than that."

Idella ran back to the car, and as soon as she told him what her ma said, he came flying to the yard. If looks could kill you, she would have died on the spot.

"Don't you ever call me a fool to my young'uns again. I bought this car to help you, and if you don't want to ride in it, I can shore find someone who will. Right now, me and *my* young'uns are going for a ride and you and yore wash can just be damned."

They took off in a cloud of dust. Myra didn't even look up from the washboard. The only thought she had was how did James learn how to drive a car and where did he get the money to buy it. She knew he hadn't been making much at the store, and he threw away what he did make. He stopped trying to make a go of the store after his pa died. She always managed to feed the young'uns, but sometimes she got real short on rations.

When she finally looked up from the scrub board, she saw Olla and her young'uns hurrying down the road. She had seen the car, because she was always watching to see what was going on at Myra's house. Myra loved her like a sister, but she was nosey. There wasn't anything to do but tell her what had happened. If she was expecting sympathy, she didn't get it from Olla.

"Myra, you are the biggest fool I have ever seen. You know how proud James is, and he couldn't wait to show that car to you. You hurt his feelings real bad. Here you are washing instead of being off with him and the young'uns havin' a good time. If Malcolm had given me that chance, I'd left the clothes in the pot. You can wash anytime."

What she said made Myra stop and think. She hadn't meant to hurt James's feelings, but it had always been her way to put work ahead of everything. He knew they had to have clean clothes, especially since he put on a clean starched shirt every day. She couldn't give Olla the satisfaction of seeing that she was bothered by her words, so she just kept on washing. Olla helped her hang the clothes, and before she left she had more to say.

"Myra, you mark my word, you are in fer trouble with that man if you don't stop thinking work is all there is and pay more attention to him."

After Olla left, Myra tried to think of what she should do, but it just wasn't in her to act like that.

Middle of the afternoon the car drove up, and James let the young'uns out. Then he took off again, sending the dust flying. The young'uns were excited and happy about having a good time with their papa.

"Idella, I reckon you young'uns ain't had a bite of dinner."

"Oh yea, Papa bought us hamburgers and drinks and ice cream."

James did know how to turn the young'ens head. She didn't bother to ask where they had gone. It was a nice sunny day, and the clothes dried quickly. She brought in the wash and was ready to iron the next day. The young'uns spent the rest of the day playing car with a big box.

She fed the young'uns, got them to bed, and then sat up wondering where James was. She didn't want to think about what he was doing. The words he said were still in her mind.

"If you don't want to come with me, I can shore find someone who will."

After a while she gave up on him coming home, so she lay down but didn't close her eyes. Way into the night she heard him coming in. She knew he was drunk as a lord and was still mad with her. He didn't come into their room. After a while she went to check on him and found him piled in the bed with Stephen. She had to laugh because Stephen still wet the bed almost every night. If it happened, it would serve him right. The next morning he didn't say a word to her as he rushed out the door and into the car. She had to find a way to talk to him and ask him how he got the car and what he did with June.

This went on for nearly a week. She wanted him to come back to their bed, but she didn't know what to say or do. He wasn't eating at home, but she saw his car at his ma's most days for dinner. She knew Olieta was enjoying this.

Finally, one night James came in and pulled off his clothes and got in their bed. She didn't say a word to him, but she couldn't help but enjoy feeling his warm body beside her again. It didn't take long for them to get back together and enjoy being man and wife.

After he ate his breakfast the next morning, he didn't race out like he usually did. He kept sitting at the table.

Finally, he said, "Myra, as soon as you get the young'uns fed, send them to Olla's, because I want to talk to you."

She didn't know what to expect when she came back in the kitchen.

"Myra, I've made a lot of changes in the last few days. I have done something that I have wanted to do for a long time. First off, I sold the store to a Jew that just came to town. I just couldn't make a go of it, and I didn't like having to stay there all the time. I know I can make better money and enjoy working more at something else. I used the money I got from the store to buy the car. You know I have always wanted a car. Besides, I have to have a car, because tomorrow I am starting to work for Hunter Furniture Company.

"You know what a good salesman I am. They want me to travel all over these parts and sell furniture. We got pictures of the furniture in a catalog. I sell it to them, and then the truck from Glencoe will deliver it right to their house. I will make money on every piece I sell. You know how good I am at selling, so we are going to have more money than ever. I will have to be on the road a lot, but I will be back home every few days. I am going to do good at this, and I will get to do everything that I want to do for you and the young'uns. You know that is all I care about. So what do you think about it?"

She was shocked and had never thought of something like that. She knew she had to say the right thing. It was already done, and there was no turning back, so she had to find a way to make the best of it.

"What did you do with June?"

James finally broke into a smile and said, "Leave it to you to think more of that mare than you do a brand-new car. I sold her to Possum Henry. He'll take good care of her. He needs her to pull his wagon when he delivers things from his farm. Now the next thing I want to know is where do you want to go in our car next Sunday. You know it will go over thirty miles in an hour, so we can go and come back from almost anywhere we want in a day."

She hadn't thought about that part of having a car, and there was a place that she really wanted to go.

"James, could we go all the way to Soperton and a little beyond to Friendship Church."

"Shore, we can get there in less than two hours. Why do you want to go there?"

"That's where my Aunt Mary Coleman lives. Her husband pastors that church, and I ain't seen her in so long."

She was afraid he wouldn't want to go to see any of her folks, but he was excited and wanted to show off the car.

"You fix us dinner to carry, and we'll head over there early Sunday morning."

"Uncle Daniel will be preachin'. There ain't no need in gettin' there so early."

"I've head of that church, and I want to get there in time for preaching."

Myra couldn't believe her ears. She was always afraid to bring up anything about her folks, because James had made it clear that he did not like to be around any of them. It was hard on her because she loved them and just plain got homesick to be with them, especially Will Rob. She went to see Angie every time she went to town, but Will Rob was usually at work. She stayed so busy with the young'uns that she didn't go to town but every week or so. James always brought home all the rations, and the only other things she bought were piece goods for her sewing.

It was Wednesday when James told her that they could go to see Aunt Mary, so she had a few days to think about getting ready. When she thought of her aunt, it made her feel like a little girl again. She wanted to show that she had done well in life. She would take the best crocheted pieces and a jar of everything she had canned.

The rest of the week flew by. It was too late to let her aunt know they were coming, and it never crossed her mind that Aunt Mary might not be there. She washed, starched, and ironed clothes for all of them. She was starting to polish up everybody's shoes when James drove in early on Saturday evening and told them to get in the car. They were going to town to get new shoes for everybody. She was so happy and felt as if she was floating on air.

She had cooked enough to feed them a good dinner after the preaching, and she was taking some little treats to give the young'uns on the way. She fried two chickens, baked a big pan of biscuits and two sweet tater pies, and she took jars of cucumber and peach pickles. Every thing could be eaten right out of their hands. She packed everything in a little trunk that James brought with him when they moved from the MacTavish house.

They got up before daylight on Sunday. She fed them a breakfast of fried eggs between biscuits like she remembered Mr. Clyde fixing the first time she went to Tennille. The car was packed and ready to go.

"James, you've shined this car so much that I can see myself in it."

"I ain't shined the car any more than you have shined the young'uns."

She was proud of how her family looked and preached them a sermon about how they were supposed to act. She knew the girls would be good, but Stephen was something else. Sometimes it seemed as though she had to whip him every time he came in the house.

Driving through the countryside on such a long trip was new to her, and she enjoyed looking at everything. The young'uns kept busy looking out the windows and waving to folks they passed.

"James, look at how good Laura James's hair curled when I put it up on rags. Ain't she pretty?"

"She shore is. She looks like a baby doll."

That didn't set well with Idella at all. She thought she was the only one her papa was supposed to brag on. It wasn't any time before they were fussing in the back seat, and Laura James ended up crying.

It turned out that Idella was saying to her, "I'm pretty and what makes me deny it."

Every time she said that, Laura James would light into her. When Stephen saw how easy it was to aggravate Laura James, he started saying it too. Myra threatened to stop and get a switch if they kept this up, but every time she wasn't looking back at them, they started tormenting Laura James again. Myra was getting really mad because they were ruining the happy time. She didn't want Laura James to look as if she had been crying when Aunt Mary saw her.

James didn't get into it until they drove through Soperton. He slowed the car down almost to a stop.

"Y'all look over there on that corner. That's the jailhouse, and that's where I'm gonna leave y'all if you don't stop this fussing and aggravating yore mama."

The young'uns eyes got as big as saucers, and they didn't say another word until they drove up in the churchyard. That didn't settle it forever though, and Idella and Stephen kept on tormenting Laura James with this saying until they were all grown. It all came from Idella just being plain jealous of Laura James for having pretty curly hair.

They drove up at the church just as the service started. The only bench with room for all of them to sit was right at the back. Uncle Daniel preached and prayed for at least an hour. There were breaks during the sermon for hymns, and the singing was good. Myra craned her neck every which way trying to see Aunt Mary. She finally spotted her up near the front, and her aunt looked just like she remembered. The young'uns sat quiet and still. James had scared them good with the talk of the jail. James had not gone to church much lately, but he seemed to be listening to the sermon and sang out on all the hymns. At the close of the service, Uncle Daniel had an altar call and asked any visitors to stand and say who they were. She knew James wouldn't like it if she did that, so she just sat tight. She was dying to get to Aunt Mary after the service and hoped her aunt would recognize her.

Uncle Daniel and some of the deacons were standing at the door greeting people when they walked out. James shook his hand and said, "We are Mr. and Miz James MacTavish from Glencoe, and these are our young'uns, sir."

Uncle Daniel stopped shaking hands and looked right at Myra and grabbed her to him in a big hug and hollered.

"Mary, Mary, come quick and see who is here."

Her aunt broke into a big smile and pushed through the crowd to get to Myra. They hugged and hugged.

She said over and over, "Myra, you made a fine lady. Myra, you made a fine lady."

She hugged and kissed all the young'uns and even hugged James. For the first time, James seemed to have found some of her family that he liked and that he thought was as good as the MacTavishes.

"Now you must come to our house for dinner. I'm going on over, and Daniel will come as soon as everyone leaves."

"We brought our dinner with us, Aunt Mary. You didn't know we wuz comin'."

"Oh, I know you've got plenty, but we will put it all together. A preacher's wife always cooks enough on Sunday to feed all that might come to dinner at her table. I want every minute I can get with you, Myra."

Their house was right next door to the church, so they walked over. It was a big white-washed house with a wide porch all across the front. First off, James had to take the young'uns to the toilet. Myra took her trunk of food to the kitchen

"Myra, you are so smart to think of carrying it like that, and look at all that good stuff."

Already, the front porch rockers were filled with folks who were waiting to be called to dinner. James sat on the porch and seemed to be enjoying talking with the men. She heard him mention Samuel, and several of the deacons knew him. Idella, Laura James, and Stephen were sitting on the front steps and playing some kind of game. Idella was good at thinking up things for them to play.

She was wondering how she would go about feeding the young'uns without sitting them at the table. Aunt Mary had already thought of that.

"Myra, I want to have as much time to be with you as I can. How about we fix plates for the young'uns and sit in the kitchen to eat. I will set the table for the other folk, and they can just pass the food around."

"Oh, Aunt Mary, I would love to do that. All that I want is to be with you."

While she was setting the food out and calling everyone into the dining room, Myra filled a plate for each of them. The table was loaded with good things to eat, but what she saw and wanted most was raisin cake, just like the one Aunt Mary had given to them on that day in Tennille. They put the young'uns up to the kitchen table, and they dug into their food.

"My, my, look at how those babies eat. I love to see children eat like that and not be finicky. You and James have sure done a fine job with them, Myra."

"My young'ens eat whatever's put in front of them. James always sees to it that we have plenty."

"He's a good husband and father, and I am so happy for you."

They took their plates and sat in two rocking chairs pulled up close together. When they started talking, Aunt Mary wanted to hear about the rest of the family. Myra told her about Joe Wiley, Will Rob, Annie Lou, Dolly, and Jesse.

"I wish I could tell you about Arno, but all I know is that he's been gone fer six years. I don't know where he is."

"Myra, I had no idea that you didn't know where Arno was. I have known all along, and I would have tried to let you know if I had known that you were worried about him. When Arno left Glencoe, he went back to Washington County. His first thought was to find Mr. Clyde, but both he and Miz Sara had passed on. Their son had sold the place, and new people were living there. The colored folks that he used to know told him that Joe Early had been elected sheriff. Arno took off for Tennille, because he thought Joe Early might give him some kind of work. Of course, Joe Early was tickled pink to see him.

"You remember he had asked your ma about raising both the little boys, and he had always worried about them. They were just too young to make it without a pa. He was glad to give him a home and put him to work doing jobs for him around the courthouse. Arno took right to it. You know what a smart boy he always was.

"Arno stayed there for five years or more, but he was just too smart a boy not to want to better himself. He talked to Joe Early a lot about what he could do to get out and learn more. Finally, Joe Early took him up near Macon to an army camp, and Arno joined the army. Joe Early thought it was a good thing for him to do. He would always have a place to live, and he could learn how to do something other than farm. He said he never did like farming. Anyway, right after that, the army sent him way off to another camp in Texas for his training, and that is where he still is, I suspect.

"He sent Joe Early a letter and told him that he liked it fine, and they had given him a lot of uniforms to wear, and he thanked Joe Early for all that he had done for him. He said when he finished the training he would get a furlough, and he was coming back to see everyone. I just bet he will turn up on your doorsteps sometime soon."

That was the best news that she had heard in a long time. Not only was Arno safe and well, but she knew he was doing what he really wanted to do.

"Myra you have a good husband and such sweet children. I am so happy for you. My one sorrow is that Daniel and I were never blessed with children. You are going to have another one, aren't you?"

Now how did she know that? Myra hadn't been sure herself until a few weeks ago, and she hadn't even told James. She knew he would be happy because he loved babies and was proud of his family. She loved her young'uns, but she didn't know how she was going to manage another one when she always had to be thinking about petting and babying their papa.

She must have looked troubled because Aunt Mary said, "What is it, Myra? I can see something is bothering you."

Myra had never talked about James to anyone but Olla, but her worries started spilling out. She didn't say anything about the bad stuff like drinking and staying out. She did tell her about the way James liked so much attention and how he was spoiled by his family and thought he should always be petted.

"Aunt Mary, it just ain't my nature to do that. Papa didn't need that kind of foolishness. He saw me workin' and that wuz enough. I ain't never learned to say the lovin' things that James seems to crave. I keep the house clean, cook plenty of good food; my sewin' keeps the young'uns in clothes. I keep a garden, a cow, and chickens. We hardly have to buy anything from the store except when James wants something different. All that should be enough fer him to know I care about him.

"Sometimes, we have bad fusses 'bout this. Like the day he brought home the car, and thought I should stop washing and go ridin' in hit."

"Myra, all of us are different. You had a hard time all your life, and I know it is hard to put yourself in James's place. He must have had it real easy, and all of his folks made him feel like he was something special. That is a good way to feel, and he wants you to keep it up. There is nothing wrong with letting go some of that work you do and take the time to enjoy being with him. I bet he would rather have you with him than to have the house spic and span. He is a nice-looking man, and he has a lot of pride. You need to let him know how much you love and appreciate him.

"Now you say that it was never the way of your family to make over people, but you are wrong. Your father was as loving a boy as there ever was, and think about how much he loved your mother to give up all that could have been his. I think you will learn, and then you and James will be much happier."

"I want to try, but I just don't know if I can change that much."

They didn't get to talk anymore because it was time to clear the table. Myra was ready to wash the dishes, but Aunt Mary told her a young girl was coming in a little later to clean up the kitchen. She said the young girl, Ava, helped her every day, but she let her off on Sunday morning to go to her own church. Before they could say more, James came in.

"Aunt Mary, this has shore been an enjoyable day, and I am pleased to finally get to meet the aunt that Myra loves so much. I hate to leave, but we need to start back to get home by dark."

"James, you just bring Myra and these fine young'uns back again. You all are welcome any time."

After hugs all around and promises to come back soon, they piled in the car and headed back to Glencoe.

Almost as soon as the car cranked, all three young'uns were asleep. It had been such a happy day for her, especially because she found out about Arno. She could tell James had enjoyed it too, and he started telling her things the men told him and advice they had given him on selling in their part of the country. She wanted to make over James and let him know how happy she felt that day. It just seemed right for her to move over in the seat close to him. He put his arm around her and drove the car with one hand. Then he started teaching her how to help him shift the gears and said that she would be driving soon.

The time seemed just right to tell him about the new baby coming. He was tickled and said he was going to spend all the time that he wasn't out on the road at home helping her and taking the other young'uns off her hands. She had to bite her tongue to keep from saying that she would believe that when she saw it. She needed to pray hard for the Lord to help her keep from saying spiteful things.

The sun had gone down when they got home, and it was almost dark. Myra just put the young'uns right to bed. They had eaten so much dinner that nobody was hungry.

The next morning James headed out to start his route. He would be gone until Thursday. He was going down south of Glencoe to McRae,

Helena, and she didn't know where else. He would spend the nights in rooming houses. She knew he was excited, and maybe this type of traveling work would keep him satisfied. She would miss him, but she was determined to make the best of this new way of living and not nag him.

Things did seem to be going good. James was gone every week from Monday to Thursday and a few times even to Saturday morning. The days he was not traveling he worked in the store or worked on his accounts. Most of the furniture was sold on credit, and he had to collect every week as well as sell. He was making good money, and every week he brought something home for them. He bought a phonograph, new lamp, pretty pillows for the divan, and some little rocking chairs for the young'uns. It was easier for her during the week when he wasn't home, because she could get all the work done and not have to worry about what he was doing or thinking. She always spruced up herself and the young'uns and had a good supper cooked when he got home. The only thing that was worrisome was never knowing when he would stay out past Thursday. He said he didn't have banker's hours and just had to stay until he finished up the route. She believed him, and thank the Lord, she did not complain to him. She was disappointed when he didn't get in on Thursday night, but she always had a smile on my face when he did get home.

-17-

By early summer, Myra was as big as a barrel. The baby was never still. Just when she got comfortable, it would start moving around. The young'uns got a kick out of feeling a little hand or foot sticking right against her skin. James said this one was all MacTavish for sure, because it was already trying to get a head start. The pregnancy was easy, and except for being heavy and awkward, she felt fine.

The morning of August sixth was a Monday, and James had his car packed to leave for the week. The doctor had figured the baby wouldn't come for a few more weeks He was wrong. Just as James was walking out the door, she was hit by a pain and yelled to James.

He rushed back into the house, put her in bed, and sent Idella to get Malcolm and Olla. The pains were coming one right after the other, and she knew this baby was in a hurry to see the world. Malcolm went for the doctor, and it was a good thing that he found him quickly. In two hours they had a new baby girl. Myra was wide awake the whole time. Afterward, she didn't feel as if she had done a thing. Olla cleaned the baby up and handed her to James.

"Myra, just look at this fine baby girl. She is filled out better than any baby I've ever seen, and listen how strong she cries."

"Give her here, James. I know how to stop that crying."

Myra put her to the breast, and she started nursing. Her little eyes looked right at Myra. They just locked eyes together. Myra had a feeling she had seen this baby before. Every time she nursed her, it was the same way. She couldn't stop looking into the baby's eyes. All babies have sort of blue eyes, but the eyes of the other three had shown signs of being dark from birth. The MacTavish all had almost black eyes, and Myra's eyes were dark. This baby's eyes were blue as beads. She just felt as though she had seen those eyes before. After a few days she realized when she looked at the baby, she was looking into her papa's blue eyes.

They hadn't talked about a name, but she knew James had one picked out. He kind of hemmed and hawed about it before saying he had promised Olieta that she could name this baby. She didn't much like it, but she could give her a nickname if she didn't like the name. The first time Olieta came to see the baby, she was the happiest that Myra had ever seen her.

"I want to name her Ovieda for my dear twin sister."

Myra hated to call that little baby such an ugly, old-timey name, but she would have to go along with it. She had started thinking up a nickname when Olieta gave her a surprise.

"My favorite story in the Bible is the story of Ruth. I name her Ruth Ovieda."

The name just fit the little, blue-eyed girl. Myra knew the story of Ruth and hoped her Ruth would have as much love in her as the Bible Ruth.

Ruth was born on August sixth, and by the time the weather started to turn cool, she was fat as a butterball. When Myra took her out, people looked at her and talked about her pretty eyes. She was different than the other young'uns in more ways than just her eyes. She cried and fretted more. The others were easy to pacify when they cried, but Ruth always seemed to want more than just something to eat or dry diapers. Her little eyes were always looking around. It was as if she wanted to see all there was to see in the world. They loved her dearly, but when she got older, Myra knew she would be a handful and harder to deal with than the others.

Olieta and Idella acted as if she was their very own baby girl. Idella took care of her just like a little mother and never got tired of it. Olieta came to see her every evening. She would rock her and talk just like Ruth was grown. Of course, the main thing that she told her was how special it was to be a MacTavish and how she had to live up to the name. Myra was tired of hearing this, but at least she kept the baby contented. It did seem like Ruth was taking in everything, Olieta said. James got a big kick out of hearing Olieta talk to Ruth—that is, whenever he happened to be home long enough.

James was staying on the road more and more, and many weeks he didn't get home until late Saturday. She was keeping her vow not to fuss at him, but it sure did make a lonely week for her. When he did get home, he seemed happy and proud of what he was doing. He was making good money, but he managed to spend most of it before he got home. Of course, he always brought home groceries and anything else they needed. He gave Myra money every week. She tried to hang on to whatever he gave her. She knew they needed to put some back because good times don't last forever.

Every time she had the chance to sit down by herself, she would think about the things Aunt Mary had told her. She was the only person whose advice Myra tried to follow. She talked things over with Olla, but that was no help. Malcolm did as bad if not worse than James, and Olla let him get away with it. There was never a chance to talk with Will Rob. He had to work hard to keep up with the money that Angie spent. Besides, every time they were together, Angie did all the talking. It was hard for him to keep ahead when they had to buy every mouthful they ate. She knew he remembered how they never bought much but flour and sugar. James bought a lot, but if it was left up to her, they would buy only what they couldn't grow. Angie would never know how to manage like that, and Will Rob never complained. Also, she hadn't talked freely with her brother since she told him that he was not to ever say anything bad to her about James.

Idella and Laura James were both going to school now. They had to walk about a mile into town, but all of the other MacTavish young'uns walked along with them. Half of the school was made up of MacTavishes. Olla and Malcolm had Tom, Emma, and Jewel, and Olla was about to have another one. Lewis and Lottie lived just down the road with Lizzie. Grace and Lonzy had built a house on the other side of the MacTavish place, and they had Louise, Fern, and Andrew. George and Birdie lived closer to town, and they had a houseful too.

Fern was the same age as Idella, and they loved to play together. Laura James and Jewel teamed up. That left Stephen, Andrew, and the rest on the outs, so what they did was pester each other and fight. Sometimes, Myra didn't know how they got through the day without killing each other. When it got so bad, either she or Olla would go out with a switch and wear them all out. Since all the young'uns always played at one of their houses, they figured it was their right. Grace got a knot in her nose more times than once about Andrew getting a switching. Myra didn't care, because she figured that boy was going to need more switching than she could give him. Stephen would mind his mama and really helped her out a lot, but he wasn't about to let anyone get the best of him. If the bigger ones picked on him, he would bide his time and find a way to get back at them. Sometimes she thought he acted like a little man, even if he was just four years old. She had expected James to be proud of having a son and really pay attention to him, but it had not worked like that. Stephen wouldn't mind James like he did his mama, and he didn't seem to care about being around his papa like the girls did. That didn't set well with James at all, because he thought everybody should make over him. She knew Stephen was natured up like her, and he would never do that.

Late one evening in the middle of the week, she was sitting in the porch swing getting Ruth to sleep when she saw two fellows coming down the road. She couldn't make out who they were until they were almost on her. Then she flew down the steps so fast that she left Ruth in the swing. They were two men, not boys, and they were Arno and Jesse. She couldn't believe her eyes. Arno was in a soldier suit, and he was a sight for sore eyes. Both of them had little satchels as if they were traveling. After she had hugged them enough, they sat on the porch, and Arno talked in his quiet way about all that he had been doing.

"I got to go to see Aunt Mary, and she told me about you bein' in the army. Now tell me about where you've been."

"I took my basic training in Texas. The base wuz right next to Mexico, and it was hotter than Georgia. It was hard work, but I did real well. See this stripe? It means they promoted me to private."

"I am proud of you. You're getting to see places just like you wanted."

"After I finished my training, they gave me two weeks off before I report to my next base. It took me nearly a week to get here on the bus, and I've tried to see everybody but Annie Lou. She lives too far. My next base is just over the line in Alabama, so I have to leave tomorrow."

"I never knowed nothin' about the army, but hit sounds like a good place fer a feller like you."

"It is, Myra. I will always have money in my pocket, a good bed to sleep in, and plenty of food to eat. It gives me a chance to work myself up and make something out of myself. I like going to different bases."

"I hope it stays that way fer you. Jesse, are you here to see him off?"

"No, I'm joining the army too."

"When I told Will Rob and Joe Wiley about how much the army had done for me, they both thought it would be a good place for him. Will Rob gave him money for the ticket, and he's going to my camp to sign up."

"I hate to see both my little brothers go off so far, but it does sound good for you."

She felt a little jealous, because they were going to go places and see things that she would never see in her life time, but she had a family that made up for it.

The young'uns were shy around Arno, and like always, he didn't have much to say. He didn't seem to want to talk about old times. She realized how hard it had been for Arno, because he was natured up different from the rest of them. He did laugh when she started telling about the time they picked all those pears and ate on them for a week. Jesse had always played with her young'uns just like another young'un, but this time he was trying to act grown up for Arno's sake. She got together a good supper, and they went to bed early because they had to get to the bus in Glencoe early the next morning. She would miss them, but she was glad that they had someplace to go. They had such a hard time coming up, and poor little Jesse hadn't had a real home since Ma died. Now his home would be the army. She prayed they wouldn't have to go to any kind of fighting across the water.

The next morning she was up before sunup, cooked a big breakfast, and packed some vittles for them to eat along on the bus ride. When they left, she stood and watched as long as she could see them walking down the road. She remembered when Pa had watched Joe Wiley leave and how Jesse and Arno had run behind Uncle Joe Early's buggy. There is nothing sadder than seeing somebody leave when you don't know when you will ever see them again.

She sat down on the porch, and her heart was so heavy it was about to burst. It was way too early to get the young'uns ready for school, so she had a little time to herself. She thought about how they all sat around the table when Papa was living, and now they were scattered everywhere. No two of them were together except for Annie Lou and Dolly. She hadn't seen them since they moved off to the coast of Georgia.

Dolly was a big girl now, and she was faring just fine with Horace and Annie Lou. She hoped Dolly helped take care of Rachel. Annie Lou had another baby now, so she needed the help. This one was a boy called Coy. She heard he was crippled in one of his arms, but he was not in nearly as bad a shape as Rachel was for the first few years of her life. She was thankful that Rachel was doing well, but after her late start, she would always be small and not real strong. Myra started to cry, which was something she hadn't let herself do in a long time. She missed them all, but most of all she missed James being by her side like a husband should be.

She didn't know how things would turn out with them. When he was on the road, she knew he was drinking, and she also knew there were a lot of low-living women around the places where he went to drink. If she let herself think like that, she just couldn't abide it. She had to remember the good things.

She hadn't thought of the blue boy in a long time, but now she wanted to see him. She wished he would come back and help her find the way. Her mind was drifting on and on. She had thought about him a lot over the years, and she knew there wasn't really a blue boy. Somehow her mind had made him up, but one thing she knew for sure. There was an Aunt Mary, and she helped her when they talked about how things were with James. She said that Papa was a loving man, but Myra only saw him showing his love by working and taking care of them. That was still how she thought it should be.

James had a side too, and like Aunt Mary said, she needed to think about his side. He did try to take good care of them, and he wanted his family to have what they needed. Of course, a lot of those things she would just as soon not have. A barrel of flour meant more to her than a flowered hat. James wasn't going to change, and if she changed to be like him, there was no way to keep the family running. One of them had to think more about the flour barrel than flowered hats, and she knew it would not be James.

All she could do was pray for God to make James a stronger man, so he wouldn't fall into drinking and all the other foolishness. Most of the time when she thought about James, it was only about the times he had hurt her or shamed himself. This would just make her mad with him all over again. This time the thoughts that came into her mind were the times he had shown what a good man he could be. She looked at the sewing machine and thought how much pleasure and help it had given to her. She thought of how Idella and Laura James just thought he was the finest pa in the world.

Some evenings in the summer when the days were long, James would come in just as she got supper ready to put on the table, and say, "Gal, lets pack up something easy and take these young'uns down to the creek to eat their supper. It will be mighty pretty down there this evening."

Sometimes she would pitch a fit and wouldn't do it, because she didn't have a thing fit to take outdoors. Other times she would pack up biscuits and fried meat, tea cakes, and peaches, berries, watermelon, or whatever was bearing, and they would head out for the creek. She never saw it as anything but more trouble for her, but the young'uns thought it was the finest thing they had ever done. She did like to sit under the same tree that she and James sat under when they were courting and watch him playing with their young'uns. Maybe some of his ways weren't foolishness. She never got to play like that when she was a young'un, and that might be something that young'uns need as much as a full belly. Maybe he showed his love for her in the only way that was natural for him.

She sat there swinging a little, and then she started to hum, and then it turned into a full hymn that she had learned from Olla. The verses reminded her of how Papa always said she had a brightness about her. She had never sung beyond the first verse before, but the words to the second verse came to her. This verse told her that she could use her brightness to lead others to a better life.

"Lord, can I do it? Can I make my life bright and lead James to a better life? I've got a tough row to hoe, but I was never one to stop and lean on my hoe. Oh, Lord, I am willin' to try. Help me, Lord. It's the only hope I got."

She had never turned to Him before. To tell the truth, she had been mad at Him ever since He took Papa in such a way and at the time that He did. When she went to church, she tried to take in the sermon and find a way to talk to the Lord. Mostly, she used that time to rest and think about times in the past. She knew there was a Lord, and he took care of what happened to folks. She knew the Lord never forget about Myra, because he sent a lot of good people her way to help her over the hardest times. Maybe since He has to be the one in charge, He sends out His love to folks through the little baby Jesus. She had always thought about Jesus as a little baby like in the Christmas programs at Sullivan's Corner. She didn't like to think of the hard times He had after He became a man.

Then it came to her. That was how it worked. The sweetness in that little baby goes out to other people, and they give it back by being good to other people. After she lost Papa, she found Miz Sara and Aunt Mary. To go on back even more, there was Miss Caroline who taught her to crochet. Nannie helped her lots just by being there and needing her help. She found Annie and her ma, who taught her to sew. There was even that good doctor who gave Dolly and her a ride to Dublin to catch the train when she came to Glencoe. Of course, there was Olla, who was more like a sister than her own sisters. She had to add Miz Rosenberg, the little Jew lady who helped her get ready to marry James. Although he never seemed like a loving man, she remembered how Judge MacTavish stood up for her the first night James brought her home. Maybe all of them had a little love from the baby Jesus in them. She knew the Lord meant the world to be a place of love and goodness, and when she looked at her own four little young'uns, she knew this was true.

She thought back to the first time she saw James and how she never dreamed he would end up being her husband. If all the things in the past had not happened, she would never have been his wife and had her four little young'uns. That must be the way it was meant to be.

Day started to break, and the sunrise was the most beautiful she had ever seen. It just seemed to hang in the sky for her to enjoy. She heard Ruth crying, and then she heard Idella up with her. She had breakfast cooked and sitting on the back of the stove for the young'uns. Two clean, starched, and ironed dresses were ready for the girls to wear. One of her best times was watching them walk off to school, carrying their little dinner pails and looking so clean and sweet. She knew they would get to go on to school and learn more than she would ever know. James would see to that.

After she got them off, she was going to sit and play with Ruth. Then she would start a new dress for herself from a flowered print that she had bought for the girls. They certainly had plenty of dresses. If it was warm enough after dinner, she would take Stephen and Ruth and walk to Glencoe. She would stop in at Miz Rosenberg's store and see how things were with her. She might just buy herself a flowered hat.

When James got home, he would have to shade his eyes. Every corner in their house would be so bright. She didn't know if she could lead James, but she could give him a way to follow. There was still a long row ahead for them to hoe, but she knew that they would work it together. If he needed help along the way, she knew how to lend him a hand.

-18-

The afternoon after Arno and Jesse left for the army was sunny and warm. Myra took that as a sign that she act on some of the thoughts she had that morning. She put Ruth in the buggy, took Stephen by the hand, and set off to buy a flowered hat. Miz Rosenberg had hats displayed all around the store. Myra kept the goal long enough to try on a few. Her practical nature just would not let her spend money on something that had no value except to look pretty. Miz Rosenberg helped her try them on, but she knew that Myra was not a customer for a flowered hat. The two had become friends during the years and enjoyed their little visits together. Myra knew what loneliness felt like, and she knew her friend had no family nearby except for her husband and children. There was not even a church of her kind that she could attend.

She thought about Miz Rosenberg a lot, and for some reason, she always felt sad when she thought of her. Rosenberg's was the best store in Glencoe and had plenty of customers. They owned a big house just off Main Street, and she was sure they had everything they needed and probably, most of the things they wanted. The Rosenberg children went to school with all the MacTavish young'uns, but she had never seen them playing with other children. They just seemed standoffish and real quiet. She brought up a picture in her mind of Miz Rosenberg sitting on the porch with her, and they were talking just like she would do with Olla. All the young'uns were playing together in the yard, and they were laughing and hollering. She couldn't hold that picture for long, because it just didn't seem right.

She tried not to question the Lord, but she couldn't help wondering why He spread His chosen people out so thin all over Georgia. If they were all in the same spot, they could have their own kind of church and not be

271

so lonely. Then again, they might be happy just knowing they came from the people in the Bible that God took to the Promised Land. She didn't know enough about this to even wonder, so she just put it out of her mind. Trying on hats had not taken very long, so she had time to stop by Angie's before heading home. Angie was always good for a laugh, because she knew all the gossip going around Glencoe. As always, Angie was sitting on the porch. Will Rob had sectioned off one corner of the porch for a little pen. Doreen sat in there on a pallet and played. Myra understood why he did this. When Angie got to talking, she didn't think about anything else. It was a good idea to keep her from running in the street or from falling off the porch, but somehow, Myra didn't want to put her young'uns in a pen. They laughed and talked about everyone who came down the street. Stephen played under the house, digging doodle bugs. Ruth was tired out and fell asleep in Myra's arms. She loved to be rocked, and Myra usually didn't have much time to sit and rock her. It was so pleasant sitting on the porch that she stayed longer than she had intended.

All of a sudden, she realized she had better hightail it home if she was to beat the young'uns getting home from school. She had never wasted an afternoon like this before in her life. Instead of feeling ashamed, she had a light-hearted feeling. As she walked up the road, she saw all the school young'uns walking ahead of her. She hung onto Ruth, took Stephen's hand, and started running to catch up with them. Idella and Laura James were tickled to see her, and she laughed and skipped all the way home with them. Even when she was a schoolgirl, she had never done this because she always had to hurry home to help Papa. This time she didn't even think about what was waiting to be done at home. She was as carefree as the young'uns, and that felt good.

As they passed the MacTavishes' house, Olieta was sitting on the porch. Just as she saw them, she was letting out a big spit of snuff. She was too proud to let anyone see her dipping, but everyone knew that she loved her snuff.

Getting caught with snuff would really upset her, so Myra yelled out, "Go right on with your snuff, Olieta. We're not plannin' to stop."

This gave her another good laugh. A lot of women used snuff, so Myra couldn't understand why she kept it a big secret. Well, now the secret was out!

When they rounded the curve heading to their house, the day got even better. The car was in front of the house, and James was sitting in the swing. The young'uns were excited to see him and all jumped in the swing. He hugged them, and they started digging in his pockets for the candy that he always brought for them.

She must have had a big smile on her face when she walked up the steps because he said, "Gal, you must be mighty proud to see your loving husband, but I will tell you that he is just as proud to see you."

She went right over and squeezed in the swing with him and the young'uns and sat Ruth in his lap. They were so tight in the swing they could hardly breathe, but it felt good to be close together, laughing and happy. The young'uns finally got the candy out of his pocket. He had bought Silver Tips, which was chocolate wrapped in silver paper. It had melted in his pocket and when they pulled it out, it smeared all over them and his shirt. They loved the chocolate and just sat there licking their fingers. Myra had to laugh, but she knew the stain would be hard to get out of his shirt. For some reason, she didn't even care about the extra work.

James sure didn't mind, for he said, "When y'all get through licking yore fingers, you can start on my shirt."

After a while it was time to start supper, but James said the young'uns had filled up on candy and for her to just sit tight for a while. They talked until after sundown. Ruth fell asleep in her papa's arms, and Idella kept the others happy playing little games that she made up. They were happy to see their mama and papa enjoying being together.

She told James all about Jesse and Arno, and he seemed real interested in them and proud they were both going to be soldiers. He said not to worry about them fighting because probably they would be given some other kind of work to do. She told him everything about her day. He got a kick about everything, especially the part about her skipping home with the school young'uns and catching Olieta spitting snuff.

When they finally went in the kitchen to make supper, James brought out the fresh bread he had brought home and the pitcher of sweet milk from her cow. She found out right then that it wasn't a rule to cook supper every night. The young'uns loved eating bread and milk by the lamplight. They all fell asleep at the table, and James carried them to their beds. Since she didn't have much cleaning up to do, she just sat at the table and waited for James to tell her why he was home so early. She couldn't help but start worrying that he had been fired off his job. Her mind was already turning to how she could help out if he was going to be without a paycheck. He sat back down at the table and reached for her hand.

"I know you're wondering why I come off my route in the middle of the week. When I checked into the hotel in Claxton, Mr. Hunter had sent me a wire. He wanted me to head right back to Glencoe to help him with a big sale that he's putting on all next week. I went right to the store when I got in. It is going to be big doings. A man from Swainsboro is coming to show us how to put on a sale. We're going to paint a big banner to hang in front of the store that tells about the sale. People can buy furniture for less money all during that week. Mr. Hunter bought a boxcar of furniture from a place in Carolina that made it. He got a cheaper price and will make just as much money."

James loved a good business deal like that. Myra didn't really understand how it would make money for him, but she was so happy to have him home that she didn't care.

"It's gonna be something. We're giving out suckers to the young'uns and fancy fans to the women. Everybody that buys something gets to put their name into a box. On the last day the man from Swainsboro will pull out one name, and that person will win a little shoat pig."

James worked the rest of the week getting ready for the sale. He was very impressed with the man from Swainsboro. He told Myra that the man went all round the state putting on sales and had got rich doing it.

Monday morning when the doors opened, almost all of Glencoe turned out, and most of them decided they needed new furniture. Every night when he came home, James told her how many sales he had made. He got the same commission on what he sold, and he was selling twice as much. He especially liked to brag about the people who came in just to see what was going on and ended up buying a piece or two of furniture. He said it made him glad, because he knew it would make their home a better place. He got home so late that she had to feed and put the young'uns to bed before he came in. She didn't worry about him being late, because he always came straight home and never smelled of liquor or cloves. He brought home a sack of hamburgers and two colas every night. It was almost like they were courting again when they sat in the lamplight and ate supper together.

She was dreading the day when the sale would end, but things took another good turn. Mr. Hunter liked having James in the store and saw what a help he was to business. James knew everybody in Glencoe and could really drum up business. Mr. Hunter decided to keep him in the store and send someone else out on the road. She knew the Good Lord was looking out for her, because that just made her happiness complete.

The store closed for an hour at dinnertime, so James came home every day to eat. She spent the morning cooking a big dinner of things he enjoyed. She could count on him being home by sundown every day. She quit firing up the stove at night when the weather started getting warm. There were always leftovers from dinner. James brought home a fresh loaf of light bread every evening, and there was plenty of cold fresh milk from her cow. She learned that eating bread and milk for supper was as good to her as it was to him. This left time to sit on the porch in the swing before bedtime. This reminded her of the happy times she had sitting on the porch with Papa. Some nights they didn't even talk. They just sat there and watched the lightning bugs, listened to the crickets, and other night noises.

The next year was happy, and it passed quickly. Stephen started to school, and Ruth was running all over the place. Myra had to watch her closely and never knew what she might do. She was a sweet and loving little thing, but she did have a strong will. James was making good money, and they had pretty much anything they wanted and everything that they needed. She kept the young'uns in clothes with her sewing and the shelves filled with jars from her canning. Every spring, she planted and worked a big garden. Her pen was always filled with laying hens, fryers, and at least two roosters. Bessie, the cow, gave good rich milk for drinking and making butter. She kept telling James that she could feed a pig just from their scraps, and then get it butchered for fresh pork. He wouldn't even talk about that. That was where he drew the line.

"You done made me look like a farmer, but you ain't making me no pig farmer."

That didn't matter, because in the fall he would buy fresh pork meat and smoked hams from farmers.

Life was good for all of them. She loved having James working in Glencoe. He was happy as long as he was able to make as much money as he thought he should. Any time that business slacked off, he would get real restless and aggravated. These were the times when he would stop off and get whiskey before he came home. She just pure hated for him to do this, but it wasn't every day, and for that she was thankful.

By the next year another baby was on the way. It seemed as if every time one was big enough not to be trouble, here came another one. They loved their young'uns, and she was thankful that she could give them a good home and all the things that were hard to come by when she was growing up. She often thought how Papa must have spent a lot of time trying to figure out how to keep them fed and in some kind of clothes. He was a smart man because he always managed somehow.

Sometime she couldn't help wondering how things would be if James was more like Papa. Everything came easy for James, and he just took for granted that it always would. When there was extra money, she wanted to put it back, but James always found ways to spend it. James liked for her to be jolly and act like she didn't have a care. She tried to be like that, but when things worried her, she couldn't keep from letting it show.

She knew the good times wouldn't last forever, and that summer things started going to hell in a hand basket again. The weather was extra hot and the flies, gnats, and skeeters were the worst that she had ever seen. The garden was not making anything and was drying up from lack of rain. She had to scrabble around to find enough to cook every day and couldn't even think about canning. James was in a short temper most of the time. He said Glencoe was like a ghost town. People were not getting out in the heat of the day. He hated the hot weather that made him sweat so much his white shirt stuck to him. He changed every day when he came home for dinner. That meant she had to stand over the washpot and ironing board twice as long. She was getting so big, and her feet were swelling just like when she was carrying Idella.

He never thought about any of that, and she wasn't about to bring it up. She was afraid he might say, "If you ain't willing to keep me in clean clothes, I will just have to find someone who will."

No matter how good he was to her, she still couldn't keep thoughts like that out of her head. She knew he was short-tempered from not selling any furniture. It was laying-by time for all the farmers. They had run out of money from last year, and they were just waiting to get the new crop in and hoping to make some money. She knew how times like that felt, and buying furniture was the last thing on a body's mind. James had never gone through those times, so he got aggravated with folks because they weren't buying chairs and tables and things. She tried not to remind him that they should have put back money last fall when truckloads of furniture were being sold.

She could hardly drag by the end of the day but managed to keep going. The garden failed to produce enough vegetables to can. Blackberries seemed to thrive in the hot, dry weather. Every day the young'uns picked all they could find. Most of her jars were filled with blackberries. James wouldn't eat a supper of stewed blackberries and biscuits, but that would surely fill up the young'un's bellies. It didn't help her feelings either when

James came home with his face as red as a beet and acting the fool. He wasn't ever drunk, but it made her mad as fire to know he had been off spending money that they needed. Sometimes she couldn't hold back and let him have it the minute he came in the door. She said a lot of things that only made things worse. After all this time she should have known that was not the way to change him. He would get just as mad and either go to bed or take off in the car.

One night she said, "My papa wouldn't have ever wasted money like you do."

If she had spit in his face, he wouldn't have gotten any madder. He snapped back, "Your pa never had two cents to rub together that he didn't owe. He is lying out there under a mound of dirt in a wiregrass graveyard, and everybody but you have forgotten he even lived."

She went to pieces and told him all the things she had been holding back.

"You don't know and don't care how bad I been feeling. This is the worst time I've ever had being pregnant, but I keep on going. You don't care how hard it is fer me to take care of yore young'uns, keep them fed, keep you in starched shirts, and put up with yore foolishness."

She didn't mean it to sound like she didn't love the young'uns, but that is how he took it. He went to their room and started pulling out his things as though he was leaving. He jerked the white shirts she had just ironed off the hangers and put them over his arm.

She shouted, "Look what you're doin' mussing up them shirts. I'll have to iron every one of 'em over."

"Damn you, woman. You know how to make a man feel as low as dirt. I notice you enjoy spending my money when I am making it, but when times get a little tight, you just throw it in my face. I'm sick and tired of your down-in-the-mouth look and quarreling at me every time I walk in the door. Every time I see them sorry-assed blackberries you're so proud of, I want to break every one of them jars. I guarantee you, my young'uns will have plenty of good things to eat this winter, and it shore as hell won't be blackberries.

"You just do things like that to make me feel worse than I already do. I'm out there every day, busting my butt trying to make a living. About the only time I have any peace is when I stop off and have a little nip and a few laughs. I'll tell you this right now, if it is so hard to take care of my young'uns, I guarantee you there will never be another after this one."

He threw his shirts in the back of the car and took off down the road. As mad as she was, she had to laugh at him. What did he think he was going to wear with shirts and no pants?

He stayed off all that night and came home late the next night smelling like liquor and, worse of all, that ol' cheap perfume. He looked awful and was still too mad to even look at her. He didn't even pay the young'uns any attention. He didn't bring his shirts in from the car. The next day he came in with two brand-new shirts from Rosenberg's. She knew he had run a bill on them, but she didn't say anything. He wasn't home except to sleep, and then he slept with his back to her and as far away as he could. This went on for more than a week. It was now into August and the worse of the dog days when there wasn't a breeze stirring or a drop of rain in sight.

One night he got in just as the young'uns were getting ready to go to bed. Idella went over and sat on his lap, and in just a minute she was sound asleep. He held her close to him, and then he said, "Myra, come feel this child. She is hot as a firecracker."

"I'm not surprised in this heat. She didn't eat all day. I think something messed up her stomach 'cause she puked two or three times."

"No, this is something else. I thought when I came in that she looked peaked. My God, haven't you paid her any mind."

She didn't say anything back to that, because she was scared too. He carried Idella to the bed, and they tried to cool her down with wet rags. She was sleeping but not easy. She would jerk, roll her head back, and shake all over. Myra had heard of people having fits, and she wondered if that was what was happening to Idella. Her firstborn might be dying. She wanted to fall down and beg the Lord's forgiveness and ask for Him to spare her, but all she did was keep bathing her with cool water. James took over and told her to send Stephen to get Malcolm. Poor little Stephen was scared to death and ran down the road in the dark. In no time, Malcolm and Olla were there. Stephen had run on to his grandma's, and she and Olieta were there as quick as they could throw some clothes on.

Miz MacTavish knew what was wrong as soon as she saw Idella. She said, "It's the fever, and it's going to be rough on her."

"Go to town and get young Dr. Joe Douglas. Tell him to come right now. I'll pay whatever it takes to help my baby." Malcolm headed out as soon as James spoke.

Idella was still having one fit right after the other. Miz MacTavish had been around people with this and knew what must be done.

"Roll up a cloth and put it between her teeth, so she won't bite her tongue off. We've got to keep all the young'uns away from her 'cause this is catching."

Laura James, Stephen, and Ruth were standing peering into the room and frightened by what they were seeing.

"You young'uns, get in the kitchen and stay there. Shoo, now go on. That means you too, Laura James." Olla shooed them away from the door and into the kitchen.

Standing over Idella, Myra moaned to herself, "Oh, Lord Jesus, I've always thought I had troubles, but there ain't nothing to compare with this. Please don't take my firstborn. I'll do yore will however you want. Don't punish me and James for our fussing and quarreling like this. Lord, I love these young'uns. I never meant that I didn't."

The life just seemed to be running out of Idella, and she couldn't bear watching her daughter die. Just before she fell to the floor in a faint, she felt a strong arm around her, and she thought the Lord was saving her. It was James, and when he pulled her over to him, she could feel tears running down his cheeks and onto her face.

They held each other, and then James said, "He ain't punishing us, Myra. That ain't his way. My baby girl might die someday, but I guarantee you it won't be tonight."

It was nearly daybreak before the doctor got there. He had been off in the country delivering a baby. He said that Miz MacTavish was right about it being the fever.

"It's typhoid fever. We don't know what causes it, but it can be passed by people who have it and can be caught by drinking bad water or food."

James swore an oath and broke down. "How can that be? Nobody around here has been sick. We have a good, clear well. There ain't no way she could have got a hold of anything to eat that would've caused it."

Myra's thought went right to the mulberries. There was a big tree at the back of the lot, and the mulberries on it have been ripe for most of the summer. She had whipped her and whipped her for eating them. She knew those berries had to be bad because worms were always crawling out of them. Why Idella loved them so, Myra couldn't understand. It couldn't be because she was hungry. She just seemed to have a taste for them. She'd sneak out and eat them, but she couldn't get away with it because her teeth would be purple. Myra had whipped her good just yesterday for eating them. It wouldn't help to say anything about the mulberries, so Myra just kept it to herself. She would chop that tree down as soon as she could. None of the other young'uns went near it after she showed them the worms.

"Oh, Lord, I try so hard to keep my young'uns from getting into things, but I just can't watch them every minute." Myra would always wonder if the fever was caused by the mulberries.

Dr. Joe didn't give any medicine but said the first thing to do was break the fever. She was having those fits because her fever was going so high. He called them convulsions, and he said a high fever could hurt her brain even if she did get well. Myra's immediately thought about Izzy and how Nannie told her he was a smart little baby until he took the fever. The Lord couldn't let this happen to her sweet, smart little girl.

Dr. Joe told them to break the fever by putting quilts on her and making her sweat even more. That didn't make sense, but he was a young doctor and should know the latest things. He told them to keep her lips wet and to put a wet rag in her mouth for thirst. She would probably choke if they tried to give her water to drink.

Myra was so scared, and all she knew to ask was if she could eat. Before the doctor could answer, Miz MacTavish said, "Feed a cold, and starve a fever."

Dr. Joe said, "Yes, ma'am, that is right. This is also contagious to anyone who is around her. Just a few of you need to come in the room. When you do, you must cover your mouth and nose with a cloth, and when you go out, wash your hands with as hot water as you can stand and plenty of soap. What is going in her favor is that she is young and healthy in other ways."

Before he left, James gave him some money and said, "Doc, you got to make my girl get well if it takes every dime all the MacTavishes can rake up."

"Sir, I'll do all I can, but it will be a rough go."

When he left, James and Myra sat by the bed until day started to break. Just as the sun was rising, her fever must have broke because she broke out in such a sweat that it soaked the bed. When they started changing the sheets and putting a gown on her, they noticed big red splotches all over her body. They were thankful the fever had broken, and she seemed to be resting.

Miz MacTavish came into the room, and Myra got a whiff of coffee and food cooking. Miz MacTavish put her arms around both of them.

"You just go on in the kitchen and eat some breakfast. I'll sit with my granddaughter. It won't do her a bit of good for you to get wore out and sick from not eating. Go on now."

When they walked out of the sick room, the house seemed like a tomb. The other young'uns had gone home with Olla. Olieta handed them plates of grits and eggs and cups of coffee. Myra wasn't a bit hungry but tried to eat a few bites to keep up her strength. James started eating, but after a few bites he pushed his plate aside.

"Myra, if we ain't two of the biggest fools in the state of Georgia, I don't know who is. We fussed and quarreled over ironed shirts and blackberries like that was something really important. Now we know what a real problem is, and we both ought to be ashamed of ourselves for the way we've been carrying on. If the Good Lord will just spare my baby, I promise him that I will change my ways. What about you?"

Myra just nodded and reached for his hand.

If there was one thing the MacTavishes did, it was help each other out when there was a need. For the next two weeks, some of the family was there night and day. They brought in food and did all the washing of the sheets that had to be changed every time her fever broke with a sweat. Olla kept Ruth, and Laura James and Stephen went home with Ada.

The whole family came just as people did when there was a death. Will Rob and Angie came and all of the MacTavishes, even Molly and Samuel who lived in Emanuel County. Annie Lou, Dolly, and Horace came and brought Jane. Myra was glad to have them come, but it made her even more scared that they thought Idella was on her deathbed. She hadn't seen Annie Lou and Dolly in over a year, but this wasn't any time to be visiting with them. Dolly was getting to be a big girl and was as pretty as a picture. Myra thought Dolly looked a lot like the way she remembered Ma looking before the bad times started. Annie Lou told her that her little boy, Coy, was a hearty little fellow, but he had a withered arm that he couldn't use much. She said that didn't stop him from doing anything he wanted to do. Myra was glad to hear it, but all she could think about was her little girl.

Idella was so thin that you could see her bones sticking out, and her color was so white that she looked blue. All she had eaten was a little of the chicken broth that Miz MacTavish always kept warm on the stove. They were thankful to get a few mouthfuls down her. During the times the fever broke, she would be easy for a spell, but then it would come back. Dr. Douglas came every day, and finally he told them he thought the worst was over.

When he left James went to the bed and picked her up and said, "I am taking her out of this room, and we are going to sit on the porch. She has been in this room long enough. She needs some fresh air."

Myra was scared it would hurt her and begged him not to take her, but as always James did what he wanted. When he picked her up, they saw something they had not noticed before. Her hair was falling out all over the bed. There were big bald spots already on her head.

"Oh, Lord, no—how can she live her life baldheaded?" She knew the MacTavish men all went bald, but she had never seen or heard of a baldheaded woman.

"Now you just hush that, Myra. Get a hold of yourself. After all that she's been through, it's no wonder her hair's coming out. I've seen it happen before from the fever, and it always comes back and even prettier. You don't remember, but I lost my girl from the fever, and all you've lost is her hair."

"I didn't mean to carry on so. I just ain't myself from the worry."

Myra had never thought about Miz MacTavish having the hurt of losing a child, and tears came to her eyes when she remembered Olieta's twin and Hannah.

She wrapped a quilt around Idella for James to carry out. They sat in the swing and Myra sat on the steps. James always had a way to make Idella laugh, and before long she was laughing just like her old self.

Then she said, "What is Grandma cooking? It shore smells good."

Miz MacTavish was standing at the door and said, "I made a pot of dumplings just for you, honey."

She brought out a bowlful, and James fed it to her sitting in the swing. It was the first solid food she had eaten. In a minute Miz MacTavish was back with some little pieces of chicken, and Idella ate that too. They had never been so happy and relieved in all their life.

For the first time in two weeks, she slept through the night All Myra could do was thank the Lord for sparing her and promising that she would be a more loving wife to James.

"Lord, I ain't nothin' like my ma, and James shore ain't nothing like Papa. I have to quit trying to make him be somethin' he ain't."

Idella got better every day. She was always hungry and quickly gained back her weight. Her hair was coming back some, but James went to see Miz Rosenberg, and they found a pretty little green hat that just covered her head. It had a band around it made out of plaid material. James said it was called a tam and was the kind of hat that the people wore in the old country where his people had come from. Myra hadn't ever seen one, but it was just perfect to cover up her head and still show her pretty face.

She was able to start to school in the middle of September. She wore her tam every day until her hair grew back. Myra was afraid she would feel ashamed for the other children to see it. James had made her feel so pretty when she wore it that the other young'uns wished they had one too. He had a way of making people feel good.

The last time Dr. Douglas came out to see Idella, he called Myra out to the porch. She was scared he was going to tell her there was still something bad wrong with Idella.

"Doctor, I knew a boy who was left real dumb in his head from havin' a high fever. Could that happen to Idella?"

"Oh no, no. There's nothing like that possible. She's already back to her old self. That would have shown up long ago.

"Mrs. Mac, you are the one I want to talk about. You must be almost to the time for having your baby. You have had a rough time, but now it is time to take care of you and this new one. You have a lot of swelling in your face and in your feet and legs."

He opened his satchel and took out a band of cloth and wrapped it around her arm real tight. He listened to the crook of her arm and to her heart. Then he felt around on her belly and her ankles and legs.

"Your blood is really high, and it is no wonder. Have you had any trouble with your kidneys?"

"They've bothered me a lot. I think the baby must be lying against them."

"This could be dangerous for you and the baby if you don't take care of yourself. I want you to turn everything over to the others. You must go to bed and stay there until it is time. You know, we have the new hospital now, and I think you should plan to let me deliver the baby there. I know Dr. Youmans brought the rest of them into the world, but I want you in the hospital for this one."

Myra had never heard of such a thing, and she was just ready to tell him so. She didn't know Miz MacTavish had come to the door and was standing there listening.

"If that is what she needs, that is just what she is going to do, starting right now. James is trying to get back to his work, but he will see to it that she takes care of herself and goes to the hospital to have the baby. There is plenty of the family that can pitch in and help with the other young'uns. I will tell James all this, and he will be seeing you to make the arrangements."

Olieta had come out by that time, and Myra just knew she would say something spiteful about her needing extra treatment, but she turned and went into the house. Miz MacTavish led her to the bedroom, and there was Olieta already making up the bed with fresh sheets. She brought in a pitcher of water because she heard the doctor tell Myra to drink plenty of water. She didn't say anything, but Myra could tell she was worried about this little MacTavish that was soon to be born. Almost as soon as her head hit the pillow, Myra was sound asleep.

When she started stirring around to wake up, James was coming into the room carrying a big plate of food. He put the plate down and started petting her.

"I am so worried about you and this baby. I couldn't make it if something happened to you. Now you're going to stay in bed and do just what the doctor tells you."

"How can I do that with four young'uns and you to tend to. I shore ain't going to the hospital just to have a baby."

He knew she was thinking about how much it would probably cost, and he said, "Yes, you will go there and get the best care in the state of Georgia. Money don't mean nothing when it comes to something like this, and besides, if it takes all I've got, I can always make more money. I can't get another Myra or this little baby boy that is coming."

Then she laughed. "James, how can you be saying this is a boy in my belly?"

"Well," he said, "I love my girls just fine, but it is time that we had another boy. I've already got his name picked out. I am naming him for the best governor the state of Georgia ever had, Wallace W. Walker. Yes, sir, he will be Wallace Walker MacTavish, and I wouldn't be surprised if he turned out to be the governor of Georgia someday.

"Another thing, I have been thinking about is how the world is changing so fast that it is going to be hard to make a living in the old ways. I want our young'uns to get all the schooling they need. I want the boys to go off to college and learn to be doctors or lawyers or something like that."

As they were talking, they had been eating the plate of food. It was a really tasty stew with lots of meat in it, and there were big hot biscuits too.

"This is good. Who cooked it?"

"Lizzie brought it from her house."

"I knew Olla didn't cook hit. I want the young'uns to come back home. It's safe now."

"No, Idella is still too weak to be of any help, but I'll see what I could figure out because I want them home too."

He took the plates out and told her to go back to sleep. She was still worn out from the siege with Idella and went right back to sleep.

A little later, he and Laura James came back into the room and he said, "Mama, you don't need to worry about a thing. I have the best helper I could find right here. During the week, they are going to school and take Ruth to Olla on the way and pick her up on the way back. In the evening before I get home, Laura James will take care of Ruth. Between Ma, Olieta, Olla, Lizzie and Callie, they will keep us fed. I can get Rosa from across the branch to come in and do the washing and ironing and anything else we need."

Myra shouldn't have but she snapped at him, "James, how can we even think about paying somebody to do the work that I should be doing? I am getting out of this bed tomorrow morning and taking care of my house and young'uns."

Laura James usually never had much to say, but she came to the bed with tears running down her face. "Oh, Mama, you can't do that. I can do it all in the evening after school. I am ten years old now, and you always tell us that you was cooking and working in the fields with your papa when you weren't any older than that."

Her thoughts ran back to those days when she had to be the one to do those things, because there wasn't any other way. She looked at little Laura James, and she reminded her so much of Will Rob and how he was always doing a man's work when he wasn't any older than Laura James. She was willing, and she would do all she could.

It all worked out. Rose came every day and did what was needed. Laura James kept Ruth busy and happy, and Stephen kept the wood box filled, took the clothes off the line, or whatever else that she needed him to do. She had to be proud of her fine young'uns. They might have been raised like MacTavishes, but they knew how to work like Stuarts.

Even with all the help, she still couldn't make herself lay around in the bed. She stayed up to make sure that everything was being done like it should be. Stephen learned to build a fire in the cook stove, and she found that cooking wasn't so hard if that was all that she had to do. By the first of October the baby had dropped, and it wouldn't be long. Dr. Douglas had been by to look her over and thought everything was going to go well. She still didn't want to go to the hospital, but James wouldn't hear of anything but that. Every time she started to talk about it, he would say that he was tired of her thinking he couldn't spend money to take good care of her. Finally, he told her that he had already paid the bill, and if she didn't go the money would just be lost.

On the sixth day of October, Myra was awakened by cramps that she recognized. It was time to go to the hospital—although she still did not think the hospital was necessary. James jumped out of bed when she called, and the first thing he did was put his pants on backward. This was the fifth time he had gone through this, but he was more nervous than she had ever seen him. When they started out to the hospital, James flooded the engine and had a hard time getting it to crank.

"Now, James, you just settle down. You are making it worse for me. You've got to stop at yore ma's and tell them, so they can go down and stay with the young'uns."

"I'm scared to stop. I might not be able to get it started again. I'll just honk the horn and tell them when they come out."

That's what he did. As they drove off, Myra could see Miz MacTavish and Olieta hurrying down the road. As always, they were happy to welcome a new MacTavish.

James acted as though he didn't know how to drive. He started out going so slow that they hardly moved. When she had a pain and grunted out, he would speed up and whip around the curves. She had never seen him so nervous.

This was her first time to even see the inside of a hospital, and she was surprised at how white and quiet everything was. A nurse took her right into a room and said she was sending for Dr. Douglas.

This baby didn't care if the doctor was there or not. It was ready to see the world. The doctor walked in just in time to help her with the last few pushes, and out popped another little MacTavish. Dr. Douglas showed the baby to her, and as weak as she was, she still let out a big laugh. Governor Wallace Walker was a little girl. She was a tiny thing and not filled out like all the others had been. The doctor said she was fine, but he was glad that she was in the hospital where he could keep an eye on her. Myra had some worries, because when she put the baby to her breast, she just didn't seem to have the strength to nurse.

James came in while she was nursing her, and he was pale as a sheet. He said that he had passed out for a few minutes after the nurse took her away. This was harder on him than when she had them at home and he just sat on the porch and waited.

He already knew it was a girl, but he didn't seem a bit disappointed. She told him they had to come up with another name.

He said, "No, sir, I am still honoring the governor. There ain't nothing wrong with a girl being named Wallace Walker."

"There's only one way I will go for that. I want her middle name to be Ann. She can be Wallace Ann MacTavish." Myra was planning to call her Wallace Ann and that sounded as good as Laura James. Besides, Ann had been Ma's name.

"That does sound right good, so she'll be Wallace Ann MacTavish."

It turned out she was glad to be in the hospital with all the nurses around. Wallace had a hard time keeping her milk down. She spit up so much, and she cried and cried. Dr. Douglas said she was colicky and would have to nurse often so she would not take too much at one time. That would be a change. The others just sucked her dry and then turned over and went to sleep with their little navels sticking out like a pot leg. She dreaded taking her home if she was going to cry so much. She knew the crying would get on James's nerves.

The day after Wallace Ann was born, James brought the three older young'uns to see her. They all got to hold their new little sister and were proud of her.

Stephen seemed to love her best and said, "Mama, when she cries, I'll rock her."

Idella said, "She shore is a scrawny little thing, ain't she?"

"Well, she can't help it, and not everybody thinks they have to be as pretty as you think you are," Laura James answered right back.

"You hush that kind of talk. She's going to fatten up as soon as she gets home, ain't she, Mama?" James did not look too convinced himself

As they were leaving, Myra heard him tell the young'uns that he was taking them by Hunters to pick out something from the candy jars. Hunters was a furniture store, but they had a case of candy to sell. She knew James would let them eat all they wanted and make them all sick. Even if things like this did make them love him better than her, she was still the one they needed when they got sick.

Wallace didn't get much better after they brought her home. She would tighten her little stomach up and scream. Myra knew she was hurting, but she didn't know a thing to do, except keep on feeding her a little bit at the time. Of course, Olieta convinced James that Myra had just spoiled the baby.

First, he would tell Myra to let her cry it out, and then he would say, "Myra, if you don't do something about that baby's squalling, I swear I am going to have to go and stay at Ma's."

Finally, she told him to just do that, because it would be easier on her if he wasn't around. The young'uns tried to help by rocking her, but even that wouldn't put her to sleep. She cried when she was hungry, and she cried when she was full.

Rosa came in from hanging out the wash and said, "Miz Mac, you pore little thing, you are plum wore out by that baby. Give her here to me, and you go get you a little rest."

Myra was glad to hand her right over. She fell asleep as soon as she stretched out on the bed. When she woke up she didn't hear a sound, and this scared her. She ran in the front room, and there was Wallace sleeping in her little basket as peaceful as could be. Rosa was sitting in the rocking chair with her head laid back, mouth open, and snoring away.

"Rosa, how did you get her sleepin' so good?"

Rosa laughed and said, "Lawse, lawse, honey, ain't you never tried a sugar tit with her. After she sucks as much as her little belly can hold, you just give her a sugar tit and she thinks she is still nursing, and in a few minutes she's right off to sleep."

Myra had completely forgotten how Ma used to give a sugar tit to Dolly to keep her satisfied. She hadn't needed it with the others, so she never thought about it. Rosa showed her how to tie up a little sugar in a clean piece of cloth and stick it in the baby's mouth. The sugar tasted good to her and also settled down her stomach. Myra was thankful and wanted to do something for Rosa in return. She gave her some of the canned goods, even though they were in short supply. Rosa was getting ready to have another baby herself, and Myra hadn't even thought about how she had to do the wash when she was just dragging around herself. Myra vowed to do something to help her when her time came. She had never counted Rosa's young'uns, but she knew there was a houseful.

"Miz Mac, I 'ppreciate these vittles. I tell ya the truth. Gettin' a little money fer doin' yore wash has been a godsend for me."

Myra's heart knew that wasn't right. Rosa's skin might be black, but she had the same feelings as anybody and loved her young'uns. Myra couldn't figure out why colored folks always sang praises to the Lord when He had put such a hardship on them. There was so much Myra couldn't understand about His ways, but maybe the colored folks knew why.

She went back to check on Wallace and found Ruth was sitting on the floor, sucking on the sugar tit. She had to laugh, but she knew that as close as they were together and with the nature of Ruth, there would always be jealousy between them.

James came in and said, "I met Rosa leaving and paid her for the wash. She told me how she got Wallace to settle down. I don't know what in the hell a sugar tit is, but you give her all she wants."

Wallace did get better, and by the next year she was eating from the table and starting to walk. There were still times when she would throw back her head and kind of twitch her little body, but after that she would go to sleep for a long time. Myra didn't worry about it and believed this was something she would outgrow. She had a lot of the looks of the MacTavish, but as much as Myra hated to say it, she just wasn't as pretty as the others. Idella and Laura James favored James, and people always commented on how pretty they looked. Stephen seemed to look like his mama, but he was such a hearty and smart little fellow that he looked fine too. Of course, Ruth was just Ruth. Her hair was dark red, the first redhead on either side of the family. She did have Papa's blue eyes.

-19-

A quick glance in the mirror told Myra that she was showing her age. She was over thirty and had filled those years with hard work. James still looked about the same except he just had a fringe of hair surrounding a bald spot on the top of his head.

The young'uns were growing up, and they all were smart in their school work. Idella was fifteen and pretty as a picture. James adored her and tried to give her anything that she wanted. He paid tuition for the two older girls to go to high school in Glencoe instead of the county school.

Olieta started giving Idella piano lesson right after she got over the fever. She took right to this and loved the piano. It wasn't long before the Hunter truck backed up to their house and unloaded a piano. She could play anything and didn't need lessons. If she heard a tune one time, she could play it. They all loved to listen to her play.

Laura James was thirteen. Myra thought she was just as pretty as Idella, but she didn't put on airs like Idella. She was a big help in the house and with the little young'uns. In some ways, the two girls made her think of herself and Annie Lou. Idella played the piano while Laura James washed the dishes.

Stephen had a little job at the dairy of the old folk's home. He left home before daybreak to get there when they started the milking. His job was to keep the calves away from the cows while they were being milked. He earned a dime a day for doing this, and he loved to save his money. He was always so scared that he wouldn't wake up in time that he slept in his clothes. One night she looked at him, and he was sound asleep in bed and already wearing his cap. It made her think of how she and Will Rob were always finding ways to earn a little bit and never spent it.

Ruth would have been a worry, except that Myra never had time to worry. All the MacTavish young'uns walked home from school together. Every day Ruth came home crying. Myra knew the others picked on her, but she would just have to learn to take it. The young'uns always had chores, so as soon as Ruth was big enough, she was given the job of staking out the cow. All she had to do was lead the cow to the good grass in the back field, tie her to a stake in the ground, and bring her back to the barn in the evening. Myra had to remind her every time, and she acted as if her head was being cut off. She cried the whole time she was doing it. Stephen couldn't milk until she brought the cow back to the barn, and he always had to sit and wait on her. When he fussed about her dragging the cow and squalling, she cried even more. When Myra complained to James, he said not to pay them any mind because they were just young'uns. That was fine for Mr. Hunter Furniture Salesman who was seldom at home. She wondered what he would say if he were with them night and day.

Wallace still had little spells, but it didn't seem to bother her. In fact, Myra thought she didn't even realize when they happened. She knew some of the MacTavish were calling it "fits" and talked about how her grandma had crazy spells. Myra didn't worry about that. Wallace was a sweet, loving little girl and as smart as the others. When Idella dressed her up and fixed her hair, she looked right pretty.

James was worried that he wasn't making as much as he thought he should. Money was getting tight for the farmers and folks who made their living off the farmers. The blight had wiped out the cotton crop for most of the county, so buying furniture was the last thing farmers were thinking about. He went back on the road to try to drum up more business. She knew he enjoyed getting away where there was nothing or nobody to aggravate him. He hadn't stopped drinking, but as far as she knew, he wasn't fooling around with women.

Wallace was almost four years old, and Myra was enjoying not having a little one to tend. She was beginning to think she was too old to have any more babies, but then she saw the signs and knew that wasn't so. When she told James, she insisted that she would be fine and would not go to the hospital. He was a little surprised at having another one on the way, but he still hoped for a second son. He agreed for her to have it at home if she would let Rosa do the wash. She was glad to hear that because she knew Rosa needed the little bit she would earn.

Rosa had two more babies since Wallace had been born. One of them had died a few weeks after it was born. There was something wrong with its breathing from the day it was born. Myra went down to her house the day it died and took more canned goods and a pretty little gown for the baby to be buried in. Myra helped her wash the baby, put on the gown, and lay it out on a board for her folks to come to see. She didn't know until she washed it that it was a little boy.

As she were leaving, Rosa said, "Miz Mac, you have always been so good to me, and I love you like a sister."

Myra cried with her and could feel how much Rosa was hurting. She couldn't bear to even think about one of her babies dying. That night the young'uns pitched a fit to go down and see the dead baby. She didn't want them to go, but James said it wouldn't hurt a thing to go and pay their respects. When they came back, James was blowing his nose and sniffling, and she knew he had to hold back the tears. He said he put some money into the pot to help pay for the burying. When she lay down that night, she thanked the Lord a long time for her living young'uns and prayed to have more patience with them and James. She tried to do everything she could to keep things going for them, but she was never able to give them the hugs and laughs that they got from James. Maybe that was how the Lord meant it to be. They kind of balanced each other out.

Myra's next pregnancy was easy even through the long dog days of summer. Since she had none of the problems she had when she was pregnant with Wallace, she knew this baby would be fine. She hoped for a boy, so James could finally have a namesake. Laura James had his name, but that wasn't like being a junior. Sometimes, she wished they had named Stephen for his papa, but Stephen wasn't a drop like James. He loved his papa, but he didn't like him all the time. Stephen only thought about working and helping, and he just didn't have time for James's foolishness. As soon as James came in, she could tell if he had been drinking. His face would be red as fire, and he fumbled around and acted silly. The other young'uns enjoyed cutting the fool with him, but not Stephen. Often he would give them more money than they needed to have. Stephen left the house when his papa came in drinking. If James gave him money, he would take it and then give it to his mama.

Her time came on the first of November. They sent for Dr. Douglas, and he just eased this one out with hardly a yell out of Myra. It was another little girl, and when he slapped her to cry, she didn't make a sound. He cleaned out her mouth and started blowing into it himself and finally she let out a little cry. When he put her in Myra's arms, she felt as if she was holding a baby angel.

Myra always thought her babies were pretty, but this one was the prettiest of all. She had a perfectly round head and her nose looked like a little button. For the first time Myra immediately felt what was called "mother love." The baby had no trouble nursing, so Myra felt relieved after the problems she had with Wallace.

"Mama, it's yore turn to name the baby. Now what are we gonna call this pretty little lady? You got a governor you want to name her for?"

"Now, James, you know I ain't gonna mess up this baby with such a name. She looks just like her name should be Mary Alice."

"I like that too. So Mary Alice MacTavish will be her name."

From the very first, Myra had a feeling that Mary Alice would not be with them long. There were times when she would stop breathing. Dr. Douglas taught Myra to blow her breath real easy into the baby's mouth to help her catch her breath. She pinched her little nose so the air wouldn't come out. Myra was able to bring her back several times. Dr. Douglas told them he was afraid her little heart just wasn't formed right, and there wasn't a thing he could do. She thought back to the heart dropsy that had killed Papa, and how people said that it ran in families. She asked the doctor and he said not to even think about that, because sometimes babies just don't get all their parts perfect the way they should be.

Myra never wanted to put her down because she was afraid she wouldn't be there to bring her back if her breathing stopped. She would sit in the rocking chair all night and hold her. James never told her to put the baby down and come to bed. He didn't have much to say, but she knew he was grieving. The day she was six weeks old, the young'uns came home from school talking about a carnival that had come to Glencoe. James had always taken them to things like that, and he loved it as much as they did. She told him to go on and take them, because they needed to get away from the house. He agreed and sent Stephen to get Rosa to come and stay while they were gone. They piled in the car and took off.

Rosa sat with her, and they watched Mary Alice have one spell after another. They didn't even bother to put on the lamp. Just after dark she heard a sound that she didn't want to hear. An owl was in a tree somewhere in the field, and it started to hoot. Rosa looked at her, and they both knew what that sign meant. James and the young'uns came in real quietly, and the young'uns went to bed. Rosa wouldn't leave, so James, Rosa, and Myra sat up together. Just before midnight, the baby had a spell, and Myra started breathing into her mouth. She didn't catch her breath back as she had before.

Myra kept trying and trying, until Rosa took Mary Alice out of her arms and said, "Miz Mac, this little baby girl is one of God's angels now."

James gathered her in his arms and they cried until both of their fronts were wet with tears. Rosa rocked the baby and sang softly to herself. Myra remembered the hurt when Papa died, but that was nothing compared to this. She fell across the bed and cried until she didn't have a sob left in her. When she got to the snubbing stage, she saw something she thought she would never see again. The lamp wasn't lit in the room, and there was just a little light coming in from the other room. Still, she could see him in the corner in his blue suit. He just looked at her with his steady eyes, and before she could blink, he was gone. She knew he was not really there, but still it gave her some peace to have a sight of him.

She tried to pray and the words that came out were, "Lord, you must know what you are doing to take my baby like this. Maybe going so young has saved her from a lot of pain later on in years, but it shore has put the pain on me. Help me to get through this as best I can."

The undertaker came and took the baby away. The next morning, she sent James to town to take a white dress and cap that she had made for her. It was the prettiest thing she had ever made and the first time she had tatted lace around a baby dress. James told her he was buying a lot in the new Pine Ridge Cemetery in Glencoe for her grave. He said the old cemetery was getting full, and he wanted enough room, so that when the time came they could all lay together. She was glad of that because the new cemetery looked like a peaceful place to be. All the grave markers were new and shiny and not old and weathered looking like in the old cemetery.

The next day the house was filled with all their family. Everyone came and brought food. James bought a little casket that was made just for a baby. It was soft and lacy inside and trimmed in pink. She looked like a sleeping doll. Two days after she died, they took her to the Baptist Church in Glencoe for the funeral. She was holding up pretty good until they closed the casket, and Will Rob and Malcolm carried it out to the hearse. It was so little they didn't need but two pallbearers to carry it, but all of James's nephews walked along as the honorary pallbearers. She felt as if she was sleepwalking.

The procession of cars and buggies followed the hearse to the cemetery. She couldn't bear to look when they put the dirt over the casket. She felt an arm around her, and it was Stephen. He was crying as much as her. Then all the other young'uns came over, and they cried together. Samuel had preached the funeral, but there were several other preachers there. When people started coming over to speak to her, she was surprised to see Aunt Mary and Uncle Daniel Coleman from Trutlen County. Will Rob sent word to them, and they were able to come.

"Oh, Aunt Mary, I just wish she could have seen her. I knew from the beginning that she was a little angel."

"Now she is up in heaven with Martin, and they are both looking over you. I thank you for naming her for me."

Myra liked that thought. Papa never got to see any of his grandchildren, and now he had one with him. She hadn't even thought about where she got the name Mary Alice. It just seemed to come to her. She hadn't given Aunt Mary a thought in a long time. Something just told her that should be the name, now that it was all over, she was glad.

"It's my favorite name. I am so thankful to ya fer comin'"

"We have to leave to get home by dark. Since we have a car now, I can come back to see you before long."

She told the young'uns to go over and get flowers from the casket spray to take home and press in their Bibles, so they would always remember her. She had pictures made of all the other young'uns, but she never got a chance to get her picture made. She didn't need a picture, because she would never forget how her little angel looked.

As they stood around the little grave, dark clouds started moving in, and the wind picked up. James said, "Everybody get in the car. We gotta leave to get ahead of that bad cloud coming up."

"No, I'm stayin' with my baby. I ain't never left one of my young'uns out in bad weather." She could not turn her back and walk away when the rain was starting to come down, thunder was rumbling, and soon there would be lightning.

"Myra, there ain't nothing you can do for her by staying here. You have to quit cutting the fool and think about the rest of us. We are hurting just as much as you, but we ain't showing out like you."

Olieta had to put her two cents worth in and said, "James, you better get a hold of her now or she will go plum crazy. You know, it runs in her family."

That was all it took. Myra gritted her teeth, looked straight at Olieta, and said, "Let's go home, James, we will come back tomorrow and check on the grave. I need to get supper on, and I know all of you are tired."

James put his arm around her shoulder, and she felt someone take her hand and knew it was Stephen. They ran for the car just as the rain started. When James tried to crank the car, it wouldn't start. He pulled up the hood and started tinkering with it. He didn't know a thing about a car except to drive it and put gas in it, so all he was doing was getting soaked. She could hear him cussing something awful, and she was ashamed that he was doing that so soon after Mary Alice's funeral. Everyone but them had already left, so Myra didn't know what they would do. He stuck his head in the car door and said there wasn't anything he could do but go to town for help and for them to just sit in the car.

He took off in his best suit of clothes, and he was soaked to the bone. As they sat there, the wind was rocking the car, and lightning was striking all around. She had heard a car was the safest place to be in lightning, but it wasn't safe for James walking to town.

All the young'uns were scared, and the little girls were crying. She didn't know anything else to do, so she started to sing. She sang the hymn that reminded her of Papa saying she had a brightness.

She remembered Rosa's soft voice praising Jesus as she bathed her dead baby boy. She had always wondered why the colored folks sang praises when they had such a hard life. As she sang, she seemed to understand why they sang. There was nowhere to turn but to the Lord.

The children joined her in the song. Then one of them started another hymn and then another. Listening to the voices of the ones God had left with her, the burden just seemed to be lifting. That didn't mean she was forgetting Mary Alice, but she knew her angel baby was in safe arms and not under the mound of dirt with the rain beating down on it. Then there was a knock on the window, and she saw the undertaker, Mr. Williamson.

"I was coming back out here to check on things when the cloud hit, and I met James walking to town. He was about drowned, so I took him on home and told him I would come back for all of you. He said to tell you not to worry about the car. He will get it fixed tomorrow, so you all run fast and get in the back of the hearse, and I'll take you home."

James had a big fire going and a pot of coffee ready to pour. They pulled off their wet clothes and wrapped up in quilts by the fire. People had brought so much food, and there was plenty left. The young'uns got whatever they wanted and sat eating by the fire. In no time, they were all fast asleep. After they got the young'uns into their beds, they sat on the floor by the fire without talking for a long time. When James started to talk, she was scared of what he would say about how she had acted at the grave.

He gave that little smirky laugh of his and said, "Myra, when you all passed Ma's house, did you look to see if Olieta was looking out?"

"No, but you can bet she was, because she knows everything that goes down the road."

Between laughs he said, "Well, I can just see her saying to Ma, 'Come quick. The hearse is pulling up to James's house. I knew Myra would kill him one day and now she has.'"

Myra hadn't given a thought to riding home in the hearse, but James's words were just what she needed. She put her head on his shoulder and felt safe with the feel and smell of him all around her. She must have fallen asleep like that, because she woke up the next morning in their bed with James snoring beside her. She did love him so, and she was going to tell him right after she started breakfast.

Of course, Myra didn't tell him for she was too busy getting the day started and the young'uns up and dressed. As soon as they got off to school, she was going to clean her house from top to bottom. Loving is good but not in a dirty house. In a few days, everyone was back to the regular way of living. Mary Alice was not forgotten, but soon talking about her brought joy, not sadness.

James was on the road every week, because he was trying to make as much as he could. Everyone said the hard times would be over as soon as the farmers got in another cotton crop. He wasn't counting on that because the blight could come right back next year. He had cleaned out his savings on the doctor's bills and funeral. He wasn't about to let Myra know that. She would raise cane about how much he had spent buying a new cemetery lot and the fancy coffin. Myra was like that. Spending money just scared her to death, and when she was scared, she sure made it hard on him. He vowed to be more thrifty until he got a little nest egg built back up.

Christmas came, and they made it as good for the young'uns as they could. They always set out Myra's sewing machine drawers on Christmas Eve for Santa Claus to fill with presents. James made sure there was plenty to fill them.

A few days before Christmas, James said, "Myra, you know that soon we will have us a grown girl. Idella is going on sixteen and she will finish up high school next year. I just hope I can keep her at Glencoe High School, 'cause that damn old W. L. Pound keeps raising the tuition. Anyhow, I think we ought to get her something really special and grown-up for Christmas this year. Let's you and me ride to the drugstore and see what we can find."

That was one time that Myra didn't complain about money. She was proud to have raised a grown girl that was as pretty and smart as Idella. They let Laura James, Ruth, and Wallace ride with them, and headed for Glencoe. James said he had seen a counter full of pretty things for women in the drugstore. They left the girls in the car and went inside. There were powders, perfumes, beads, hair clips, hand mirrors, and lots of other things. What caught James's eye was a small round gold box. The clerk showed them how to push a little clip to flip open the top. In the top part was a mirror, and the bottom had a place to put powder, and it had a little powder puff. Myra didn't really know what it was for, but the clerk said it was called a compact and was for girls to carry their powder with them in their handbag. If they needed to freshen up, they could just look in the little mirror and put on their powder. As prissy as Idella was, they knew she would love it. They bought the compact and a box of face powder in her shade. The price came to one dollar and thirty cents. When they showed the girls, their eyes were as big as saucers. Myra knew how much Laura James would love a compact, and she vowed to buy her one when she was a little older. This was to be a present from her mama and papa, because Idella was too big for Santa Claus.

Everyone had a good Christmas, and as always, Myra outdid herself cooking a big dinner. She baked a fresh ham until it was falling off the bone tender. Nobody could beat her making dressing. She always cooked about six pies and a raisin cake. This year James did not even slip off and find a bottle. Even though Mary Alice wasn't with them long, her little life seemed to have brought them closer.

Myra kept busy during the winter months to keep her mind from turning to the sadness. The shelves were filled with canned goods, so cooking didn't take up much time. She spent many hours at the sewing machine. She was always mending Stephen's clothes or taking up or letting out clothes for the big girls to hand down to the smaller ones. She kept piece goods on hand and often surprised Idella or Laura James with a new dress. She didn't need patterns. She would just decide how the dress should look and cut it out according to their measurements. She was also sneaking in a little sewing for others. Miz Rosenberg would send ladies who needed a dress made. She had to keep this real secret, because James would raise cane. It kept her in extra money to buy what she needed to sew for the girls. James never even thought about how she got this money, and if he ever ran into one of the ladies coming out of the house, he just thought they were visiting Myra. Every once in a while she would sew up some dresses and give to Rosa for one of her girls. Rosa's oldest, Geneva, now had two babies of her own. She was the little girl who had helped Myra on the day Idella was born. They still lived in the same little house, and Myra never had been able to count how many stayed there.

Myra started her early garden and planned what she would plant for the rest of the year. When the weather warmed, the chickens started laying good, and Bessie was giving plenty of milk. They could have custard nearly every day. These were the times when she felt the most happy and content. She liked to know that she had plenty for her family, and it made her thankful that she didn't have to go through times like she had in her childhood when every day was a struggle to find enough to fill the bellies of her big family. James was a good provider, and she knew how to manage what she had.

-20-

Myra was always happy to gather the first onions, lettuce, and radishes from her spring garden. These made a tasty dish when wilted down with hot meat grease. She pulled up enough to take a mess down to Olla.

Olla was standing with her hands on her hips and staring as if she couldn't believe her eyes.

"Myra, I watched you walking up here. You shore have put on weight. You musta abeen really doin' some eatin' lately."

Myra hadn't thought about it, but her dresses were hard to button. Her stomach had been unsettled for a few weeks, so she had been eating less, not more. By now she should have known the signs. She tried to count back to her last monthly and thought it was some time in February or it could have been March.

"Lord, Olla, I can't be having another one this quick, but I must be. That's downright shameful fer a woman as old as I am. I thought surely I was through after Mary Alice."

"Well, don't be talking that way," Olla replied. "I think I have another one coming along too. Lord, ain't they enough MacTavish young'uns already?"

Within a few weeks there was no question about it, both of them were in the family way. James was always happy to know he was going to be a papa again. This time he didn't say a word about hoping for a boy.

He did say, "The Lord is giving us another chance, and I know this one will be fine."

As summer went by, Myra felt good and had no difficulties. Carrying Mary Alice through the summer had been so easy, that feeling good almost troubled her. She wouldn't let herself think like that.

They had a good time during that summer. On the hottest days, James took them to the creek to swim. He kept them in plenty of ice, so there was always tea, cold watermelons, and sometimes colas. The garden just outdid itself. Every time she finished one crop, there was another one coming in. She had plenty of snap beans, peas, butter beans, corn, squash, tomatoes, and okra to cook, can, and share. She filled many jars with peaches, blackberries, and plums. James and the young'uns loved her jam on their biscuits. The scuppernong vine she rooted when she first moved to the house now covered a large arbor and hung with grapes. James wanted to try to make wine, but she dared him to touch her grapes. She made pickles with cucumbers, peaches, and pears. James could make a meal from a relish that she made with green tomatoes, onions, and hot peppers.

James usually brought home something extra in the evening. She never knew what it would be, but she cooked it for him. He loved mullet fish and bought them from trucks that came from the coast. On Saturday nights, he would bring home a big mess, and she would fry them up with corn dodgers and cabbage slaw. There was always plenty if company stopped by.

On the Fourth of July all the MacTavishes gathered for the family reunion and barbecue at North Connolly Church. Miz MacTavish's people were named Connolly, and they had settled out there and built the church. A lot of them still lived around the church. Everybody pitched in to buy the hogs. There would always be at least two hogs split down the middle and cooked over coals. A few men tended the barbeque all night and had it ready by dinnertime. A big pot of stew hung over the fire. Hog heads were boiled in the pot until all the sweet tender meat fell off into the broth. The bones were removed and vegetables and seasonings were added. The pot of stew hung over the coals and simmered until the barbeque was ready to serve. Myra always helped with the stew and seasoned it up to her liking.

Tater salad, cabbage slaw, fresh vegetables, sliced tomatoes, pickles, cakes, pies, and loaves of light bread covered the long tables. Big milk jugs of tea were ready to pour over ice in the cups. Watermelons floated in washtubs filled with ice. Everyone who had any tie to the Connolly family looked forward to this reunion.

Myra started cooking a week ahead and filled her little trunk with as much as it would hold. She carried a big cake on her lap.

It wasn't a day for preaching, but since there were several preachers in the family, each one was called on to give grace. Some of the prayers were almost a sermon. They always gave thanks for their grandpas, Daniel MacTavish and Caleb Connolly, who had come to Georgia after their families came over from the old country, Scotland. They gave thanks for the country and the brave men who had served in the War Between the States. While this was going on, the women were busy keeping the young'uns still and fanning gnats off the food. They always joked that if gnats got in the stew, folks would just think it was pepper.

Myra and James were proud to show off their fine family and people did brag on them. She made sure her young'uns knew how to behave and how to say please and thank you. They knew better than to hog the food. She wouldn't call any names, but some of the MacTavish young'uns hadn't been taught these things.

After the big dinner was eaten, the tables were covered over with cloths. Then everyone sat back to do some visiting. The young'uns ran and played and didn't need any attention. If they fought and argued, nobody noticed.

This year Annie Lou and Horace came and brought Jane, Dolly, and their young'uns, Coy and Rachel. After dinner, the three sisters got together for a visit. Dolly was a grown girl now, had already finished school, and was working at a dentist's office. Annie Lou and Horace had done a good job of raising her. Dolly didn't have much to say, but Myra wanted to tell her about things that she could not remember. She told her about bringing her to Glencoe on the train and about how Pa always fed her sweet taters.

"We've planned to stay over for two days. Horace is very busy now that he is running the sawmill by himself. But I told him we were going to stay over a day or two since we haven't seen the family in so long."

Annie Lou had to be sure to let Myra know that Horace was running the sawmill now that his pa was dead.

"Dolly, will you come home and spend that time with me? I haven't had time to be with you in so long."

She smiled for the first time and said, "I would love to go home with you if I wouldn't be too much trouble."

"You'd never be trouble. I got plenty of room. You can sleep in the room with Idella and Laura James."

Usually, Myra would have asked James before giving an invitation, but she knew he wouldn't object since Dolly was considered part of the MacTavish family. He thought the world of his sister Jane and always tried to please her.

Annie Lou kept looking over where the young'uns were playing and seemed worried about them getting hurt. Myra couldn't much blame her because the Glencoe young'uns were all used to playing together and one was just as rough as the next one. Annie Lou told Dolly to go bring Rachel and Coy to the shade before they got too hot. Dolly came back with Rachel, but Coy was having a good time, and he wouldn't come. She tried to pull him by his good arm, and his little withered arm was just flinging around trying to fight her off. Myra was glad that he wanted to stay, and in a minute she saw him wrestling with Thurmond, George's boy. She laughed because even with only one good arm, Coy was getting the best of Thurmond.

Rachel came over and sat down right beside Annie Lou. This was Myra's first good look at her, and it showed that she didn't get a good start in life. She was real small for her age. In fact, she wasn't any bigger than Wallace. She whined the rest of the time. She was too hot or the gnats were biting her, or there was a sandspur on her sock, and on and on. She begged to go back home. Finally, Myra had heard enough.

"Rachel, gnats don't bite. All they do is aggravate. What ya gotta do is act like they ain't botherin' ya, and they'll go away. Now you leave yore mama alone and go on over and play with Wallace and Ruth."

She just made an ugly face and crawled into Annie Lou's lap. Myra felt sorry for her, but she knew Annie Lou wasn't helping by letting her act that way. Annie Lou spent the time telling about how well Horace was doing, about their nice house, and how much she liked living right on the coast and so close to Savannah.

"Horace is just too busy now that he has taken over. The sawmill has grown so much that he's had to hire a whole bunch of new workers. It's just so hard to get good workers nowadays.

"I wish you could come to see us. We could go into Savannah. There are so many stores, and you can always find just what you want—not like here in Glencoe.

"I love the coast. Most folks have never even seen the Atlantic Ocean and that's such a shame. Myra, I bet you ain't never had shrimp. We eat them all the time."

Myra just listened as she had always done with her sister. The next time she saw Will Rob, he would get a laugh when she mocked his sister's fancy talk.

Later in the evening, everybody had another turn at the table and divided up what was left to take home. Myra was proud to see every morsel she brought had been eaten. While they were eating supper, the men started teasing James and Malcolm about their wives being in the family way again.

"Ain't you boys found out what causes it yet?"

"I think they're in a race to see which one can have the most."

Everybody was laughing, and they meant no harm. James and Malcolm enjoyed it and grinned with pride. It sort of embarrassed Myra, but she went along with their jokes. Before leaving, many of the women came over and told her they were glad that she decided to have another one to take the place of Mary Alice. She didn't tell them, but she hadn't even considered having another, until she found out she was expecting. She knew she would love this one, but it would not take the place of her angel baby.

James was agreeable and happy to have Dolly go home with them. From the minute she got in their car, Dolly acted like a different person. Eight people, the trunk, and Dolly's satchel were packed in the car. The young'uns were used to sitting all over each other. Myra knew being squeezed in a car was new for Dolly. But she laughed and giggled just like the young'uns when someone yelled, "You're squishing me." She picked back at James when he teased her about thinking she was uppity because she lived close to Savannah.

Myra was glad to learn that her little sister was very smart and knew how to get along. Something didn't seem quite right about her. While she was around Annie Lou, she hardly said a word and never smiled. Now she was laughing and talking like a girl her age ought to act.

When they got home, the young'uns and James washed up and went right to bed. Myra went out to sit in the swing for a breath of cool air, and Dolly followed her. They sat in the swing and talked about how good it was to be together, but Myra could tell her little sister needed to talk more.

Finally, she said, "Myra, is there any way that I could live here with you and James and not have to go back home with Annie Lou? I can get a job in Glencoe and pay you board."

"Honey, I'd love to have you, but I don't think Annie Lou and Horace would let you do that. Why would you even want to? They can give you a lot better home than here with my houseful of young'uns.

She started to cry and said, "It's him, Horace, I can't go back where he is."

"Why not?"

"He tried to mess with me in a way that a man shouldn't with someone who ain't his wife. He tried it three times, and I had to fight him off."

"Did you tell, Annie Lou?"

Dolly was really sobbing and shaking and said, "I tried just before we left to come here, but she took his side and said that I was making up lies. She said Horace told her that I had been after him ever since I was little, but I swear on our papa's grave that ain't true. She said she would tell all the MacTavishes that lie if I told any of you."

Myra had never been so mad in her life. She wanted to snatch Annie Lou as baldheaded as Horace.

"No, ma'am, you do not have to go back with them. You have a home with us as long as you want it, and we will see about Mr. Horace and his lies."

"Just let me stay here. Please don't cause any trouble."

There was no way he was getting away with that. Myra held her close and sat in the swing, comforting her until she almost fell asleep.

The next morning, Myra got up early and woke James so they could talk before the rest were up. When she told him what Horace had done, he turned as red as fire and banged his fist on the table.

"I'll kill him. I hadn't ever liked that little weasel-eyed rat, and he is not getting away with this. His ma might be my sister, but I swear, there ain't one drop of MacTavish blood in a man who would do that. I'm going right now to find him, and I'll kill him. He won't ever bother her or any other little girl again."

"No, no, you ain't gonna kill him. That would just put you in the pen and leave me and Annie Lou with young'uns to raise without a pa."

He settled down a little before taking off for town. Myra worried all day and kept expecting someone to come to the door and tell her James was in jail for killing Horace. She was relieved when he got home that evening.

"It's all settled. Dolly, you're stayin' here with us from now on. They're goin' home tomorrow and will send the rest of her clothes on the bus."

As soon as they were alone, she asked him what happened when he talked to Horace.

"I told him that I had come to kill him, but he wasn't worth killing. I told him if he ever came near her again, I would kick his ass all over Glencoe, and then I would tell his ma all about it. He knows I will, and he knows she will believe anything I tell her. He was shaking and could hardly talk. The little coward didn't even try to defend himself. Anyway, that is the way it was left. Annie Lou won't know any of this, except that she is to send Dolly's clothes."

From that day on, Dolly was part of their family. She got a good job with Dr. Sasser, the dentist, and paid board every week. She fit right in with the family, and Myra loved being able to help her because she had never really known what it was like to have a ma or pa.

The new baby was coming around the first of the year, so she didn't get too big and heavy until the weather begin to cool off. She was surprised to feel good and be able to keep up with her work. Dolly and the older children were a big help and could keep things running just as smoothly as she could. She was surprised at how good James and Dolly got along. He seemed to feel good about being able to help her out, and he felt ashamed that a member of his family had mistreated her. Every morning he let her ride with him into town, but she walked home in the evening because you never knew when James would be coming in. He was happy now that business was picking up. He just couldn't stand it when money was tight.

Three days before Christmas, Olla had a baby boy. This was her second boy, and they named him Charles Edwin. Malcolm was as proud as a peacock.

They had a good Christmas planned for the young'uns, and Myra was hoping and praying that she could hold out until it was over. Usually she only made the pies and cakes on Christmas Eve and cooked the dinner the next morning. She had a feeling that she might not make it through Christmas Day. By sundown on Christmas Eve, she had everything ready enough that they could have sat down to eat. It wouldn't take much to heat it up, even if her pains did start.

Christmas morning, she was starting to cramp a little. Ruth and Wallace were the only ones little enough to still believe in Santa, but the big ones still played like they did. She had a good time seeing them enjoy their presents. They had bought silk stockings for Dolly, and she wondered if this would seem like much of a gift to her. She knew Annie Lou and Horace always spent a lot more on her.

"Thank you, Myra and James. I haven't had silk stockings before. I wasn't expecting anything, but I love you for it. I didn't know what to get you, but I wanted to let you know how much staying here means to me."

She handed Myra three dollars. That was a lot of money for her to give. She didn't make but five dollars a week and paid Myra two dollars for her board.

Everyone pitched in to help get dinner on the table. Miz MacTavish and Olieta came to eat with them. Even if she had hurried it up, it was as good a Christmas dinner as she had ever cooked. While they were eating, Dolly asked what Christmas was like when she was little and when Papa was alive. She had no memories of that time. Myra wondered why Annie

Lou had never told her. Myra had to wait a bit to think of something that wouldn't sound like bad times to her. She told her about how Papa bounced her on his knee and sang all the Christmas songs that he knew and how Ma cooked the best dumplings you had ever tasted.

She said, "Well, she must have showed you how, Myra, because when I tasted your dumplings, it made me think about how it must have been when I was little."

After they finished eating, James told her to sit down, put her feet up, and let the young'uns clean up. She had tried to keep it hidden, but her pains were already getting close together.

"There ain't time fer that. I hate to call Dr. Douglas away from his Christmas, but you need to go fer him right now and quick."

"That's what doctors have to do. I'm on my way. Olieta, you take Ruth and Wallace home with you and Ma. The rest of y'all go visit some of the family. Don't come home 'til you see the doctor's car gone. Tell them all what is happening."

Her water broke just as she got in the bedroom. James hurried off to get the doctor, and the others cleaned up the kitchen quickly and left. James came back and said the doctor was on his way. James sat in the room with her, and he put in to talking.

"Myra, I don't tell you things like this as much as I ought to. I want ya to know that I am proud of how things have turned out for us. We got fine young'uns, and you have always helped me, even when I wasn't worth helpin'."

"It's gonna all be good from now on. I'm lookin' for business to really pick up in the New Year. I know 1929 will get this country moving again. I didn't vote for him, but they say Herbert Hoover is gonna make a good president. He is a mining engineer and should really know how to get the country moving.

"Yes, sir, the good times are ahead of us in this country, and I'm gonna get my part of it. We're gonna live good and send all of our young'uns—even the girls—through as much schooling as they can take."

That sounded good to her, and even though the pains were coming fast and hard, she felt on top of the world.

Dr. Douglas came just in time to ease the baby out. Tears came to her eyes when she saw him for the first time. She knew he would be her last, and would always be her baby. He was a really hearty little fellow and reminded her of Stephen, but he had a MacTavish look about him. When she put him to her breast, there was no question about anything being wrong with him. He knew just what to do and nursed like he was starved to death. James acted as if he had done it all himself.

He said over and over, "Yes, sir, I've got me another boy, and he is going to be the smartest boy to ever come out of Glencoe. People are going to sit up and take notice of this boy." They hadn't talked about a name, but she was having her way about this one. He was Brian James MacTavish Jr.

While she lay in bed nursing her baby boy and looking out on the pretty starry night, she thought about how far she had come. She was not the same little girl who left Washington County riding on the back of a wagon and wondering what her future would be. She remembered how Papa always told her that when the cotton row was long and hard, she just had to keep on chopping. She hadn't been in a cotton patch in a long time, but maybe that was the way with life too. Her life changed the first day she met James. It hadn't always been the way she would have it to be, but they had stuck together. It didn't matter if the future turned out to be as good as James expected, or if times took a turn for the worse. There was one thing she knew for sure that would get them through. She loved James MacTavish with all her heart, and she knew he loved her just as much. That was better than cotton in Augusta. God had done right by Papa's little girl.

James came back into the room and fumbled in his pocket to bring out an envelope.

"Here, Myra, this came in the mail for you last week. I kept forgettin' to give it to ya."

"What is hit?"

He ripped open the envelope and said, "It's a Christmas greeting from yore Aunt Mary." He unfolded the paper and started to read.

> Dear Myra,
>
> Christmas greetings to you and your dear family. I hope you, James, and your precious children are well and happy.
>
> I want you to have this photograph of your father, Martin, and myself. I think he was about eight years old, and I was six. I remember how handsome he looked in his new blue suit that just matched his eyes.
>
> With love always,
>
> Aunt Mary

A faded tintype fell out of the envelope. Myra studied it for a minute and recognized someone she had seen many times before.

EPILOGUE

Myra was correct that Brian James Jr. would be her last child. James's belief that the year 1929 was going to be the beginning of good times for all did not hold true. Soon the Great Depression hit the entire country, and small town Georgia merchants faced times that were harder than anyone had ever known.

Myra did keep on chopping a long row with James, and she never stopped brightening the way. The years passed, and as she moved through her life, she continued to carry the load that had been given to her. She never remembered a childhood of her own. Her weak mother, hardworking father, and circumstances gave her a load that was not meant for a child to carry. James remained childlike throughout his life. They had a deep abiding love, but neither could understand or accept the other's nature.

Throughout the years there were good times, hard times, and even harder times. Myra had times to rejoice and times to grieve. During the hardest of times, she kept her family going by the skills she had learned in her childhood—sewing, gardening, and canning. She never sat her children down to a table that did not have a filling meal on it. She lived to see all of her children grown, married, and successful. Her greatest triumph was seeing her youngest, called B. J. by all, graduate from the University of Georgia. Many times his tuition was paid partly with crumpled dollar bills earned from her sewing.

James never changed his nature, and he never lost his charm. Myra never lost the excitement that she always felt when she heard his footstep on the porch. He was a natural born salesman and was always successful in times of prosperity. As economic times changed the name, MacTavish, did not have the status in Glencoe that it once had. This was hard for

James to accept. The family continued to grow, and future generations of MacTavish would be known in the medical and legal profession, business, education, agriculture, and government. While the MacTavish name might have lost some of its prestige, people all over Aberdeen County got to know and respect "Miz Mac." Her sewing became known throughout the county. Her talent and skill in designing and making clothes could have led her into a successful career in fashion, if she had lived in a later time. She brightened her way and made it bright for all around her. She never stopped trying to guide James to a better life, and there was never a time when she did not need to be his guide. He knew how much he needed and loved her, and he never strayed so far that he couldn't get back to her by suppertime.

From the little girl walking down the red clay road in Washington County to the grand lady that she became was a long row, and she chopped as hard as she could all of the way. She made her peace with God and accepted her lot in life on that long-ago day when she sat in the swing and figured out how His love was shown through the goodness of His people. She never lost her faith or her love for all mankind.

Her children shall rise up and call her blessed;
Her husband also and He praiseth her.
—Proverbs 31:28

Edwards Brothers, Inc.
Thorofare, NJ USA
November 9, 2011